A TEXT BOOK OF

NANO ELECTRONICS AND MEMS

(ELECTIVE IV)
FOR
SEMESTER - II

FINAL YEAR (BE) DEGREE COURSE IN ELECTRONICS/ ELECTRONICS AND TELECOMMUNICATION ENGINEERING

According to New Revised Syllabus of Savitribai Phule Pune University, Pune.
(2012 Pattern)

Dr. Sandipann P. Narote
M. E. (EC), Ph.D. (E & TC),
Professor
Dept. of E & TC Engineering
M.E.S. College of Engineering.
Pune.

Dr. S.T. Patil
M.Tech. (CSE), Ph.D. (Computer)
Professor,
Dept. of Computer Engineering,
Vishwakarma Institue of Technology
Pune.

NIRALI PRAKASHAN
ADVANCEMENT OF KNOWLEDGE

N 3733

NANO ELECTRONICS AND MEMS (BE E&TC SEM. II)   ISBN 978-93-5164-892-5

Second Edition :   January 2017

© :   Authors

Published By :

NIRALI PRAKASHAN

Abhyudaya Pragati, 1312, Shivaji Nagar,
Off J.M. Road, PUNE – 411005
Tel - (020) 25512336/37/39, Fax - (020) 25511379
Email : niralipune@pragationline.com

☞ **DISTRIBUTION CENTRES**

PUNE

Nirali Prakashan   : 119, Budhwar Peth, Jogeshwari Mandir Lane, Pune 411002, Maharashtra
Tel : (020) 2445 2044, 66022708, Fax : (020) 2445 1538
Email : bookorder@pragationline.com, niralilocal@pragationline.com

Nirali Prakashan   : S. No. 28/27, Dhyari, Near Pari Company, Pune 411041
Tel : (020) 24690204 Fax : (020) 24690316
Email : dhyari@pragationline.com, bookorder@pragationline.com

MUMBAI

Nirali Prakashan   : 385, S.V.P. Road, Rasdhara Co-op. Hsg. Society Ltd.,
Girgaum, Mumbai 400004, Maharashtra
Tel : (022) 2385 6339 / 2386 9976, Fax : (022) 2386 9976
Email : niralimumbai@pragationline.com

☞ **DISTRIBUTION BRANCHES**

JALGAON

Nirali Prakashan   : 34, V. V. Golani Market, Navi Peth, Jalgaon 425001,
Maharashtra, Tel : (0257) 222 0395, Mob : 94234 91860

KOLHAPUR

Nirali Prakashan   : New Mahadvar Road, Kedar Plaza, 1st Floor Opp. IDBI Bank
Kolhapur 416 012, Maharashtra. Mob : 9850046155

NAGPUR

Pratibha Book Distributors   : Above Maratha Mandir, Shop No. 3, First Floor,
Rani Jhanshi Square, Sitabuldi, Nagpur 440012, Maharashtra
Tel : (0712) 254 7129

DELHI

Nirali Prakashan   : 4593/21, Basement, Aggarwal Lane 15, Ansari Road, Daryaganj
Near Times of India Building, New Delhi 110002
Mob : 08505972553

BENGALURU

Pragati Book House   : House No. 1, Sanjeevappa Lane, Avenue Road Cross,
Opp. Rice Church, Bengaluru – 560002.
Tel : (080) 64513344, 64513355,Mob : 9880582331, 9845021552
Email:bharatsavla@yahoo.com

CHENNAI

Pragati Books   : 9/1, Montieth Road, Behind Taas Mahal, Egmore,
Chennai 600008 Tamil Nadu, Tel : (044) 6518 3535,
Mob : 94440 01782 / 98450 21552 / 98805 82331,
Email : bharatsavla@yahoo.com

niralipune@pragationline.com | www.pragationline.com

Also find us on [f] www.facebook.com/niralibooks

PREFACE TO THE SECOND EDITION

We are glad and excited to announce that the First Edition of this book received an overwhelming response from the engineering student community, compelling us to release its **Second Edition** within a very short period of time.

This thoroughly revised **Second Edition** has been **updated** with **additional matter**, many solved problems, including **all University Examination Papers** and Numerous Exercises for practice.

Special care has been taken to maintain high degree of accuracy in the theory and numericals throughout the book.

We take this opportunity to express our sincere thanks to Dineshbhai Furia of Nirali Prakashan, a reputed pioneer in the publication field. Our special thanks to Jignesh Furia for their effective cooperation and great care in bringing out this revised edition. We also appreciate the efforts of M. P. Munde and the entire staff of Engineering Books Deptt. of Nirali Prakashan namely Mrs. Deepali Lachake (Co-ordinator) and Mrs. Shilpa Kale for bringing this book to the students in a timely manner.

We sincerely hope that this "**Second Edition**" will also be warmly received by all concerned as in the past.

Valuable suggestions from our esteemed readers to improve the book are most welcome and highly appreciated.

Pune   **–Authors**

PREFACE TO THE FIRST EDITION

It gives us great pleasure to bring out the book on **"Nano Electronics and MEMS"**. This book is strictly written as per the New Revised Syllabus of Savitribai Phule Pune University, (2012 Pattern) for the students of final year Degree Course in Electronics / Electronics and Telecommunication Engineering.

This book is as per New Revised Examination Scheme which has been implemented from this academic year. According to this, In-Semester Examination carries 30 Marks over first three Units and End-Semester Examination carries 70 Marks over entire syllabus of which is first three units will carry 20 Marks and Units 4, 5, and 6 will carry 50 Marks.

Last but not the least, we have provided a **Sample Question Papers for In-Semester Examination (30 Marks) and End-Semester Examination (70 Marks)** are given to students for practice.

The subject matter is presented in simple form so as to enable the students to understand the subject easily. Sufficient care is taken to present the subject matter in the point wise form in most of the Units. The book consists of six units, which cover the entire syllabus.

This book has been written to satisfy the needs of undergraduate syllabus of the Electronics/Electronics and Telecommunication Engineering Course in most of the Universities. We are quite sure that this book will serve its purpose very well for Electronics/Electronics and Telecommunication Students.

We are sincerely thankful to **Shri Dineshbhai K. Furia, Shri. Jignesh C. Furia, Mrs. Nirali Verma, Shri. M. P. Munde** and the entire team of **Nirali Prakashan** namely **Mrs. Deepali Lachake** (Co-ordinator) who really has taken keen interest and untiring efforts in publishing this text.

Despite the best efforts taken by authors, it is possible that some unintentional errors might have taken place. Authors would gratefully acknowledge if any of these are pointed out.

16th February 2016   **Authors**

SYLLABUS

Unit I: Introduction to Materials in Nano Electronics   6L

Band structures in Silicon, Historical development and basic concepts of crystal structure, defects, crystal growth and wafer fabrication, crystal planes and orientation. Modern CMOS technology, construction of MOS Field Effect Transistor, Electrical characterization: IV/CV characterization, temperature dependent characterization.

Unit II: Semiconductor Nano Electronic Manufacturing   6L

Basic understanding of contaminations, Levels of contaminations, Wafer cleaning methods, Lithography: basic concepts of optics, photoresists, wafer exposure systems, methods and equipment. Thermal Oxidation: formations of Si and SiO_2 interface, types of thermal oxidations and their comparisons. Dopant Diffusion and Ion implantation fundamentals, Thin film deposition, sputtering methods and types, etching process and types.

Unit III: Nano Electronic Devices   6L

Single Electron devices and Transistors, Quantum particle, Quantum Dot, Logic circuits using quantum dots, nanowires construction and applications, FinFETs, construction of FinFET, properties of FinFETs.

Unit IV: Introduction to MEMS   6L

Intrinsic characteristics of MEMS, miniaturization, Sensors and actuators, sensor noise and design complexity, packaging and integration, stress and strain, intrinsic stress, torsion deflections, types of beams and deflection of beams.

Unit V: MEMS Based Sensors and Actuators   6L

Electrostatic sensors and Actuators, Thermal sensing and actuation, piezoresistive sensing and actuation, Magnetic actuation. Comparison of major sensing and actuation methods. Case studies of selected MEMS: Acceleration sensors, gyros etc.

Unit VI: Measurements Methods and Tools   6L

Electrical methods: Hot probe method, Sheet resistance, Hall effect measurements. Physical measurements: Fourier Transform Infrared Spectroscopy, Electron microscopy, Atomic Force Microscope, X-Ray photoelectron Spectroscopy, Profilometers, Reflectrometers.

CONTENTS

Unit I : Introduction to Materials in Nano-Electronics   **1.1-1.58**

1.1   Introduction   1.1
1.2   Band Structures in Silicon   1.3
    1.2.1   Full Band Approach   1.6
1.3   Historical Development and Basic Concepts of Crystal Structure and Defects   1.7
    1.3.1   Crystal Defects   1.9
    1.3.2   Crystal Growth and Wafer Fabrication   1.13
    1.3.3   Crystal Planes and Orientation   1.17
1.4   Modern Cmos Technology   1.18
    1.4.1   Construction of MOS Field Effect Transistor   1.27
1.5   Electrical Characterization   1.31
    1.5.1   Current-Voltage (I-V)/Capacitance-Voltage (C-V) Characterization   1.33
    1.5.2   Temperature Dependent Characterization   1.38
    •   Summary   1.57
    •   Exercise   1.58

Unit II : Semiconductor Nano Electronic Manufacturing   **2.1-2.44**

2.1   Introduction   2.1
2.2   Basic Understanding of Contaminations   2.1
    2.2.1   Levels of Contaminations   2.2
    2.2.2   Contamination Analysis and Monitoring   2.4
    2.2.3   Wafer Cleaning Methods   2.4
2.3   Lithography   2.6
    2.3.1   Basic Concepts of Optics   2.21
    2.3.2   Photo-Resists   2.23
    2.3.3   The Difference between Positive and Negative Photo Resist   2.25
2.4   Thermal Oxidation   2.26
    2.4.1   Formations of Si and SiO_2 Interface   2.28
    2.4.2   Thermal Oxidations or Incineration   2.29
    2.4.3   Dopant Diffusion   2.30
    2.4.4   Ion Implantation Fundamentals   2.30
    2.4.5   Annealing After Implantation   2.32
    2.4.6   Advantages of Ion Implantation   2.32
    2.4.7   High-Current High-Energy Implantation Machines   2.33
    2.4.8   Problems in VLSI Processing   2.33
    2.4.9   Importance of Ion Implantation for VLSI Technology   2.34
    2.4.10   Thin Film Deposition   2.35
    2.4.11   Applications of Thin Films   2.35

2.5	Sputtering Methods	2.39
2.6	Etching Process	2.42
	• Summary	2.43
	• Exercise	2.43

Unit III : Nano Electronic Devices   **3.1-3.34**

3.1	Introduction	3.1
3.2	Single Electron Devices and Transistors	3.3
	3.2.1 Single-Electron Box	3.3
3.3	Quantum Particle	3.7
	3.3.1 Quantum Dot	3.9
	3.3.2 Logic Circuits With Quantum Dots	3.13
	3.3.3 Quantum Dots Applications	3.15
	3.3.4 Advantages of Quantum Dots	3.16
	3.3.5 Nano Wires Construction and Applications	3.18
3.4	Finfets	3.20
	3.4.1 Finfet : The Promises and the Challenges	3.24
	3.4.2 Finfet : A Technology Primer	3.25
	3.4.3 The Finfet Tool Story	3.28
	3.4.4 Construction of Finfet	3.32
	3.4.5 Properties of Finfet	3.32
	3.4.6 Advantages of Finfet Technology	3.33
	• Summary	3.33
	• Exercise	3.34

Unit IV : Introduction to MEMS   **4.1-4.24**

4.1	Introduction	4.1
4.2	Overview of MEMS	4.2
	4.2.1 The Intrinsic Characteristics of MEMS	4.3
4.3	Sensors and Actuators	4.6
	4.3.1 Energy Domains and Transducers	4.6
	4.3.2 Sensor Noise and Design Complexity	4.9
4.4	Packaging and Integration	4.11
	4.4.1 Functions of MEMS Packages	4.11
	4.4.2 Types of MEMS Packages	4.12
	4.4.3 Integrating MEMS	4.14
4.5	Stress and Strain	4.15
	4.5.1 Intrinsic Stress	4.19
	4.5.2 Types of Beams	4.21
	4.5.3 Deflection of Beams	4.22
	• Summary	4.23
	• Exercise	4.24

Unit V : Mems Based Sensors and Actuators   **5.1-5.52**

5.1	Introduction	5.1
5.2	Electrostatic Sensors and Actuators	5.2

	5.2.1	Electrostatic Induction	5.4
	5.2.2	Electrostatic Actuators	5.5
	5.2.3	Electrostatic Type Instruments Construction Principle Torque Equation	5.10
	5.2.4	Thermal Sensing and Actuation	5.14
	5.2.5	Thermal Actuator Applications	5.25
	5.2.6	Piezo Resistive Sensing	5.26
	5.2.7	Areas of Applications	5.29
5.3		Magnetic Actuation	5.30
	5.3.1	Magnetic Materials for MEMS	5.36
	5.3.2	MEMS Switch Uses Magnetic Actuation	5.36
5.4		Comparison of Major Sensing And Actuation Methods	5.37
5.5		Case Studies of Selected MEMS: Acceleration Sensors	5.40
	5.5.1	Simple Steps to Selecting the Right Accelerometer	5.40
	5.5.2	Type of Measurement	5.40
	5.5.3	Ground Isolation	5.44
	5.3.4	Gyroscope	5.50
	•	Summary	5.52
	•	Exercise	5.52

Unit VI : Measurements Methods and Tools   **6.1-6.38**

6.1		Introduction	6.1
6.2		Electrical Methods	6.2
	6.2.1	Hot Probe Method	6.3
	6.2.2	Sheet Resistance	6.6
	6.2.3	Hall Effect	6.9
6.3		Physical Measurements	6.15
	6.3.1	Fourier Transform Infrared Spectroscopy	6.16
	6.3.2	Electron Microscopy	6.25
	6.3.3	Atomic Force Microscope	6.31
	6.3.4	X–Ray Photoelectron Spectroscopy	6.33
	6.3.5	Profilometers	6.35
	6.3.6	Reflectrometers	6.36
	•	Summary	6.38
	•	Exercise	6.38

Sample Question Paper for In-Semester Examination (30 Marks)   **SQP.1-SQP.1**
Sample Question Paper for End-Semester Examination (70 Marks)   **SQP.2-SQP.2**
• Reference   **Ref. 1**
• University Question Papers (May 2016 to Nov. 2016)   **P.1 – P.2**

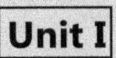

INTRODUCTION TO MATERIALS IN NANO–ELECTRONICS

1.1 INTRODUCTION

- The word Nanoelectronics consists of two parts: Nano and Electronics. One nanometer (nm) equals 0.000 000 001 metre. This very tiny length goes almost beyond our imagination and cannot be seen using traditional microscopes. A nanometer to a meter is the same as a marble compared to the size of the earth. A hair is around 100.000 nm thick. Nanoelectronics studies the flow of charge through various devices and materials such as semiconductors, metals, resistors, inductors and nano–structures. Electronic parts are important for many tools we use in daily life: cell phones, computers, television, home equipment sand cars. Nanoelectronics is the branch of electronics dealing with miniaturised electronic circuits integrated on semiconductor 'chips'. Its basic element is the transistor. Up to recently, transistor dimensions were in the micrometer range but today they are manufactured at 65 nanometer or below. Nanoelectronics research is dealing with devices of dimensions of 22 nm and smaller, the technology and equipment to make them, the competences to design them with integrated circuits and electronic components and the art to manufacture them cheap in large volumes. The smaller the technology, the smaller, faster, more powerful and cheaper electronic equipment can be.

- The scientists have established a universal system for the classifying the size, it is typically based on the metric system with the base unit as meter. The metric system has a prefixes size of the centimeters. 100 or 0.01. It is expressed as 10^{-2}. The Nano is third smallest increment described on the metric scale its value 0.00000001 or 1 billion base value. Now–a–days nano–technology and nanoelectronics used to interchangeably. They have a number of innovations of the modern ability to work and see with very small units. This small units are on atomic or molecular scale.

- Nananoelectronics signifies to the products of the evolutionary development of silicon–based micro electronic transistor technology categorized by the miniaturization and increased integration of elements which does not indicate instrumental implementation of quantum size effects.

- Nananoelectronics is also applied to a combination of electronic instruments, devices and their production techniques based on new effects.

- The scale of several tens of nanometers, the specific sizes of elements become comparable to certain fundamental physical values, such as, shielding distance, electron path, de Broglie wavelength, which involves the emergence of new physical effects and the existence of some fundamental physical restrictions of the capabilities of such devices. This is how nanoelectronics differ from microelectronics, which depends on the macroscopic laws of classical physics.

- The modern electronics are on the turn–around point in materials. The past, Al or SiO_2 which has an attraction to Si has been used and the functionalities are conveyed by manufactured devices.

- Consequently, the device structures have been intricate progressively and now it almost closes to the fabrication limit. Therefore, for the future Nano device needs new materials which give superior performance in Nano scale.

- The future Nano devices comprising LSI consist of a lots of interfaces with numerous materials. Basically nanoelectronics materials invented by the silicon, gallium, arsenic, and others, all these materials, Silicon is one of the most commonly available element on the earth. Silicon is cheaper, abundant and it requires low power only. Nanotechnology gives the more consistent small size devices and it gives faster working.

- The emerging potential for the science of nanoelectronics can be used in development of medicine technology.

Some of the several perspectives to the concept of nanoelectronics are:

1. Nanoscale dimensions of nanoelectronic components allow for systems of giga–scale complexity measured in terms of component on a chip or in a package. This scaling feature and the giga–scale systems can be described as the 'More Moore' domain of development.

2. Another is that nanotechnology is very diverse and allows the integration of purely electronic devices with mechanical devices, bio–devices, chemical devices, etc. Also, digital systems can be combined with analog/RF circuits. This technology fusion can be described as the 'More than Moore' domain of development.

3. A third is that traditional scaling limits in standard CMOS technology are reached during the next decade, fundamentally, new nanoscale electronic devices. This development of nanoelectronic components can be denoted the 'Beyond CMOS' domain of development.

- Over the years, semiconductor technologists have pushed transistors to smaller and smaller feature sizes. This steady shrinking of device size has resulted in an information revolution that today impacts on virtually every facet of our lives. Even though transistors are close to reaching their ultimate size limitation relative to integrated circuit performance, the stunning achievements in fabrication tool development in the last several decades as part of the microelectronics revolution now allow for molecular–level structural tailoring of materials not available or explorable except through naturally occurring atomic processes. Indeed, the age of nanoscience has arrived.

- Nanoscience is the study of material manipulation and its intended physical consequences at the molecular scale, that is, on a scale of the order of a few hundred

Angstoms less than one thousandth of a human hair. The extraordinary feature of nanoscience is that it allows for the tailoring and combining of the physical, biological, and engineering properties of matter at a common level of manipulation and control; this feature provides an enormous opportunity to fabricate, tailor, and embed novel, specifically targeted chemical, biological, physical, and material attributes at the lowest level of material building block. The challenge of nanotechnology is to scale up or suitably package nano–based material concepts to a robust, usable macroscopic level while preserving the desired embedded nano features.

- The early techniques of molecular and cluster beam epitaxy, and more recently, the chemistry of self–assembly and molecular design, have facilitated the fabrication of structures with atomic layer resolution; as well, advanced lithographic and replication methods have provided the capability for defining lateral dimensions with an accuracy of Angstroms.

- Over the evolving years of progressive microelectronics, these revolutionary nanofabrication techniques have ushered microelectronics into the nanoelectronic regime by providing quantum wells, wires, and dots to serve as the basic workhouse structures for the study of many novel quantum phenomena and device concepts.

- Today, with new and emerging chemical processes, nanoscience has the potential to provide a unique spectrum of new concepts and capabilities for future generations of electronics as well as other areas including nanoelectromechanical structures, designer functional materials and textile fabrics, medical sensors and probes, and the like.

- This potential will be realized through a systems–level approach which concurrently integrates nano–embedded properties with new paradigms for device physics, flexible architectures, and hierarchical design principles.

- The perspective includes a discussion of the need to transition from the classical to the quantum picture of nature, a view of life in the nano lane, a discussion of quantum engineering – the application of quantum principles to nano objects including some of the author's own interests, an observation concerning a materials explosion toward new applications of nanoscience and technology, and a discussion of future directions relevant to nanoscience and engineering.

1.2 BAND STRUCTURES IN SILICON

- Silicon is a type of semiconductor material in which number of free electrons is less than conductor but more than that of insulator. Silicon has an enormous application in the field of electronics, for having this unique characteristic.
- There are two types of energy bands in silicon which are conduction band and valance band. A series of energy levels having valance electrons forms the valance band in the solid.

- At absolute temperature (0°K) the energy levels of the valance band is filled with electrons. When the electrons are in valance band, this band consists of extreme amount of energy, no current flows due to such electrons.
- As shown in Fig. 1.1 energy band of silicon levels of energies of electrons in the material. there are two types of energy bands one is conduction band and second is valance band. Valance electrons band with highest energy level. Free electrons are in conduction band with minimum amount of energy.
- Valance and conduction bands are separated by the amount of energy known as the forbidden energy gap. This amount is nearly 1.2 eV at 300° K. In intrinsic silicon, the Fermi level lies in the middle of the donor atoms, it becomes n–type when Fermi level moves higher, i.e. closer to conduction band.
- When intrinsic silicon is doped with acceptor atoms, it becomes p – type and Fermi level moves in the direction of valance band.

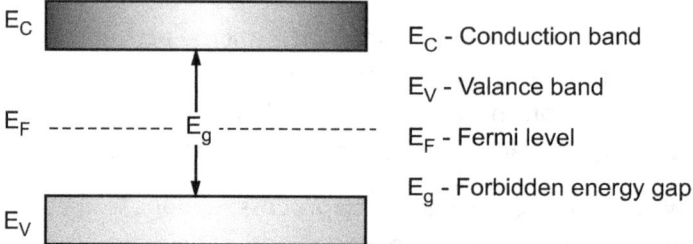

E_C - Conduction band

E_V - Valance band

E_F - Fermi level

E_g - Forbidden energy gap

Fig. 1.1: Energy bands in Silicon

- Fabrication of Silicon nanoelectronics materials plays two important things, that is, quantum effect and single electron effect.
- The advantages of fabrication of silicon nanoelectronics are to decrease the size and power consumption.
- Fabrication of silicon nanoelectronics involves the quantum dot, quantum wire, quantum wel is and single electron transistor device (nano MOS) used to the lower power consumtion.

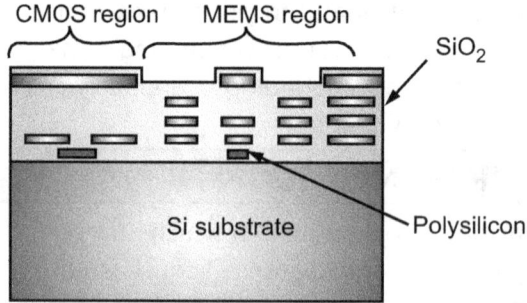

Fig. 1.2: Silicon based nano CMOS

- Especially for silicon, semiconductor band structures are hard to describe with an analytical formula. The plot is drawn for energy values along particular edges.

- The energy dispersion along the straight line from point T to point X, which is called Δ line. For silicon the conduction band minima lie on the six equivalent Δ lines along (100) directions and occur at about 0.85% of the way to the zone boundary. These are the well–known, equivalent ellipsoidal constant energy valleys. When electrons gain 0.13 eV of energy, they can cross the zone boundary.

- There is a second minimum in the first conduction band at point L , which lies 1.0 eV above the first valley. The second conduction band valley is only 0.1 eV above the minimum of the first conduction band.

- Carriers above 0.1 eV in kinetic energy may reside in either of the two conduction bands before the second valley of the first band is occupied. Under large electric fields, electrons populate the entire Brillion zone and the band structure at energy minima cannot be described by simple analytical approximations.

- The valence band maximum for the heavy–hole, light–hole and for the split–off band is positioned precisely at the T–point. It is clear that for a small electric field the concentration of holes is higher in the region around the T–point. It is thus important to use, for full band Monte Carlo simulations, a discretization of the momentum space, which demonstrate a higher mesh density around the T–point.

- The complexity of semiconductor band structures forces different approximations to reduce intensity and computational costs. Two analytical models, namely the parabolic and the non–parabolic model are widely used.

- The FBMC method produces a more general description, suitable also for higher energy values. This description is commonly based on the pseudo potential method.

Analytical Approximations

Silicon band structure simplest model is centered on the effective mass. If the band structure is identified, the energy wave vector relation E(k) in one dimension can be stretched in a Taylor series as:

$$E(k) \; = \; E(0) + \left.\frac{\partial E(k)}{\partial k}\right|_{k=0} k + \frac{1}{2}\left.\frac{\partial^2 E(k)}{\partial k^2}\right|_{k=0} k^2 + \dots \qquad \dots(1.1)$$

When the band minimum occurs at k = 0, the gradient of E(k) is zero at k = 0, so, the lowest order,

$$E(k) \; = \; E(0) + \frac{h^2 k^2}{2m^*} \qquad\qquad \dots(1.2)$$

where
$$\frac{1}{m^*} \; = \; \frac{1}{h^2}\frac{\partial^2 E(k)}{\partial k^2} \qquad\qquad \dots(1.3)$$

The effective mass, and h = $\dfrac{h}{(2\pi)}$ = 1.05457168 (18) · 10^{-34} Js is Planck's constant.

For diamond crystals such as silicon the conduction band has three minima, one at k = 0 (called the T point), another along (111) directions at the boundary of the first Brillouin zone (called L) and a third one near the zone boundary along (100) directions. cf. If the first conduction band minimum E(k) is described by,

$$E(k) = \frac{h^2 k^2}{2m^*} \qquad \qquad ...(1.4)$$

The constant energy surface in k–space of the band approximation, forms a sphere and the effective mass m^* is isotropic. When the conduction band does not lie at k= 0, the effective mass depends on the crystallographic orientation of the minimum. In common cubic semiconductors, we find that

$$E(k) = \frac{h}{2}\left(\frac{k_l^2}{m_l^*} + \frac{k_t^2}{m_t^*} + \frac{k_t^2}{m_t^*}\right) \qquad \qquad ...(1.5)$$

Equation (1.5) expresses a band with ellipsoidal constant energy surfaces. The effective mass is a different longitudinal and transverse effective masses, m_l^* and m_t^* , respectively. Material specific values for m_l^* and m_t^*. Formula (1.5) is referred to as the parabolic energy band approximation.

In this case, high applied fields, carriers may be far above the minimum, and the higher order terms in the Taylor series expansion cannot be ignored. For the conduction band, this is approximated by a relation of the form

$$E(1 + \alpha E) = \frac{h^2 k^2}{2m^*} \qquad \qquad ...(1.6)$$

where m^* is determined from formula (1.2) at the minimum. For a minimum at k = 0,

$$\alpha_T = \frac{1}{E_T} = \left(1 - \frac{M_T^*}{m_0}\right)^2 \qquad \qquad ...(1.7)$$

where E_T is the direct bandgap. Formula (1.6) is referred to as the non–parabolic energy band approximation.

1.2.1 Full Band Approach

According to the higher energies the conduction band approximates with non–parabolic parameter α as in equation (1.6). Nevertheless a non–parabolic band provides a reasonable approximation only up to an energy of about 1 eV . For example in silicon MOSFETs an important reliability problem is caused by injection of electrons from the channel into the gate oxide. The energy barrier at the SiO_2, Si interface is 3.1 eV. For these problems simple expressions for E(k) are not valid any more and a numerically generated table of E(k) must be used.

A very useful approach to a numerical evaluation of E(k) is the so called pseudo potential method. To evaluate E(k) the Schrödinger equation for the electrons is solved for a bulk semiconductor in the absence of scattering and without any built–in potential. The pseudo potential method relies on the fact that the band structure is largely determined by the valence electrons. In addition empirical form factors have been derived to fit band gaps at the high symmetry locations.

1.3 HISTORICAL DEVELOPMENT AND BASIC CONCEPTS OF CRYSTAL STRUCTURE AND DEFECTS

- Many solids and some crystalline liquids have a consistent, repeating, three–dimensional arrangement of atoms referred to as a crystal lattice or crystal structure. In contrast, an amorphous solid is a kind of solid material, for instance glass, which deficiencies such a long–range repeating structure.

- Many of the physical, optical, and electrical properties of crystalline solids or liquids are thoroughly associated to crystal structure. The repeating units of a crystalline structure are referred to as "cells." These units are made up of small boxes or other three–dimensional shapes.

- Many of these cells are grouped together in a repeating, orderly structure to make up the overall structure.

- The crystal structure of a given crystalline material can affect many of that material's overall properties.

- It is one of the major defining factors affecting the optical properties of the material, for instance.

- The crystal structure affects the reactivity of the crystallize material. It regulates the reactive atoms on the outside edges and faces of the crystalline solid or liquid arrangement.

- In other way material traits, as well as electrical and magnetic properties of some materials, are also determined largely by crystal structure. Most of the time atoms self–organize in crystals.

- The crystalline lattice is a periodic array of the atoms. When the solid is not crystalline, it is called amorphous. Examples of crystalline solids are metals, diamond and other precious stones, ice, graphite. Glass, amorphous carbon (aC), amorphous Si, most plastics are common examples of amorphous solids.

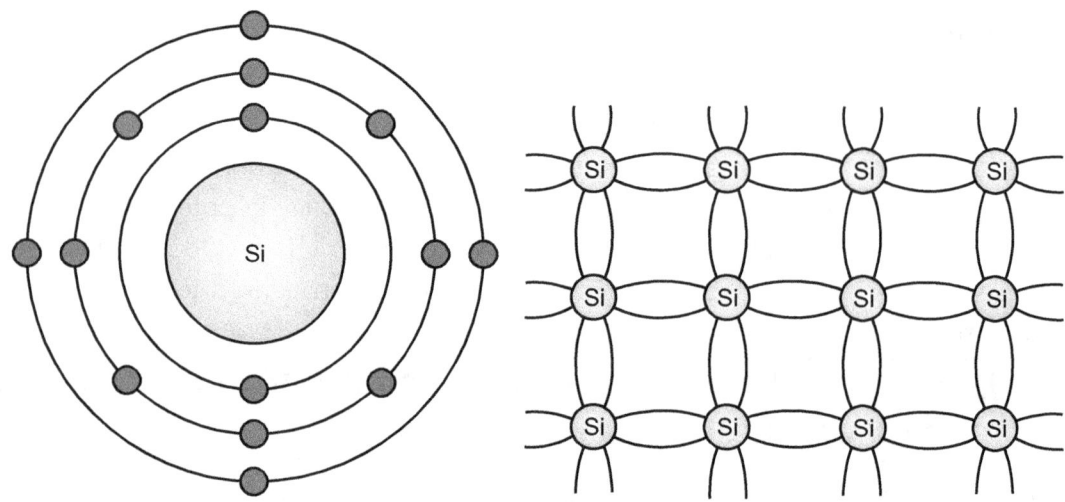

Fig. 1.3: Silicon atoms

- The above Fig. 1.3 shows the arrangement of the silicon atoms in a unit cell, with the numbers representing the height of the atom above the base of the cube as a fraction of the cell dimension.

- Silicon crystallines in the same pattern as diamond, in a structure which Ashcroft and Mermin call "two interpenetrating face–centered cubic" primitive lattices.

- The lines between silicon atoms in the lattice illustration specify nearest–neighbor bonds. The cube side for silicon is 0.543 nm. Germanium has the same diamond structure with a cell dimension of 0.566 nm.

- A crystal structure consists of a unit cell, a set of atoms arranged in a particular way which is periodically repeated in three dimensions on a lattice.

Important properties of the unit cells are:

- The type of atoms and their radii R.

- Cell dimensions (side in cubic cells, side of base a and height c in HCP) in terms of R.

- Number of atoms per unit cell. For an atom that is shared with m adjacent unit cells, we only count a fraction of the atom, 1/m.

- The coordination number, which is the number of closest neighbors to which an atom is bonded.

- The atomic packing factor, which is the fraction of the volume of the cell actually occupied by the hard spheres.

$$APF = \frac{\text{Sum of atomic volumes}}{\text{Volume of cell}}$$

Table 1.1

Unit Cell	n	CN	a/R	APF
SC	1	6	2	0.52
BCC	2	8	4Ö3	0.68
FCC	4	12	2Ö2	0.74
HCP	6	12		0.74

The closest packed direction in a BCC cell is along the diagonal of the cube; in a FCC cell is along the diagonal of a face of the cube. The unit cell is the smallest structure that repeats itself by translation through the crystal. We construct these symmetrical units with the hard spheres. The most common types of unit cells are faced–centered cubic (FCC), Body–Centered Cubic (BCC) and Hexagonal Close–Packed (HCP). Other types exist, particularly among minerals. The Simple Cube (SC) is often used for didactical purpose.

1.3.1 Crystal Defects

The structure of real crystals differs from that of ideal ones. Real crystals always have certain defects or imperfections, and therefore, the arrangement of atoms in the volume of a crystal is far from being perfectly regular.

Natural crystals always contain defects, often in abundance, due to the uncontrolled conditions under which they were formed. The presence of defects which affect the colour can make these crystals valuable as gems, as in ruby (chromium replacing a small fraction of the aluminium in aluminium oxide: Al_2O_3). Crystal prepared in laboratory will also always contain defects, although considerable control may be exercised over their type, concentration, and distribution.

The importance of defects depends upon the material, type of defect, and properties, which are being considered. Some properties, such as density and elastic constants, are proportional to the concentration of defects, and so a small defect concentration will have a very small effect on these. Other properties, e.g. the colour of an insulating crystal or the conductivity of a semiconductor crystal, may be much more sensitive to the presence of small number of defects. Indeed, while the term defect carries with it the connotation of undesirable qualities, defects are responsible for many of the important properties of materials and much of material science involves the study and engineering of defects so that solids will have desired properties. A defect free, i.e. ideal silicon crystal would be of little use in modern electronics; the use of silicon in electronic devices is dependent upon small concentrations of chemical impurities such as phosphorus and arsenic which give it desired properties. Some simple defects in a lattice are shown in Fig. 1.4.

There are some properties of materials such as stiffness, density and electrical conductivity which are termed structure–insensitive, are not affected by the presence of defects in crystals while there are many properties of greatest technical importance such as mechanical strength, ductility, crystal growth, magnetic

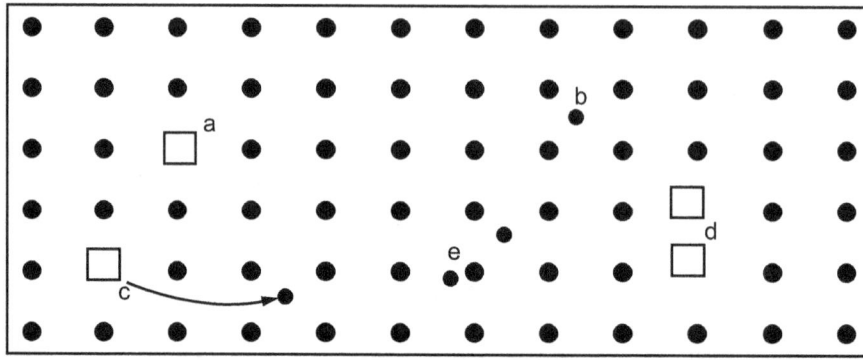

a = vacancy (Schottky defect)

b = interstitial

c = vacancy – interstitial pair (Frenkel defect)

d = divacancy

e = split interstitial

☐ = vacant site

Fig. 1.4 Some Simple defects in a lattice

Hysteresis, dielectric strength, condition in semiconductors, which are termed structure sensitive are greatly affected by the–relatively minor changes in crystal structure caused by defects or imperfections. Crystalline defects can be classified on the basis of their geometry as follows:

(i)   Point imperfections

(ii) Line imperfections

(iii) Surface and grain boundary imperfections (iv) Volume imperfections

The dimensions of a point defect are close to those of an interatomic space. With linear defects, their length is several orders of magnitude greater than the width. Surface defects have a small depth, while their width and length may be several orders larger. Volume defects (pores and cracks) may have substantial dimensions in all measurements, i.e. at least a few tens of A^0. We will discuss only the first three crystalline imperfections.

Point Defects in Ionic Crystals and Metals

The point imperfections, which are lattice errors at isolated lattice points, take place due to imperfect packing of atoms during crystallisation. The point imperfections also take place due to vibrations of atoms at high temperatures. Point imperfections are completely local in effect, e.g. a vacant lattice site. Point defects are always present in crystals and their present results in a decrease in the free energy. One can compute the number of defects at equilibrium concentration at a certain temperature as,

$$n = N \exp [-E_d / kT]$$

Where n – number of imperfections, N – number of atomic sites per mole, k – Boltzmann constant, E_d – free energy required to form the defect and T – absolute temperature. E is typically of order of 1 eV since k = 8.62 X 10^{-5} eV /K, at T = 1000 K, n/N = exp[$-1/(8.62$ x 10^{-5} x 1000)] $\approx 10^{-5}$, or 10 parts per million. For many purposes, this fraction would be intolerably large, although this number may be reduced by slowly cooling the sample.

(i) Vacancies: The simplest point defect is a vacancy. This refers to an empty (unoccupied) site of a crystal lattice, i.e. a missing atom or vacant atomic site [Fig. 1.5] such defects may arise either from imperfect packing during original crystallization or from thermal vibrations of the atoms at higher temperatures. In the latter case, when the thermal energy due to vibration is increased, there is always an increased probability that individual atoms will jump out of their positions of lowest energy. Each temperature has a corresponding equilibrium concentration of vacancies and interstitial atoms (an interstitial atom is an atom transferred from a site into an interstitial position). For instance, copper can contain 10^{-13} atomic percentage of vacancies at a temperature of 20–25°C and as many as 0.01 % at near the melting point (one vacancy per 10^4 atoms). For most crystals the–said thermal energy is of the order of I eV per vacancy. The thermal vibrations of atoms increases with the rise in temperature. The vacancies may be single or two or more of them may condense into a di–vacancy or trivacancy. We must note that the atoms surrounding a vacancy tend to be closer together, thereby distorting the lattice planes. At thermal equilibrium, vacancies exist in a certain proportion in a crystal and thereby leading to an increase in randomness of the structure. At higher temperatures, vacancies have a higher concentration and can move from one site to another more frequently. Vacancies are the most important kind of point defects; they accelerate all processes associated with displacements of atoms: diffusion, powder sintering, etc.

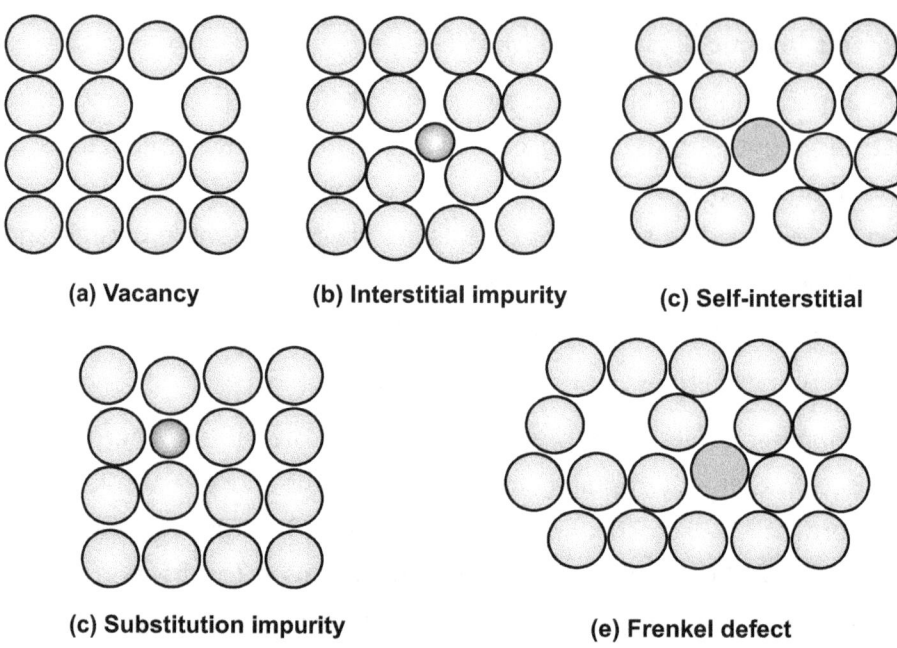

(a) Vacancy   (b) Interstitial impurity   (c) Self-interstitial

(c) Substitution impurity   (e) Frenkel defect

Fig. 1.5: Point defects in a crystal lattice

(ii) Interstitial Imperfections: In a closed packed structure of atoms in a crystal if the atomic packing factor is low, an extra atom may be lodged within the crystal structure. This is known as interstitial position, i.e. voids. An extra atom can enter the interstitial space or void between the regularly positioned atoms only when it is substantially smaller than the parent atoms [Fig. 2(b)], otherwise it will produce atomic distortion. The defect caused is known as interstitial defect. In close packed structures, e.g. FCC and HCP, the largest size of an atom that can fit in the interstitial void or space have a radius about 22.5% of the radii of parent atoms. Interstitialcies may also be single interstitial, di–interstitials, and tri–interstitials. We must note that vacancy and interstitialcy are inverse phenomena.

(iii) Frenkel Defect: Whenever a missing atom, which is responsible for vacancy occupies an interstitial site (responsible for interstitial defect) as shown in Fig. 2(c), the defect caused is known as Frenkel defect. Obviously, Frenkel defect is a combination of vacancy and interstitial defects. These defects are less in number because energy is required to force an ion into new position. This type of imperfection is more common in ionic crystals, because the positive ions, being smaller in size, get lodged easily in the interstitial positions.

(iv) Schottky Defect: These imperfections are similar to vacancies. This defect is caused, whenever a pair of positive and negative ions is missing from a crystal [Fig. 1.5(e)]. This type of imperfection maintains charge neutrality. Closed–packed structures have fewer interstitialcies and Frenkel defects than vacancies and Schottky defects, as additional energy is required to force the atoms in their new positions.

(v) Substitutional Defect: Whenever a foreign atom replaces the parent atom of the lattice and thus occupies the position of parent atom (Fig. 1.5(d)], the defect caused is called substitutional defect. In this type of defect, the atom which replaces the parent atom may be of same size or slightly smaller or greater than that of parent atom.

(vi) Phonon: When the temperature is raised, thermal vibrations takes place. This results in the defect of a symmetry and deviation in shape of atoms. This defect has much effect on the magnetic and. electric properties.

All kinds of point defects distort the crystal lattice and have a certain influence on the physical properties. In commercially pure metals, point defects increase the electric resistance and have almost no effect on the mechanical properties. Only at high concentrations of defects in irradiated metals, the ductility and other properties are reduced noticeably.

In addition to point defects created by thermal fluctuations, point defects may also be created by other means. One method of producing an excess number of point defects at a given temperature is by quenching (quick cooling) from a higher temperature. Another method of creating excess defects is by severe deformation of the crystal lattice, e.g., by hammering or rolling. We must note that the lattice still retains its general crystalline nature, numerous defects are introduced. There is also a method of creating excess point defects is by external bombardment by atoms or high–energy particles, e.g. from the beam of the cyclotron or the neutrons in a nuclear reactor. The first particle collides with the lattice atoms and displaces them, thereby causing a point defect. The. number of point defects created in this manner depends only upon the nature of the crystal and on the bombarding particles and not on the temperature.

1.3.2 Crystal Growth and Wafer Fabrication

The preparation of silicon or gallium arsenide wafer is required before the fabrication of the integrated circuit. The preparation of wafer involves 4 steps.

1.　Distillation and reduction/synthesis,

2.　Crystal growth,

3.　Grind/saw/polish, and

4.　Electrical and mechanical characterizations.

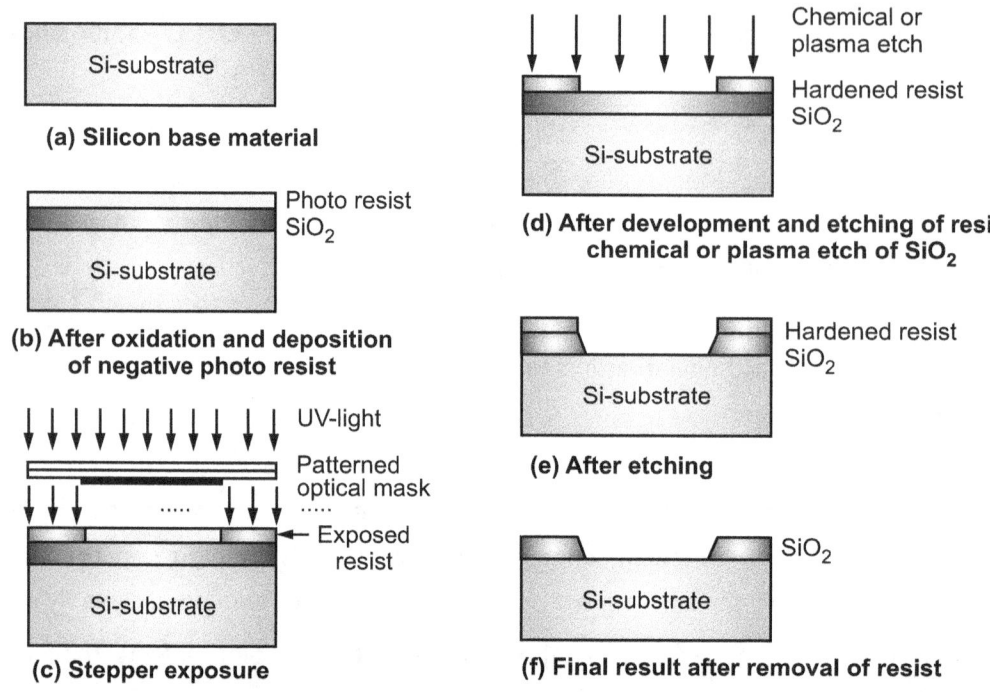

Fig. 1.6: Crystal growth and wafer fabrication

The starting material is silicon dioxide for making silicon wafer. It is chemically processed to form a high–purity crystal polycrystalline semiconductor for which single crystal is formed.

The single crystal is shaped to define diameter and is sawed into wafer. The wafer is then etched and polished to provide smooth surface. Pure form of sand SiO_2 called quartzite is placed in high temperature furnace with various forms of carbon like coke, coal, and even wood chip. Owing silicon dioxide is very stable, carbon is used to replace silicon to form carbon dioxide at reduced temperature. Although there are numbers of reaction take place and the overall reaction follows equation

$$SiO_2 + 2C \rightarrow Si + 2CO \uparrow \qquad \qquad ...(1.8)$$

This process generates polycrystalline silicon with about 98% to 99% purity called crude silicon or metallurgical–grade silicon MGS.

In next process step is the silicon purification step. Silicon is pulverized and treated with hydrochloric acid gas HCl at temperature 300°C to form trichlorosilane $SiHCl_3$ vapor. The chemical reaction follows equation

$$Si + 3HCl \xrightarrow{300°C} SiHCl_3 + H_2 \uparrow \qquad \qquad ...(1.9)$$

Trichlorosilane TCS vapor is then gone to fractional distillation to remove unwanted impurities through a series of filters, condensers (boiling point 32°C), and purifiers to finally get an ultra high purity liquid of purity higher than 99.9999999% at room temperature. Then, high–purity TCS is used in the hydrogen reduction reaction at temperature 1,1000C to produce the electronic grade silicon EGS.

$$SiHCl_3 + H_2 \xrightarrow{1100°C} Si + 3HCl \uparrow \qquad \ldots(1.10)$$

The reaction takes place in a reactor containing resistance heated silicon rod, which serves as the nucleation point for deposition of EGS in polycrystalline form of high purity. This is the raw material used to prepare device quality single crystal. Pure EGS has impurity concentration generally in part per billion. The pure EGS is then ready to be pulled into silicon ingot for making wafer for integrated circuit fabrication. There are a number of methods used to grow silicon crystalline ingot.

Silicon Wafer Fabrication Process

- More than 90% of the earth's crust is composed of Silica (SiO_2) or Silicate, making silicon the second most abundant element on earth. When sand glitters in sunlight, that's silica.

- Silicon is found in compounds in nature. Silicon is the principle platform for semiconductor devices.

- Now–a–days semiconductor is the most advanced technology requires the monocrystalline silicon with uniform chemical characteristics to control doping and oxygen content.

- The process to transform raw silicon into a useable single–crystal substrate for modern semiconductor processes begins by mining for relatively pure Silicon Dioxide.

- Most silicon now is made by reducing temperature of SiO_2 with Carbon in an electric furnace from 1500 to 200 °C. With carefully selected pure sand, the result is commercial brown Metallurgical Grade Silicon of 97% purity or better.

- This is the silicon eventually used for semiconductors, but it must be further purified to bring impurities below the parts–per–billion level. Now that a high level of purity has been attained (99.999999999%), the atomic structure of the silicon must be dealt with a process termed as Crystal Growing which transforms polycrystalline silicon into samples with a singular crystal orientation, known as ingots.

- The Polysilicon is mechanically broken into 1 to 3 inch chunks and undergoes stringent surface etching and cleaning in a clean room environment. These chunks are then packed into quartz crucibles for meltdown (at 1420 °C) in a CZ furnace.

- A mono crystalline Silicon seed is installed into a seed shaft in the upper chamber of the furnace. Slowly, the seed is lowered so that it dips approximately 2 mm into the Silicon melt.

- Next, the seed is slowly retracted from the surface allowing the melt to solidify at the boundary.

- As the seed pulls the Silicon from the melt, both the crucible and the seed are rotated in opposite directions to allow for an almost round crystal to form. CZ furnaces also must be very stable and isolated from vibrations.

- The crystal diameter is properly achieved by increasing the seed lift along with the heat transfer from heating elements it will control the diameter of the crystal. In this growth process, the crucible slowly dissolves oxygen and melt that into the final crystal.

- Additionally, to pull speed and heat transfer at the solid–liquid interface, heat dissipation during crystal cooling strongly determines microscopic defect characteristics in the final crystal. For modern CZ pulling systems, those variables can be accurately predicted by numerical simulations which allow designing the geometrical and thermal configuration of the CZ puller to the desired outcome of the crystals. Once the growth process is complete, the crystal is cooled inside the furnace for up to 7 hours. This gradual cooling allows the crystal lattice to stabilize and makes handling easier before transport to the next operation.

- It is important, for some applications, to have even lower concentrations of impurity atoms (e.g. Oxygen) than what can be achieved by CZ crystal growth. In this case, Float Zone Crystal Growth is used.

- In this process the end of a long polysilicon rod is locally melted and brought in contact with a monocrystalline Silicon seed. The melted zone slowly migrates through the poly rod leaving behind a final uniform crystal. Ingots coming from crystal growing are slightly over–sized in diameter and typically not round.

- Hence, a machine employing a grind wheel shapes the ingot to the precision needed for wafer diameter control. Other grinding wheels are then used to carve a characteristic notch or a flat in order to define the proper orientation of the future wafer versus a particular crystallographic axis.

- Wafer shaping contains a series of precise mechanical and chemical process steps that are necessary to turn the ingot segment into a functional wafer.

- It is during these steps that the wafer surfaces and dimensions are perfected to exacting detail. Each step is designed to bring the wafer into compliance with each customer specification.

- The first of these critical steps is Multi–Wiring Slicing. The dominant state of the art slicing technology refers to Multi–Wire Sawing (MWS). Here, a thin wire is arranged over cylindrical spools so that hundreds of parallel wire segments simultaneously travel through the ingot.

- While the saw as a whole slowly moves through the ingot, the individual wire segments conduct a translational motion always bringing fresh wire into contact with the Silicon.

- The sawing effect is actually achieved by SiC or other grinding agents that run along the rotating wire.

- After MWS the wafers are cleaned and consolidated into process lots and transported to the next operation.

- The sideward deflection of the wire saw can lead to marks or "waviness" on the wafer surface and wire–to–wire thickness variations cause wafer thickness variations of up to several microns. Thus wafers are exposed to a complex polishing process.

1.3.3 Crystal Planes and Orientation

- The orientation of a plane in a lattice is stated by Miller indices. They referred as intercept of the plane with the axes along the primitive translation vectors A_1, A_2 and A_3. Let us these intercepts be X, Y, and Z, so that X is fractional multiple of A_1, Y is a fractional multiple of A_2 and Z is a fractional multiple of A_3. Therefore we can measure X, Y, and Z in units A_1, A_2 and A_3 respectively. We have a triplet of integers (X Y Z) then we invert it (1/X 1/Y 1/Z) and reduce this set to a similar one having the smallest integers by multiplying by a common factor. This set is called Miller indices of the plane (hkl).

For example, if the plane intercepts X, Y, and Z in points 1, 3, and 1, the index of this plane will be (313) as shown in Fig. 1.7.

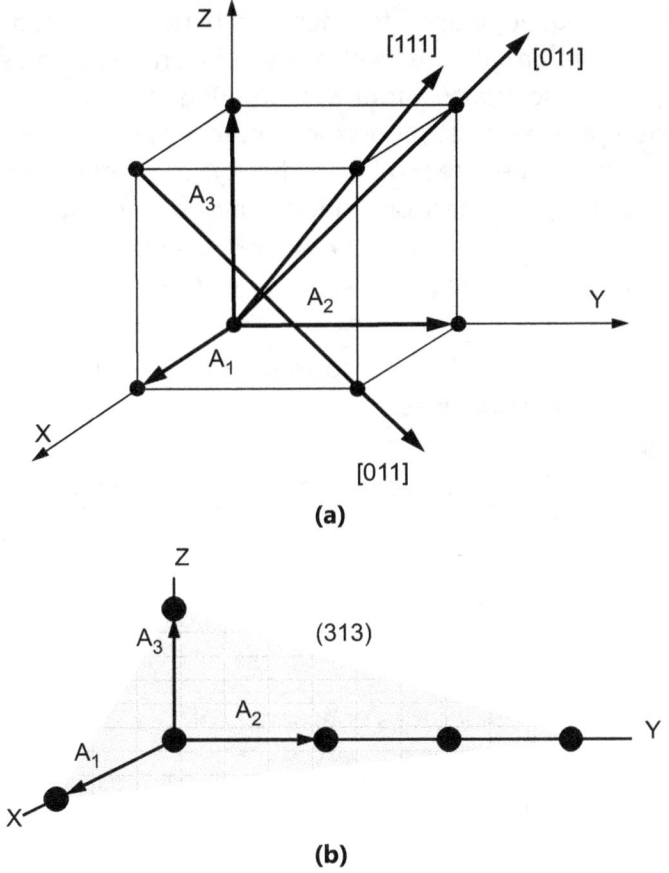

Fig. 1.7: Crystal plane intercept

The orientation of a crystal plane is determined by three points in the plane, provided they are not collinear. If each point lay on a different crystal axis, the plane could be specified by giving the coordinates of the points in terms of the lattice constants a, b, c. A notation conventionally used to describe lattice points (sites), directions and planes is termed as Miller Indices. A crystal lattice may be considered as an assembly of equidistant parallel planes passing through the lattice points and are known as lattice planes. In order to specify the orientation one employs the so called Miller indices. For simplicity, let us start with a two dimensional lattice and then generalized to three dimensional case.

The equation of plane in 2D and 3D having the intercepts a, b and a, b, c respectively are:

$$\frac{x}{a} + \frac{y}{b} = 1 \text{ and } \frac{x}{a} + \frac{y}{b} + \frac{z}{c} = 1$$

Crystal direction is the direction (line) of axes or line from the origin and denoted as [111], [100], [010] etc.

1.4 MODERN CMOS TECHNOLOGY

A Complementary Metal Oxide Semiconductor (CMOS) is a kind of integrated circuit technology. The term is frequently used to refer to a battery–powered chip found in many PCs that holds some basic information, as well as the date and time and system configuration settings, required by the Basic Input/Output System (BIOS) to start the computer. However, this name is rather deceptive as most modern computers no longer use these chips for this function; on the other hand they depend on other types of non–volatile memory. CMOS chips are still found in many other electronic devices, including digital cameras.

In addition to NMOS and PMOS transistors, the technology offers:

* A deep n–well that can be utilized to reduce substrate noise coupling.
* A MOS varactor that can serve in VCOs
* At least six levels of metal that can form many useful structures such as inductors, capacitors, and transmission lines.

Why CMOS Technology?

Comparison of BJT and MOSFET technology from an analog viewpoint as follows:

Feature	BJT	MOSFET
Cutoff Frequency (f_T)	100 GHz	50 GHz (0.25 µm)
Noise (thermal about the same)	Less 1/f	More 1/f
DC Range of operation	9 decades of exponential current versus vBE	2–3 decades of square law behavior
Small Signal Output Resistance	Slightly larger	Smaller for short channel.
Switch Implementation	Poor	Good
Capacitor Implementation	Voltage dependent	Reasonably good

- Almost every comparison favors the BJT, however a similar comparison made from a digital viewpoint would come up on the side of CMOS.
- Therefore, since large–volume technology will be driven by digital demands, CMOS is an obvious result as the technology of availability.
- The potential for technology improvement for CMOS is greater than for BJT.
- Performance generally increases with decreasing channel length.

Basic Steps of CMOS Technology

1. Oxide growth
2. Thermal diffusion
3. Ion implantation
4. Deposition
5. Etching
6. Epitaxial

Photolithography is the means by which the above steps are applied to selected areas of the silicon wafer as shown in following Fig. 1.8.

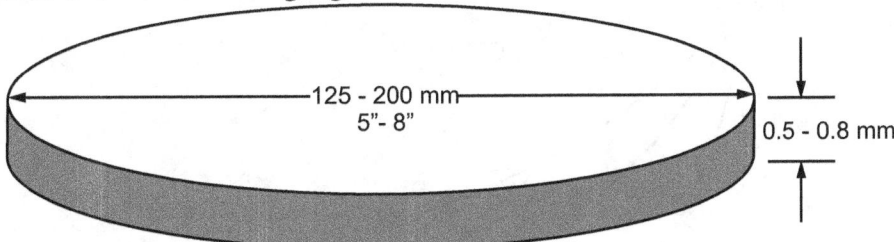

125 - 200 mm
5"- 8"
0.5 - 0.8 mm

n-type : 3 - 5 Ω-cm
p-type : 14 - 16 Ω-cm

Fig. 1.8: Si wafer

1. Oxidation

Oxidation is the process by which a layer of silicon dioxide is grown on the surface of a silicon wafer.

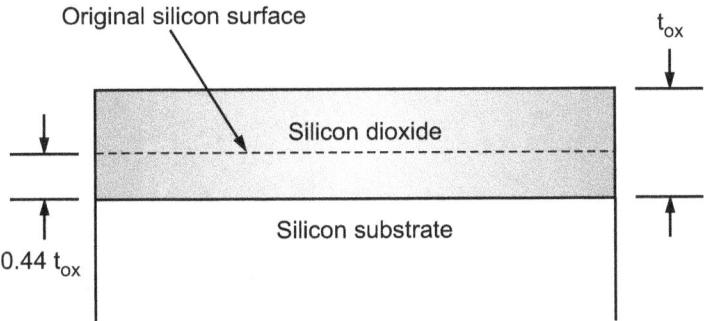

Original silicon surface

t_{ox}

Silicon dioxide

Silicon substrate

0.44 t_{ox}

Fig. 1.9: Oxidation

Uses

- Protect the underlying material from contamination.
- Provide isolation between two layers.

Very thin oxides (100 °A to 1000 °A) are grown using dry oxidation techniques. Thicker oxides (>1000 °A) are grown using wet oxidation techniques.

2. Diffusion

The process of movement of impurity atoms at the surface of the silicon into the bulk of the silicon. It is always in the direction from higher concentration to lower concentration.

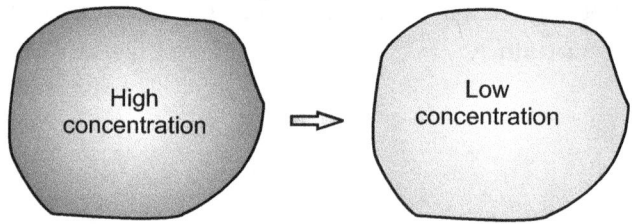

Fig. 1.10: Diffusion

It is typically done at high temperatures: 800 to 1400 °C

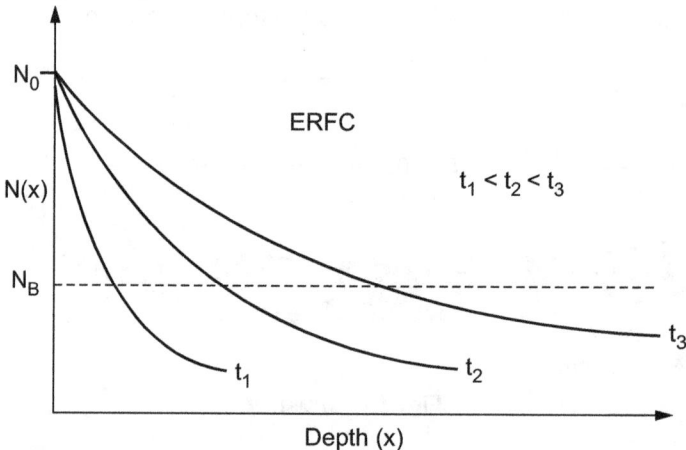

Fig. 1.11 : Infinite source of impurities at the surface

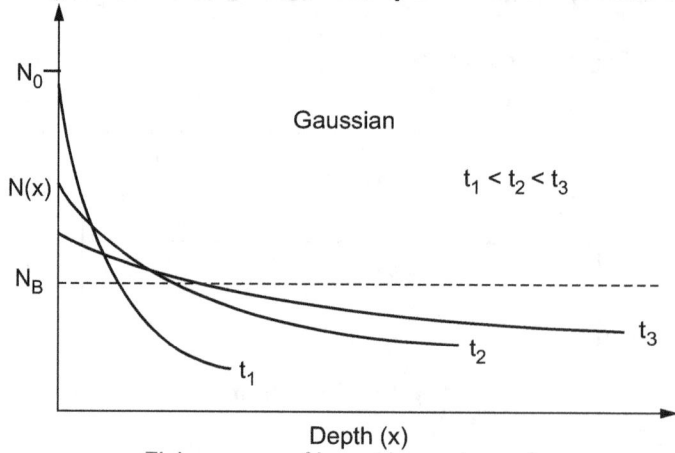

Fig. 1.12 : Finite source of impurities at the surface

3. Ion Implantation

The process by which impurity ions are accelerated to a high velocity and physically lodged into the target material.

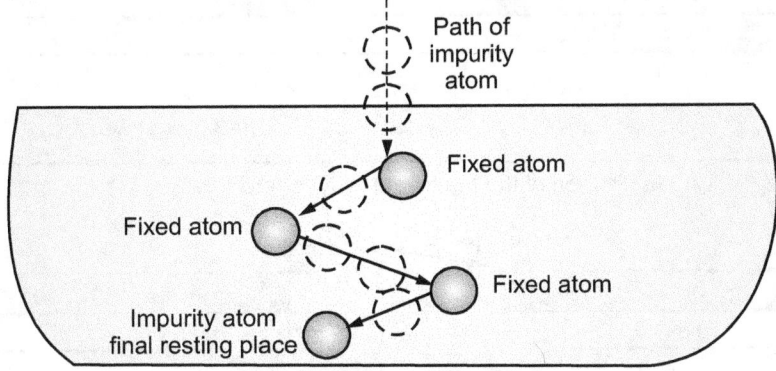

Fig. 1.13: Ion implantation

- Annealing is required to activate the impurity atoms and repair the physical damage to the crystal lattice. This step is done at 500 to 800°C.
- Ion implantation is a lower temperature process compared to diffusion.
- Can implant through surface layers, thus it is useful for field–threshold adjustment.
- Can achieve unique doping profile such as buried concentration peak.

4. Deposition

The deposition means by which various materials are deposited on the silicon wafer.

Examples:

- Silicon nitride (Si_3N_4)
- Silicon dioxide (SiO_2)
- Aluminum
- Polysilicon

There are various ways to deposit a material on a substrate:

- Chemical–Vapor Deposition (CVD)
- Low–Pressure Chemical–Vapor Deposition (LPCVD)
- Plasma–Assisted Chemical–Vapor Deposition (PACVD)
- Sputter deposition material that is being deposited using these techniques covers the entire wafer.

5. Etching

The Etching process of selectively removing a layer of material. When etching is performed, the etchant may remove portions or all of:

- The desired material.

- The underlying layer.
- The masking layer.

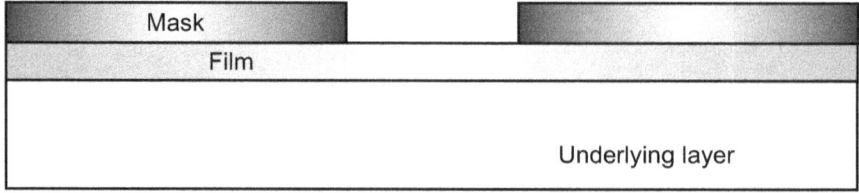

(a) Portion of the top layer ready for etching.

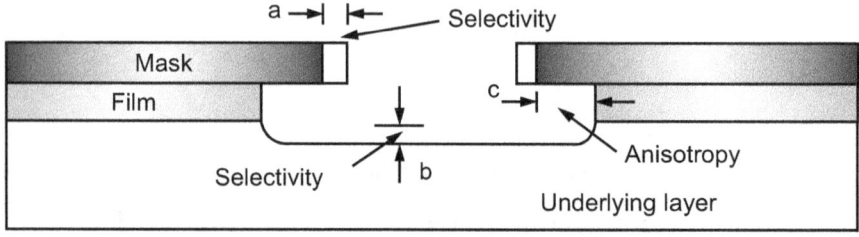

(b) Horizontal etching and etching of underlying layer.

Fig. 1.14: Etching

Important Considerations:

- Anisotropy of the etch is defined as, A = 1–(lateral etch rate/vertical etch rate)
- Selectivity of the etch (film to mask and film to substrate) is defined as,

$$S_{film-mask} = \frac{\text{film etch rate}}{\text{mask etch rate}}$$

$$A = 1 \text{ and } S_{film-mask} = \infty \text{ are desired}$$

There are basically two types of etches:

- Wet etch which uses chemicals
- Dry etch which uses chemically active ionized gases.

5. Epitaxial

Epitarial of growth is the formation of a layer or of single crystal silicon on the surface of the silicon material so that the crystal. Structure of the silicon is continuous across the following interfaces.

- It is done externally to the material as opposed to diffusion which is internal.
- The epitaxial layer (epi) can be doped differently, even opposite, of the material on which it grown.
- It accomplished at high temperatures using a chemical reaction at the surface.
- The epi layer can be any thickness, typically 1–20 microns.

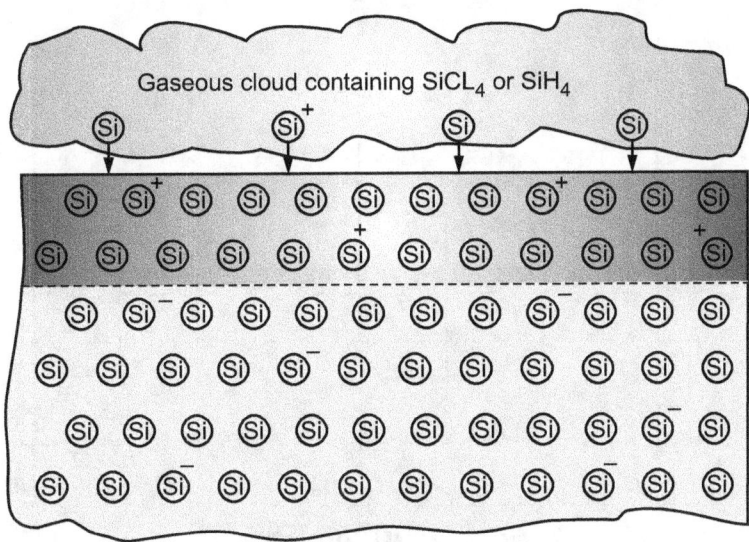

Fig. 1.15: Epitaxial Layer

Basic CMOS Concepts

A transistor behaves like a switch. For NMOS transistors, if the input is a 1 the switch is on, otherwise it is off. Conversely, for the PMOS, if the input is 0 the transistor is on, then the transistor is off. Here, it is a graphical representation of these facts:

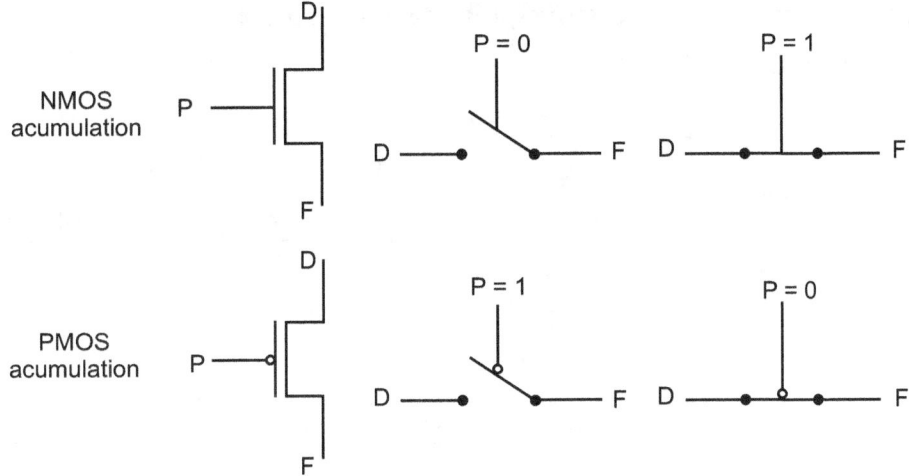

Fig. 1.16: Accumulation of NMOS and PMOS

- When a circuit contains both NMOS and PMOS transistors, we say it is implemented in CMOS (Complementary MOS) Understanding the basics of transistors, we can now design a simple NOR gate.

- Following Fig. 1.17 shows the implementation in transistors of the NOT gate and how it works for different inputs (1 and 0). On the left there is the implementation, on the right the behavior. The symbol VDD is the source voltage (or the logic 1), GND is the ground (or the logical 0).

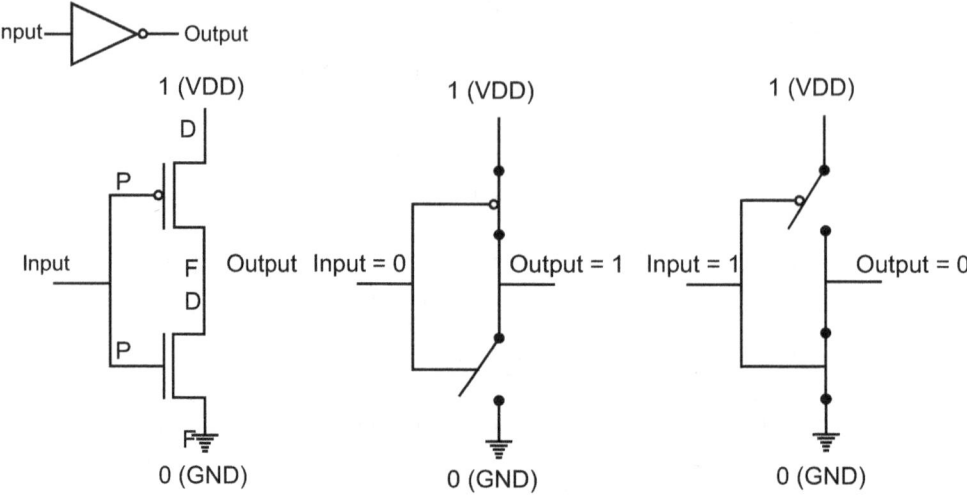

Fig. 1.17: NOT operation

- We have just seen how to implement a simple logic gate using transistors. To implement the rest of logical gates (and whatever circuit we might think off), we will analyze first the behavior of the transistors when connected in a "series" fashion or in a "parallel" way.

- If we connect two NMOS transistors in series, we get the behavior shown in following Fig. 1.18. It is triangle in the bottom representation of ground (GND).

Output = 0, Si S1 = 1, S2 = 1

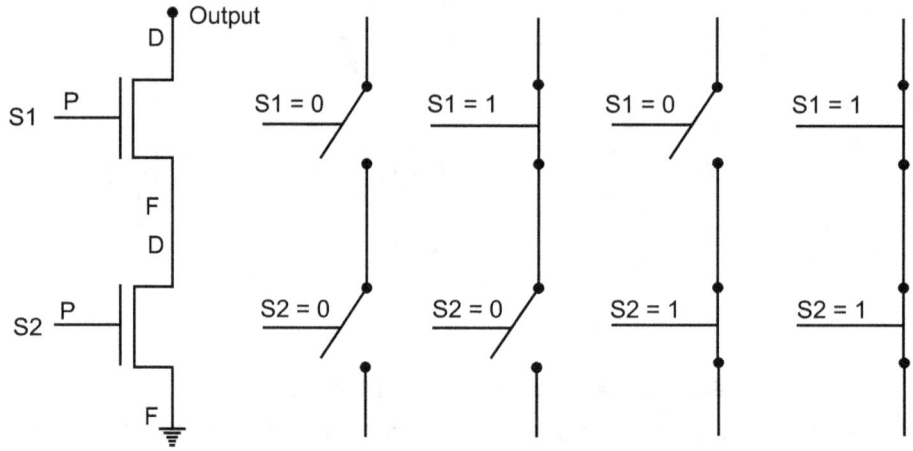

Fig. 1.18: Series connection of NMOS transistor

- Following Fig. 1.18 shows the behaviour of the PMOS when connected in series. It is horizontal line on the top of the first transistor representation of V_{DD}.

Output = 1 Si S1 = 0 ; S2 = 0

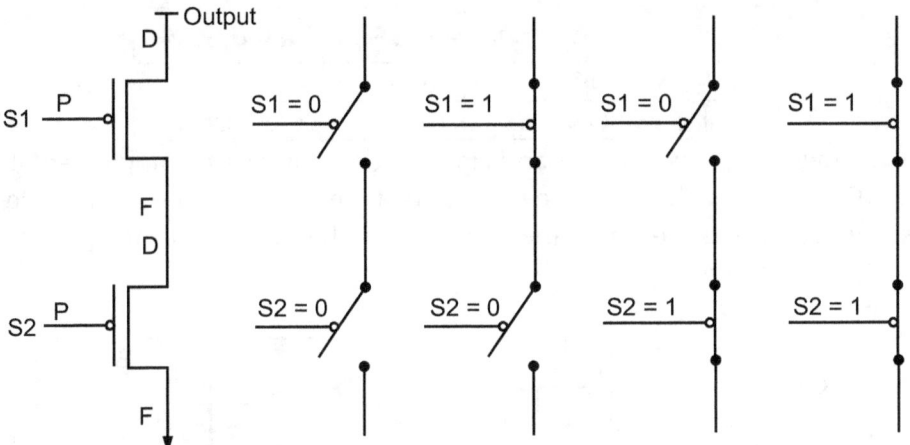

Fig. 1.19: Series connection of PMOS transistor

- When using CMOS technology, precisely static CMOS, we will design the circuits with two clearly defined parts. One (called pull–up) will be built of PMOS transistors and it has the duty of setting the output to 1 whenever the implemented function defines it.

- The other part (called pull–down) will be built of NMOS transistors and it will set the output to 0 whenever the implemented function defines it. All circuits will either set the output to 1 or 0 for any combination of the input values. Both pull–up and pull–down cannot be active at the same time (when the output set 1 and input set 0 at the same time). Similarly, both the pull–up and the pull–down cannot be off at the same time (logic functions have always a defined output either 0 or 1).

- Nevertheless, we will see further down the course that when not implementing logic functions we might be interested sometimes in setting the output to undetermined in certain cases.

Complementary CMOS Logic Gates

- nMOS pull–down network

- pMOS pull–up network and static CMOS

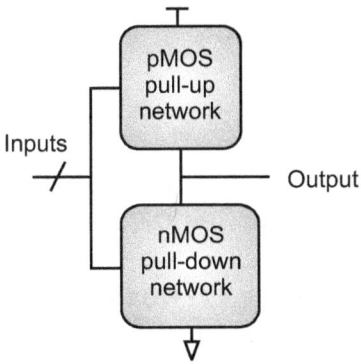

Fig. 1.20: Pull–down network of CMOS

	Pull–up OFF	Pull–up ON
Pull–down OFF	Z (float)	1
Pull–down ON	0	X (crossbar)

As shown in following Figures Fig. 1.21 and Fig. 1.22 demonstrate the implementations of the NAND and NOR gates in CMOS. For each one of them, there is the truth table and clear indications of what outputs are set by the pull–up and what outputs for the pull–down.

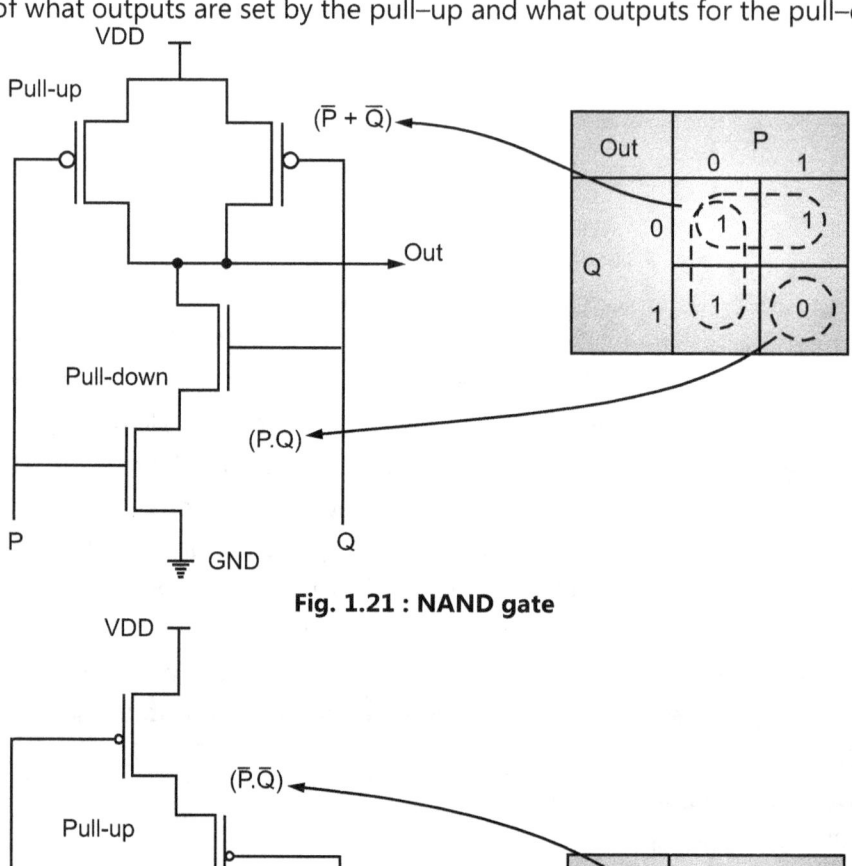

Fig. 1.21 : NAND gate

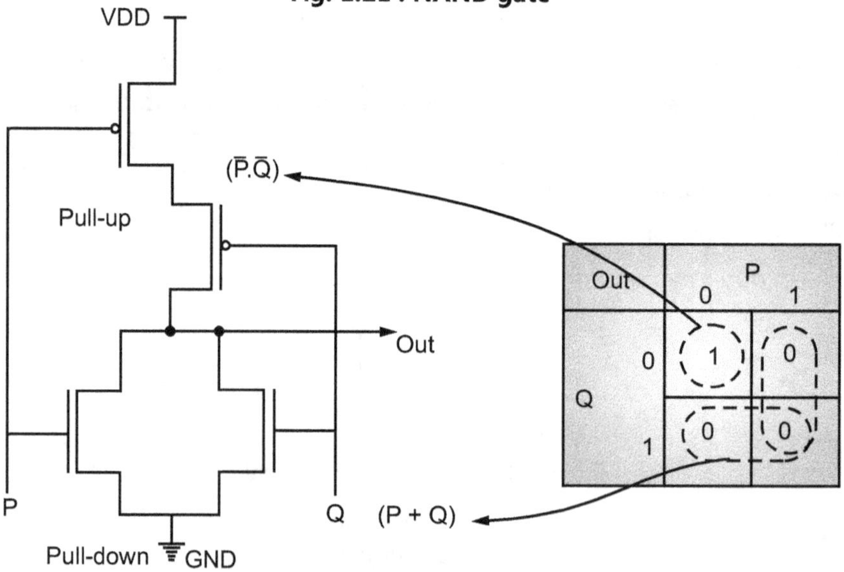

Fig. 1.22 : NOR gate

In the same way we implement the logic gates, or we can implement the logic function. Following Fig. 1.23 shows the implementation of the logic function:

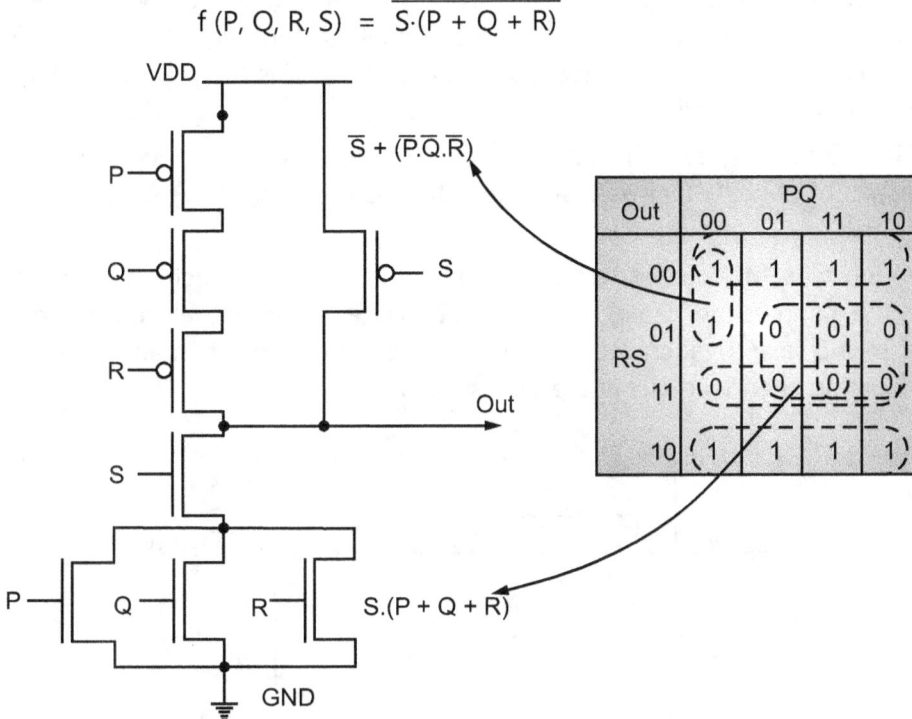

$$f(P, Q, R, S) = \overline{S \cdot (P + Q + R)}$$

Fig. 1.23: Implementaion of logical function

We can design methodology for turning logical functions into CMOS circuits:

- The logic function must be complemented. (i.e., it must look like f(x,y,z) = NOT (expression); in a logic expression,

$$f(x, y, z) = \overline{\text{expression}}$$

- AND operator ("·"):
- Pull–down: NMOS transistors NMOS in series
- Pull–up: PMOS transistors in parallel
- OR operator ("+"):
- Pull–down: NOMS transistors in parallel
- Pull–up: PMOS transistors in series

1.4.1 Construction of MOS Field Effect Transistor

- The term MOSFET is an acronym for Metal Oxide Semiconductor Field Effect Transistor, and the name indicates a hint to its manufacturer. The devices had been known about for several years but only became important in mid and late 1960s.
- Primarily, semiconductor research had focused in developing the bipolar transistor, and problems had been experienced in fabricating MOSFETs because of process problems, particularly with the insulating oxide layers.
- Now the technology is one of the most widely used semiconductor techniques, having become one of the principle elements in integrated circuit technology today.

- Their performance has enabled power consumptions in ICs to be reduced. This has reduced amount of heat being dissipated and enabled the large ICs, we take for granted today to become a reality. As a result of this the MOSFET is the most widely used form of transistor in existence today.

- MOSFET have metal gates which are insulated from the semiconductor by a layer of SiO_2 or dielectric. In EMOSFET of gate voltage activates the channel by inducing carriers layer between the source and drain under the terminal.

- In depletion type MOSFETs, there is a small strip of semiconductor of the same type as that of the source and drain, and the gate voltage can either reduce (by depleting carriers) or increase (by increasing carriers) the channel current. In an n channel MOSFET, the conducting channel exists in a p type substrate.

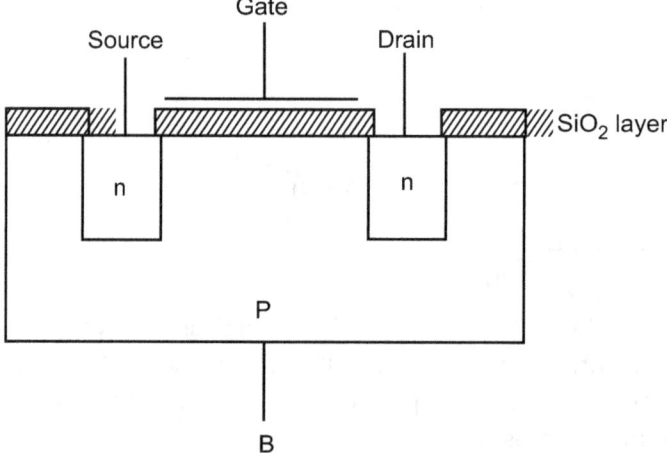

Fig. 1.24 : *n*–channel EMOSFET structure

Note : The additional B terminal on the substrate, which is often connected directly to the source.

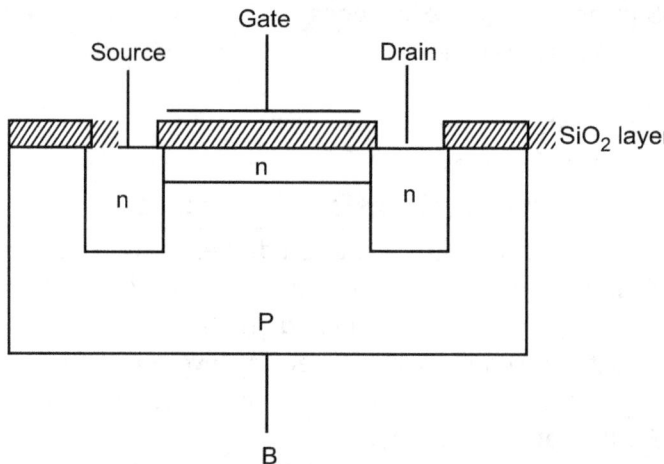

Fig. 1.25 : n–channel DMOSFET structure

Working Principle of MOSFET

- MOSFET depends on the MOS capacitor; the main part of MOSFET is the semiconductor surface at below the oxide layer and between the drain and source terminal can be inverted from p–type to n–type by applying a positive or negative gate voltages separately.

- When applying positive gate voltage the holes present beneath the oxide layer repulsive force are pushed downward with the substrate. The depletion region is populated by the bound negative charges, which are associated with the acceptor atoms.

- The positive voltage also attracts to electrons from the n+ source and drain regions into the channel. The electron reach channel is formed.

- If a voltage is applied between the source and the drain, current flows freely between the source and drain gate voltage controls the electrons concentration the channel becomes positive, if we apply negative voltage, a hole channel will be formed beneath the oxide layer. The controlling of source to gate voltage is responsible for the conduction of current between source and the drain. If the gate voltage exceeds a given value, called the three voltage only the conduction begins.

- The current equation of MOSFET in triode region is :

$$I_D = u_n \, C_{ax} \frac{W}{2} \left[(V_{GS} - V_{TH}) \, V_{DS} - \frac{1}{2} V_{DS}^2 \right]$$

Where, u_n = Mobility of the electrons C_{ox} = Capacitance of the oxide layer W = Width of the gate area L = Length of the channel V_{GS} = Gate to Source voltage V_{TH} = Threshold voltage V_{DS} = Drain to Source voltage.

P–Channel MOSFET

- MOSFET which has p – channel region between sources and gate is called as p – channel MOSFET. Terminals are gate, drain, source and substrate or body. The drain and source is heavily doped p+ region and the substrate is in n–type.

- The current flows through positively charged holes that's why it is called as p–channel MOSFET.

- If we apply negative gate voltage to the gate terminal of MOSFET, the electrons present beneath of the oxide layer, then repulsive force is pushed downward into the substrate. The depletion region of this case populated by the bound positive charges it has associated with donor atoms.

- The negative gate voltage also attracts holes from p+ source and drain region in to the channel region, thus holes which channel is formed now if a voltage between the source and the drain is applied current flows. The gate voltage controls the hole concentration of the channel.

- The following Fig. 1.26 showing of p–channel enhancement and depletion MOSFET are given below.

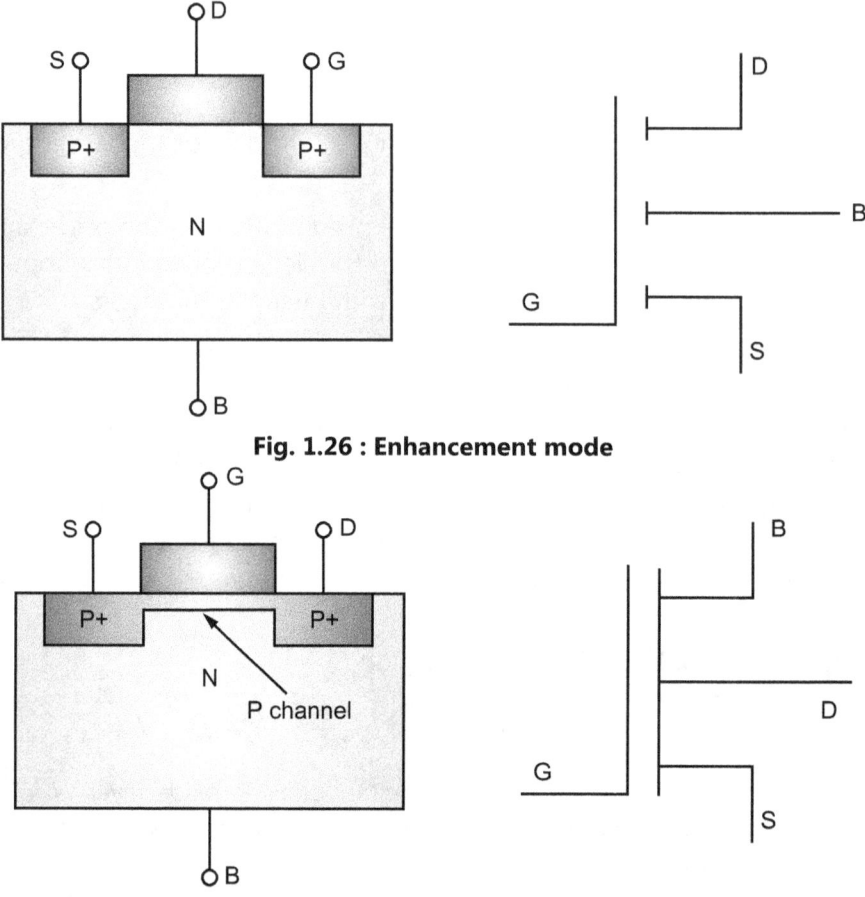

Fig. 1.26 : Enhancement mode

Fig. 1.27 : Depletion mode

N–Channel MOSFET

- MOSFET having n–channel region between source and drain is called as n–channel MOSFET.

- The terminals are gate, drain and source and substrate or body. The drain and source is heavily doped n+ region and the substrate is p–type. The current flows because of flow of the negatively charged electrons, that's why it is called as n– channel MOSFET.

- If we apply the positive gate voltage to the gate terminal the holes present beneath the oxide layer, repulsive force (holes) are pushed downwards into the bound negative charge associated with the acceptor atoms.

- The positive gate voltage also attracts to electrons from n+ source and drain region into the channel, thus an electron which channel is formed, now if a voltage is applied between the source and drain.

- The gate voltage controls the electron concentration in the channel n–channel MOSFET is preferred over p–channel MOSFET as the mobility of electrons are higher than holes. The diagrams of enhancements mode and depletion mode are given below.

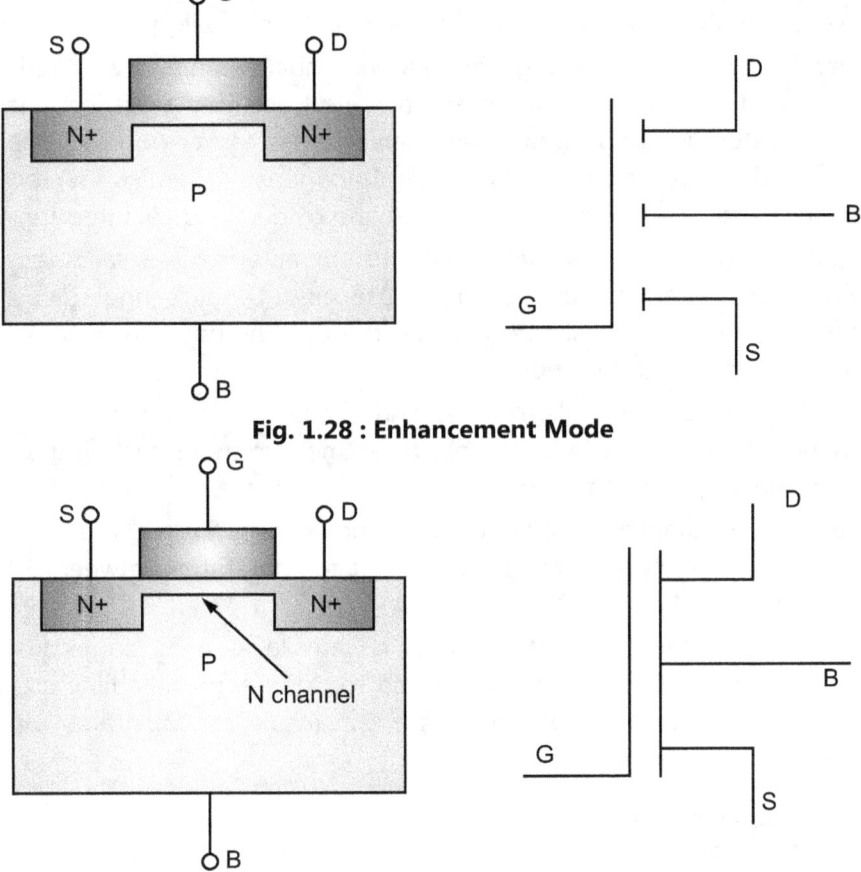

Fig. 1.28 : Enhancement Mode

Fig. 1.29 : Depletion mode

1.5 ELECTRICAL CHARACTERIZATION

- Electrical Characterization can be used to determine resistivity, carrier concentration, mobility, contact resistance, barrier height, depletion width, oxide charge, interface states, carrier lifetimes, and deep level impurities.

- Electrical characterization techniques are used to dielectric–semiconductor edges and to transmit the results of these measurements to the reliability of the device or component. Use this techniques investigators prefer to do not require special test structures. It is used to easily and readily applied to standard test structure to manufactured for the process of file development.

- The continued evolution of semiconductor devices with smaller dimensions to improve performance speed, functionality and integration density, all at reduced cost require layers or films of semiconductors, insulators and metals with increasingly higher quality that are well characterized and can be deposited and patterned to very high precision.

- However, it is not always the case that improvements in materials' quality have kept pace with the evolution of integrated circuit dimensional down–scaling.

- An important aspect of assessing the material quality and device reliability is the development and use of fast, non–destructive, and accurate electrical characterization techniques to determine important parameters such as carrier doping density, type and mobility of carriers, interface quality, oxide trap density. Semiconductor bulk defect density. contact and other parasitic resistances and oxide electrical integrity.

- Electrical Characterization is the key means to characterize and validate your product quality, but from tester to nano–probing, use cases and technologies involved are different: from a simple oscilloscope/ probing through the pads down to most advanced nano–probing solutions/ applications.

- The characterization of materials, devices and circuits is unthinkable without electrical measurements. A broad spectrum of electrical measurement techniques and analysis methods for device characterization.

- This includes capacitance measurements, such as C(V), C(T) and C(f), current measurements with femto–ampere resolution at temperatures between 5 K and 450 K and voltages up to 3000 V.

- Samples can be analyzed by direct probing on wafer level using single probes or probe cards. Package level testing can be performed for long–term reliability characterization. Additionally, carrier lifetime measurements are available on substrates with microwave detected photoconductivity.

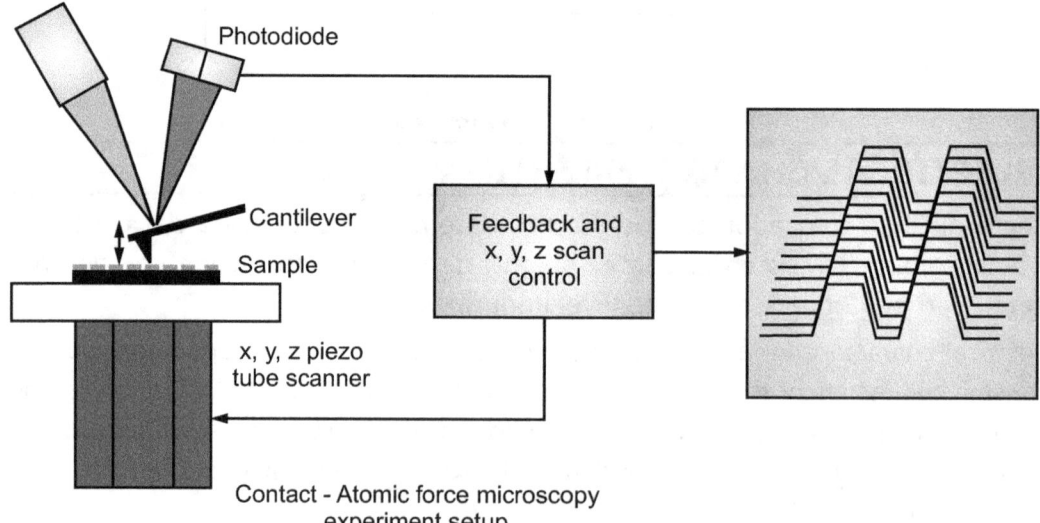

Contact - Atomic force microscopy experiment setup

Fig. 1.30 : Characterization of material

The established methods involve:

- Analysis of single memory cells (memory window, retention, endurance, ...) by static and pulsed measurements.

- Determination of transistor and capacitor characteristic curves by C–V and I–V measurements.
- Determination of sheet resistance for thin layers.
- Determination of doping profiles by Scanning Spreading Resistance Microscopy (SSRM).
- Reliability characterization of dielectric and transistors.
- Defect characterization by charge pumping and charge trapping analysis and defect spectroscopy.
- Measurement of charge carrier mobility with Hall and split–C(V).

Low temperature measurements open the door to investigate effects of charge discreteness or the quantum nature of electrons in devices. In–house fabricated Si–Nanowire transistors operated in the quantum dot regime at T = 5 K show characteristic coulomb oscillations. Here, the periodic peak spacing (21 mV) is directly linked to the specific capacitance and energy structure of the respective nanowire device. Moreover, magneto–transport measurements on transistor devices can be performed up to a magnetic field B= +/– 2.5 T.

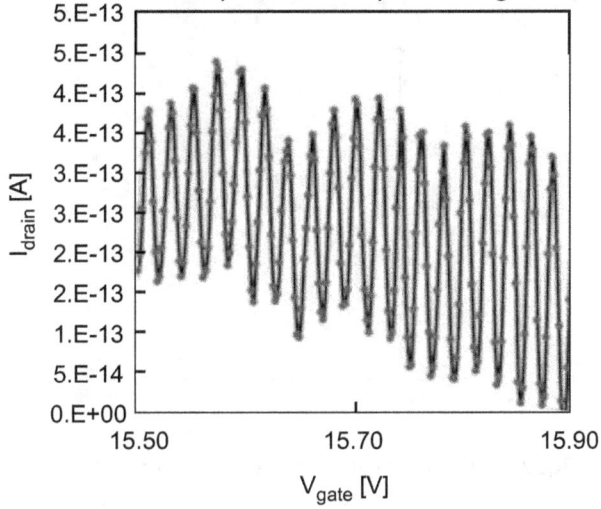

Fig. 1.31: Low temperature measurement

A powerful characterization software was developed enabling automatic wafer mapping, easy measurement flow setup in Extensible Markup Language (XML), control of various probe stations and all kinds of measurement equipment, real time parameter extraction and dynamic measurement flow control as well as data export into standard formats (.xlsx, .opj) and user defined formats. The characterization software provides the needed flexibility in handling of all different kinds of samples and the whole band of characterization techniques.

1.5.1 Current–Voltage (I–V)/Capacitance–Voltage (C–V) Characterization

- Low current measurement challenges such as error sources for example leakage currents, noise, offset currents, piezoelectric currents, and environmental conditions can have a serious impact on measurement accuracy.

- Precision DC I–V measurements are the foundation of electrical characterization for cutting–edge devices, materials, and semiconductors. With proper measurement techniques and practices, these critical measurement challenges can be met.

- Now–a–days, many parametric measurements require a fast, pulsed I–V measurement using pulsed I–V signals to characterize devices rather than DC signals makes it possible to study or reduce the effects of self–heating (joule heating) or to minimize current drift/degradation in measurements.

- Many applications require pulsed I–V along with C–V and DC I–V measurements. Learn how to combine all three measurement types into one test system while maintaining the measurement performance.

IV measurements are a process to determine devices characteristics and performance. Depending on the device in hands we will attain different information.

lets consider a ohmic device, that is, is obeys Ohm law, V = RI then as the equation shows we would obtain a linear relation between voltage and current, as showed:

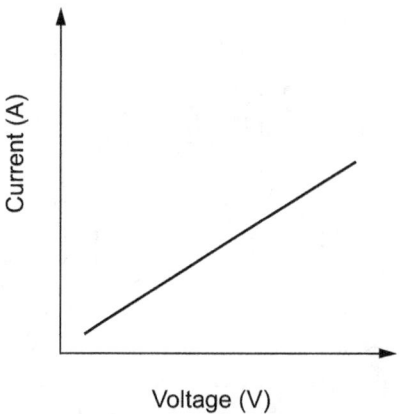

Fig. 1.32 : Linear relation between voltage and current

The resistance we measure has a contribution from the sample, the wires and the contacts:

$$R = R_{wires} + R_{contact} + R_{sample}$$

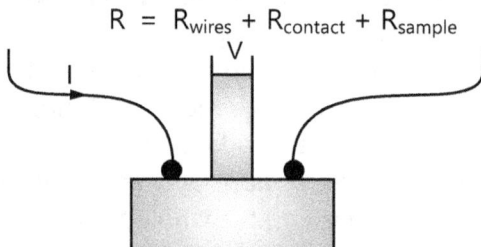

Fig. 1.33 : Resistance measurement

In order to minimise the contact and wires resistances the measurements are usually done with four probes; we are initially considering diodes. Below is sketch an IV curve. from observing the curve we can determine if we have a good quality device, since the bigger Δ is, better will the device perform. The threshold voltage is taken from the extrapolation to V=0 of the IV curve in forward bias.

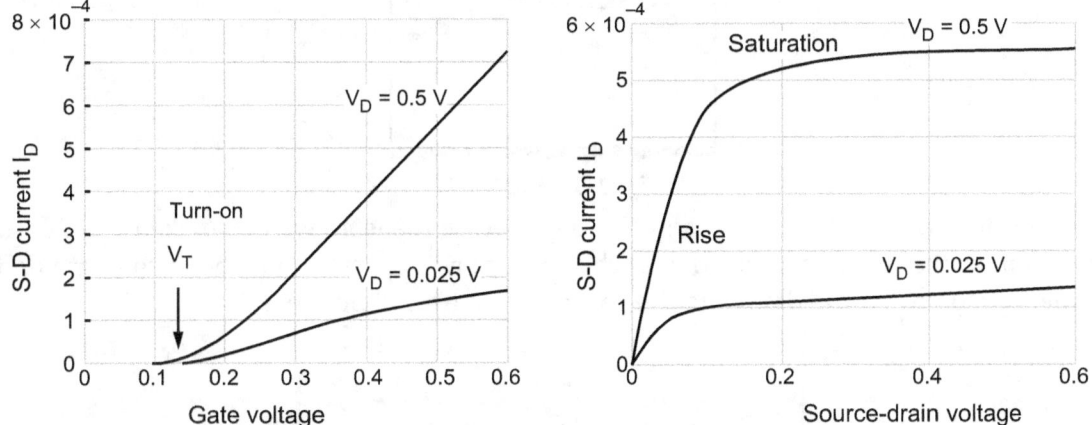

Fig. 1.34: VI characteristics

Another parameter that is possible to take is the Schoottky barrier height. A sketch of the band structure can be seen below:

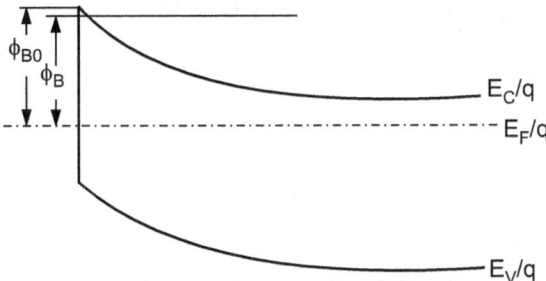

Fig. 1.35 : Band structure of schoottkydiode

In order to get the barrier height (φ_B) we need to consider the thermionic current voltage relationship:

$$I = I_s \left(\exp \frac{qV}{nkT} - 1 \right)$$

where I_s is the saturation current and

$$I_s = AA^* T^2 \exp - \frac{q\phi B}{kT}$$

from this last equation we get

$$\phi_B = \frac{kT}{q} \ln \left(\frac{AA^* T^2}{I_s} \right)$$

with being the area of the diode and A*=120(m*/m). If we plot a semilog curve of $I_s$vs. V and extrapolate the curve to V=0 we will get φ_B for zero bias.

Lets consider now a MOSFET. Below is a sketch of one:

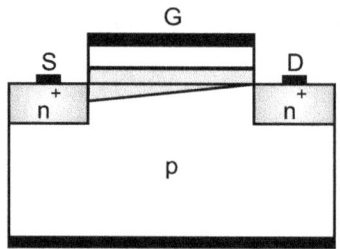

Fig. 1.36: MOSFET

where S is the source, D the drain and G the gate. One measure we can make is to measure the current at the drain and the source while we apply a constant voltage in the gate and a variable voltage along the drain and the source. What we will obtain is:

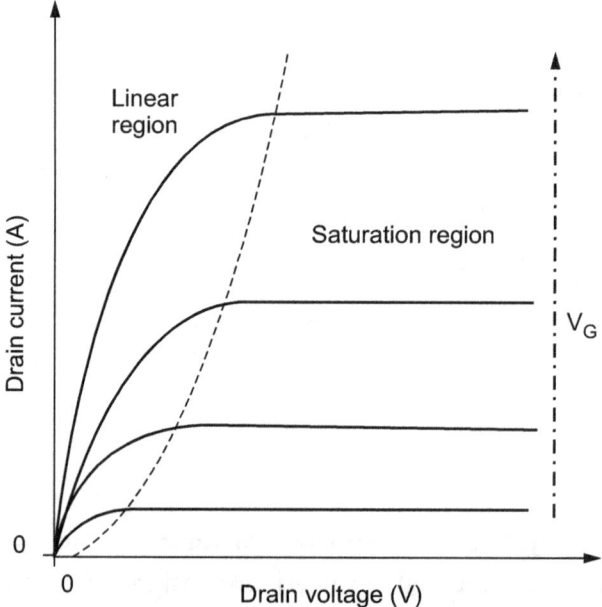

Fig. 1.37 : Output Characteristics

In above Fig. 1.37 shows we can see two different regions: the linear region and the saturation region. In the linear region the conduction channel acts like a resistor. if we continue to increase the voltage the channel potential will reduce the current, translating in the lost of linearity, if we continue to increase the voltage we will get to a point where the inversion charge reaches zero and we no longer see a change in the current, we reach the saturation regime.

The threshold voltage is the gate bias at which the devices turn on. And, it can be determine from the transfer characteristic, for that we need to measure the drain current while we change the gate voltage and extrapolate the curve to V=0. If we then plot the same curve in a semi log scale we will get the sub threshold swing.

There are many parameters could be extracted from IV measurement such as thershold voltage sub threshold slope and resistance which will discuss in next section.

Capacitance–Voltage (C–V) Measurements

For example, in order to measure effective field, it is common to use Split CV. With this technique we are able to determine charge depletion and charge inversion which are need.

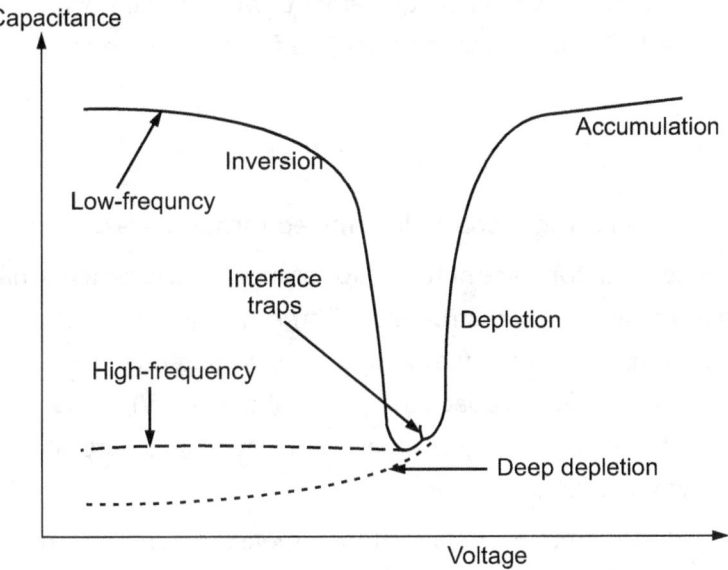

Fig. 1.38: Capacitance Voltage characteristics

In the gate channel configuration, C_{gc}, the substrate is connected to Earth while we apply voltage at the gate. The capacitance will be measured through the drain and source. The charge inversion will determine integrating the CV curve from the flatband voltage:

$$Q_{inv} = \frac{1}{WL} \int_{V_{FB}}^{V_G} C_{gc} d\, V_G$$

In the gate body configuration, C_{gb}, the drain and the source are connected to the Earth while we apply voltage at the gate. the capacitance will now be measure through the substrate and the charge depletion will be determined integrating the CV curve, also, from the flatband voltage:

$$Q_{dep} = \frac{1}{WL} \int_{V_{FB}}^{V_G} C_{gc} d\, V_G$$

From the above expressions it can be perceive that another important parameter is the flatband voltage. This can be determined from the $1/C^2$ vs V_G curve, by extrapolating the linear part to V = 0.

The effective field is given by

$$\varepsilon_{eff} = \frac{\eta \, Q_{int} + Q_{dep}}{k\varepsilon_0}$$

with η = ½ for electron mobility and η = 1/3 for hole mobility.

Combining this measurements with IV measurements we can see how mobility changes with the effective field since the mobility can be obtained from the drain conductance in the linear region:

$$\mu_{eff} = \frac{L}{W} \frac{gD}{q \cdot N_s}$$

where $q.N_S$ is the inversion carrier density determined through the gate channel capacitance.

- A variety of semiconductor parameters, capacitance measurements have been used on numerous different devices and structures. Three measurement techniques are used to derive critical parameters from a wide range of new materials, processes, devices. Multi–frequency capacitance offers capacitance vs. voltage (C–V), capacitance vs. frequency (C–f), and capacitance vs. time (C–t) measurements to evaluate at frequencies ranging from 10 MHz down to 1 kHz.

- Sometimes even lower frequency capacitance measurements are necessary to evaluate test parameters of thin film transistors, MEMS structures, and other high impedance devices is called very low frequency (VLF) C–V, this newer technique performs C–V measurements in the range of 10 mHz to 10 Hz.

- To characterize slow trapping and de–trapping phenomenon in some materials, a capacitance measurement technique called quasi static (or almost DC) measurements can be used.

1.5.2 Temperature Dependent Characterization

- Advanced technology regards the measurement of the temperature, Silicon (Si) power devices have been saturated in terms of higher temperature and higher power operation by advantage of their physical properties.

- Silicon Carbide (SiC) has been recognized as a material with the potential to replace Si devices due to their superior material advantages such as large band gap, high thermal conductivity, and high critical breakdown field strength.

- SiC devices are capable of operating at high voltages, high frequencies, and at higher junction temperatures. SiC unipolar devices such as Schottky diodes, VJFETs, MOSFETs, etc. have much higher breakdown voltages compared to their Si counterparts which makes them suitable for use in traction drives.

- The power devices in traction applications should be able to handle extreme environments which include a wide range of operating temperature.

SiC Schottky Diodes

The **Schottky diode** (named after German physicist Walter H. Schottky), also known as **hot carrier diode**, is a semiconductor diode with a low forward voltage drop and a very fast switching action. The cat's–whisker detectors used in the early days of wireless and metal rectifiers used in early power applications can be considered primitive Schottky diodes.

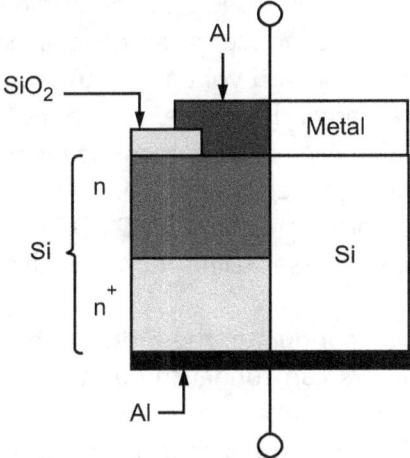

Fig: 1.39 : Construction of Schottky Diode

Fig: 1.40 : Symbol of Schottky diode

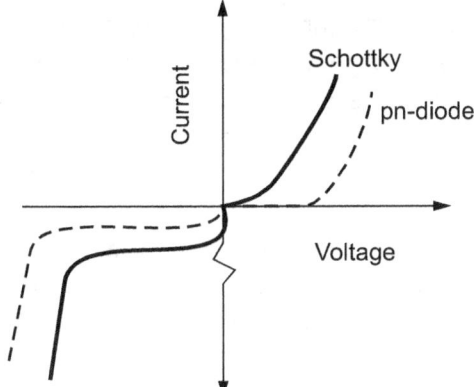

Fig. 1.41 : VI characteristics of Schottky diode

When forward current flows through a solid–state diode, there is a small voltage drop across its terminals. A silicon diode has a typical voltage drop of 0.6–0.7 V, while a Schottky diode has a voltage drop of 0.15–0.45 V. This lower voltage drop can be used to give higher switching speeds and better system efficiency.

A metal–semiconductor junction is formed between a metal and a semiconductor, creating a Schottky barrier (instead of a semiconductor–semiconductor junction as in conventional diodes). Typical metals used are molybdenum, platinum, chromium or tungsten, and certain silicides (e.g., palladium silicide and platinum silicide), whereas the semiconductor would typically be n–type silicon. The metal side acts as the anode, and n–type semiconductor acts as the cathode of the diode. This Schottky barrier results in both very fast switching and low forward voltage drop.

The combination of the metal and semiconductor determines the forward voltage of the diode. Both n–type and p–type semiconductors can develop Schottky barriers. However, the p–type typically has a much lower forward voltage. As the reverse leakage current increases dramatically with lowering the forward voltage, it can not be too low, so the usually employed range is about 0.5–0.7 V, and p–type semiconductors are employed only rarely. Titanium silicide and other refractory silicides, which are able to withstand the temperatures needed for source/drain annealing in CMOS processes, usually have too low a forward voltage to be useful, so processes using these silicides therefore usually do not offer Schottky diodes.

With increased doping of the semiconductor, the width of the depletion region drops. Below a certain width, the charge carriers can tunnel through the depletion region. At very high doping levels, the junction does not behave as a rectifier anymore and becomes an ohmic contact. This can be used for the simultaneous formation of ohmic contacts and diodes, as a diodes will form between the silicide and lightly doped n–type region, and an ohmic contact will form between the silicide and the heavily doped n– or p–type region. Lightly doped p–type regions pose a problem, as the resulting contact has too high a resistance for a good ohmic lapis contact, but too low a forward voltage and too high a reverse leakage to make a good diode.

As the edges of the Schottky contact are fairly sharp, a high electric field gradient occurs around them, which limits how large the reverse breakdown voltage threshold can be. Various strategies are used, from guard rings to overlaps of metallization to spread out the field gradient. The guard rings consume valuable die area and are used primarily for larger higher–voltage diodes, while overlapping metallization is employed primarily with smaller low–voltage diodes.

Schottky diodes are often used as antisaturation clamps in Schottky transistors. Schottky diodes made from palladium silicide (PtSi) are excellent due to their lower forward voltage (which has to be lower than the forward voltage of the base–collector junction). The Schottky temperature coefficient is lower than the coefficient of the B–C junction, which limits the use of PtSi at higher temperatures.

For power Schottky diodes, the parasitic resistances of the buried n+ layer and the epitaxial n–type layer become important. The resistance of the epitaxial layer is more important than it is for a transistor, as the current must cross its entire thickness. However, it serves as a distributed ballasting resistor over the entire area of the junction and, under usual conditions, prevents localized thermal runaway.

In comparison with the power p–n diodes the Schottky diodes are less rugged. The junction is direct contact with the thermally sensitive metallization, a Schottky diode can therefore dissipate less power than an equivalent–size, p–n diodes counterpart with a deep–buried junction before failing (especially during reverse breakdown). The relative advantage of the lower forward voltage of Schottky diodes is diminished at higher forward currents, where the voltage drop is dominated by the series resistance.

Key specification parameters

In view of the particular properties of the Schottky diode there are several parameters that are of key importance when determining the operation of one of these diodes against the more normal PN junction diodes.

• **Forward Voltage Drop:** In view of the low forward voltage drop across the diode, this is a parameter that is of particular concern. As can be seen from the Schottky diode IV characteristic, the voltage across the diode varies according to the current being carried. Accordingly any specification given provides the forward voltage drop for a given current. Typically the turn–on voltage is assumed to be around 0.2 V.

• **Reverse Breakdown:** Schottky diodes do not have a high breakdown voltage. Figures relating to this include the maximum Peak Reverse Voltage, maximum Blocking DC Voltage and other similar parameter names. If these figures are exceeded then there is a possibility the diode will enter reverse breakdown. It should be noted that the RMS value for any voltage will be $\dfrac{1}{\sqrt{2}}$ times the constant value. The upper limit for reverse breakdown is not high when compared to normal PN junction diodes. Maximum figures, even for rectifier diodes only reach around 100 V. Schottky diode rectifiers seldom exceed this value because devices that would operate above this value even by moderate amounts would exhibit forward voltages equal to or greater than equivalent PN junction rectifiers.

• **Capacitance:** The capacitance parameter is one of great importance for small signal RF applications. Normally the junctions areas of Schottky diodes are small and therefore the capacitance is small. Typical values of a few pico Farads are normal. As the capacitance is dependent upon any depletion areas, etc, the capacitance must be specified at a given voltage.

• **Reverse Recovery Time:** This parameter is important when a diode is used in a switching application. It is the time taken to switch the diode from its forward conducting or 'ON' state to the reverse 'OFF' state. The charge that flows within this time is referred to as the reverse recovery charge. The time for this parameter for a Schottky diode is normally measured in nanoseconds, ns. Some exhibit times of 100 ps. In fact what little recovery time is required mainly arises from the capacitance rather than the majority carrier recombination. As a result there is very little reverse current overshoot when switching from the forward conducting state to the reverse blocking state.

• **Working Temperature:** The maximum working temperature of the junction, T_j is normally limited to between 125 to 175°C. This is less than that which can be sued with ordinary silicon diodes. Care should be taken to ensure heat sinking of power diodes does not allow this figure to be exceeded.

- **Reverse Leakage Current:** The reverse leakage parameter can be an issue with Schottky diodes. It is found that increasing temperature significantly increases the reverse leakage current parameter. Typically for every 25°C increase in the diode junction temperature there is an increase in reverse current of an order of magnitude for the same level of reverse bias.

Limitations:

The most evident limitations of Schottky diodes are their relatively low reverse voltage ratings, and their relatively high reverse leakage current. For silicon–metal Schottky diodes, the reverse voltage is typically 50 V or less. Some higher–voltage designs are available (200 V is considered a high reverse voltage). Reverse leakage current, since it increases with temperature, leads to a thermal instability issue. This often limits the useful reverse voltage to well below the actual rating.

While higher reverse voltages are achievable, they would present a higher forward breakdown voltage, comparable to other types of standard diodes. Such Schottky diodes would have no advantage [3] unless great switching speed is required.

Silicon Carbide Schottky Diode

Schottky diodes constructed from silicon carbide have a much lower reverse leakage current than silicon Schottky diodes, as well as higher forward voltage and reverse voltage. As of 2011 they were available from manufacturers in variants up to 1700 V of reverse voltage.

Silicon carbide has a high thermal conductivity, and temperature has little influence on its switching and thermal characteristics. With special packaging, silicon carbide Schottky diodes can operate at junction temperatures of over 500 K (about 200 °C), which allows passive radiative cooling in aerospace applications.

Applications

1. Voltage Clamping

While standard silicon diodes have a forward voltage drop of about 0.6 V and germanium diodes 0.2 V, Schottky diodes' voltage drop at forward biases of around 1mA is in the range of 0.15 V to 0.46 V, which makes them useful in voltage clamping applications and prevention of transistor saturation. Due to the higher current density in the Schottky diode.

2. Reverse Current and Discharge Protection

A Schottky diode's low forward voltage drop, less energy is wasted as heat making them the most efficient choice for applications sensitive to efficiency. For instance, they are used in stand–alone ("off–grid") photovoltaic (PV) systems to prevent batteries from discharging through the solar panels at night, called "blocking diodes". They are also used in grid–connected systems with multiple strings connected in parallel, in order to prevent reverse current flowing from adjacent strings through shaded strings if the "bypass diodes" have failed.

Switched–Mode Power Supplies

Schottky diode are also used as rectifiers in switched–mode power supplies. The low forward voltage and fast recovery time leads to increased efficiency.

They can also be used in power supply "OR"ing circuits in products that have both an internal battery and a mains adapter input, or similar. However, the high reverse leakage current presents a problem, in this case, as any high–impedance voltage sensing circuit (e.g., monitoring the battery voltage or detecting whether a mains adapter is present) will see the voltage from the other power source through the diode leakage.

SiC Schottky diodes are majority carrier devices and are attractive for high frequency applications because they have lower switching losses compared to p–n diodes. However, Schottky diodes have higher leakage currents, which affect the breakdown voltage rating of the device.

Characteristics of Schottky Diode

Temperature affects every semiconductor device, and diodes are no exception. Temperature can have considerable effect on the characteristics of diode. The goal of this section is to understand how temperature affects the characteristics of diode. We shall study the effects of temperature on both forward and reverse characteristics.

We studied about the characteristics of diode by applying Shockley's equation. Shockley's equation is as follows.

$$I_D = I_S \left(e^{V_D/\eta V_J} - 1 \right)$$

Consider the term V_T given in above equation. This term is called thermal voltage and is dependent on temperature by the relation $V_T = kT/q$, where k is Boltzmann's constant, q is the charge on an electron and T is the temperature in Kelvin. **This term indirectly suggests the dependence of diode characteristics on temperature.**

Effect of temperature on forward characteristics :

The characteristics curve of a Si diode shifts to the left at the rate of –2.5 mV per degree centigrade change in temperature in forward bias region.

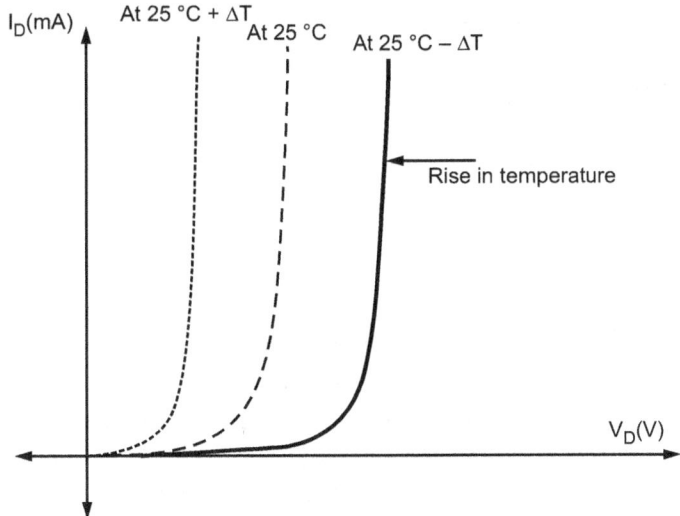

Fig. 1.42 : Effect of temperature on forward bias

Above Fig. 1.42 shows the curves are shown far apart just for illustration purpose and are not to scale. The curve shifts to the left at the rate of –2.5 mV per degree centigrade change in temperature. Hence if the temperature increases from room temperature (25° C) to 80° C, the voltage drop across the diode will be (80–25) x 2.5 mV = 137.5 mV.

Effect of temperature on reverse characteristics :

In the reverse bias region, the reverse saturation current of Si and Ge diodes doubles for every 10° C rise in temperature. Let us take an example to understand how much the reverse saturation current changes with temperature. Consider an increase of temperature from 25 °C to 85 °C, where the reverse saturation current at 25 °C is 100 nA. The temperature increases by 60 °C (25 °C to 85 °C), which is 6 × 10. Hence the reverse saturation current would increase by a factor of 2^6 = 64. Hence the reverse saturation current at 85 °C will be 100 nA x 64 = 6400 nA.

A showing in Fig. 1.43 the variation of reverse saturation current with temperature is shown below. The difference between the curve is exaggerated for illustration purpose.

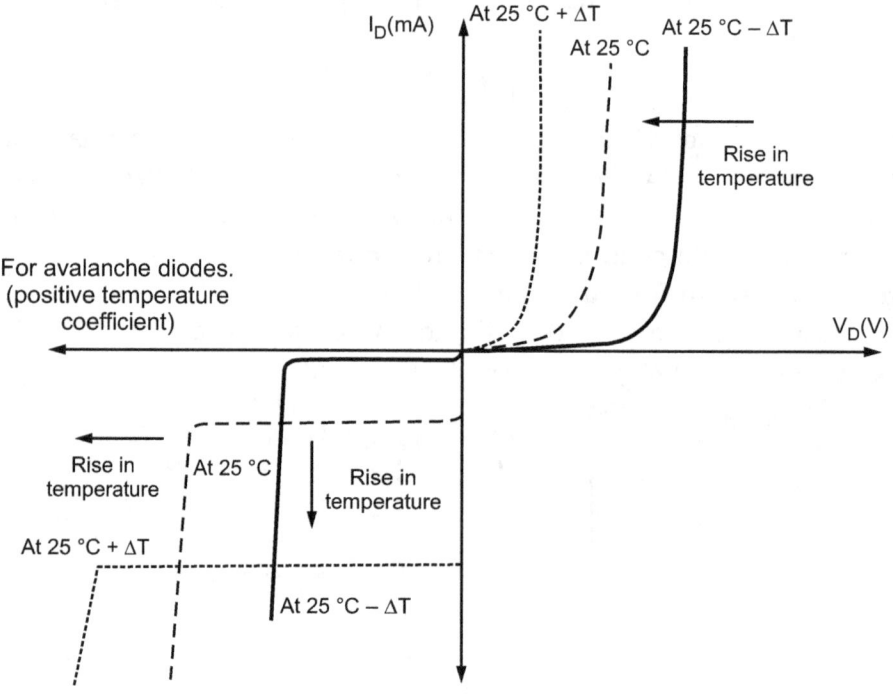

Fig. 1.43: Effect of temperature on Reverse bias

From the above Fig. 1.43 shows that the reverse saturation current increases with increase in temperature. The graph also shows how the reverse breakdown voltage changes with temperature. It is indicated in the above graph that the reverse breakdown voltage increases with an increase in temperature. However, it is only true for avalanche diodes. The reverse breakdown voltage for Zener diodes decreases with an increase in temperature, which is shown in the Fig. 1.44 below.

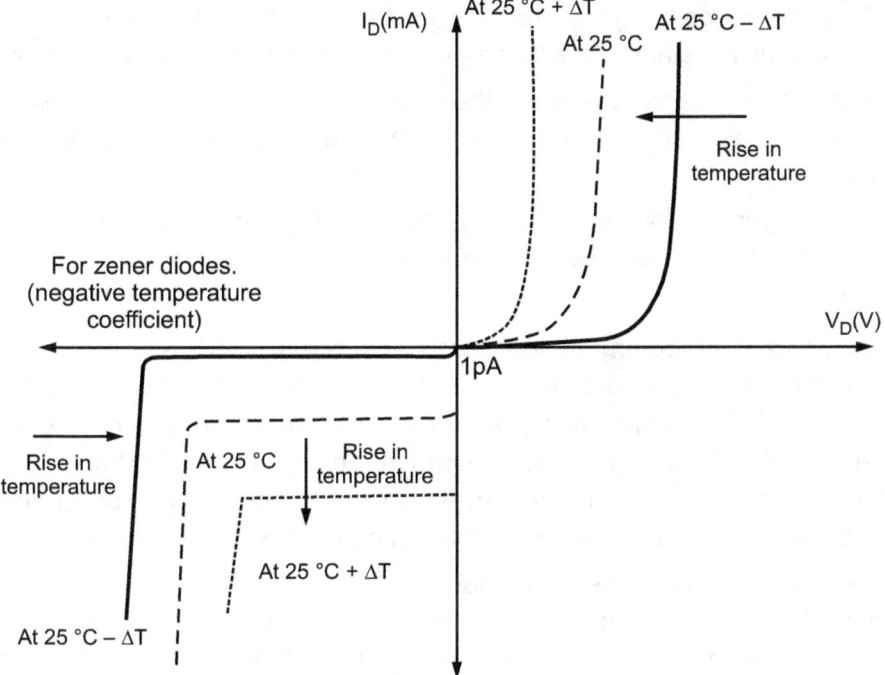

Fig 1.44: Effect of temperature on Zener diode

• The threshold voltage or the knee voltage are the on–state resistance is different for the diodes because of differences in device dimensions for different ratings. The static characteristics of diodes for a temperature range of –50 °C to 175 °C. The on–state voltage drop of a Schottky diode is dependent on barrier height and the on–state resistance. Both parameters vary with temperature and hence contribute to the temperature dependence of forward characteristics.

• At lower current levels the built–in potential (barrier potential) decreases with increasing temperature due to reduction in barrier height.

• As the temperature increases, the thermal energy of electrons increase which causes lowering of the barrier height.

Dynamic Characteristics

• A buck chopper with an inductive load is built for evaluating the switching characteristics of the diodes. An IGBT is used as the main switch and is switched at 20 kHz with a 25% duty ratio.

• The power losses for various forward peak currents and different temperatures are shown for the Si diode and diode S_4. The power losses for the Si diode increase with temperature, because of the increase in peak reverse recovery current.

• The switching loss for diode S_4 is almost independent of the change in temperature. The reverse recovery current is dependent on charge stored in the drift region.

- The SiC Schottky diode has no stored charge because it is a majority carrier device, and hence has virtually constant turn on energy loss for a wide temperature range.

- The reverse recovery current reduces the oscillation due to ringing and sunbber circuit for the limiting recovery. As a result of this condition efficiency as the losses or minimized.

- The blocking layer of thickness, due to the high electric breakdown field of the SiC material, contributes to the low switching losses of the SiC diode.

SiC Vertical JFET (VJFET)

We saw previously that a bipolar junction transistor is constructed using two PN–junctions in the main current carrying path between the emitter and the collector terminals. The **Junction Field Effect Transistor** (JUGFET or JFET) has no PN–junctions but instead has a narrow piece of high resistivity semiconductor material forming a "channel" of either N–type or P–type silicon for the majority carriers to flow through with two ohmic electrical connections at either end commonly called the drain and the source respectively.

There are two basic configurations of junction field effect transistor, the N–channel JFET and the P–channel JFET. The N–channel JFET's channel is doped with donor impurities meaning that the flow of current through the channel is negative (hence the term N–channel) in the form of electrons.

Likewise, the P–channel JFET's channel is doped with acceptor impurities meaning that the flow of current through the channel is positive (hence the term P–channel) in the form of holes. N–channel JFET's have a greater channel conductivity (lower resistance) than their equivalent P–channel types, since electrons have a higher mobility through a conductor compared to holes. This makes the N–channel JFET's a more efficient conductor compared to their P–channel counterparts.

We have said previously that there are two ohmic electrical connections at either end of the channel called the drain and the source. But within this channel there is a third electrical connection which is called the gate terminal and this can also be a P–type or N–type material forming a PN–junction with the main channel. The relationship between the connections of a junction field effect transistor and a bipolar junction transistor are compared below.

Table 1.2 : Comparison of Connections between a JFET and a BJT

Bipolar Transistor	Field Effect Transistor
Emitter – (E) >>	Source – (S)
Base – (B) >>	Gate – (G)
Collector – (C) >>	Drain – (D)

The symbols and basic construction for both configurations of JFETs are shown in Fig. 1.45 below.

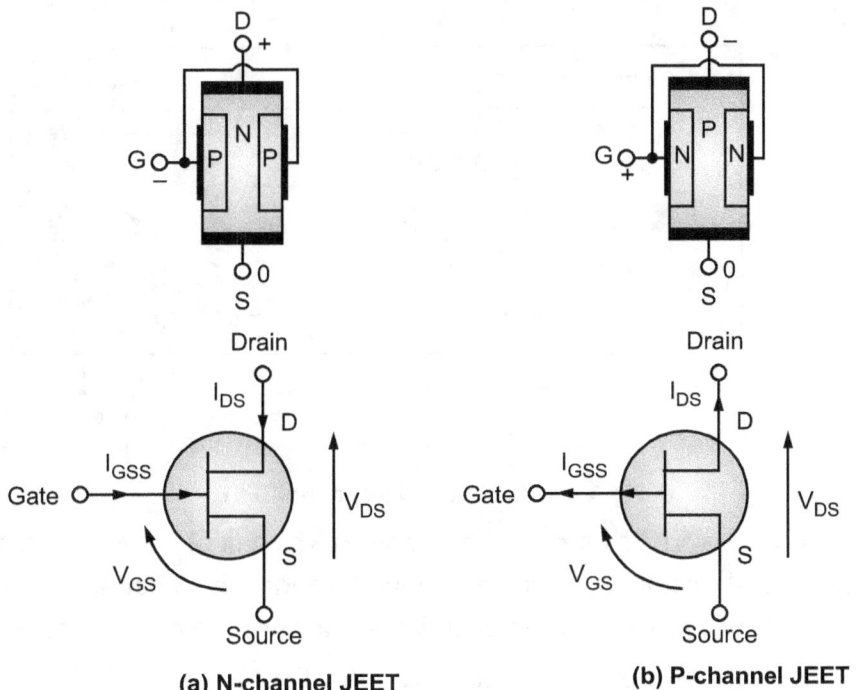

(a) N-channel JEET   (b) P-channel JEET

Fig 1.45: Construction of JFET

The semiconductor "channel" of the **Junction Field Effect Transistor** is a resistive path through which a voltage V_{DS} causes a current I_D to flow and as such the junction field effect transistor can conduct current equally well in either direction. As the channel is resistive in nature, a voltage gradient is thus formed down the length of the channel with this voltage becoming less positive as we go from the drain terminal to the source terminal.

The result is that the PN–junction therefore has a high reverse bias at the drain terminal and a lower reverse bias at the source terminal. This bias causes a "depletion layer" to be formed within the channel and whose width increases with the bias.

The magnitude of the current flowing through the channel between the drain and the Source terminals is controlled by a voltage applied to the gate terminal, which is a reverse–biased. In an N–channel JFET this Gate voltage is negative while for a P–channel JFET the Gate voltage is positive. The main difference between the JFET and a BJT device is that when the JFET junction is reverse–biased the Gate current is practically zero, whereas the Base current of the BJT is always some value greater than zero.

The above Fig. 1.46 shows an N–type semiconductor channel with a P–type region called the gate diffused into the N–type channel forming a reverse biased PN–junction and it is this junction which forms the *depletion region* around the gate area when no external voltages are applied. JFETs are therefore known as depletion mode devices.

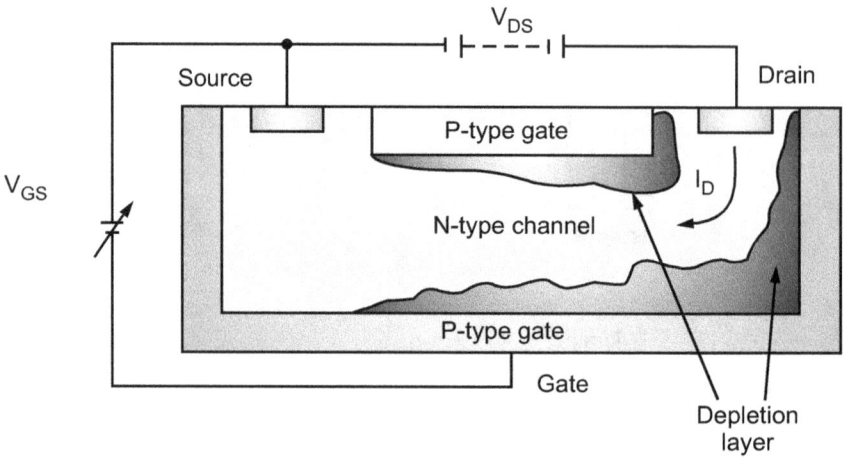

Fig 1.46: Biasing on N–channel JFET

This depletion region produces a potential gradient which is of varying thickness around the PN–junction and restrict the current flow through the channel by reducing its effective width and thus increasing the overall resistance of the channel itself.

Then we can see that the most–depleted portion of the depletion region is in between the gate and the drain, while the least–depleted area is between the gate and the source. Then the JFET's channel conducts with zero bias voltage applied (ie, the depletion region has near zero width).

With no external Gate voltage ($V_G = 0$), and a small voltage (V_{DS}) applied between the drain and the Source, maximum saturation current (I_{DSS}) will flow through the channel from the drain to the Source restricted only by the small depletion region around the junctions.

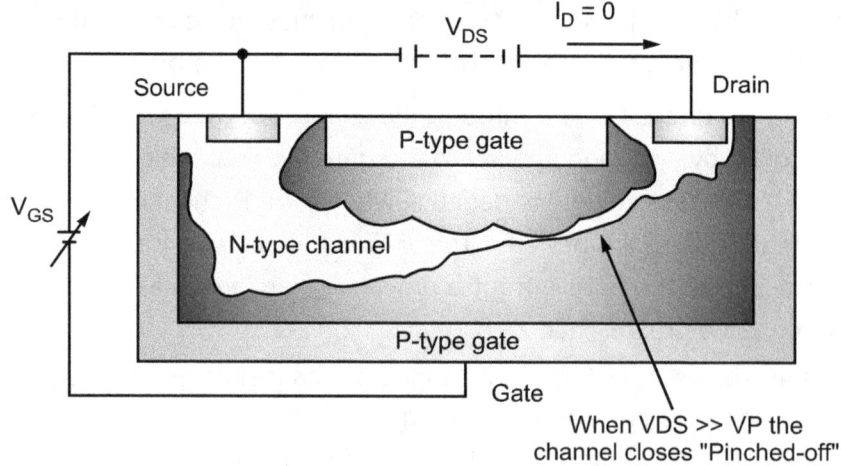

Fig 1.47: JFET Channel Pinched–off

If a small negative voltage ($-V_{GS}$) is now applied to the gate the size of the depletion region begins to increase reducing the overall effective area of the channel and thus reducing the current flowing through it, a sort of "squeezing" effect takes place. So by applying a reverse bias voltage increases the width of the depletion region which in turn reduces the conduction of the channel.

Since the PN–junction is reverse biased, little current will flow into the gate connection. As the Gate voltage ($-V_{GS}$) is made more negative, the width of the channel decreases until no more current flows between the drain and the source and the FET is said to be "pinched–off" (similar to the cut–off region for a BJT). The voltage at which the channel closes is called the "pinch–off voltage", (V_P).

In this pinch–off region the gate voltage, V_{GS} controls the channel current and V_{DS} has little or no effect.

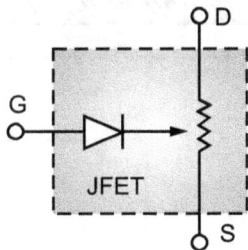

Fig. 1.48: JFET Model

The result is that the FET acts more like a voltage controlled resistor which has zero resistance when $V_{GS} = 0$ and maximum "ON" resistance (R_{DS}) when the gate voltage is very negative. Under normal operating conditions, the JFET gate is always negatively biased relative to the source.

It is essential that the gate voltage is never positive since if it is all the channel current will flow to the gate and not to the Source, the result is damage to the JFET. Then to close the channel:

1. No Gate voltage (V_{GS}) and V_{DS} is increased from zero.

2. No V_{DS} and Gate control is decreased negatively from zero.

3. V_{DS} and V_{GS} varying.

The P–channel **Junction Field Effect Transistor** operates the same as the N–channel above, with the following exceptions: (1) Channel current is positive due to holes, (2) The polarity of the biasing voltage needs to be reversed.

The output characteristics of an N–channel JFET with the gate short–circuited to the source is as shown in following Fig. 1.49.

Output characteristic V–I curves of a typical junction FET.

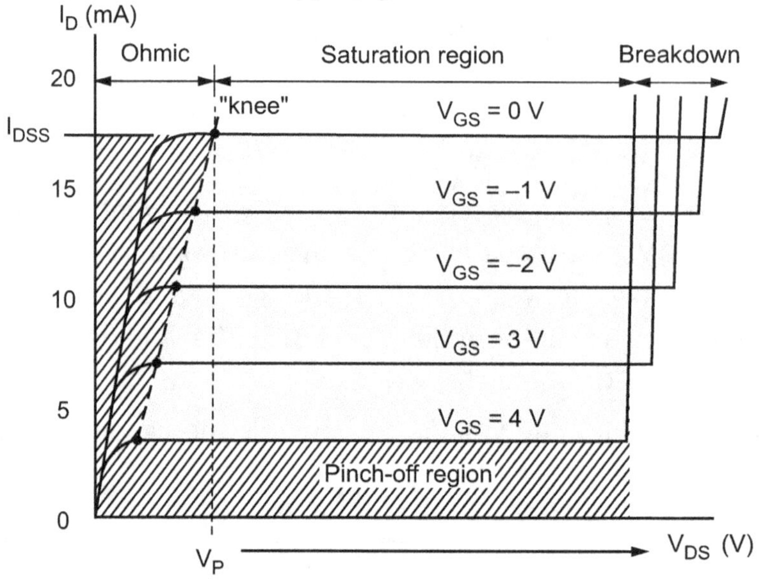

(a)

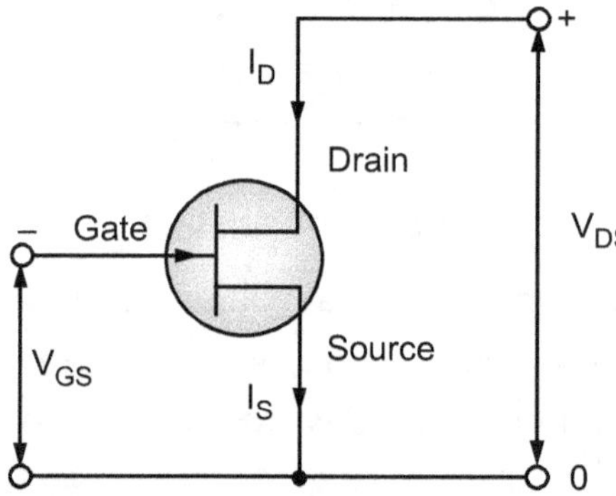

(b)

Fig 1.49: Output Characteristics of JFET

The voltage V_{GS} applied to the gate controls the current flowing between the drain and the source terminals. V_{GS} refers to the voltage applied between the gate and the source while V_{DS} refers to the voltage applied between the drain and the Source.

Because a **Junction Field Effect Transistor** is a voltage controlled device, "No current flows into the gate!" then the source current (I_S) flowing out of the device equals the drain current flowing into it and therefore ($I_D = I_S$).

The characteristics curves example shown in above in Fig. 1.49 (a) shows the four different regions of operation for a JFET and these are given as:

1. **Ohmic Region :** When $V_{GS} = 0$ the depletion layer of the channel is very small and the JFET acts like a voltage controlled resistor.

2. **Cut–off Region :** This is also known as the pinch–off region were the gate voltage, V_{GS} is sufficient to cause the JFET to act as an open circuit as the channel resistance is at maximum.

3. **Saturation or Active Region :** The JFET becomes a good conductor and is controlled by the Gate–Source voltage, (V_{GS}) while the drain–source voltage, (V_{DS}) has little or no effect.

4. **Breakdown Region :** The voltage between the drain and the source, (V_{DS}) is high enough to causes the JFET's resistive channel to break down and pass uncontrolled maximum current.

The characteristics curves for a P–channel junction field effect transistor are the same as those above, except that the drain current I_D decreases with an increasing positive gate–source voltage, V_{GS}.

The drain current is zero when $V_{GS} = V_P$. For normal operation, V_{GS} is biased to be somewhere between V_P and 0. Then we can calculate the drain current, I_D for any given bias point in the saturation or active region as follows:

Drain current in the active region.

$$I_D = I_{DSS} \left[1 - \frac{V_{GS}}{V_P} \right]^2$$

Note that the value of the Drain current will be between zero (pinch–off) and I_{DSS} (maximum current). By knowing the Drain current I_D and the drain–source voltage V_{DS} the resistance of the channel (I_D) is given as:

Drain–Source channel resistance.

$$R_{DS} = \frac{\Delta V_{DS}}{\Delta I_D} = \frac{1}{g_m}$$

Where: g_m is the "transconductance gain" since the JFET is a voltage controlled device and which represents the rate of change of the Drain current with respect to the change in Gate–Source voltage.

Modes of FET's

Like the bipolar junction transistor, the field effect transistor being a three terminal device is capable of three distinct modes of operation and can therefore be connected within a circuit in one of the following configurations.

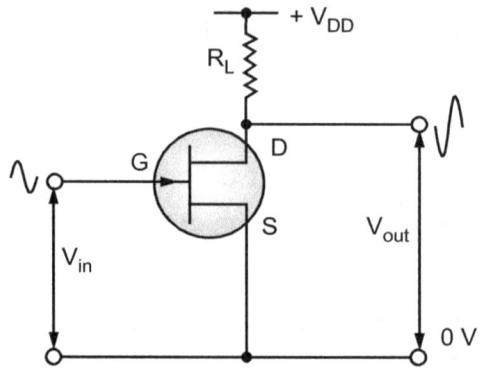

Fig 1.50: Common Source (CS) Configuration

In the **Common Source** configuration (similar to common emitter), the input is applied to the gate and its output is taken from the drain as shown. This is the most common mode of operation of the FET due to its high input impedance and good voltage amplification and as such common source amplifiers are widely used.

The common source mode of FET connection is generally used audio frequency amplifiers and in high input impedance pre–amps and stages. Being an amplifying circuit, the output signal is 180° "out–of–phase" with the input.

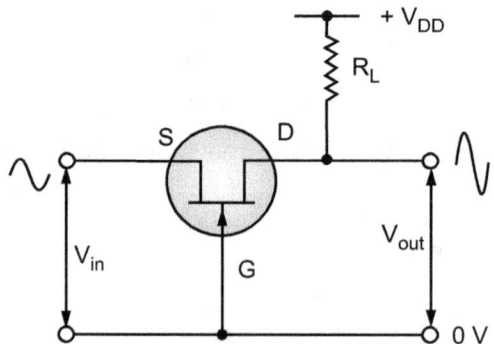

Fig. 1.51: Common Gate (CG) Configuration

In the **Common Gate** configuration (similar to common base), the input is applied to the Source and its output is taken from the drain with the gate connected directly to ground (0V) as shown. The high input impedance feature of the previous connection is lost in this configuration as the common gate has a low input impedance, but a high output impedance.

This type of FET configuration can be used in high frequency circuits or in impedance matching circuits were a low input impedance needs to be matched to a high output impedance. The output is "in–phase" with the input.

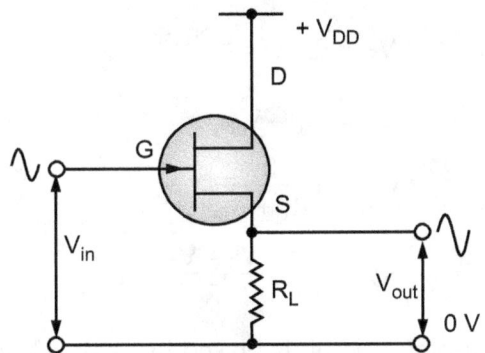

Fig 1.52: Common Drain (CD) Configuration

In the **Common Drain** configuration (similar to common collector), the input is applied to the gate and its output is taken from the source. The common drain or "source follower" configuration has a high input impedance and a low output impedance and near–unity voltage gain so is therefore used in buffer amplifiers. The voltage gain of the source follower configuration is less than unity, and the output signal is "in–phase", 0° with the input signal.

This type of configuration is referred to as "Common Drain" because there is no signal available at the drain connection, the voltage present, $+V_{DD}$ just provides a bias. The output is in–phase with the input.

The JFET Amplifier

Just like the bipolar junction transistor, JFET's can be used to make single stage class A amplifier circuits with the JFET common source amplifier and characteristics being very similar to the BJT common emitter circuit. The main advantage JFET amplifiers have over BJT amplifiers is their high input impedance which is controlled by the Gate biasing resistive network formed by R1 and R2 as shown.

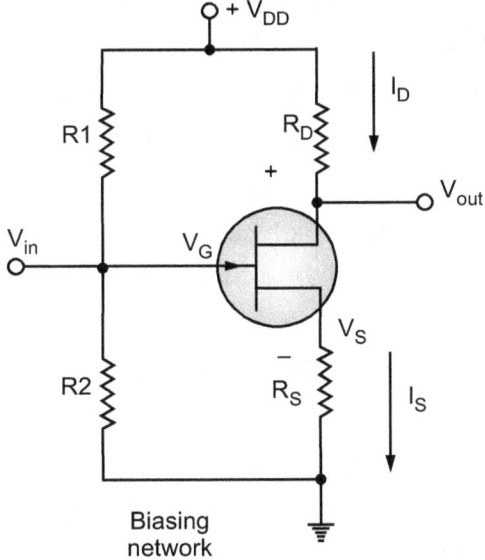

Fig 1.53: JFET Amplifier

$$V_S = I_D R_S = \frac{V_{DD}}{4}$$

$$V_S = V_G - V_{GS}$$

$$V_G = \left(\frac{R_2}{R_1 + R_2}\right) V_{DD}$$

$$ID = \frac{V_S}{R_S} = \frac{V_G - V_{GS}}{R_S}$$

This Common Source (CS) amplifier circuit is biased in class "A" mode by the voltage divider network formed by resistors R1 and R2. The voltage across the source resistor R_S is generally set to be about one quarter of V_{DD}, ($V_{DD}/4$). The required gate voltage can then be calculated using this R_S value. Since the gate current is zero, ($I_G = 0$) we can set the required DC quiescent voltage by the proper selection of resistors R1 and R2.

The control of the drain current by a negative gate potential makes the **Junction Field Effect Transistor** useful as a switch and it is essential that the gate voltage is never positive for an N–channel JFET as the channel current will flow to the gate and not the drain resulting in damage to the JFET. The principals of operation for a P–channel JFET are the same as for the N–channel JFET, except that the polarity of the voltages need to be reversed.

Transistors, we will look at another type of Field Effect Transistor called a **MOSFET** whose gate connection is completely isolated from the main current carrying channel.

- JFET, a unipolar device, has several advantages compared to MOSFET devices. It has low voltage drop and higher switching speed. It is free from the gate oxide interface problems not like the MOSFET.

- JFET is a normally–on device and conducts even though there is no gate voltage applied. Therefore it requires protection circuit for system power failures to prevent a short circuit.

- This normally–on feature demands special gate drive designs increasing the complexity of design. The VJFET can be used in high current and voltage applications, unlike Si JFET because of the vertical structure and the intrinsic properties of SiC.

- A normally–on SiC VJFET rated at 1200V and 2A was tested to study the high temperature behavior of the device. The on–resistance of the VJFET increases from 0.36 at – 50 °C to 1.4 at 175 °C.

- The values of the on–resistance are high; however, these devices have positive temperature coefficient which enables easy paralleling of devices and the on–state resistance would decrease

Transfer Characteristics
JFET Output Characteristic

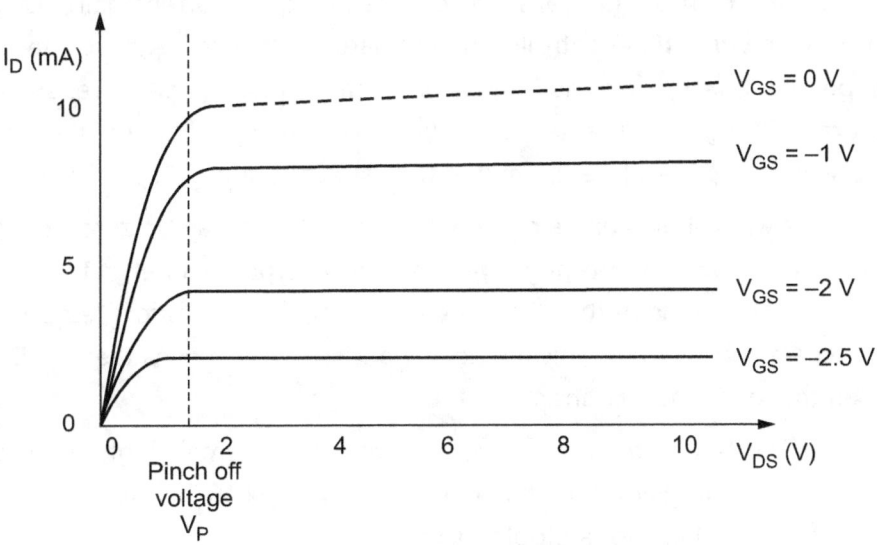

Fig 1.54: JFET Output Characteristics

In the JFET output characteristics shown in Fig. 1.54, the Drain current I_D shows very little change, and the curves are very nearly horizontal at voltages greater than the pinch off voltage. Almost all of the expected increase in current, due to the increase in voltage between Source and Drain (V_{DS}), is offset by the narrowing of the conducting channel due to the growing depletion layers.

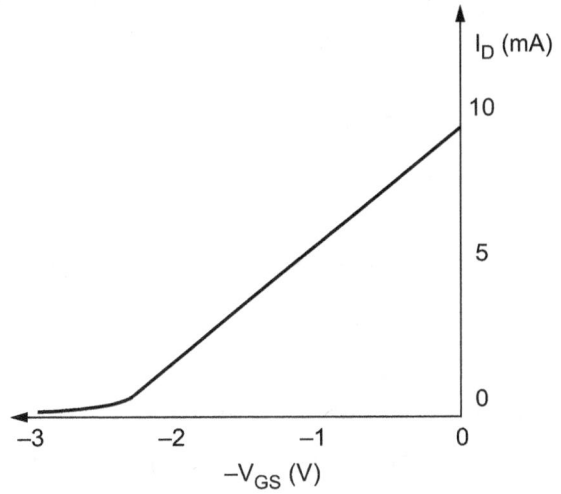

Fig. 1.55 : JFET Transfer Characteristic

The transfer characteristic for a JFET, which shows the change in drain current (I_D) for a given change in gate–source voltage (V_{GS}), is shown in Fig 1.55. Because the JFET input (the gate) is voltage operated, the gain of the transistor cannot be called current gain, as with bipolar transistors. The drain **current** is controlled by the gate–source **voltage**, so the graph shows milliamperes per volt (mA / V), and as I / V is conductance (the inverse of resistance V / I) the slope of this graph (the gain of the device) is called the forward or mutual transconductance, which has the symbol g_m. Therefore the higher the value of g_m the greater the amplification.

Notice that V_{GS} is always shown as being negative; in reality it may be zero or slightly above zero, but the gate is always more negative than the N-type channel between source and drain. Note also that the slope of the curve in the transfer characteristic is less steep than that of the transfer characteristic for a typical bipolar transistor. This means that a JFET will have a lower gain than that of a bipolar transistor.

This disadvantage is offset by the advantage of having an extremely high input resistance. A typical input resistance for a JFET would be in the region of 1×10^{10} ohms (10,000 Megohms!) compared with 2K to 3K Ohms for a bipolar device.

This makes the JFET ideal for applications where the circuit or device driving the JFET amplifier cannot supply any appreciable current, an example being the Electret microphone, which uses a FET within the microphone to amplify the tiny voltage variations appearing across the vibrating diaphragm element.

Another feature of the JFET that makes it more suited to very high frequency use than bipolar transistors, is the absence of junctions in the JFET conducting channel. In a bipolar transistor two PN junctions forming tiny capacitances, exist between base and emitter, and base and collector, due to the PN junctions. These capacitances will limit high frequency performance, as they provide negative feedback paths at high frequencies. Because the JFET is in effect just a slab of silicon between Source and Drain, the stray capacitances that exist in bipolar devices are absent, so high frequency performance is improved, making JFETs usable even at hundreds of MHz.

The negative gate pinch–off voltage required to turn–off the device does not vary much with an increase in drain to source voltage V_{ds}.

This pinch–off voltage determines the voltage requirement of the gate drive circuit. A gate drive was developed for the VJFET for high frequency and high temperature operation. Based on the transfer characteristics, the gate drive was designed for a voltage of 30V and a 250 kHz operation was achieved for peak gate currents of 0.8 A.

Gate Drive Requirements

- SiC VJFET switches can be operated at higher switching frequencies and higher temperatures; therefore, they have different gate drive requirements than traditional Si power switches.

- SiC VJFET are devices can be turned OFF by applying a negative voltage this condition requires the higher than the typical switch Si.

- One of the important parameters in gate drive design for VJFETs is that they have a large stray capacitance between the gate and the other terminals.

- Total input capacitance of VJFET, CISS, determines the current required by the gate and the rate at which the applied gate voltage is built across the gate and source terminals.

- These capacitances are due to the geometrical design of the device and also because of the parasitic body diode.

- Therefore, the circuit that drives the gate terminal should be capable of supplying a reasonable current so the stray capacitance can be charged up as quickly as possible.

- The gate drive was tested with several capacitors as load before testing the driver circuit with the device.

- When these are operated at high frequencies, they also need high peak gate currents. The CISS of VJFET is higher and a resistor is added between the gate driver and the source terminal.

- This is to limit the current to the gate so that the maximum voltage on the gate terminal does not overshoot.

SUMMARY

- Basically nanoelectronics materials fabricated by the silicon, gallium and arsenic etc.

- Silicon nanoelectronics materials fabrication plays the important role in two important things. i.e quantum effect and single electron effect.

- Semiconductor band structures in general and especially for silicon are hard to describe with an analytical formula.

- The crystalline lattice is a periodic array of the atoms. When the solid is not crystalline, it is called amorphous.

- A crystal structure is composed of a unit cell, a set of atoms arranged in a particular way; which is periodically repeated in three dimensions on a lattice.

- Crystal defect, imperfection in the regular geometrical arrangement of the atoms in a crystalline solid.
- Point defects include self interstitial atoms, interstitial impurity atoms, substitution atoms and vacancies.

EXERCISE

1. What do you understand by the crystal defects? Explain.

2. Explain the crystal growth and wafer fabrication.

3. What are the crystal planes and its orientation?

4. Recognize the basic steps of CMOS.

5. Discuss I–V/C-V characterization.

6. Explain the temperature dependent characterization.

7. Write a short note on the CMOS technology.

8. State and explain the construction of mass field effect transistor.

9. Explain the water fabrication techniques.

10. State the working principal of N and P-MOSFET transistor.

SEMICONDUCTOR NANO ELECTRONIC MANUFACTURING

2.1 INTRODUCTION

- Semiconductor materials are manufactured using Flexible electronic components, large area and economical for instance sensors, transistor and diodes on a scale from micro to nano range.

- A semiconductor is a material, typically a solid chemical element or compound that can conduct electricity under some conditions, making it a good medium for the control of electrical current.

- Conductance differs depending on the current or voltage applied to a control electrode, or on the strength of Infrared Radiation (IR), visible light, ultraviolet (UV), or X rays.

- The precise properties of a semiconductor vary based on the impurities or dopants added to it. An N-type semiconductor conveys current primarily as negatively-charged electrons, in this way the conduction of current in a wire.

- A P-type semiconductor conveys current mainly as electron deficiencies known as holes, a positive electric charge equal and opposite to the charge on an electron.

- The flows of holes, in a semiconductor material, takes place in a direction opposite to the flow of electrons.

- Element of semiconductors consist of antimony, germanium, selenium, silicon, arsenic, boron, carbon, sulfur and tellurium. All these, silicon is the best-known forming the basis of Integrated Circuits (ICs).

- Common semiconductor compounds consist of gallium arsenide, indium antimonide and the oxides of most metals. Gallium Arsenide (GaAs) is widely used, in low-noise, high-gain and weak-signal amplifying devices.

2.2 BASIC UNDERSTANDING OF CONTAMINATIONS

- **Contamination** is the presence of an unwanted constituent, contaminant or impurity in a material, physical body, natural environment, workplace, etc.

- Contaminations from the ambient storage ambient air with the process of gases chemicals, water and materials used in the processes of fabrication.

- Metallic contamination in semiconductors adversely affects device performance. The line widths decrease the allowable levels of metal contamination get smaller and smaller.

- Contamination is accountable for 75% of the yield loss in Integrated Circuit (IC) manufacture though, it is also arises in the Back-End-Of-the-Line (BEOL) processes with patterned wafer surfaces. The semiconductor industry faces the ongoing challenge of removal of contamination.
- The need for clean substrates in the fabrication of microelectronic devices has been well recognized since the solid-state device technology. Particles larger than about 1/4 of the minimum line-width may cause fatal device defects. A 64 Mb 0.25 μm DRAM process flow had 60 to 70 cleaning steps.
- For 0.18 μm CMOS technology about 80 of 400 process steps were cleaning. As semiconductor device geometry endures to shrink and wafer sizes surge, the limitations of existing cleaning methods on devices yield will become more critical as the size of "killer" particles also shrinks.
- Physical substrate-independent cleaning processes are highly desirable since they do not have to be modified for different substrates and potential for modifying the surface.
- Thus innovative cleaning processes are needed to specifically target removal of strongly adherent, nano-scale particles and contaminants. These processes do not have to be modified by chemical based cleaning process and etching roughening.
- In semiconductor manufacturing process, cleaning of deep submicron offers a tremendous challenge. Manufacturers should be using stable flow or pulsating flow cleaning techniques.
- These techniques are even more competent for semiconductor manufacturing. Most of the particle removal techniques depend on weakening the adhesion force before or during cleaning for effective removal, so a fundamental phenomenon that needs to be understood is particle adhesion and how it changes during and after the manufacturing process.
- There are reliable and accurate continuous monitoring of the impurities in the vacuum ultra pure gases. It is mostly used in semiconductor processing also manufacturing process.

2.2.1 Levels of Contaminations

The mechanism of contamination of silicon wafer is summarized as

1. Source of contamination
2. Transportation of the contamination
3. Location of the contamination: surface, bulk
4. Evolution of the contamination.

Source of Contamination :

Foreign Materials :

- Fluid impurities : Chemicals, gas
- Tools impurities : corrosion, outgasing, handling
- Particles : Suspensions within fluid, abrasion.

Parasitic Reactions:

- Between reactive materials
- Corrosion, outgasing, dissolution of tool parts

Transportation of the Contamination:

Brownian movement and convection, molecular diffusion, chemical diffusion, electromagnetic diffusion

Contamination within the bulk of the silicon water

- Implantation : Ionic implantation or plasma induced implantation
- Diffusion during hot process
- Through deposition process

Adherence and surface phenomena

- Chemical bounding (covalent, ionic, van der waals, hydrogen)
- Surface tension : Capillarity, electrochemical effects
- Wetting according the surface layer (Silicon, Silicon oxide, polymer, silicon nitride)

Cleaning Effect : How is the contamination removed ? What contamination is brought up during the cleaning steps ?

- Cleaning solutions as SC1, SC2, HF, piraha
- Surface state : Hydrophobic or hydrophilic
- Mechanical actions : Brush megasonics, jet rinse, bath motion
- Chemical actions :
- Impurity oxy do-reduction reaction
- Basis/acids dissolution
- Surface pitting
- Particles removals
- Filtration for particles and / or ionic contamination
- Gettering : Capture of the defects outside the active area of the components.
- Precipitation of the defect on the backside of the wafer.
- Precipitation of the defect due to oxygen precipitate.
- Charges within dielectric films as doped silicon films (Phosphorus silicon glass, Boron phosphorus Silicon Glass) and Silicon nitride films.

The chemistries of the cleaning solutions, which are described within contamination work flow are able to remove particles or metallic contamination. They can also bring both of these contaminants. Here, the source of contamination explore and the way to measure it. Another way to consider wafer contamination source is the environment of the wafer:

Contact with the Wafer: Chemicals, Gases, Ultra pure de-ionized Water, resist, ionic implantation, deposition layers, etching process.

Environment for the Process: Tool, network for gases and chemicals distribution, boxes for wafer handling and transportation. General environment: Facilities, human, external pollution (traffic, industrial).

*   Contamination by the semiconductor devices are sensitive due to the different root causes such as device sensitivities on process steps, cross contamination, device reduction size, ultra pure water and gases.
*   The environment is also contributing to the contamination effect on the wafer as tools, transportation boxes and clean-room. Contamination can be divided in three categories: ionic contamination, airborne molecular contamination particles (defect density).

2.2.2 Contamination Analysis and Monitoring

The analytical techniques for measurements of the different contaminants defined in the break down within four categories :

1. Metallic contamination analysis.
2. Ions impurities analysis with ion chromatography.
3. Chemical composition analysis as gas chromatography (GC), Total Organic Compound (TOC), Analyser for Deionized water (DI water).
4. Liquid particle measurement with liquid particle counters for particle size above or equal 0.1 μm diameter for chemicals. Tools for the characterization of the particles size distribution are also interesting, but not in the scope of this presentation.

2.2.3 Wafer Cleaning Methods

The general stragies of cleaning wafers as shown in Fig. 2.1.

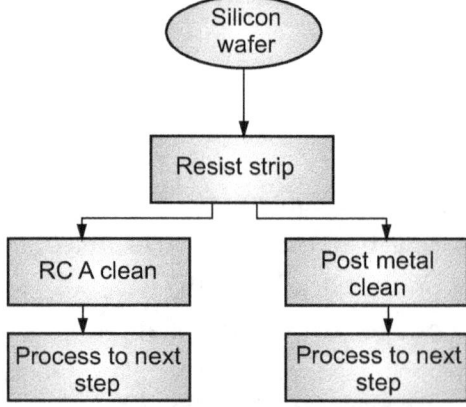

Fig. 2.1 : Cleaning wafer stragies

- Most of the cleaning process begins with photo resist removal photo lithography. Photo resist are organic compounds. In front end processing no metal on the wafers. We photo can use acid H_2SO_4 and strong oxidant H_2O_2. Another method uses oxygen plasma method. It reduces pollution and good selectivity of the materials.

- In semiconductor processing, the avoidance of contamination is enormously important and the wafers will undergo many cleaning operations during the process. The wafers must be kept covered as much as possible and constant attention is required to prevent them from coming into contact with contaminated surfaces.

- The success of the process will depend largely on your ability to keep wafers free from contamination. Recall that impurity levels, which are normally measured in terms of atoms per cubic centimeter, can have very important effects.

- The importance of clean substrate surfaces in the fabrication of semiconductor micro electronic devices has been recognized since the early days of the 1950s. As the requirements for increased device performance and reliability have become more stringent in the era of VLSI and ULSI silicon circuit technology, this technique to avoid contamination and processes to generate very clean wafer surfaces have become critically important. Besides, over 50% of yield losses in integrated circuit fabrication are generally accepted to be micro contamination.

- Trace impurities, such as sodium ions, metals and particles, are especially detrimental if present on semiconductor surfaces during high-temperature processing (thermal oxidation, diffusion, epitaxial growth) it may spread and diffuse into the semiconductor interior.

- Impurities must also be removed from surfaces before and/or after lower temperature steps, such as chemical vapor deposition, dopant implanting and plasma reactions.

- Post cleaning after photo resist stripping is necessary for every mask level throughout the production process.

- Many wafer cleaning techniques have been tested and several are being used.

- In this approach for silicon wafers without metallization used on wet chemical based on hydrogen oxide chemistry. This process remained unchanged during the past year.

1. Early Cleaning Procedures

- The beginning of silicon wafer processing till about 1970, one used mixtures as cleaning chemicals, organic solvent extraction, boiling nitric acid, aqua regia, concentrated hydrofluoric acid, and hot acid.

- Mixtures of sulfuric acid-chromic acid led to chromium contamination and caused ecological problems of disposal. Mixtures of sulfuric acid and hydrogen peroxide caused sulfur contamination. Aqueous solutions containing hydrogen peroxide had long been used for cleaning electron tube components but not for semiconductors.

- The levels of impurity and particles in process chemicals are high and lead to surface contamination.

- Particle impurities were removed by ultrasonic treatment in detergent solutions or by brush scrubbing.
- The first caused frequent wafer breakage and the second often deposited more debris from the bristles than it removed from the wafer surfaces.

2. Alternative Cleaning Techniques

- Generally so many techniques for cleaning silicon wafers have been tried over the years with various degrees of success. Some techniques are useful only for specific applications or may introduce undesirable side effects. For instance, glow discharge techniques such as plasma etching, effectively strip photo resist films but leave inorganic contaminants and metals behind.
- Numerous types of sputter-etching can cause surface damage. For example, plasma treatments for preparing small-geometry devices for metallization or wet chemical etching of the silicon to remove entire surface layers by etch dissolution.

3. Wafer Rinsing and Drying

- Wafer rinsing and drying is vital because the wafers very easily recontaminate appropriately.
- Rinsing after wet cleaning is done, usually at room temperature, with flowing high purity and ultra filtered high resistivity DI water.
- Mega sonic rinsing is beneficial. Centrifugal spray rinsing and rinsing in a closed system have the advantage that wafers are not removed between cleaning, rinsing and drying.
- Wafer drying after rinsing must be done by physical removal of the water rather than by allowing it to evaporate. Spin drying accomplishes it has been the most widely used technique Hot forced-air drying is a desired technique with less chance for particle recontamination.

2.3 LITHOGRAPHY

Semiconductor Lithography (Photolithography)

Starting with an uniformly doped silicon wafer, the fabrication of Integrated Circuits (IC's) needs hundreds of sequential process steps. The most important process steps used in the semiconductor fabrication are :

Lithography

Lithography is used to transfer a pattern from a photomask to the surface of the wafer. For example, the gate area of a MOS transistor is defined by a specific pattern. The pattern information is recorded on a layer of photo resist which is applied on the top of the wafer. The photo resist changes its physical properties when exposed to light (often ultraviolet) or another source of illumination (e.g. X-ray). The photo resist is either developed by (wet or dry) etching or by conversion to volatile compounds through the exposure itself. The pattern defined by the mask is either removed or remained after development, depending if the type of resist is positive or negative. For example, the developed photo resist can act as an etching mask for the underlying layers.

Etching

Etching is used to remove material selectively in order to create patterns. The pattern is defined by the etching mask, because the parts of the material, which should remain, are protected by the mask. The unmasked material can be removed either by wet (chemical) or dry (physical) etching. Wet etching is strongly isotropic which limits its application and the etching time can be controlled difficultly. Because of the so-called under-etch effect, wet etching is not suited to transfer patterns with sub-micron feature size. However, wet etching has a high selectivity (the etch rate strongly depends on the material) and it does not damage the material. On the other side dry etching is highly anisotropic but less selective. But it is more capable for transfering small structures.

Deposition

A multitude of layers of different materials have to be deposited during the IC fabrication process. The two most important deposition methods are the physical vapor deposition (PVD) and the Chemical Vapor Deposition (CVD). During PVD accelerated gas ions sputter particles from a sputter target in a low pressure plasma chamber. The principle of CVD is a chemical reaction of a gas mixture on the substrate surface at high temperatures. The need of high temperatures is the most restricting factor for applying CVD. This problem can be avoided with Plasma Enhanced Chemical Vapor Deposition (PECVD), where the chemical reaction is enhanced with radio frequencies instead of high temperatures. An important aspect for this technique is the uniformity of the deposited material, especially the layer thickness. CVD has a better uniformity than PVD.

Chemical Mechanical Planarization

Processes like etching, deposition, or oxidation which modify the topography of the wafer surface lead to a non-planar surface. Chemical Mechanical Planarization (CMP) is used to plane the wafer surface with the help of a chemical slurry. First, a planar surface is necessary for lithography due to a correct pattern transfer. Furthermore, CMP enables indirect pattering, because the material removal always starts on the highest areas of the wafer surface. This means that at defined lower lying regions like a trench the material can be left. Together with the deposition of non-planar layers, CMP is an effective method to build up IC structures.

Oxidation

Oxidation is a process which converts silicon on the wafer into silicon dioxide. The chemical reaction of silicon and oxygen already starts at room temperature but stops after a very thin native oxide film. For an effective oxidation rate the wafer must be settled to a furnace with oxygen or water vapor at elevated temperatures. Silicon dioxide layers are used as high-quality insulators or masks for ion implantation. The ability of silicon to form high quality silicon dioxide is an important reason, why silicon is still the dominating material in IC fabrication.

Ion Implantation

Ion implantation is the dominant technique to introduce dopant impurities into crystalline silicon. This is performed with an electric field which accelerates the ionized atoms or molecules so that these particles penetrate into the target material until they come to rest because of interactions with the silicon atoms. Ion implantation is able to control exactly the distribution and dose of the dopants in silicon, because the penetration depth depends on the kinetic energy of the ions which is proportional to the electric field. The dopant dose can be controlled by varying the ion source. Unfortunately, after ion implantation the crystal structure is damaged which implies worse electrical properties. Another problem is that the implanted dopants are electrically inactive, because they are situated on interstitial sites. Therefore after ion implantation a thermal process step is necessary which repairs the crystal damage and activates the dopants.

Diffusion

Diffusion is the movement of impurity atoms in a semiconductor material at high temperatures. The driving force of diffusion is the concentration gradient. There is a wide range of diffusivities for the various dopant species, which depend on how easy the respective dopant impurity can move through the material. Diffusion is applied to anneal the crystal defects after ion implantation or to introduce dopant atoms into silicon from a chemical vapor source. In the last case the diffusion time and temperature determine the depth of dopant penetration. Diffusion is used to form the source, drain and channel regions in a MOS transistor. But diffusion can also be an unwanted parasitic effect, because it takes place during all high temperature process steps.

The fabrication of an Integrated Circuit (IC) requires a variety of physical and chemical processes performed on a semiconductor (e.g., silicon) substrate. In general, the various processes used to make an IC fall into three categories: film deposition, patterning, and semiconductor doping. Films of both conductors (such as polysilicon, aluminum and more recently copper) and insulators (various forms of silicon dioxide, silicon nitride and others) are used to connect and isolate transistors and their components. Selective doping of various regions of silicon allow the conductivity of the silicon to be changed with the application of voltage. By creating structures of these various components millions of transistors can be built and wired together to form the complex circuitry of a modern microelectronic device. Fundamental to all of these processes is lithography, i.e., the formation of three-dimensional relief images on the substrate for subsequent transfer of the pattern to the substrate.

The word lithography comes from the Greek lithos, meaning stones, and graphia, meaning to write. It means quite literally writing on stones. In the case of semiconductor lithography (also called photolithography) our stones are silicon wafers and our patterns are written with a light sensitive polymer called a photoresist. To build the complex structures that make up a transistor and the many wires that connect the millions of transistors of a circuit, lithography and etch pattern transfer steps are repeated at least 10 times, but more typically are done 20 to 30 times to make one circuit. Each pattern being printed on the wafer is aligned to the previously formed patterns and slowly the conductors, insulators, and selectively doped regions are built up to form the final device.

The importance of lithography can be appreciated in two ways. First, due to the large number of lithography steps needed in IC manufacturing, lithography typically accounts for about 30 % percent of the cost of manufacturing. Second, lithography tends to be the technical limiter for further advances in feature size reduction and thus transistor speed and silicon area. Obviously, one must carefully understand the trade-offs between cost and capability when developing a lithography process. Although lithography is certainly not the only technically important and challenging process in the IC manufacturing flow, historically, advances in lithography have gated advances in IC cost and performance.

Optical lithography is basically a photographic process by which a light sensitive polymer, called a photoresist, is exposed and developed to form three-dimensional relief images on the substrate. In general, the ideal photo resist image has the exact shape of the designed or intended pattern in the plane of the substrate, with vertical walls through the thickness of the resist. Thus, the final resist pattern is binary: parts of the substrate are covered with resist while other parts are completely uncovered. This binary pattern is needed for pattern transfer since the parts of the substrate covered with resist will be protected from etching, ion implantation, or other pattern transfer mechanism.

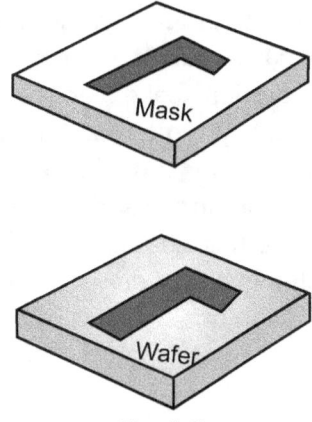

Fig. 2.2

The general sequence of processing steps for a typical photolithography process is as follows: substrate preparation, photo resist spin coat, prebake, exposure, post-exposure bake, development, and postbake. A resist strip is the final operation in the lithographic process, after the resist pattern has been transferred into the underlying layer. This sequence is shown diagrammatically in Fig. 2.2 and is generally performed on several tools linked together into a contiguous unit called a lithographic cluster. A brief discussion of each step is given below, pointing out some of the practical issues involved in photo resist processing.

1. Substrate Preparation

Substrate preparation is intended to improve the adhesion of the photo resist material to the substrate. This is accomplished by one or more of the following processes: substrate cleaning to remove contamination, dehydration bake to remove water, and addition of an adhesion promoter. Substrate contamination can take the form of particulates or a film and can be either organic or inorganic. Particulates result in defects in the final resist pattern, whereas film contamination can cause poor adhesion and subsequent loss of linewidth control. Particulates generally come from airborne particles or contaminated liquids (e.g., dirty adhesion promoter). The most effective way of controlling particulate contamination is to eliminate their source. Since this is not always practical, chemical/mechanical cleaning is used to remove particles. Organic films, such as oils or polymers, can come from vacuum pumps and other machinery, body oils and sweat, and various polymer deposits leftover from previous processing steps. These films can generally be removed by chemical, ozone, or plasma stripping. Similarly, inorganic films, such as native oxides and salts, can be removed by chemical or plasma stripping. One type of contaminant adsorbed water is removed most readily by a high temperature process called a dehydration bake.

A dehydration bake, as the name implies, removes water from the substrate surface by baking at temperatures of 200°C to 400°C, usually for 30 to 60 minutes. The substrate is then allowed to cool (preferably in a dry environment) and coated as soon as possible. It is important to note that water will re-adsorb on the substrate surface if left in a humid (non-dry) environment. A dehydration bake is also effective in volatilizing organic contaminants, further cleaning the substrate. Often, the normal sequence of processing steps involves some type of high temperature process immediately before coating with photoresist, for example thermal oxidation. If the substrate is coated immediately after the high temperature step, the dehydration bake can be eliminated. A typical dehydration bake, however, does not completely remove water from the surface of silica substrates (including silicon, polysilicon, silicon oxide, and silicon nitride). Surface silicon atoms bond strongly with a monolayer of water forming silanol groups (SiOH). Bake temperatures in excess of 600°C are required to remove this final layer of water. Further, the silanol quickly reforms when the substrate is cooled in a non-dry environment. Since this approach is impractical, the preferred method of removing this silanol is by chemical means.

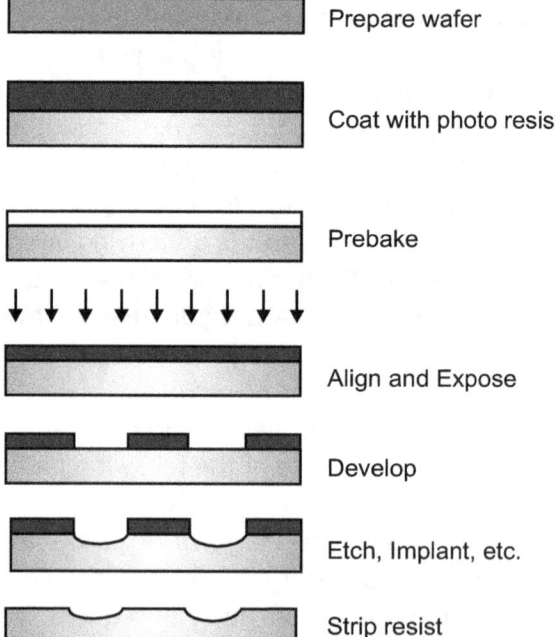

Fig. 2.3 Typical sequence of lithographic processing steps
(with no post-exposure bake in this case)

Adhesion promoters are used to react chemically with surface silanol and replace the -OH group with an organic functional group that, unlike the hydroxyl group, offers good adhesion to photoresist. Silanes are often used for this purpose, the most common being hexamethyl disilizane (HMDS). (Note : HMDS adhesion promotion was first developed for fiber glass applications, where adhesion of the resin matrix to the glass fibers is important.) The HMDS can be applied by spinning a diluted solution (10-20% HMDS in cellosolve acetate, xylene, or a fluorocarbon) directly on to the wafer and allowing the HMDS to spin dry (HMDS is quite volatile at room temperature). If the HMDS is not allowed to dry properly dramatic loss of adhesion will result. Although direct spinning is easy, it is only effective at displacing a small percentage of the silanol groups. By far the preferred method of applying the adhesion promoter is by subjecting the substrate to HMDS vapor, usually at elevated temperatures and reduced pressure. This allows good coating of the substrate without excess HMDS deposition, and the higher temperatures cause more complete reaction with the silanol groups. Once properly treated with HMDS the substrate can be left for up to several days without significant re-adsorption of water. Performing the dehydration bake and vapor prime in the same oven gives optimum performance.

2. Photo Resist Coating

A thin, uniform coating of photo resist at a specific, well controlled thickness is accomplished by the seemingly simple process of spin coating. The photoresist, rendered into a liquid form by dissolving the solid components in a solvent, is poured onto the wafer, which is then spun on a turntable at a high speed producing the desired film. Stringent requirements for thickness control and uniformity and low defect density call for particular attention to be paid to this process, where a large number of parameters can have significant impact on photo resist thickness uniformity and control. There is the choice between static dispense (wafer stationary while resist is dispensed) or dynamic dispense (wafer spinning while resist is dispensed), spin speeds and times, and accelerations to each of the spin speeds. Also, the volume of the resist dispensed and properties of the resist (such as viscosity, percent solids, and solvent composition) and the substrate (substrate material and topography) play an important role in the resist thickness uniformity. Further, practical aspects of the spin operation, such as exhaust, temperature and humidity control, and spinner cleanliness often have significant effects on the resist film. Fig. 2.4 shows a generic photo resist spin coat cycle. At the end of this cycle a thick, solvent-rich film of photo resist covers the wafer, ready for post-apply bake.

Although theory exists to describe the spin coat process rheologically, in practical terms the variation of photo resist thickness and uniformity with the process parameters must be determined experimentally. The photo resist spin speed curve (Fig. 2.5) is an essential tool for setting the spin speed to obtain the desired resist thickness. The final resist thickness varies as one over the square root of the spin speed and is roughly proportional to the liquid photo resist viscosity.

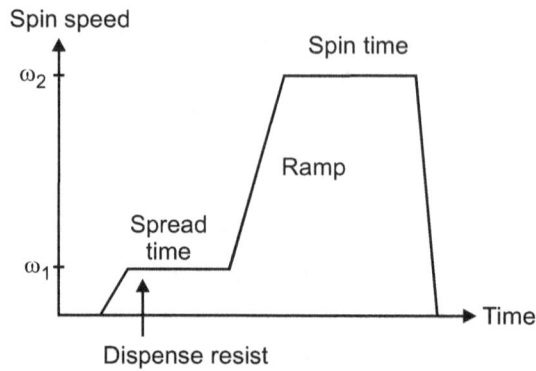

Fig. 2.4 : Pictorial representation of a simple photo resist spin coat cycle. If w 1 > 0, the dispense is said to be dynamic

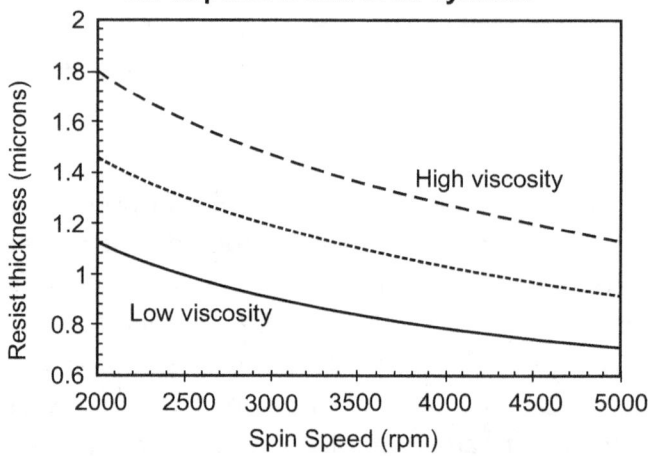

Fig. 2.5 : Photo resist spins speed curves for different resist viscosities showing how resist thickness varies as spin speed to the -1/2 power

3. Post-Apply Bake

After coating, the resulting resist film will contain between 20 – 40% by weight solvent. The post-apply bake process, also called a softbake or a prebake, involves drying the photo resist after spin coat by removing this excess solvent. The main reason for reducing the solvent content is to stabilize the resist film. At room temperature, an unbaked photo resist film will lose solvent by evaporation, thus changing the properties of the film with time. By baking the resist, the majority of the solvent is removed and the film becomes stable at room temperature.

There are four major effects of removing solvent from a photo resist film:

- Film thickness is reduced,
- Post-exposure bake and development properties are changed,
- Adhesion is improved, and
- The film becomes less tacky and thus less susceptible to particulate contamination.

Typical prebake processes leave between 3 and 8 % residual solvent in the resist film, sufficiently small to keep the film stable during subsequent lithographic processing.

Unfortunately, there are other consequences of baking most photo resists. At temperatures greater than about 70°C the photosensitive component of a typical resist mixture, called the Photoactive Compound (PAC), may begin to decompose . Also, the resin, another component of the resist, can crosslink and/or oxidize at elevated temperatures. Both of these effects are undesirable. Thus, one must search for the optimum prebake conditions that will maximize the benefits of solvent evaporation and minimize the detriments of resist decomposition. For chemically amplified resists, residual solvent can significantly influence diffusion and reaction properties during the post-exposure bake, necessitating careful control over the post-apply bake process. Fortunately, these modern resists do not suffer from significant decomposition of the photosensitive components during prebake.

There are several methods that can be used to bake photo resists. The most obvious method is an oven bake. Convection oven baking of conventional photo resists at 90°C for 30 minutes was typical during the 1970s and early 1980s. Although the use of convection ovens for the prebaking of photo resist was once quite common, currently the most popular bake method is the hot plate. The wafer is brought either into intimate vacuum contact with or close proximity to a hot, high-mass metal plate. Due to the high thermal conductivity of silicon, the photo resist is heated to near the hot plate temperature quickly (in about 5 seconds for hard contact, or about 20 seconds for proximity baking). The greatest advantage of this method is an order of magnitude decrease in the required bake time over convection ovens, to about one minute, and the improved uniformity of the bake. In general, proximity baking is preferred to reduce the possibility of particle generation caused by contact with the backside of the wafer.

When the wafer is removed from the hotplate, baking continues as long as the wafer is hot. The total bake process cannot be well controlled unless the cooling of the wafer is also well controlled. As a result, hotplate baking is always followed immediately by a chill plate operation, where the wafer is brought in contact or close proximity to a cool plate (kept at a temperature slightly below room temperature). After cooling, the wafer is ready for its lithographic exposure.

4. Alignment and Exposure

The basic principle behind the operation of a photo resist is the change in solubility of the resist in a developer upon exposure to light (or other types of exposing radiation). In the case of the standard diazonaphthoquinone positive photoresist, the Photoactive Compound (PAC), which is not soluble in the aqueous base developer, is converted to a carboxylic acid on exposure to UV light in the range of 350 – 450 nm. The carboxylic acid product is very soluble in the basic developer. Thus, a spatial variation in light energy incident on the photo resist will cause a spatial variation in solubility of the resist in developer.

Contact and proximity lithography are the simplest methods of exposing a photo resist through a master pattern called a photomask (Fig. 2.6). Contact lithography offers high resolution (down to about the wavelength of the radiation), but practical problems such as mask damage and resulting low yield make this process unusable in most production environments. Proximity printing reduces mask damage by keeping the mask a set distance above the wafer (e.g., 20 µm). Unfortunately, the resolution limit is increased to greater than 2 to 4 µm, making proximity printing insufficient for today's technology. By far the most common method of exposure is projection printing.

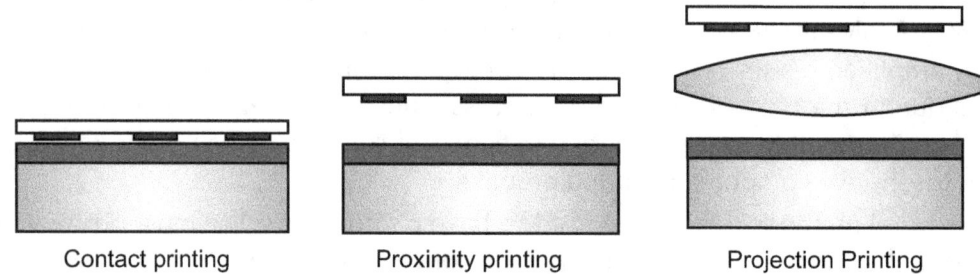

Contact printing   Proximity printing   Projection Printing

Fig. 2.6 : Lithographic printing in semiconductor manufacturing has evolved from contact printing (in the early 1960s) to projection printing (from the mid 1970s to today).

Projection lithography derives its name from the fact that an image of the mask is projected onto the wafer. Projection lithography became a viable alternative to contact/proximity printing in the mid 1970s when the advent of computer-aided lens design and improved optical materials allowed the production of lens elements of sufficient quality to meet the requirements of the semiconductor industry. In fact, these lenses have become so perfect that lens defects, called aberrations, play only a small role in determining the quality of the image. Such an optical system is said to be diffraction-limited, since it is diffraction effects and not lens aberrations which, for the most part, determine the shape of the image.

There are two major classes of projection lithography tools – scanning and step-and-repeat systems. Scanning projection printing, pioneered by the Perkin-Elmer company, employs reflective optics (i.e., mirrors rather than lenses) to project a slit of light from the mask onto the wafer as the mask and wafer are moved simultaneously by the slit. Exposure dose is determined by the intensity of the light, the slit width, and the speed at which the wafer is scanned. These early scanning systems, which use polychromatic light from a mercury arc lamp, are 1:1, i.e., the mask and image sizes are equal. Step-and-repeat cameras (called steppers for short) expose the wafer one rectangular section (called the image field) at a time and can be 1:1 or reduction. These systems employ refractive optics (i.e., lenses) and are usually quasi-monochromatic. Both types of systems (Fig. 2.7) are capable of high-resolution imaging, although reduction imaging is required for the highest resolutions.

Scanners replaced proximity printing by the mid-seventies for device geometries below 4 to 5 µm. By the early 1980s, steppers began to dominate as device designs pushed below 2 µm. Steppers have continued to dominate lithographic patterning throughout the 1990s as minimum feature sizes reached the 250nm levels. However, by the early 1990s a hybrid step-

and-scan approach was introduced by SVG Lithography, the successor to Perkin-Elmer. The step-and-scan approach uses a fraction of a normal stepper field (for example, 25 mm × 8 mm), then scans this field in one direction to expose the entire 4 × reduction mask. The wafer is then stepped to a new location and the scan is repeated. The smaller imaging field simplifies the design and manufacture of the lens, but at the expense of a more complicated reticle and wafer stage. Step-and-scan technology is the technology of choice today for below 250 nm manufacturing.

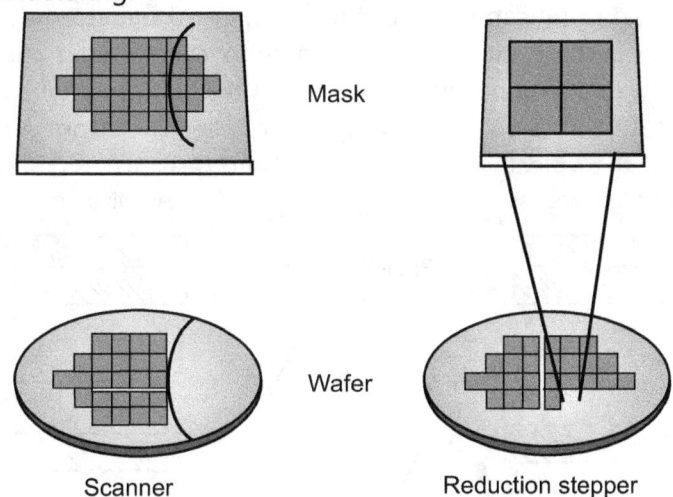

Fig. 2.7 : Scanners and steppers use different techniques for exposing a large wafer with a small image field

Resolution, the smallest feature that can be printed with adequate control, has two basic limits: The smallest image that can be projected onto the wafer, and the resolving capability of the photo resist to make use of that image. From the projection imaging side, resolution is determined by the wavelength of the imaging light (λ) and the numerical aperture (NA) of the projection lens according to the Rayleigh criterion:

$$R \: \alpha \: \frac{\lambda}{NA}$$

Lithography systems have progressed from blue wavelengths (436 nm) to UV (365 nm) to deep-UV (248 nm) to today's mainstream high resolution wavelength of 193 nm. In the meantime, projection tool numerical apertures have risen from 0.16 for the first scanners to amazingly high 0.93 NA systems today producing features well under 100 nm in size.

Before the exposure of the photo resist with an image of the mask can begin, this image must be aligned with the previously defined patterns on the wafer. This alignment, and the resulting overlay of the two or more lithographic patterns, is critical since tighter overlay control means circuit features can be packed closer together. Closer packing of devices through better alignment and overlay is nearly as critical as smaller devices through higher resolution in the drive towards more functionality per chip.

Important aspect of photo resist exposure is the standing wave effect :

Monochromatic light, when projected onto a wafer, strikes the photo resist surface over a range of angles, approximating plane waves. This light travels down through the photo resist and if the substrate is reflective, is reflected back up through the resist. The incoming and reflected light interfere to form a standing wave pattern of high and low light intensity at different depths in the photo resist. This pattern is replicated in the photo resist, causing ridges in the sidewalls of the resist feature as seen in Fig. 2.8. As pattern dimensions become smaller, these ridges can significantly affect the quality of the feature. The interference that causes standing waves also results in a phenomenon called swing curves, the sinusoidal variation in line width with changing resist thickness. These detrimental effects are best cured by coating the substrate with a thin absorbing layer called a Bottom Antireflective Coating (BARC) that can reduce the reflectivity seen by the photo resist to less than 1 %.

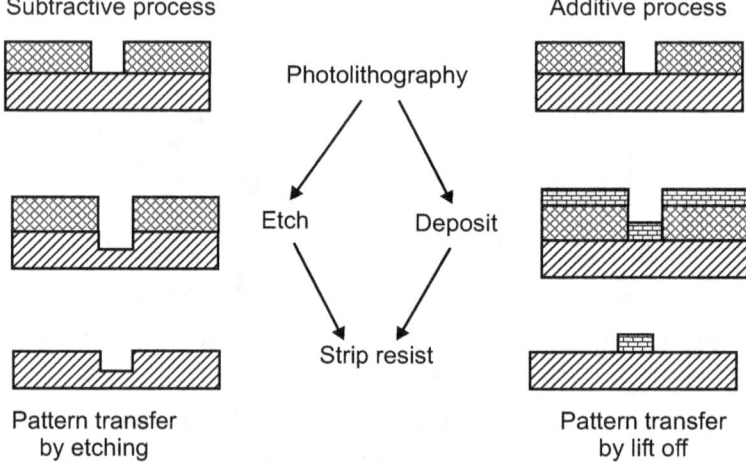

Fig. 2.8 : Photo Resist Exposure

5. Post-Exposure Bake

One method of reducing the standing wave effect is called the Post-Exposure Bake (PEB). Although there is still some debate as to the mechanism, it is believed that the high temperatures used (100°C – 130°C) cause diffusion of the photoactive compound, thus smoothing out the standing wave ridges (Fig. 2.9). It is important to note that the detrimental effects of high temperatures on photo resist discussed concerning prebaking also apply to the PEB. Thus, it becomes very important to optimize the bake conditions. It has also been observed that the rate of diffusion of the PAC is dependent on the prebake conditions. It is thought that the presence of solvent enhances diffusion during a PEB. Thus, a low temperature prebake results in greater diffusion for a given PEB temperature.

For a conventional resist, the main importance of the PEB is diffusion to remove standing waves. For another class of photo resists, called chemically amplified resists, the PEB is an essential part of the chemical reactions that create a solubility differential between exposed and unexposed parts of the resist. For these resists, exposure generates a small amount of a strong acid that does not itself change the solubility of the resist. During the post-exposure bake, this photo generated acid catalyzes a reaction that changes the solubility of the polymer resin in the resist. Control of the PEB is extremely critical for chemically amplified resists.

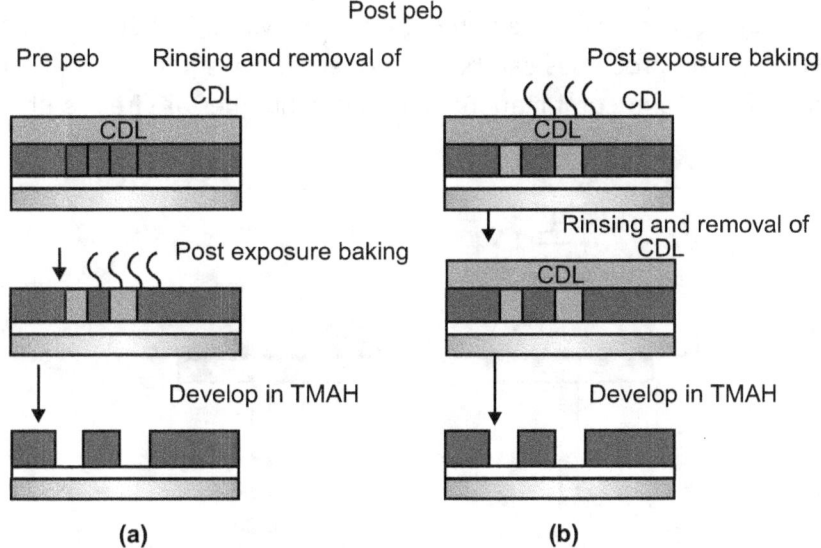

Fig. 2.9 : Post-Exposure Bake

Diffusion during a post-exposure bake is often used to reduce standing waves. Photo resist profile simulations as a function of the PEB diffusion length.

6. Development

Once exposed, the photo resist must be developed. Most commonly used photo resists use aqueous bases as developers. In particular, tetramethyl ammonium hydroxide (TMAH) is used in concentrations of 0.2 - 0.26 N. Development is undoubtedly one of the most critical steps in the photo resist process. The characteristics of the resist-developer interactions determine to a large extent the shape of the photo resist profile and, more importantly, the linewidth control.

The method of applying developer to the photo resist is important in controlling the development uniformity and process latitude. In the past, batch development was the predominant development technique. A boat of some 10-20 wafers or more are developed simultaneously in a large beaker, usually with some form of agitation. With the push towards in-line processing, however, other methods have become prevalent. During spin development wafers are spun, using equipment similar to that used for spin coating, and developer is poured onto the rotating wafer. The wafer is also rinsed and dried while still spinning. Spray development has been shown to have good results using developers specifically formulated for this dispense method. Using a process identical to spin development, the developer is sprayed, rather than poured, on the wafer by using a nozzle that produces a fine mist of developer over the wafer (Fig. 2.10). This technique reduces developer usage and gives more uniform developer coverage. Another in-line development strategy is called puddle development. Again using developers specifically formulated for this process, the developer is poured onto a stationary wafer that is then allowed to sit motionless for the duration of the development time. The wafer is then spin rinsed and dried. Note that all three in-line processes can be performed in the same piece of equipment with only minor modifications, and combinations of these techniques are frequently used.

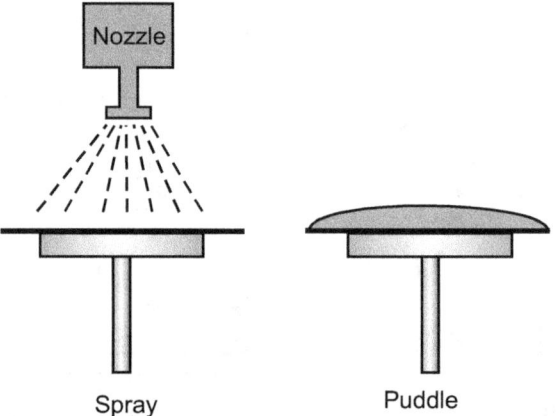

Fig. 2.10 : Different developer application techniques are commonly used

7. Postbake

The postbake (not to be confused with the post-exposure bake that comes before development) is used to harden the final resist image so that it will withstand the harsh environments of implantation or etching. The high temperatures used (120°C - 150°C) crosslink the resin polymer in the photoresist, thus making the image more thermally stable. If the temperature used is too high, the resist will flow causing degradation of the image. The temperature at which flow begins is related to the glass transition temperature and is a measure of the thermal stability of the resist. In addition to cross-linking, the postbake can remove residual solvent, water, and gasses and will usually improve adhesion of the resist to the substrate.

Other methods have been proposed to harden a photo resist image. Exposure to high intensity deep-UV light crosslinks the resin at the surface of the resist forming a tough skin around the pattern. Deep-UV hardened photo resist can withstand temperatures in excess of 200°C without dimensional deformation. Although it is commonly thought that the deep-UV radiation causes the crosslinking reaction directly, there is some evidence to suggest that ozone generated by the interaction of the light with atmospheric oxygen may cause (or enhance) the crosslinking reaction. Plasma treatments and electron beam bombardment have also been shown to effectively harden photoresist. Commercial deep-UV hardening systems are now available and are widely used.

8. Pattern Transfer

After the small patterns have been lithographically printed in photoresist, these patterns must be transferred into the substrate. There are three basic pattern transfer approaches: subtractive transfer (etching), additive transfer (selective deposition), and impurity doping (ion implantation). Etching is the most common pattern transfer approach. A uniform layer of the material to be patterned is deposited on the substrate. Lithography is then performed such that the areas to be etched are left unprotected (uncovered) by the photoresist. Etching is performed either using wet chemicals such as acids, or more commonly in a dry plasma environment. The photo resist "resists" the etching and protects the material covered by the resist. When the etching is complete, the resist is stripped leaving the desired pattern etched into the deposited layer. Additive processes are used whenever workable etching processes are not available, for example for copper interconnects. Here, the lithographic pattern is used to open areas where the new layer is to be grown (by electroplating, in the case of copper). Stripping of the resist then leaves the new material in a negative version of the patterned photoresist. Finally, doping involves the addition of controlled amounts of contaminants that change the conductive properties of a semiconductor. Ion implantation uses a beam of dopant ions accelerated at the photoresist-patterned substrate. The resist blocks the ions, but the areas uncovered by resists are embedded with ions, creating the selectively doped regions that make up the electrical heart of the transistors.

9. Strip

After the imaged wafer has been processed (e.g., etched, ion implanted, etc.) the remaining photo resist must be removed. There are two classes of resist stripping techniques: wet stripping using organic or inorganic solutions, and dry (plasma) stripping. A simple example of an organic stripper is acetone. Although commonly used in laboratory environments, acetone tends to leave residues on the wafer (scumming) and is thus unacceptable for semiconductor processing. Most commercial organic strippers are phenol-based and are somewhat better at avoiding scum formation. However, the most common wet strippers for positive photo resists are inorganic acid-based systems used at elevated temperatures.

Wet stripping has several inherent problems. Although the proper choice of strippers for various applications can usually eliminate gross scumming, it is almost impossible to remove the final monolayer of photo resist from the wafer by wet chemical means. It is often necessary to follow a wet strip by a plasma descum to completely clean the wafer of resist residues. Also, photo resist which has undergone extensive hardening (e.g., deep-UV hardening) and been subjected to harsh processing conditions (e.g., high energy ion implantation) can be almost impossible to strip chemically. For these reasons, plasma stripping has become the standard in semiconductor processing. An oxygen plasma is highly reactive towards organic polymers but leaves most inorganic materials.

Isolation Techniques

Thermal grown oxide is mainly used as isolation material in semiconductor fabrication. For the isolation of neighboring MOS transistors there exist two techniques, namely Local Oxidation of Silicon and Shallow Trench Isolation. The differences in their process flow and their final oxide shapes are described in the following.

Local Oxidation of Silicon

Local Oxidation of Silicon (LOCOS) is the traditional isolation technique. At first a very thin silicon oxide layer is grown on the wafer, the so-called pad oxide. Then a layer of silicon nitride is deposited which is used as an oxide barrier. The pattern transfer is performed by photo lithography. After lithography the pattern is etched into the nitride. The result is the nitride mask, which defines the active areas for the oxidation process. The next step is the main part of the LOCOS process, the growth of the thermal oxide. After the oxidation process is finished, the last step is the removal of the nitride layer. The main drawback of this technique is the so-called bird's beak effect and the surface area which is lost to this encroachment. The advantages of LOCOS fabrication are the simple process flow and the high oxide quality, because the whole LOCOS structure is thermally grown.

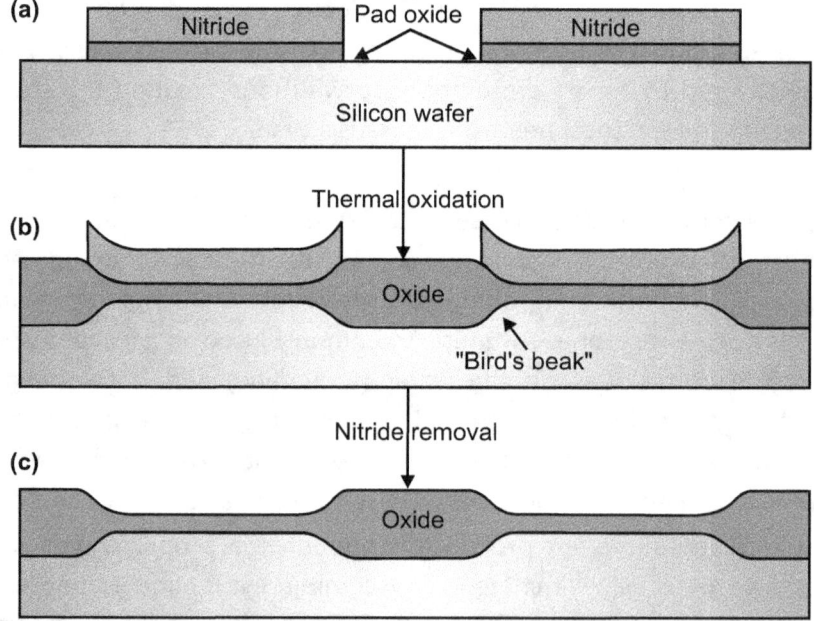

Fig. 2.11 : Process sequence for local oxidation of silicon (LOCOS)

Shallow Trench Isolation

The Shallow Trench Isolation (STI) is the preferred isolation technique for the sub-0.5 μm technology, because it completely avoids the bird's beak shape characteristic. With its zero oxide field encroachment STI is more suitable for the increased density requirements, because it allows to form smaller isolation regions. The STI process starts in the same way as the LOCOS process. The first difference compared to LOCOS is that a shallow trench is etched into the silicon substrate, after underetching of the oxide pad, also a thermal oxide in the trench is grown, the so-called liner oxide. But unlike with LOCOS, the thermal oxidation process is stopped after the formation of a thin oxide layer, and the rest of the trench is filled with a deposited oxide. Next, the excessive (deposited) oxide is removed with chemical mechanical planarization. At last the nitride mask is also removed. The price for saving space with STI is the larger number of different process steps.

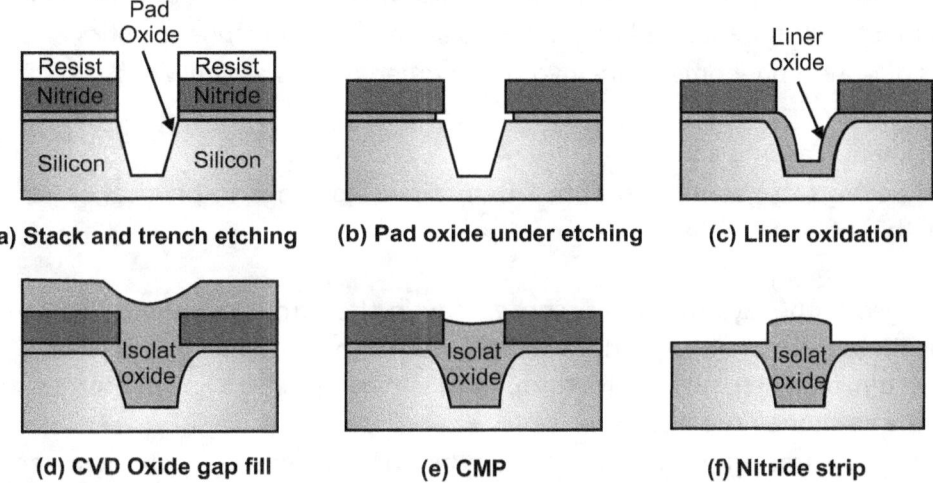

Fig. 2.12 : Steps in a typical shallow trench isolation (STI) process flow

2.3.1 Basic Concepts of Optics

- Light and optical systems it is the applications of lithography systems.
- When the light travels as an electromagnetic wave through a free space then the behavior of an optical system in all dimensions are large compared to the optical components, this problem is known as tracing ray. This approach can be used in the optic source and lens condenser to remember that light as it passes through the mask, the objective lens, the wafer. Following Fig. 2.13 shows that the passage of pattern strikes the screw or image place and straight line.

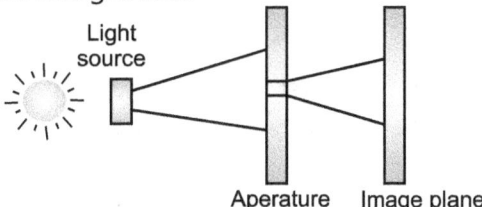

Fig. 2.13: Image plane formation

- The smallest aperture because the more spread this screen image. In morden lithography light passes through a mask with aperatures.
- The science of light is known as optics. If you have no idea about optics, here, the basic facts understand how mirages, green flashes, and other refraction phenomena work. Traditionally, optics is separated into two main areas:

- **Geometrical Optics:** Which deals with how light moves and where it goes; and
- **Physical Optics :** Which deals with the nature of light itself (which we don't need to get into here) and with the interaction between light and matter (which we will need to use a little bit).

- There are also numerous associated fields, such as vision, and the science of color. The science of the color one is atmospheric optics, which deals with how light interacts with our atmosphere. Mirages and green flashes are part of atmospheric optics.

Two kinds of optical phenomena are involved in green flashes and mirages:

- Atmospheric refraction
- Atmospheric transmission

Refraction belongs to geometrical optics; transmission belongs to physical optics. Let's look at both of these fields.

Refraction

The bending of light rays by the varying *density* in the atmosphere is called **atmospheric refraction**. Refraction process produces both green flashes and mirages hence it is requires a separate web page. The paths of rays through which medium with any properties so it can be compute the path of a ray accurately.

This process of "tracing rays" through the air, or through an optical system, is what geometrical optics is all about.

Limitations of Refraction: When obstacles or apertures are very small, the (actual) wave nature of light makes very narrow beams or shadows spread out and become fuzzy at the edges. Then the wide-beam assumptions that lie beneath geometrical optics are no longer true, and "ray-tracing" fails. As we have had to mention the "nature of light" here, this brings us to physical optics.

Physical Optics

We need to use the part of physical optics that deals with the loss of light from a beam. There are two main processes:

- Absorption
- Scattering

Absorption: Light can absorbed completely turned into heat, dark colored surface absorb the light that falls on the surface. In sunny days air absorbs the lights air molecules at a particular wavelength spectrum.

The absorptions that are most important in producing green flashes are those in the yellow and orange part of the spectrum, caused by ozone and water vapor. These absorptions are fairly weak; but when the Sun is near the horizon, the path of the sunlight through the air is long enough that most of the yellow and orange light is absorbed. In fact, during twilight, the blue color of the sky overhead is mostly due to absorption of orange light by ozone.

Scattering: Scattering changing the direction of light which changes the direction of a beam without making broader but a redistribution of the light in all directions. Rough surfaces scatter light but the particles of air suspended in scatters light. The sky is blue because air molecules scatter blue and violet light much more strongly than the colors with longer wavelengths, like yellow and red. Wherever you look in a clear sky, you see blue light that has been scattered toward your eye from the air along your line of sight. The scattering produced by air molecules alone is termed as "Rayleigh scattering" because it was first clarified, in 1871, by Lord Rayleigh.

Rayleigh scattering entails particles that are "small" compared to the wavelength of light. Air molecules are roughly a thousand times smaller than visible wavelengths, so they certainly satisfy this requirement. Larger solid or liquid particles suspended in the air usually called "dust" or "aerosol" particles also scatter light. But particle scattering is mostly into directions near the original direction of the light; so it appears brightest in the part of the sky near the Sun. The bright aureole around the Sun seen in all but the clearest air is caused by this "forward scattering" by aerosols.

Particle scattering is also much more neutral in color than molecular scattering; so the aureole (due to particle scattering) is nearly white.

If there is a lot of aerosol scattering, the sky looks whitish instead of a clear blue. And aerosol scattering between you and the distant landscape produces a bluish-white haze, which can even hide objects some distance away.

The wavelength of light scatters almost equally in all directions. The larger particles are more scattered to the forward direction. If the particles are larger then it produces spherical raindrops. If the scattering is selected at certain direction then it produces rainbows.

Phenomena of atmospheric optics that require aerosol scattering are crepuscular rays and iridescent clouds.

2.3.2 Photo-Resists

A photo resist is a light-sensitive material used in several industrial processes, such as photo lithography and photo engraving, to form a patterned coating on a surface.

There are two types of photo resist:

1. Positive and
2. Negative.

For positive resists, the resist is exposed with UV light wherever the underlying material is to be removed. In these resists, exposure to the UV light changes the chemical structure of the resist so that it becomes more soluble in the developer.

The exposed resist is then washed away by the developer solution, leaving windows of the bare underlying material. In other words, "whatever shows, goes." The mask, therefore, contains an exact copy of the pattern which is to remain on the wafer.

Negative resists behave in just the opposite manner. Exposure to the UV light causes the negative resist to become polymerized, and more difficult to dissolve. Therefore, the negative resist remains on the surface wherever it is exposed, and the developer solution removes only the unexposed portions. Masks used for negative photo resists, therefore, it contain the inverse (or photographic "negative") of the pattern to be transferred. The Fig. 2.14 below shows the pattern differences generated from the use of positive and negative resist.

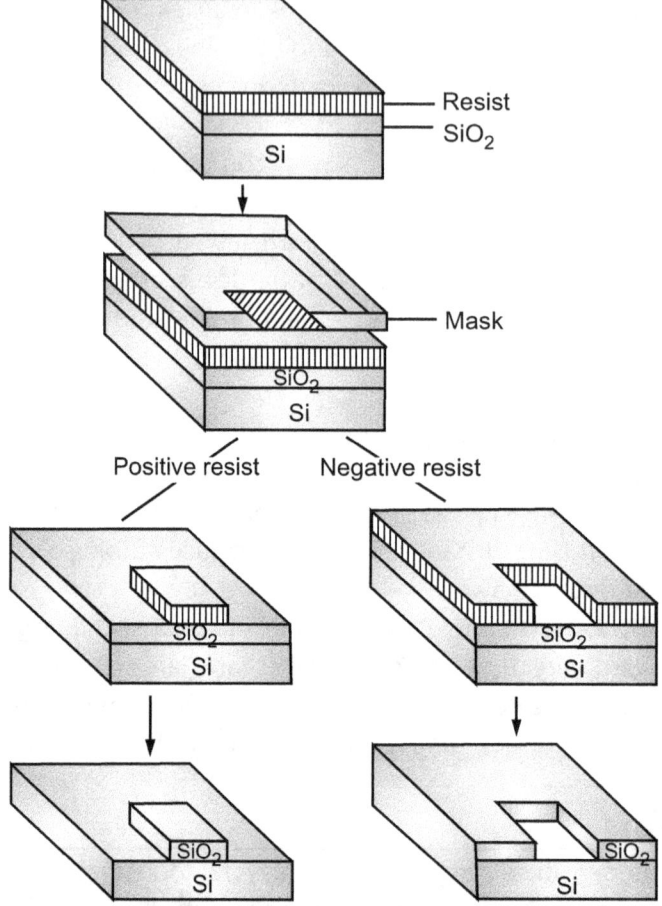

Fig. 2.14 : Positive and negative photo resists

Negative resists were popular in the early history of integrated circuit processing, but positive resist gradually became more widely used since they offer better process controllability for small geometry features. Positive resists are now the dominant type of resist used in VLSI fabrication processes.

Positive Tone Resists

The resist is exposed with UV light where the underlying material is to be removed. In these resists, exposure to the UV light changes the chemical structure of the resist so that it becomes more soluble in the developer. The exposed resist is then washed away by the developer solution, leaving windows of the bare underlying material. The mask, therefore, contains an exact copy of the pattern which is to remain on the wafer, as a stencil for subsequent processing.

Negative Tone Resists

Negative tone resists behave in the opposite manner.

When exposed to the UV light, the negative resist becomes cross linked /polymerized, and more difficult to dissolve in developer. Therefore, the negative resist remains on the surface of the substrate where it is exposed, and the developer solution removes only the unexposed areas. Masks used for negative photo resists, therefore contain the inverse or photographic "negative" of the pattern to be transferred. The Fig. 2.14 shows the pattern differences generated from the use of a positive and negative resist.

2.3.3 The Difference Between Positive and Negative Photo Resist

As semiconductor suppliers, photo resist is a material that is continuously worked with. This light sensitive material has two types, positive and negative, that react very differently when exposed to UV light; therefore, it is essential to understand each reaction in order to produce the best results in the semiconductor manufacturing industry.

Positive photo resists

With positive photo resists, UV light strategically hits the material in the areas that the semiconductor supplier intends to remove. When the photo resist is exposed to the UV light, the chemical structure changes and becomes more soluble in the photo resist developer. These exposed areas are then washed away with the photo resist developer solvent, leaving the underlying material. The areas of the photo resist that aren't exposed to the UV light are left insoluble to the photo resist developer. When working with positive photo resists in the semiconductor manufacturing industry, you receive an identical copy of the pattern, which is exposed as a mask on the wafer.

Negative photo resists

With negative resists, exposure to UV light causes the chemical structure of the photo resist to polymerize, which is just the opposite of positive photo resists. Instead of becoming more soluble, negative photo resists become extremely difficult to dissolve. As a result, the UV exposed negative resist remains on the surface while the photo resist developer solution works to remove the areas that are unexposed. This leaves a mask that consists of an inverse pattern of the original, which is applied on the wafer.

Both positive and negative photo resists are still used in the semiconductor manufacturing industry today, but many semiconductor suppliers opt for positive photo resists due to their higher resolution capabilities. Positive photo resists are able to maintain their size and pattern as the photo resist developer solvent doesn't permeate the areas that have not been exposed to the UV light. With negative resists, both the UV exposed and unexposed areas are permeated by the solvent, which can lead to pattern distortions.

While positive photo resists seem to have the advantage, negative photo resists aren't necessarily a thing of the past. Negative resists are a great material to use for those semiconductor supplies that don't require such high resolutions. As opposed to positive photo resists, negative resists have a faster photo speed, wider process latitude and a significantly lower operating cost. Negative photo resists also have better adhesion capabilities to certain substrate materials.

Both positive and negative photo resists have their place in the semiconductor manufacturing industry, and help to produce a range of high quality products.

2.4 THERMAL OXIDATION

- Thermal oxidation refers to a chemical process, where silicon dioxide (SiO_2) is grown in an ambient with elevated temperatures.

- A simple form of thermal oxidation even takes place at room temperature, if silicon is exposed to an oxygen or air ambient. There, a thin native oxide layer with 0.5 to 1 nm will form on the surface rapidly.

- After that, the growth slows down and effectively stops after a few hours with a final thickness in the order of 1 to 2 nm, because the oxygen atoms have too small energy at room temperature to diffuse through the already formed oxide layer.

- SiO_2 is used to isolate one device from another, to act as gate oxide in MOS structures, and to serve as a structured mask against implant of dopant atoms.

- In the beginning of this unit is described, why thermal grown SiO_2 is the most appropriate material for such requirements ?

- Thermal oxidation should be mentioned that SiO_2 layers produced by deposition technique like vapour deposition chemical vapour position.

- Deposition normally involves a much smaller thermal budget than thermal oxidation and so it is the only option when wafers have already metal on them.

- Usually deposited oxides are not used for thin layers under 10 nm because the control of the deposition process is not so good as the thermal oxidation process.

- Another disadvantage is the interface between a deposited oxide and the underlying silicon, which is electrically not so good as thermal oxide. Furthermore, deposited oxide does not have the same it requires high density for thermal grown oxide.

- Thermal oxidation is a complex process it is used to diffusion of oxidants, volume increase and a chemical reaction, it occur simultaneously convert to the silicon substrate into SiO_2.

- This process is strongly influenced by the used oxidant species, the oxidation ambient with temperature and pressure, and also the crystal orientation of the substrate. With these parameters the quality and the growth of the oxide during the manufacturing process can be controlled.

- The small dimensions and high performance of modern MOS devices require ultrathin SiO_2 layers for gate dielectrics. Apart from the exact thickness control, pure SiO_2 has some difficulties to fulfill all requirements at such thin thicknesses.

- Especially the dopant penetration and direct tunneling for ultra thin oxides cannot be handled. It was found that silicon oxynitrides are more suitable materials for such applications. Oxynitrides can be produced by different methods which depend on the desired nitrogen profile and, therefore, on the application.

- Silicon dioxide (SiO_2) is a main insulating material used in microtechnology. The most common technique used to produce insulating oxide layer is thermal oxidation performed in a furnace.

There are Two Methods of Oxidation:

- **Dry Oxidation :** When the wafer is exposed to an oxygen at 1000°C, high quality oxide for MOS gate insulation is produced in this manner.

- **Wet Oxidation :** When mixture of high-purity oxygen and hydrogen at 1000°C is burned, giving water vapour environment; the advantage of this procedure is higher growth rate, although "wet" oxide features not so good quality and may be used only as a masking layer for instance. An aim of the exercise is to grow the layer of the oxide and measure its thickness employing an ellipso-meter. This method used for growth due to safety regulations, hydrogen it must be used in lab oxidation performed in atmosphere of oxygen or nitrogen saturated with water wafer.

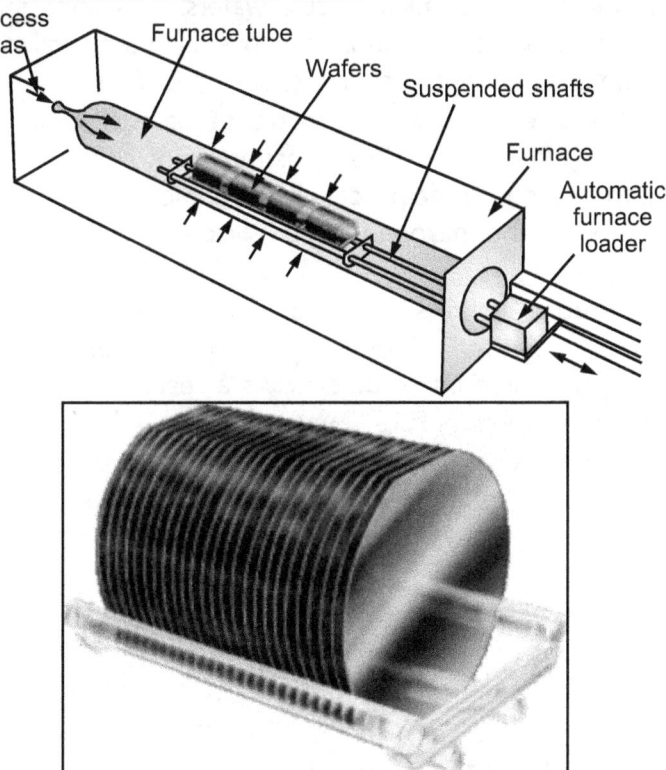

Fig. 2.15: Manufacturing processes of Si wafer

To perform an oxidation :

- Turn furnace on and heat it up. This operation will be performed by the lab staff before an exercise as heating up takes 1 to 2 hours.

- Set the temperature 1000 °C on the temperature controller. Use the thermocouple calibration.

- Once set-point temperature has been reached, put the wafers into a quartz boat and load it into the tube utilising a furnace loader (loading speed 30 cm/s). When working in the vicinity of the tube, always wear heat-resistant, protective gloves.

- During heating up, pure oxygen or nitrogen flows through the processing tube. To start process, put the gas flow through the water bubbler this is where gas saturation with water vapour takes place. Use the gas system scheme shown on the gas section of the furnace.

- After 1 hour, unload the wafers from the tube (use the 20 cm/s speed). Leave the wafers for 10 minutes to cool down.

2.4.1 Formations of Si and SiO$_2$ Interface

- A highly important precondition for the production of quality integrated circuits is the well mastered production of semiconductor wafers. It is imperative for the substrate wafer to contain as little defects as possible, above all in the subsurface functional region in which active elements of integrated circuits are located.

- Another important requirement is a small scatter of material parameters across the wafer. In effort to produce the best possible substrate with suitable parameters, numerous procedures are introduced into the process of manufacture. Recently, much attention has been paid to the properties of nitrogen-doped silicon substrates grown by the method of Czochralski.

- The presence of nitrogen in the silicon substrate has been known for several decades already. In the past, however, nitrogen in silicon was understood as an undesired impurity causing a large amount of defects. As a result, the generation recombination parameters of the silicon substrate are worsened.

- In the case of substrates with large diameters there is a possibility to utilize Si wafers containing nitrogen in the production of integrated circuits, particularly thanks to the good mechanical and electrophysical properties of silicon. Motivation for further research is the expected improvement in reliability and production yield of devices based on nitrogen-doped silicon.

- To create the best subsurface region with a low concentration of electrically active defects (of the so-called denuded zone), it is inevitable to remove from it primarily metallic impurities that give rise to deep levels in the forbidden band of the semiconductor. One of the ways how to create a high-quality denuded zone is intrinsic gettering by means of oxygen precipitates.

- These behave like gettering centres for metallic impurities. Oxygen is introduced into silicon during the Czochralski growth. In the course of the multistage process of thermal treatment, oxygen precipitates are created in the bulk of the semiconducting substrate, whereas in the subsurface region oxygen diffuses to the interface and contributes to the creation of SiO2.

- In this way, metallic impurities are drawn into the bulk of Si, where they are bonded to precipitates. Nitrogen, even in small amounts, possesses the ability to support precipitation of oxygen and hereby to improve the process of intrinsic gettering. Precipitates created in the nitrogen doped Czochralski-grown substrate (NCZ) have smaller dimensions and a higher density than in an undoped Czochralski-grown (CZ) structure.

- In the case of a standard CZ silicon structure, the use of intrinsic gettering by means of oxygen precipitates can only be considered for silicon wafers of small diameters. In the case of larger diameters, a decrease in the creation of precipitates occurs in peripheral regions.

- This decreases the gettering efficacy and, as a result, a big scatter in parameters occurs across the wafer. In an NCZ structure, nitrogen supports creation of precipitates also in the peripheral regions and improves the radial uniformity of the denuded zone. Nitrogen allows locking of dislocations resulting in an improvement of the mechanical strength of semiconducting wafers, which is another advantage of nitrogen doping of silicon substrates.

2.4.2 Thermal Oxidations or Incineration

- It is the process of oxidizing combustible materials by raising their temperature above the auto-ignition point in the presence of oxygen and maintaining it at a high temperature for sufficient time to complete combustion to carbon dioxide and water.

- The heart of the thermal incinerator is a nozzle-stabilized flame maintained by a combination of auxiliary fuel, waste gas compounds, and supplemental air as required. When the waste gas passes through the flame, it is heated from the preheated inlet temperature to the ignition temperature. The ignition temperature varies for different compounds and is usually determined empirically.

- The combustion of the VOC and fuel (if air is needed) takes place in the combustion chamber, where the high velocities of the inlet streams provide good turbulent mixing. From the combustion chamber the gases pass to an insulated retention chamber, where they remain long enough at high temperature for the reactions to complete the destruction of the VOCs begun in the combustion chamber. The hot gases leave the retention chamber and flows to the stack.

- The amount of oxygen mixing time temperature, turbulence it affect to the rate of efficiency of the combustion process the basic design parameters for VOC and HAP oxidation systems. For safety considerations, the maximum concentration of the VOCs/HAPs in the waste gas must be substantially below the Lower Explosive Limit (LEL) of the specific compounds) being controlled.

- As a rule, a safety factor of four (i.e. 25% of the LEL) is used, although some direct-flame oxidizers are able to operate safely above this level. The waste gas may be diluted with ambient air, if necessary, to lower the concentration.
- The required level of VOC/HAP control that must be achieved in the time that the waste gas spends in the thermal combustion chamber dictates the reactor temperature. The shorter the residence time, the higher the reactor temperature.
- Thermal oxidizers are designed to provide no more than one second of residence time to the waste gas with typical temperatures of 650 $^\circ$C to 1,100 $^\circ$C (1,200 to 2,000 $^\circ$F).
- To save fuel cost, a heat exchanger can be added to the clean gas outlet. In this arrangement the hot clean gas leaving the retention chamber is used to heat up the incoming contaminated gas stream, thus reducing the amount of fuel needed to bring the mixture of VOC-air-fuel stream up to the temperature at which the VOC destruction reaction proceeds. Such heat exchangers are usually expensive and have severe corrosion problems.

2.4.3 Dopant Diffusion

- Dopant diffusion in semiconductors is an interesting phenomenon from both technological and scientific points of view.
- Firstly, dopant diffusion is taking place during most of the steps in electronic device fabrication and, secondly, diffusion is related to fundamental properties of the semiconductor, often controlled by intrinsic point defects: self-interstitials and vacancies.
- This investigates the diffusion of P, B and Sb, in Si as well as in strained and relaxed SiGe. Most of the measurements have been performed using secondary ion mass spectrometry on high purity epitaxially grown samples, having in-situ incorporated dopant profiles, fabricated by reduced pressure chemical vapor deposition or molecular beam epitaxy.
- The samples have been heat treated both under close-to-equilibrium conditions (i.e., long time annealings in an inert ambient) and conditions which resulted in non-equilibrium diffusion (i.e., vacuum annealing, oxidation, short annealing duration, and proton irradiation).

Mechanisms of Diffusion

Knowledge of the mechanisms that govern dopant diffusion on a microscopic level are crucial for the understanding and modeling of diffusion, and it is well established that the important dopants in Si will diffuse by interacting with native point defects, such as vacancies (V) or Si self-interstitials (I), which are always present in the crystal. The impurity traps a point defect and forms a highly mobile complex that is able to move through the crystal, until the complex breaks up and the impurity again occupies a substitutional site is called concerted exchange mechanism, where no point defect are required, because the dopant simply changes place with a neighboring Si atom, is usually regarded to be negligible in silicon.

2.4.4 Ion Implantation Fundamentals

- This method is used as an alternative to a deposition diffusion, and it produces shallow surface region of dopant atoms deposited into a silicon wafer.

- In this process a beam of impurity ions is accelerated to kinetic energies in the range of several tens of kV and is directed to the surface of the silicon. As the impurity atoms enter the crystal, they give up their energy to the lattice in collisions and finally come to rest at some average penetration depth, called the projected range expressed in micro meters.

- Depending on the impurity and its implantation energy, the range in a given semiconductor may vary from a few hundred angstroms to about 1 µm. Typical distribution of impurity along the projected range is approximately Gaussian. By performing several implantations at different energies, it is possible to synthesize a desired impurity distribution, for example a uniformly doped region.

Ion Implantation System

A typical ion-implantation system is shown in the Fig. 2.16 below.

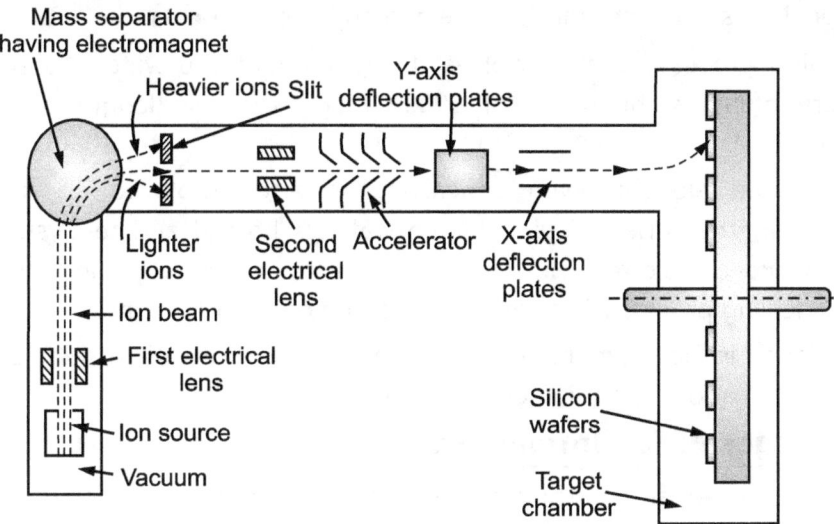

Fig. 2.16 : Ion implanation system

- A gas containing the desired impurity is ionized within the ion source. The ions are generated and repelled from their source in a diverging beam that is focused before if passes through a mass separator that directs only the ions of the desired species through a narrow aperture.

- A second lens focuses this resolved beam which is passes through an accelerator that brings the ions to their required energy before they strike the target and become implanted in the exposed areas of the silicon wafers. The accelerating voltages may be from 20 kV to as much as 250 kV.

- The mass separation the ions are accelerated to high energy. The ion beam is small it mean that for the scanning across the wafers it focused on ion beam is scanned electro statically over the surface of the wafer in chamber target.

- Repetitive scanning in a raster pattern provides exceptionally uniform doping of the wafer surface. The chamber target commonly includes automatic wafer handling facilities to speed up the process of implanting many wafers per hour. The depth of penetration of any particular type of ion will increase with increasing accelerating voltage. The penetration depth will generally be in the range of 0.1 to 1.0 μm.

2.4.5 Annealing After Implantation

- After the ions have been implanted they are lodged principally in interstitial positions in the silicon crystal structure, and the surface region into which the implantation has taken place will be heavily damaged by the impact of the high-energy ions. The disarray of silicon atoms in the surface region is often to the extent that this region is no longer crystalline in structure, but rather amorphous.

- The surface region well ordered crystalline state and it allow the implanted ions to substitutional sites in the crystal structure and annealing process.

- The annealing process usually involves the heating of the wafers to some elevated temperature often in the range of 1000°C for a suitable length of time such as 30 minutes.

- Laser beam and electron-beam annealing are also employed. In such annealing techniques only the surface region of the wafer is heated and re-crystallized. An ion implantation process is often followed by a conventional-type drive-in diffusion, in which case the annealing process will occur as part of the drive-in diffusion.

- Ion implantation is more expensive process than conventional deposition diffusion, both in terms of the cost of the equipment and the throughput.

2.4.6 Advantages of Ion Implantation

- It provides more precise control over the density of dopants deposited into the wafer, and hence the sheet resistance this is possible because both the accelerating voltage and the ion beam current are electrically controlled outside of the apparatus in which the implants occur.

- Since, the beam current can be measured accurately during implantation, a precise quantity of impurity can be introduced. Tins control over doping level, along with the uniformity of the implant over the wafer surface, make ion implantation attractive for the IC fabrication, since this causes significant improvement in the quality of an IC.

- Due to precise control over doping concentration, it is possible to have very low values of dosage so that very large values of sheet resistance can be obtained. These high sheet resistance values are useful for obtaining large-value resistors for ICs. Very low-dosage, low-energy implantations are also used for the adjustment of the threshold voltage of MOSFET's and other applications.

- Low temperatures, means that doped layers can be implanted without previously diffused regions, this means a lesser tendency for lateral spreading.

2.4.7 High-Current High-Energy Implantation Machines

- The minimum implantation energy is usually set by the extraction voltage, i.e. the voltage causing the ions to move out of the ion source into the mass separator.

- This voltage (which is usually 20 keV) cannot be reduced too far without drastically reducing beam current. The maximum implantation energy is set by the design of the high voltage equipment. The only way to circumvent this is to implant multiply-charged ions. High beam currents are obtained by using multiple extraction electrodes and higher voltages. To get a final beam of suitable energy a combination of acceleration and deceleration modes of operation is used.

- The electrostatic scanning is not suitable for high-beam currents, because it disrupts space charge neutrality and leads to beam "blow-up". Therefore a mechanical scanning system is used. The wafer is scanned past a stationary beam for this condition. This method has the added advantage of keeping the same beam angle across the whole wafer, whereas an electrostatic system can vary by ±2 for 100 mm wafers. However, mechanical scanning puts new requirements on the wafer holder.

- High-energy implantation, at MeV energies, makes possible several new processing techniques required for VLSI. High-energy implantation machines however introduce high-voltage breakdown problem. At about 400 keV of energy electrical breakdown of the air around the high voltage equipment occurs. Hence, above 400 keV, conventional equipment is used.

- Also, high energy implants frequently require water stages heated up to 600°C, so that self annealing during implantation minimizes damage in the surface layer. Mechanical scanning is used because of the difficulty of electrostatically scanning a high-energy beam.

2.4.8 Problems in VLSI Processing

- Now a day's large diameter wafers are feasible. Large size wafers are necessary for VLSI. This makes the task of uniformly implanting a wafer increasingly difficult. This in turn has effect on sheet resistance. Ion implantation is basically clean process because contaminant ions are separated from the beam before they hit the target.

- There are still several sources of contamination possible near the end of the beam line, which can result in contaminant dose up to 10 percent of the intended ion dose, for example, metal atoms knocked from chamber walls, water holder, masking aperature and so on.

- Annealing, as discussed earlier, is required to repair lattice damage and put dopant atoms on substitutional site where they will be electrically active. The success of annealing is often measured in terms of the fraction of the dopant that is electrically active, as found experimentally using a Hall Effect technique. For VLSI, the challenge in annealing is not simply to repair damage and activate dopant, but to do so while minimizing diffusion so that shallow implants remain shallow.

- This has motivated much work in rapid thermal annealing (RTA), where annealing times are on the order of seconds. RTA uses tungsten-halogen lamps or graphite resistive strips to heat the wafer from one or both sides as against conventional furnace annealing where times or on the order of minutes.

- Modern device structures, such as the lightly-doped drains (LDD) for MOSFET, require precise control of dopant distribution vertically and lateral on a very fine scale. For VLSI CMOS structure, we need to form shallow n and layers with implantation energies within the reach of standard machines.

- As stated earlier, the ion velocity, perpendicular to the surface, determines the projected range of an implanted ion distribution. If the water is tilted at a large angle to the ion beam then the effective ion energy is greatly reduced tilted ion beams, thus, make it possible to achieve extremely shallow dopant distributions using comparatively high implantation energies.

- We can circumvent the problem of implanting a shallow layer in silicon completely if instead we implant entirely into a surface layer and then diffuse the dopant into the substrate.

- This is most often done when the surface film is to be used as a conductor making contact to the substrate. Diffusion results in steep dopant profiles without damage to the silicon lattice. Dopant diffusion in silicides and polysilicon is generally much faster than in single-crystal silicon, so the implanted atoms soon become uniformly distributed in the film.

2.4.9 Importance of Ion Implantation for VLSI Technology

- Ion implantation is a very popular process for VLSI because it provides more precise control of dopants (as compared to diffusion). With the reduction of device sizes to the submicron range, the electrical activation of ion-implanted species relies on a rapid thermal annealing technique, resulting in as little movement of impurity atoms as possible.

- Thus, diffusion process has become less important than methods for introducing impurity atoms into silicon for forming very shallow junctions, an important feature of VLSI circuits. Ion, implantation permits introduction of the dopant in silicon that is controllable, reproducible and free from undesirable side effects.

- Over the past few years, ion implantation has been developed into a very powerful tool for IC fabrication. Its attributes of controllability and reproducibility make it a very versatile tool, able to follow the trends to finer-scale devices. Ion implantation continues to find new applications in VLS technologies

2.4.10 Thin Film Deposition

- Thin Film Deposition is the technology of applying a very thin film of material – between a few nanometers to about 100 micrometers, or the thickness of a few atoms – onto a "substrate" surface to be coated, or onto a previously deposited coating to form layers.
- Thin Film Deposition manufacturing processes are at the heart of today's semiconductor industry, solar panels, CDs, disk drives, and optical devices industries.
- Thin Film Deposition is usually divided into two broad categories – Chemical Deposition and Physical Deposition.

Chemical Deposition and Physical Deposition:

1. **Chemical Deposition:** It is when a volatile fluid precursor produces a chemical change on a surface leaving a chemically deposited coating. One example is Chemical Vapor Deposition or CVD used to produce the highest-purity, highest-performance solid materials in the semiconductor industry today.

2. **Physical Deposition:** It refers to a wide range of technologies where a material is released from a source and deposited on a substrate using mechanical, electromechanical or thermodynamic processes. The two most common techniques of Physical Vapor Deposition or PVD are Evaporation and Sputtering.

- Thin film materials are the key elements of continued technological advances made in the fields of optoelectronic, photonic, and magnetic devices. The processing of materials into thin films allows easy integration into various types of devices. The properties of material significantly differ when analyzed in the form of thin films.
- Most of the functional materials are rather applied in thin film form due to their specific electrical, magnetic, optical properties or wear resistance.
- This technologies make the properties can used particularly controlled by the thickness parameter mostly thin films deposition used as either chemical or physical.
- Both crystalline and amorphous, have immense importance in the age of high technology. Few of them are: microelectronic devices, magnetic thin films in recording devices, magnetic sensors, gas sensor, A.R. coating, photoconductors, IR detectors, interference filters, solar cells, polarizer's, temperature controller in satellite, superconducting films, anticorrosive and decorative coatings.

2.4.11 Applications of Thin Films

- The thin film phenomena dates back well over a century, it is really to the last four decades that they have been used to a significant extent in practical situations.
- The requirement of micro miniaturization made the use of thin and thick films virtually imperative.

- The development of computer technology led to a requirement for very high density storage techniques and it is this which has stimulated most of the research on the magnetic properties of thin films. Many thin film devices have been developed which have found themselves looking for an application or, perhaps more importantly market. These devices are resulted from research into the physical properties of thin films.

- These devices are in other generating ideas for new devices, fundamental research has led to a dramatic improvement in understanding of thin films and surfaces.

- This in turn has resulted in a greater ability to fabricate devices with predictable, controllable and reproducible properties. The cleanliness and nature of the substrate, the deposition conditions, post deposition heat treatment and passivation are vital process variables in thin film fabrication.

- Thirdly, the finance for early thin film research originated from space and defence programmes to which the device cost is less important than its light weight and other advantages, the major applications of thin film technology are not exclusively in these areas but rather often lie in the domestic sector in which low cost is essential.

- Thin film materials have used in semiconductor devices, wireless communications, telecommunications, integrated circuits, rectifiers, transistors, solar cells, light-emitting diodes, photoconductors, light crystal displays, magneto-optic memories, audio and video systems, compact discs, electro-optic coatings, memories, multilayer capacitors, flat-panel displays, smart windows, computer chips, magneto optic discs, lithography, Micro Electromechanical Systems (MEMS), and multifunctional emerging coatings, as well as other emerging cutting technologies.

1. Optical Coatings

- An optical coating is one or more thin layers of material deposited on an optical component such as a lens or mirror, when the optic reflects and transmits light.

- One type of optical coating is an antireflection coating, which reduces unwanted reflections from surfaces, and is commonly used on spectacle and photographic lenses.

- Another type is the high-reflector coating which can be used to produce mirrors which reflect greater than 99.99% of the light which falls on them.

- Optical coatings more complex and exhibit high reflection over some range of wavelengths, and anti-reflection over another range, allowing the production of dichroic thin-film optical filters.

2. Photovoltaic

- The energy of incoming photons is converted to electricity in cells containing two thin layers of crystalline silicon.

- The roll-to-roll production of flexible film solar products possible is replacement of the crystalline silicon with amorphous silicon, supplied in high-solids slurries that can be deposited onto substrates by web-converting processes like slot die coating.

- EDE microlayer can counter cast film dies with a new system the dow chemical company makes the production of produce film of standard thickness with many thin microlayers.

- The multiple layer-to-layer interfaces create a torturous path for gas molecules and thus substantially increase the barrier properties of the film.

- This is critical for photovoltaic applications, which require barrier layers to prevent performance losses caused by infiltration of oxygen or moisture vapour.

- "Though as yet little known in the solar industry, the continuous-web production methods familiar to EDI and its converter customers are a key to developing high volume, low-cost production of solar electric systems," said Miller.

- "In with working of solar product manufacturers, EDI draws on extensive experience in other applications that require thin-gauge, optically clear, close-tolerance films and coatings with critical functionalities, including films and coatings for flat panel displays and flexible batteries particularly relevant, since solar cells are a kind of battery.

- The conventional coating methods, such as spray, roll, and spin coating, slot dies provide greater control over coating weight and distribution because they are closed systems into which coating material is pumped at closely pre-determined rates; in turn this greater control makes possible thinner coatings.

- Many in the solar power industry and the investment community, believe the arrival of grid parity, the point when cost of electricity generated by a rooftop photovoltaic (PV) cell system is equivalent to that purchased from an electrical utility will mark a major inflection point for the market that will deliver a huge increase in growth.

- However, grid parity arrives, it's unlikely to generate an abrupt rise in solar system installations due to the high upfront costs and the long-term return of investing in a rooftop photovoltaic system, according to iSuppli Corp. The growth is a set of moderate during when grid parity arrives for the regions for the word industry.

3. Semiconductor

- The semiconductor industry has relied on flat, two-dimensional chips upon which to grow and etch the thin films of material that become electronic circuits for computers and other electronic devices.

- This thin layer (only a couple of hundred nanometers thick) can be transferred to glass, plastic or other flexible materials, opening a wide range of possibilities for flexible electronics. The semiconductor film can be transferred to new substrate, it makes to other side for use of more components.

- This possible number of devices can be placed on the film. By repeating the process, layers of double-sided, thin film semiconductors can be stacked together, creating powerful, low-power, three-dimensional electronic devices. These are single-crystal films of strained silicon or silicon germanium. The strain is introduced in the way we form the membrane.

- Introducing strain changes the arrangement of atoms in the crystal such that we can achieve "much faster device speed while consuming less power." For non-computer applications, flexible electronics are beginning to have significant impact.
- Solar cells, smart cards, Radio Frequency Identification (RFID) tags, medical applications, and active-matrix flat panel displays could all benefit from the development.
- The techniques could allow flexible semiconductors to be embedded in fabric to create wearable electronics or computer monitors that roll up like a window shade.
- To create fast, low power multiplayer ectronics application Sio and Ge membrane are used in semiconductor proces Germanium has a much higher adsorption for light than silicon. By including the germanium without destroying the quality of the material, we can achieve devices with two to three orders of magnitude more sensitivity."
- That increased sensitivity could be applied to create superior low-light cameras, or smaller cameras with greater resolution.

4. **Photo Electrochemical Cells (PEC)**
- In photo electrochemical experiments, Irradiation of an electrode with light that is absorbed by the electrode material causes the production of a current (a photocurrent).
- The photocurrent dependence on wavelength, solution composition and electrode potential it provides the photo process nature, its more energetic S and kinetics.
- Photocurrents at electrodes can also arise because of photolytic processes occurring in the solution near the electrode surface.
- Photo electrochemical studies are frequently carried out to obtain a better understanding of the nature of the electrode-solution interface. Photo electrochemistry and electro generated chemiluminescence photocurrent can represent the conversion of light energy to electrical and chemical energy; such processes are also investigated for their potential practical applications.
- Photo electrochemical reactions occur at semiconductor electrodes, we will review briefly the nature of semiconductors and their interfaces with solutions. Consideration of semiconductor electrodes also helps in gaining a microscopic understanding of electron-transfer processes at solid-solution interfaces.

5. **Optoelectronic**
- An optoelectronic thin-film chip, comprising at least one radiation-emitting region in an active zone of a thin-film layer and a lens disposed downstream of the radiation emitting region, said lens being formed by at least one partial region of the thin-film layer, the lateral extent of the lens being greater than the lateral extent of the radiation emitting region.
- The thin-film layer is provided for example by a layer sequence which is deposited epitaxially on a growth substrate and from which the growth substrate is at least partly removed.

- Thickness of the substrate is reduced in the surbstrate is thinned this possibility for the entire growth of substrate to be removed from the layer. The thin-film layer has at least one active zone suitable for generating electromagnetic radiation. The active zone may be provided for example by a layer or layer sequence which has a pn junction, a double heterostructure, a single quantum well structure or a multiple quantum well structure.

- Particularly preferably, the active zone has at least one radiation-emitting region. In this case, the radiation-emitting region is formed for example by a partial region of the active zone.

- Electromagnetic radiation is generated in said partial region of the active zone during operation of the optoelectronic thin-film chip.

2.5 SPUTTERING METHODS

- In sputtering, the target material and the substrate is placed in a vacuum chamber as shown in Fig. 2.17.

- A voltage is applied between them such that the target is the cathode and the substrate is attached to the anode.

- A plasma is created by ionizing a sputtering gas generally it is using chemically inert or heavy gas e.g. Argon.

- The sputtering gas bombards the target and sputters off the material.

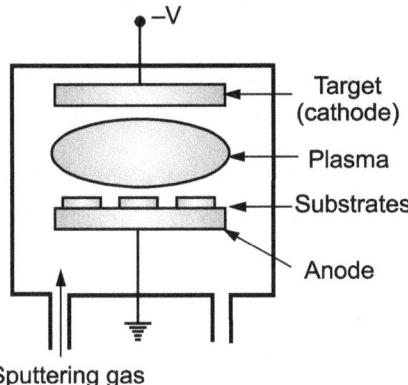

Fig. 2.17: Sputtering vacuum chamber

In Alternatively Sputtering Method

- Instead of using heat to eject material from a source, we can bombard them with high speed particles.

- The momentum transfer from the particles to the surface atoms can impart enough energy to allow the surface atoms to escape.

- Once ejected, these atoms (or molecules) can travel to a substrate and deposit as a film.

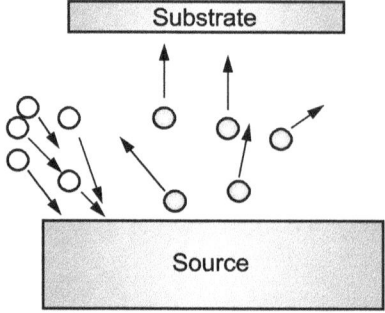

Fig. 2.18: Alternatively sputtering method

- There are following considerations as :

  (a) Creating, controlling and directing a high speed particle stream.

  (b) Interaction of these particles with the source surface and emission yields.

  (c) Deposition of the emitted atoms on the substrate and film quality.

Generating and Controlling the Plasma

- Ions can be generated by the collision of neutral atoms with high energy electrons. interaction.

- The interaction of the ions and the target are determined by the velocity and energy of the ions.

- Since ions are charged particles, electric and magnetic fields can control these parameters.

- The process begins with a stray electron near the cathode is accelerated towards the, anode and collides with a neutral gas atom converting it to a positively charged ion.

$$e^- + A \rightarrow 2e^- + A^+$$

- The process results in two electrons which can then collide with other gas atoms and ionize them creating a cascading process until the gas breaks down.

- The breakdown voltage depends on the pressure in the chamber and the distance between the anode and the cathode.

- At too low pressures, there are not enough collisions between atoms and electrons to sustain a plasma.

- At too high pressures, there are so many collisions that electrons do not have enough time to gather energy between collisions to be able to ionize the atoms.

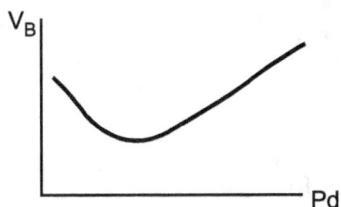

Fig. 2.19: High pressures graph

Parameters :

1. Argon Pressure

- Optimum deposition rate around 100 m.
- Compromise between :
  (a) Increasing number of Ar ions.
  (b) Increasing scattering of Ar ions with neutral Ar atoms.
- If you can increase the number of ions without increasing the number of neutrals, you can operate at lower pressures

2. Sputter Voltage

- Maximize sputter yield (S)
- Typically –2 to –5 kV

3. Substrate Bias Voltage

- Substrate is being bombarded by electrons and ions from target and plasma.
- Sputtering film while you deposit anode (substrate).
- Neutral atoms deposit independently.
- Put negative bias on the substrate to control.
- Can significantly change film properties.

4. Substrate Temperature

- Control with substrate heater.
- Eating from deposited material.
  - Increases with increasing sputter voltage.
  - Decreases with increasing substrate bias.

5. Particle Energy

- Increases with increasing sputter voltage.
- Decreases with increasing substrate bias.

- Decreases with increasing Ar pressure.

Advantages :

- Not a line of sight method.
    - Can use diffusive spreading for coating
    - Can coat around corners
- Can process alloys and compounds.
    - High temperatures are not needed
    - Even organic compounds have been sputtered.
- Can coat large areas more uniformly.
- Large target sources mean less maintenance.

2.6 ETCHING PROCESS

- After thin deposition techniques on the wafer surface is usually removed by etching to the desired pattern of the film surface.

- The etching part of a layer without reaching an underlying material multiplayer structures can be etched sequentially using same masking layer.

- Etching has a two types (i) Wet Etching (ii) Dry Etching

- Wet etching uses liquid etchants. The wafer is exposed material etched by chemical processes. Dry etching uses gas phase etchants in a plasma. This etching is a combination of chemical and physical processes.

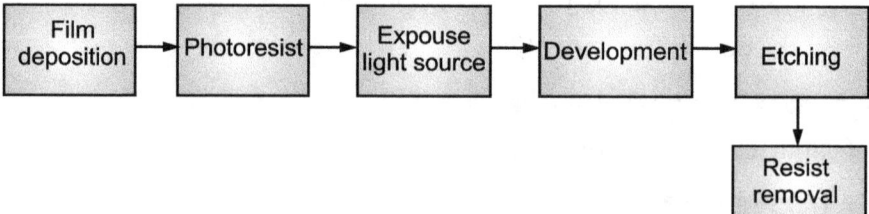

Fig. 2.20: Block diagram of etching process

Above Fig. 2.20 shows the ideal etch profile under the edge of the mask. The etching is both lateral and vertical. The photo resists mask and non-vertical sidewalls in the film. This leads the more lateral etching of the film since the photo resist mask gets narrower as the etching continues.

Etch selectivity is the ratio of the etch rates of the different materials in an etch process. The etch rates of the mask and underlying substrate are nearly zero. The etch selectivity of the film is with respect to both the mask and high substrate. The etch rate of the mask or substrate is significant then the selectivity is poor. Normally selectivity of the materials in range 25 to 50 it is usually considered as a reasonable.

SUMMARY

- Semiconductors are very promising candidates as starting materials for the manufacture of cheap, large area and flexible electronic components such as transistors, diodes and sensors on a scale ranging from micro to nano.

- Contaminants originate from the ambient air, storage ambient, as well as from process gases, chemicals, materials, and water, used in the fabrication processes.

- The need for clean substrates in the fabrication of microelectronic devices has been well recognized since the dawn of solid-state device technology.

- Centrifugal spray rinsing and rinsing in a closed system have the advantage that the wafers are not removed between cleaning, rinsing, and drying.

- The "top-down" approach to lithography begins with a suitable starting material and then "sculpts" the functionality from the material.

- Historically, the semiconductor industry has relied on flat, two-dimensional chips upon which to grow and etch the thin films of material that become electronic circuits for computers and other electronic devices.

- Innovations in micro technology and the evolution of new nonmaterial and devices have been playing a key role in the development of very accurate and reliable sensors.

- The technology of sensors has developed tremendously in the last few years owning many scientific achievements from various experiments, offering newer challenges and opportunity to the quest for every smaller devices capable of molecular level imaging and monitoring of pathological samples and the macromolecules has lately gained the focus of attention of the scientific community, particularly for remote monitoring due to the increasing need for environmental safety and health monitoring.

EXERCISE

1. What is contamination and what are the different levels of contamination? Explain.
2. Explain wafer cleaning method.
3. Why is silicon best-known forming the basis of utmost integrated circuits?

4. What are ongoing challenges of removal of contamination faced by semiconductor industry?

5. Describe lithography in detail.

6. Explain photoresist.

7. Explain thermal conduction.

8. How interface between Si and SiO_2 is carried out.

9. Explain thin film deposition.

10. Describe sputtering methods.

11. Explain etching process.

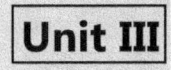
NANO ELECTRONIC DEVICES

3.1 INTRODUCTION

In the Era of 21st Century, everyone has a computer and every computer consist of nearly a billion Field Effect Transistors (FET's) working in concert, it appears safe to say that the most common electronic device is an FET, which is mainly a resistor containing an active region named the channel with two very conductive contacts at its two ends named the source and the drain (Fig. 3.1). What makes it more than just a resistor is the fact that a fraction of a volt applied to a third terminal named the gate terminal the resistance by several orders of magnitude. Electrical switches are at the heart of any computer and what has made computers more and more powerful every year is the cumulative number of switches that have been packed into one by making each switch smaller and smaller. For instance, a distinctive FET these days has a channel length (L) of ~ 50 nm, which aggregates to a few hundred atoms!

Nanoscale electronic devices have not only empowered miniature switches for computers but are also of great importance for all types of applications as well as energy conversion and sensing. The objective, however, is not to discuss specific devices or applications. Rather it is to deliver the conceptual framework that has arisen over the last twenty years, which is significant not only due to the practical insights it provides into the design of nanoscale devices, but also because of the conceptual insights it affords regarding the meaning of resistance and the essence of all non-equilibrium phenomena in general.

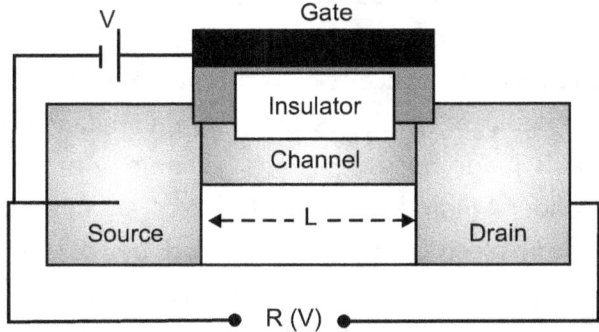

Fig. 3.1 : Schematic representing a Field Effect Transistor (FET), which consists of a channel with two contacts (labeled "source" and "drain"), whose resistance R can be controlled through a voltage V applied to a third terminal labeled the "gate", which ideally carries negligible current.

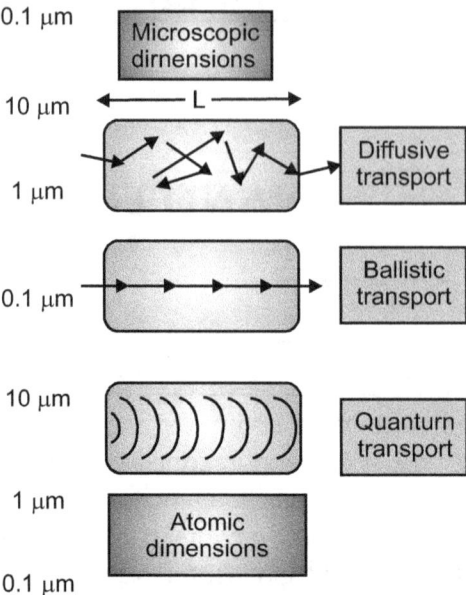

Fig. 3.2 : As the length "L" of the channel in Fig. 3.1 is reduced the nature of electronic transport from one contact to the other changes qualitatively from diffusive to ballistic to quantum

This new conceptual framework provides a unified description for all kinds of devices from molecular conductors to carbon nanotubes to silicon transistors covering different transport regimes from the diffusive to the ballistic limit (Fig. 3.2). As the channel length L is reduced, the nature of electronic transport changes qualitatively. With long channels, transport layer is diffusive, meaning that the electron gets from one contact to another via a random walk, but as the channel length is reduced below a mean free path, transport layer becomes ballistic, or "bullet-like". At even shorter lengths the wave nature of electrons can lead to quantum effects such as interference and tunneling. Historically our understanding of electrical resistance and conduction has progressed top-down: from large macroscopic conductors to small atomic scale conductors. Indeed thirty years ago it was common to argue about what, if anything, the concept of resistance meant on an atomic scale. Since then there has been significant progress in our understanding, spurred by actual experimental measurements made possible by the technology of miniaturization. However, despite this progress in understanding the flow of current on an atomic scale, the standard approach to the problem of electrical conduction continues to be top-down rather than bottom-up. This makes the problem of nanoscale devices appear unduly complicated, as we have argued extensively. The purpose of this chapter is to summarize a unified bottom-up viewpoint to the subject of electrical conduction of particular relevance to nanoelectronic devices.

3.2 SINGLE ELECTRON DEVICES AND TRANSISTORS

Single-electron devices are devices that can control, motion of even a single electron and consist of quantum dots having tunnel junctions. The operation and operation principle of single-electron devices are explained. Firstly, the concept of single-electron phenomena and Coulomb blockade effects are explained by referring to a single-electron box, the simplest single-electron device.

3.2.1 Single-Electron Box

Structure of Single-Electron Box

The smallest set of the functional single-electron device is composed of a quantum dot connected with two electrodes. One electrode is connected with the quantum dot through a tunneling junction. The other electrode, called the gate electrode, is coupled with the quantum dot via insulator through which electron cannot pass by quantum tunneling (Fig. 3.3). Therefore, electrons are injected/ejected into/from the quantum dot through the tunneling junction.

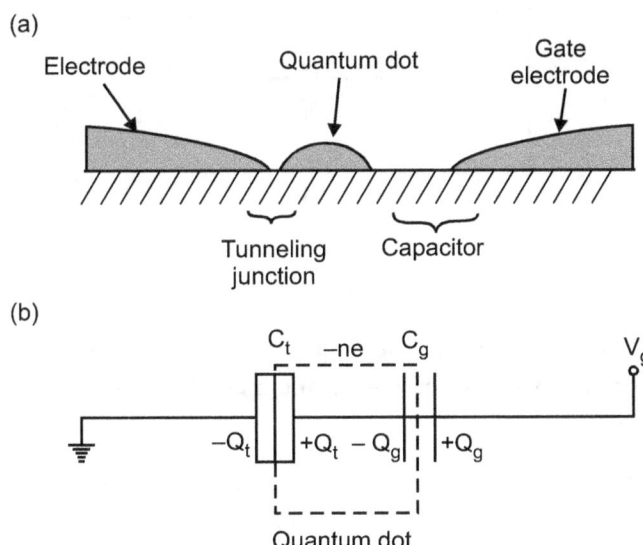

Fig. 3.3 : (a) Schematic structure of single-electron box. The single-electron box consists of a quantum dot, an electrode connected to the dot through a tunneling junction, and an electrode coupled to the dot through an ideal, infinite-resistance, capacitor.
(b) Equivalent circuit of single-electron box.

Basic Operation of Single-Electron Box :

As the size of the quantum dot decreases, the charging energy Wc of a single excess charge on the dot increases. If the quantum-dot size is sufficiently small and the charging energy Wc is much greater than thermal energy kBT, no electron tunnels to and from the quantum dot. Thus, the electron number in the dot takes a fixed value, say zero, when both the electrodes are grounded. The charging effect, which blocks the injection/ejection of a single charge into/from a quantum dot, is called Coulomb blockade effect. Therefore, the condition for observing Coulomb blockade effects is expressed as following equation (3.1),

$$W_c = \frac{e^2}{2C} >> k_B T \qquad \qquad ...(3.1)$$

where C is the capacitance of the quantum dot and T is the temperature of the system. However, it should be noted that by applying a positive bias to the gate electrode we could attract an electron to the quantum dot. The increase of the gate voltage attracts an electron more strongly to the quantum dot. When the gate bias exceeds a certain value an electron finally enters the quantum dot and the electron number of the dot becomes one. Further increase of the gate voltage makes it possible to make the electron number two. Thus, in the single-electron box, the electron number of the quantum dot is controlled, one by one, by utilizing the gate electrode as shown in Fig. 3.4.

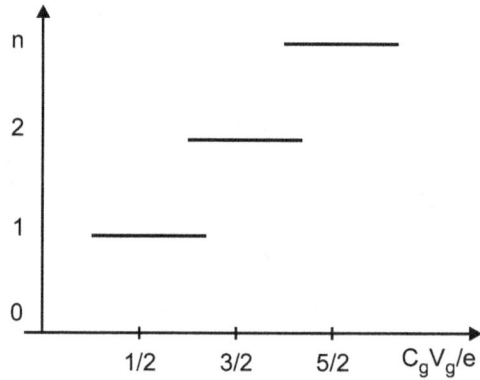

Fig. 3.4 : Electron number versus gate voltage characteristics of single-electron box. The number of electron in the quantum dot increases one by one as the gate voltage increases

Single Electron Transistors

Electrical force, is the increased resistance at small bias voltages of an electronic device comprising at least one low-capacitance tunnel junction. Because of the CB, the resistances of devices are not constant at low bias voltages, but increase to infinity for biases under a certain threshold (i.e. no current flows). When few electrons are involved and an external static magnetic field is applied, Coulomb blockade provides the ground for spin blockade (also called Pauli blockade) and valley blockade which includes quantum mechanical effects due to spin and orbital interactions respectively between the electrons.

Coulomb blockade in a tunnel junction

The tunnel junction is, in the simplest form, a thin insulating barrier between two conducting electrodes. If the electrodes are superconducting, Cooper pairs (with a charge of two elementary charges) carry the current. In the case that the electrodes are *normal conducting*, i.e. neither superconducting nor semiconducting, electrons (with a charge of one elementary charge) carry the current. The following reasoning is for the case of tunnel junctions with an insulating barrier between two normal conducting electrodes (NIN junctions).

According to the laws of classical electrodynamics, no current can flow through an insulating barrier. According to the laws of quantum mechanics, however, there is a non-vanishing (larger than zero) probability for an electron on one side of the barrier to reach the other side (see quantum tunnelling). When a bias voltage is applied, this means there will be a current, and, neglecting additional effects, the tunnelling current will be proportional to the bias voltage. In electrical terms, the tunnel junction behaves as a resistor with a constant resistance, also known as an ohmic resistor. The resistance depends exponentially on the barrier thickness. Typical barrier thicknesses are on the order of one to several nanometers.

An arrangement of two conductors with an insulating layer in between not only has a resistance, but also a finite capacitance. The insulator is also called dielectric in this context, the tunnel junction behaves as a capacitor.

Due to the discreteness of electrical charge, current through a tunnel junction is a series of events in which exactly one electron passes (*tunnels*) through the tunnel barrier (we neglect cotunneling, in which two electrons tunnel simultaneously). The tunnel junction capacitor is charged with one elementary charge by the tunnelling electron, causing a voltage buildup $U = e/C$, where 'e' is the elementary charge of 1.6×10^{-19} coulomb and C the capacitance of the junction. If the capacitance is very small, the voltage buildup can be large enough to prevent another electron from tunnelling. The electric current is then suppressed at low bias voltages and the resistance of the device is no longer constant. The increase of the differential resistance around zero bias is called the Coulomb blockade.

Observing the Coulomb blockade

In order for the Coulomb blockade to be observable, the temperature has to be low enough so that the characteristic charging energy (the energy that is required to charge the junction with one elementary charge) is larger than the thermal energy of the charge carriers. In the past, for capacitances above 1 femtofarad(10^{-15} farad), this implied that the temperature has to be below about 1 kelvin. This temperature range is routinely reached for example by 3He refrigerators. Thanks to small sized quantum dots of only few nanometers, Coulomb blockade has been observed next above liquid helium temperature, up to room temperature.

To make a tunnel junction in plate condenser geometry with a capacitance of 1 femtofarad, using an oxide layer of electric permittivity 10 and thickness one nanometer, one has to create electrodes with dimensions of approximately 100 by 100 nanometers. This range of dimensions is routinely reached for example by electron beam lithography and appropriate pattern transfer technologies, like the Niemeyer-Dolan technique, also known as shadow evaporation technique. The integration of quantum dot fabrication with standard industrial technology has been achieved for silicon. CMOS process for obtaining massive production of single electron quantum dot transistors with channel size down to 20 nm × 20 nm has been implemented.

Single-electron transistor

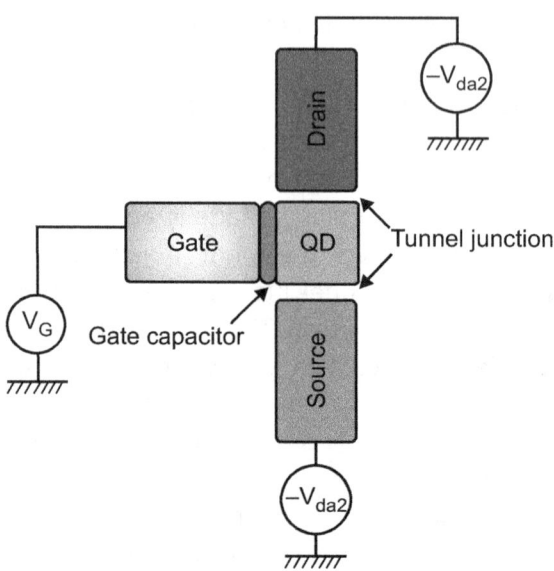

Fig 3.5: Schematic of a single-electron transistor

The simplest device in which the effect of Coulomb blockade can be observed is called **single-electron transistor**. It consists of two electrodes known as the *drain* and the *source*, connected through tunnel junctions to one common electrode with a low self-capacitance, known as the *island*. The electrical potential of the island can be tuned by a third electrode, known as the *gate*, capacitively coupled to the island.

In the blocking state no accessible energy levels are within tunneling range of the electron (red) on the source contact. All energy levels on the island electrode with lower energies are occupied.

When a positive voltage is applied to the gate electrode the energy levels of the island electrode are lowered. The electron can tunnel onto the island, occupying a previously vacant energy level. From there it can tunnel onto the drain electrode, where in elastically scatters and reaches the drain electrode Fermi level.

The energy levels of the island electrode are evenly spaced with a separation of ΔE. This gives rise to a self-capacitance C of the island, defined as

$$C = \frac{e^2}{\Delta E}$$

To achieve the Coulomb blockade, three criteria have to be met:

1. The bias voltage must be lower than the elementary charge divided by the self-capacitance of the island: $V_{bais} < \dfrac{e}{C}$;

2. The thermal energy in the source contact plus the thermal energy in the island, i.e. k_BT must be below the charging energy: $k_BT < \dfrac{e^2}{2C}$ or else the electron will be able to pass the QD via thermal excitation; and

3. The tunneling resistance, R_t should be greater than $\dfrac{h}{e^2}$ which is derived from Heisenberg's uncertainty principle.

3.3 QUANTUM PARTICLE

Subatomic (quantum) particles are particles much smaller than atoms. There are two types of subatomic particles: elementary particles, which according to current theories are not made of other particles; and *composite* particles. Particle physics and nuclear physics study these particles and how they interact.

In particle physics, the concept of a particle is one of several concepts inherited from classical physics. But it also reflects the modern understanding that at the quantum scale matter and energy behave very differently from what much of everyday experience would lead us to expect.

The idea of a particle underwent serious rethinking when experiments showed that light could behave like a stream of particles (called photons) as well as exhibit wave-like properties. This led to the new concept of wave–particle duality to reflect that quantum-scale "particles" behave like both particles and waves. Another new concept, the uncertainty principle, states that some of their properties taken together, such as their simultaneous position and momentum, cannot be measured exactly.[4] In more recent times, wave–particle duality has been shown to apply not only to photons but to increasingly massive particles as well.

Interactions of particles in the framework of quantum field theory are understood as creation and annihilation of *quanta* of corresponding fundamental interactions. This blends particle physics with field theory.

Quantum theory is the theoretical basis of modern physics that explains the nature and behavior of matter and energy on the atomic and subatomic level. The nature and behavior of matter and energy at that level is sometimes referred to as quantum physics and quantum mechanics. In 1900, physicist Max Planck presented his quantum theory to the German Physical Society. Planck had sought to discover the reason that radiation from a glowing body changes in color from red, to orange, and, finally, to blue as its temperature rises. He found that by making the assumption that energy existed in individual units in the same way that matter does, rather than just as a constant electromagnetic wave - as had been formerly assumed - and was therefore quantifiable, he could find the answer to his question. The existence of these units became the first assumption of quantum theory.

Planck wrote a mathematical equation involving a figure to represent these individual units of energy, which he called quanta. The equation explained the phenomenon very well; Planck found that at certain discrete temperature levels (exact multiples of a basic minimum value), energy from a glowing body will occupy different areas of the color spectrum. Planck assumed there was a theory yet to emerge from the discovery of quanta, but, in fact, their very existence implied a completely new and fundamental understanding of the laws of nature. Planck won the Nobel Prize in Physics for his theory in 1918, but developments by various scientists over a thirty-year period all contributed to the modern understanding of quantum theory.

Just as light waves sometimes exhibit particle-like properties, it turns out that massive particles sometimes exhibit wave-like properties. For instance, it is possible to obtain a double-slit interference pattern from a stream of mono-energetic electrons passing through two closely spaced narrow slits. Now, the effective wavelength of the electrons can be determined by measuring the width of the light and dark bands in the interference pattern. It is found that

$$\lambda = \frac{h}{p} \qquad \qquad \text{... (3.2)}$$

- The same relation is found for other types of particles. The above wavelength is called the de Broglie wavelength, after Louis de Broglie who first suggested that particles should have wave properties in 1923.

- **Note:** The de Broglie wavelength is generally pretty small. For instance, that of an electron is,

$$\lambda_e = 1.2 \times 10^{-9} \, [E(eV)]^{-1/2} \, m \qquad \text{... (3.3)}$$

where the electron energy is conveniently measured in units of electron-volts (eV). (An electron accelerated from rest through a potential difference of 1000 V acquires energy of 1000 eV, and so on.) The de Broglie wavelength of a proton is,

$$\lambda_p = 2.9 \times 10^{-11} \, [E(eV)]^{-1/2} \, m \qquad \text{... (3.4)}$$

Given the smallness of the de Broglie wavelengths of common particles, it is actually quite difficult to do particle interference experiments. In general, in order to perform an effective interference experiment, the spacing of the slits must not be too much greater than the wavelength of the wave. Hence, particle interference experiments require either very low

energy particles (since $\lambda \propto E^{-1/2}$), or very closely spaced slits. Usually the "slits" consist of

crystals, which act a bit like diffraction gratings with a characteristic spacing of order the inter-atomic spacing (which is generally about 10^{-9} m). Equation (3.2) can be rearranged to give

$$p = \hbar k \qquad \qquad \text{... (3.5)}$$

which is exactly the same as the relation between momentum and wave number that we obtained earlier for photons. In this case of a particle moving the three dimensions, the above relation generalizes to give,

$$p = \hbar k \qquad \qquad \text{... (3.6)}$$

where p is the particle's vector momentum, and k its wave vector. It follows that the momentum of a quantum particle, and, hence, its velocity, is always parallel to its wave vector. Since the relation between momentum and wave number applies to both photons and massive particles, it seems plausible that the closely related relation between energy and wave angular frequency should also apply to both photons and particles. If this is the case, and we can write

$$E = \hbar \omega \qquad \qquad \text{... (3.7)}$$

$$\omega = \frac{\hbar k^2}{2m} \qquad \qquad \text{... (3.8)}$$

A plane wave propagates at the so-called phase velocity,

$$v_p = \frac{\omega}{k} \qquad \qquad \text{... (3.9)}$$

However, according to the above dispersion relation, a particle plane wave propagates at

$$v_p = \frac{p}{2m} \qquad \qquad \text{... (3.10)}$$

that this is only half of the classical particle velocity. Does this imply that the dispersion relation (3.8) is incorrect?

3.3.1 Quantum Dot

Quantum dots (**QD**) are semiconductor devices that tightly confine electrons or holes in all three spatial dimensions. They can be made via several possible routes including colloidal synthesis, plasma synthesis, or mechanical fabrication. The term "quantum dot" was coined by Mark Reed in 1988 however, they were first discovered in a glass matrix[2] by Alexey Ekimovin 1981 and in colloidal solutions by Louis E. Brus in 1985.[6] The electronic properties of the quantum dots fall between those of bulk semiconductors and those of discrete molecules of comparable size, and optoelectronic properties such as band gap, can be tuned as a function of particle size and shape for a given composition. For example, the photo luminescence of a QD can be manipulated to specific wavelengths by controlling particle diameter. Larger QDs (radius of 5-6 nm, for example) emit longer wavelengths resulting in emission colors such as orange or red. Smaller QDs (radius of 2-3 nm, for example) emit shorter wavelengths resulting in colors like blue and green, although the specific colors and sizes vary depending on the exact composition of the QD.

The high tunability of properties, QDs are of interest in many research applications such as transistors, solar cells, LEDs, and diode lasers. For example, the ability of QDs to precisely convert and tune a spectrum makes them ideal for LCD displays. Previous LCD displays can waste energy converting red-green poor, blue-yellow rich white light into a more balanced lighting. By using QDs, only the necessary colors for ideal images are contained in the screen. The result is a screen that is brighter, clearer, and more energy-efficient. The first commercial application of quantum dots was the Sony XBR X900A series of flat panel televisions released in 2013. QDs are also being researched as possible qubits for quantum computing. Beyond electronic applications, QDs are also being investigated in the medical field for medical imaging. Additionally, their small size allows for QDs to be suspended in solution which leads to possible uses in inkjet printing and spin-coating. These processing techniques result in less-expensive and less time consuming methods of semiconductor fabrication.

A quantum dot is a semiconductor nano structure that confines the motion of conduction band electrons, valence band holes, or excitons (bound pairs of conduction band electrons and valence band holes) in all three spatial directions. The confinement can be due to electrostatic potentials (generated by external electrodes, doping, strain, impurities), the presence of an interface between different semiconductor materials (e.g. in core-shell nanocrystal systems), the presence of the semiconductor surface (e.g. semiconductor nanocrystal), or a combination of these.

- A quantum dot has a discrete quantized energy spectrum.

- The corresponding wave functions are spatially localized within the quantum dot, but extend over many periods of the crystal lattice.

- A quantum dot contains a small finite number (of the order of 1-100) of conduction band electrons, valence band holes, or excitons, i.e., a finite number of elementary electric charges.

- Small quantum dots, such as colloidal semiconductor nano crystals, can be as small as 2 to 10 nanometers, corresponding to 10 to 50 atoms in diameter and a total of 100 to 100,000 atoms within the quantum dot volume.

- Self-assembled quantum dots are typically between 10 and 50 nm in size.

- Quantum dots defined by lithographically patterned gate electrodes, or by etching on two-dimensional electron gases in semiconductor hetero structures can have lateral dimensions exceeding 100 nm.

- At 10 nm in diameter, nearly 3 million quantum dots could be lined up end to end and fit within the width of a human thumb

Quantum dots are tiny particles or nano crystals of a semiconducting material with diameters in the range of 2-10 nanometers (10-50 atoms). They were first discovered in 1980. Quantum dots display unique electronic properties, intermediate between those of bulk semiconductors and discrete molecules that are partly the result of the unusually high surface-to-volume ratios for these particles. The most apparent result of this is fluorescence, wherein the nano crystals can produce distinctive colors determined by the size of the particles.

Due to their small size, the electrons in quantum dots are confined in a small space (quantum box), and when the radii of the semiconductor nano crystal is smaller than the exciton Bohr radius (exciton Bohr radius is the average distance between the electron in the conduction band and the hole it leaves behind in the valence band), there is quantization of the energy levels according to Pauli's exclusion principle (Figure 3.5). The discrete, quantized energy levels of quantum dots relate them more closely to atoms than bulk materials and have resulted in quantum dots being nicknamed 'artificial atoms'. Generally, as the size of the crystal decreases, the difference in energy between the highest valence band and the lowest conduction band increases. More energy is then needed to excite the dot, and concurrently, more energy is released when the crystal returns to its ground state, resulting in a color shift from red to blue in the emitted light. As a result of this phenomenon, quantum dots can emit any color of light from the same material simply by changing the dot size. Additionally, because of the high level of control possible over the size of the nano-crystals produced, quantum dots can be tuned during manufacturing to emit any color of light.

Quantum dots can be classified into different types based on their composition and structure.

Core-Type Quantum Dots :

Quantum dots can be single component materials with uniform internal compositions, such as chalcogenides (selenides or sulfides) of metals like cadmium or zinc, example, CdSe or CdS. The photo- and electroluminescence properties of core-type nano crystals can be fine-tuned by simply changing the crystallite size.

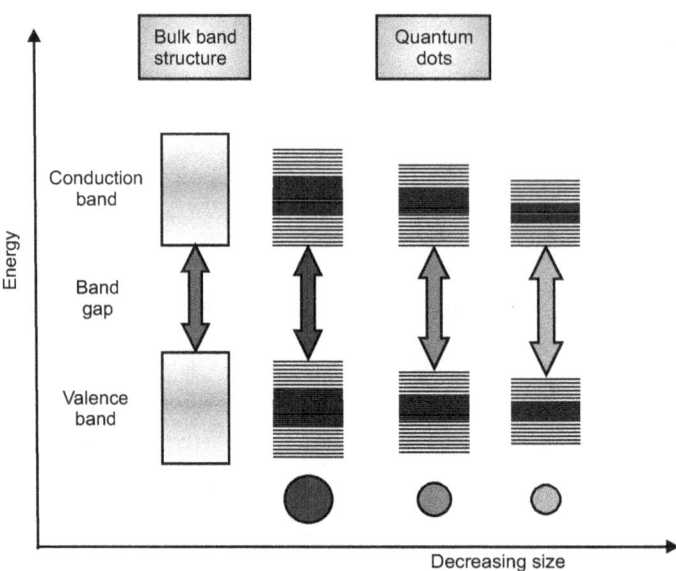

Fig. 3.5 : Splitting of energy levels in quantum dots due to the quantum confinement effect, semiconductor band gap increases with decrease in size of the nanocrystal

Core-Shell Quantum Dots :

The luminescent properties of quantum dots arise from recombination of electron-hole pairs (exciton decay) through radiative path. However, the exciton decay can also occur through nonradiative methods, reducing the fluorescence quantum yield. One of the methods used to improve efficiency and brightness of semiconductor nano crystals is growing shells of another higher band gap semiconducting material around them. These quantum dots with small regions of one material embedded in another with a wider band gap are known as core-shell quantum dots (CSQDs) or core-shell semiconducting nano crystals (CSSNCs). For example, quantum dots with CdSe in the core and ZnS in the shell available from Aldrich Materials Science exhibit greater than 80% quantum yield. Coating quantum dots with shells improves quantum yield by passivizing nonradiative recombination sites and also makes them more robust to processing conditions for various applications. This method has been widely explored as a way to adjust the photophysical properties of quantum dots.

Alloyed Quantum Dots :

The ability to tune optical and electronic properties by changing the crystallite size has become a hallmark of quantum dots. However, tuning the properties by changing the crystallite size could cause problems in many applications with size restrictions. Multi component quantum dots offer an alternative method to tune properties without changing crystallite size. Alloyed semiconductor quantum dots with both homogeneous and gradient internal structures allow tuning of the optical and electronic properties by merely changing the composition and internal structure without changing the crystallite size. For example, an alloyed quantum dot of the compositions CdS_xSe_{1-x}/ZnS of 6nm diameter emits light of different wavelengths by just changing the composition (Figure 3.6). Alloyed semiconductor quantum dots formed by alloying together two semiconductors with different band gap energies exhibited interesting properties distinct not only from the properties of their bulk counterparts but also from those of their parent semiconductors. Thus, alloyed nanocrystals possess novel and additional composition-tunable properties aside from the properties that emerge due to quantum confinement effects.

Fig. 3.6 : Photoluminescence of alloyed CdS_xSe_{1-x}/ZnS quantum dots of 6 nm diameter. The material emits different color of light by tuning the composition

3.3.2 Logic Circuits with Quantum Dots

The nanoelectronic logic circuits derived from single electron interactions in quantum dots has been a busy field. Additionally, the possibility of building reversible and non-dissipative gates with such systems have also been explored. The original concept of building logic circuits based on interactions between single electrons in closely spaced quantum dots. They showed that in an array of rectangular quantum dots (termed "quantum dashes"), each hosting a single electron, the lone electron in each dash is displaced towards one or the other edge of the dash as a result of mutual Coulomb repulsion. This causes spontaneous charge polarization in each dash with adjacent dashes having opposite polarizations. Therefore, any two neighboring dashes constitute a natural inverter. If the polarization in one dash encodes the input bit and that in the other encodes the output bit, then the output is always the logic complement of the input. Other logic gates (AND, XOR, etc.) can also be configured in similar fashion. Computation proceeds by aligning the polarizations in input dashes with an external source and allowing the system to relax to the thermodynamic ground state by dissipating energy. Once the ground state is reached, the polarization states in the output dashes represent the result of the computation in response to the input string.

Universal Gate: NAND and NOR Gate as Universal Gate

- The logical gates AND, NOT and OR gates are the basic gates; we can create any logic gate or any Boolean expression by combining them. Now NOR and NAND gates have the particular property that any one of them can create any logical Boolean expression if designed in a proper way.

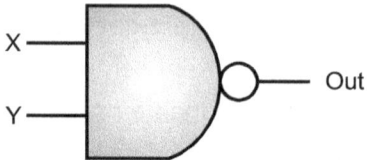

Fig. 3.7: Symbol of NAND gate

- The above Fig. 3.7 shows a two input NAND gate. The first part is an AND gate and second part is a bubble after it represents a NOT gate. So it is clear that during the operation of NAND gate, the inputs are first going through AND gate and after that the output is reversed and we get the final output. Now we will look at the truth table of NAND gate.

- The truth table of the above NAND gate i.e. a two input gate.

Truth Table of NAND Gate

X	Y	Output
0	0	1
1	0	1
0	1	1
1	1	0

Fig. 3.8: NOT gate using NAND gate

- The Fig. 3.8 shows the circuit diagram of a NAND gate used to make work like a NOT gate, the original logic gate diagram of NOT gate is given beside above Fig. 3.8.

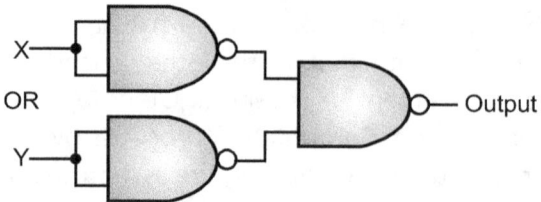

Fig. 3.9: OR gate using NAND gate

Truth Table OR Gate

X	Y	Output
0	0	0
0	1	1
1	0	1
1	1	1

- The above Fig. 3.9 shows OR gate made from combinations of NAND gates, arranged in a proper manner. The truth table of an OR gate is also given above. The design of an AND gate from NAND gates.

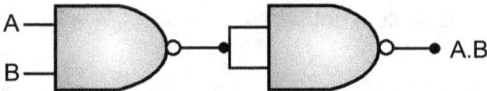

Fig. 3.10: AND gate using NAND gate

- The above Fig. 3.10 is of an AND gate made from NAND gate. So we can see that all the three basic gates can be made by only using NAND gates, that's why this gate is called Universal Gate and it is appropriate.

3.3.3 Quantum Dots Applications

- The unique size and composition tunable electronic property of these very small, semiconducting quantum dots make them very appealing for a variety of applications and new technologies as following :

1. Quantum dots are particularly significant for optical applications owing to their bright, pure colors along with their ability to emit rainbow of colors coupled with their high efficiencies, longer lifetimes and high extinction coefficient. Examples include LEDs and solid state lighting, displays and photovoltaics.

2. Being zero dimensional, quantum dots have a sharper density of states than higher-dimensional structures. Their small size means that electrons do not have to travel as far as with larger particles, thus electronic devices can operate faster. Examples of applications the unique electronic properties include transistors, solar cells, ultrafast all-optical switches and logic gates, and quantum computing, among many others.

3. The small size of quantum dots allows them to go anywhere in the body making them suitable for different bio-medical applications like medical imaging, biosensors, etc. At present, fluorescence based biosensors depend on organic dyes with a broad spectral width, which limits their effectiveness to a small number of colors and shorter lifetimes to tag the agents. On the other hand, quantum dots can emit the whole spectrum, are brighter and have little degradation over time thus proving them superior to traditional organic dyes used in biomedical applications.

4. Aldrich Materials Science offers semiconductor, core-shell and alloyed quantum dots tuned to emit different colors in the visible spectrum while exhibiting high quantum yield. Nano crystals are available in both aqueous and organic formulations suitable for use in different applications.

What Can We Do With Quantum Dots?

- Quantum dots' ability to precisely convert and tune a spectrum of light makes them ideal for LCD displays. From smart phones to tablets to TVs, all the colors we see even better by remixing white light into red, green and blue components. Until now, the white light that LCDs have had to work with the it contained a lot of blue and yellow but not very much red or green. This means displays had to waste a lot of energy to make enough red and green for a bright display while also making for broad primary colors.

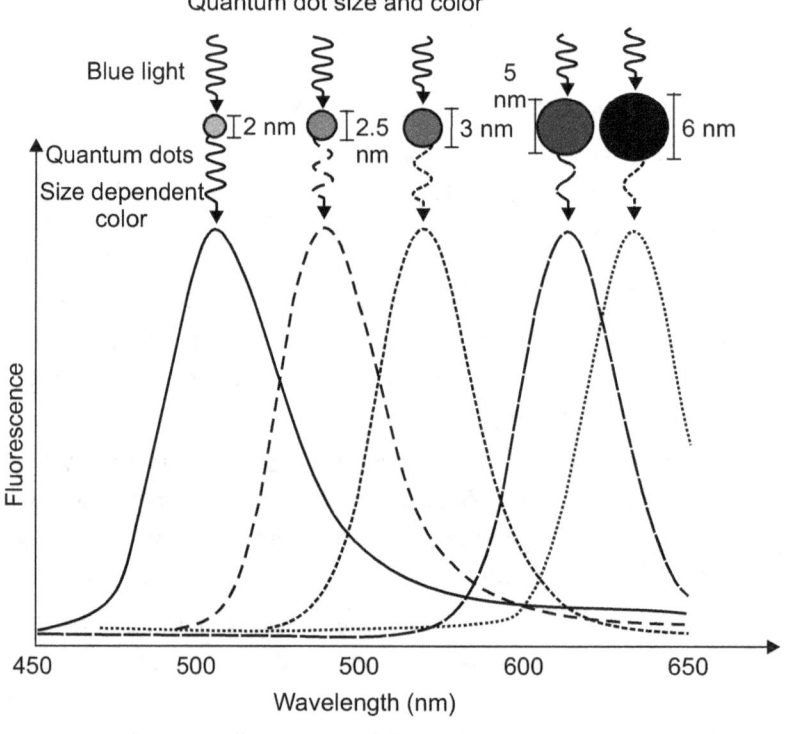

Fig. 3.11: Spectrum of light with quantum dot

With quantum dots we can designed an ideal spectrum of white light for an LCD, one that contains only the red, green and blue that the display needs to make a great image. The precise spectrum created by the dots makes colors pure. And since we're only making the colors the display needs we can use less power. The result is a display that's brighter, more power efficient and incredibly vibrant.

3.3.4 Advantages of Quantum Dots

For LCD screens, the benefits are numerous. They are the kind of benefits that are simply no-brainers.

1. Higher Peak Brightness :

- One of the reasons TV manufacturers like quantum dots is that they allow them to produce TVs with much higher peak brightness. This opens up some interesting possibilities, such as enabling support for 'high dynamic range' TVs that support standards such as Dolby Vision.
- Dolby Vision is a film standard that, when used, results in content that retains more colour and contrast information than existing standards. The result is pictures that have greater differences in the brightest and darkest parts of the image and look more 'dynamic' and real as a result.
- Imagine shots where looking into the sun actually feels like looking in to the sun for real and you get an idea. To do this you need brighter TVs and quantum dots deliver exactly that.

Following the acceptance of 4K resolutions, HDR in general is the next big feature of TVs, and all of the top TV sets announced at CES 2016 this year have made bold claims about their 'high dynamic range' capabilities. Quantum Dot technology, like OLED, goes hand in hand with this advance.

2. Better Color Precision :

Another big benefit of quantum dots is improved colour accuracy. The light produced by quantum dots is so closely tied to their size that they can be tuned very precisely to emit the exact kind of light needed. This means purer, cleaner whites and more precise colours.

3. Higher Color Capacity :

One advantage, though some might call it a disadvantage in some contexts, of OLED screens over LCDs is colour saturation. Colors on OLED screens simply 'pop' more due to the huge color gamut OLED screens can achieve. Quantum dots can, according to Dr. Soneira, increase the color gamut on LCD screens by in the region of 40 to 50 per cent.

This is great, but it's the combination of high color gamut and great accuracy that's really exciting. OLED screens look fantastic to the untrained eye, but many of those found in phones aren't very accurate or 'faithful' to the actual colors they're presenting. This can create imbalances, such as radioactive colors and iffy skin tones in videos and photos.

Taking a long term view, the impact of more devices with larger color gamuts could mean a serious increase in the quality of video and other content. Specifically, in the level of detail you can see due to greater number of colors available.

This improvement in color production is what's driving the move towards HDR, which means adopting new standards for color that cover more of the colors we can see in the real world. Current standards, like sRGB and Rec.709, only cover 80% of the color available in the P3 color space used by HDR TVs and content mastered for HDR.

None of this would be possible, on an LCD TV at least, without quantum dots.

4. Improved Battery Life in Mobile Gadgets :

One of the contradictions of modern tech is that people say they want better battery life, but when it comes to it they'll choose a slimmer, sleeker and 'sexier' phone over a chunky one with better battery life. Some of you reading this will be jumping up and down saying that's not you, but it is most people. Phones haven't been getting slimmer and lighter by accident. Companies make them that way because that's what sells.

Another truism is that the most effective way, by far, to improve your phone, tablet or laptop's battery life is to simply turn the brightness down. You can fiddle with the settings as much as you like, but it's the screen that sucks down the most power. Which is why the potential power savings of quantum dots, believed to be up to 20%, are so attractive.

What quantum dots promise, on paper, is superior image quality and a reduction in power use. That's a powerful combination, especially for a company like Apple that's loathed to compromise on design for the sake of practical things like larger batteries.

3.3.5 Nano Wires Construction and Applications

A **nanowire** is a nanostructure, with the diameter of the order of a nanometer (10^{-9} meters). It can also be defined as the ratio of the length to width being greater than 1000. Alternatively, nanowires can be defined as structures that have a thickness or diameter constrained to tens of nanometers or less and an unconstrained length. At these scales, quantum mechanical effects are important which coined the term "quantum wires". Many different types of nanowires exist, including superconducting (e.g., YBCO), metallic (e.g., Ni, Pt, Au), semiconducting (e.g., Si, InP,GaN, etc.), and insulating (e.g., SiO_2, TiO_2). Molecular nanowires are composed of repeating molecular units either organic (e.g. DNA) or inorganic (e.g. $Mo_6S_{9-x}I_x$).

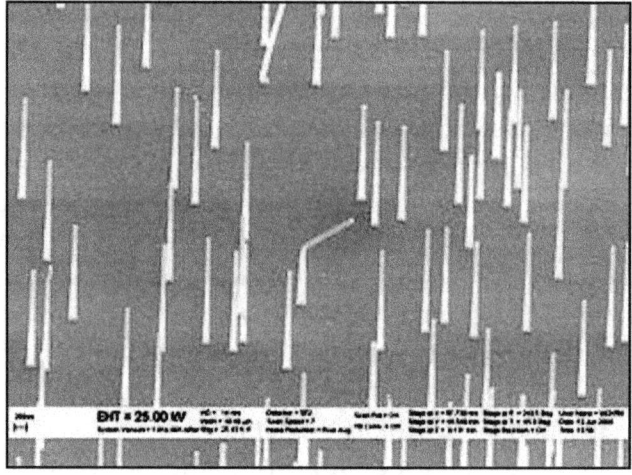

Fig 3.12 : Nanowires

Typical nanowires exhibit aspect ratios (length-to-width ratio) of 1000 or more. As such they are often referred to as one-dimensional (1-D) materials. Nanowires have many interesting properties that are not seen in bulk or 3-D (three-dimensional) materials. This is because electrons in nanowires are quantum confined laterally and thus occupy energy levels that are different from the traditional continuum of energy levels or bands found in bulk materials.

Peculiar features of this quantum confinement exhibited by certain nanowires manifest themselves in discrete values of the electrical conductance. Such discrete values arise from a quantum mechanical restraint on the number of electrons that can travel through the wire at the nanometer scale. These discrete values are often referred to as the quantum of conductance and are integer multiples of

$$\frac{2e^2}{h} \cong 77.41 \ \mu S$$

They are inverse of the well-known resistance unit h/e^2, which is roughly equal to 25812.8 ohms, and referred to as the von Klitzing constant R_K (after Klaus von Klitzing, the discoverer of exact quantization). Since 1990, a fixed conventional value R_{K-90} is accepted.

Examples of nanowires include inorganic molecular nanowires ($Mo_6S_{9-x}I_x$, $Li_2Mo_6Se_6$), which can have a diameter of 0.9 nm and be hundreds of micrometers long. Other important examples are based on semiconductors such as InP, Si, GaN, etc., dielectrics (e.g. SiO_2, TiO_2), or metals (e.g. Ni, Pt).

There are many applications where nanowires may become important in electronic, opto-electronic and nanoelectromechanical devices, as additives in advanced composites, for metallic interconnects in nanoscale quantum devices, as field-emitters and as leads for biomolecular nanosensors.

Conductivity of nanowires

Several physical reasons predict that the conductivity of a nanowire will be much less than that of the corresponding bulk material. First, there is scattering from the wire boundaries, whose effect will be very significant whenever the wire width is below the free electron mean free path of the bulk material. In copper, for example, the mean free path is 40 nm. Copper nanowires less than 40 nm wide will shorten the mean free path to the wire width.

Nanowires also show other peculiar electrical properties due to their size. Unlike single wall carbon nanotubes, whose motion of electrons can fall under the regime of ballistic transport (meaning the electrons can travel freely from one electrode to the other), nanowire conductivity is strongly influenced by edge effects. The edge effects come from atoms that lay at the nanowire surface and are not fully bonded to neighboring atoms like the atoms within the bulk of the nanowire. The unbonded atoms are often a source of defects within the nanowire, and may cause the nanowire to conduct electricity more poorly than the bulk material. As a nanowire shrinks in size, the surface atoms become more numerous compared to the atoms within the nanowire, and edge effects become more important.

Furthermore, the conductivity can undergo a quantization in energy: i.e. the energy of the electrons going through a nanowire can assume only discrete values, which are multiples of the Von Klitzing constant $G = 2e^2/h$ (where e is the charge of the electron and h is the Planck constant).

The conductivity is hence described as the sum of the transport by separate *channels* of different quantized energy levels. The thinner the wire is, the smaller the number of channels available to the transport of electrons.

This quantization has been demonstrated by measuring the conductivity of a nanowire suspended between two electrodes while pulling it: as its diameter reduces, its conductivity decreases in a stepwise fashion and the plateaus correspond to multiples of G.

The quantization of conductivity is more pronounced in semiconductors like Si or GaAs than in metals, due to their lower electron density and lower effective mass. It can be observed in 25 nm wide silicon fins, and results in increased <u>threshold voltage</u>. In practical terms, this means that a MOSFET with such nanoscale silicon fins, when used in digital applications, will need a higher gate (control) voltage to switch the transistor on.

A nanowire is a wire of dimensions of the order of a nanometer (10^{-9} meters). Alternatively, nanowires can be defined as structures that have a lateral size constrained to tens of nanometers or less and an unconstrained longitudinal size. A nanowire is a nanostructure with a diameter of the order of a nanometer (10-9 meters). Alternatively, nanowires can be defined as structures that have a thickness or diameter constrained to tens of nanometers or less and an unconstrained length. High-aspect-ratio semiconductors have led to significant breakthroughs in conventional electrical, optical, and energy harvesting devices. Among such structures, III-V semiconductor nanowires offer unique properties arising from their high electron mobility and absorption coefficients, as well as their direct bandgaps.

A common technique for creating a nanowire is Vapor-Liquid-Solid (VLS) synthesis. This process can produce crystalline nanowires of some semiconductor materials. However, metal catalysts, usually expensive noble metals, should be used for initiating the VLS mechanism. In addition, these metal catalysts are known to significantly degrade the quality of semiconductor nanowires by creating deep levels, thus limiting practical applications of nanowires into opto-electronic devices.

In this work, however, Prof. Choi's group developed a novel technique of growing III-V semiconductor nanowires without metal catalysts or nano-patterning. Metal-organic chemical vapor deposition (MOCVD, AIXTRON A200) was used for the growth of the InAsyP1-y. 2 inch Si (111) wafer was cleaned with buffer oxide etch for 1 minute and deionized (DI) water for 2 seconds. Then, the wafer was immediately dipped in poly-L-lysine solution (Sigma-Aldrich inc.) for 3 minutes then rinsed in DI water for 10 seconds. The Si substrate was then loaded into the MOCVD reactor without any delay. The reactor pressure was lowered to 50 mbar with 15liter/min of hydrogen gas flow. Then the reactor was heated to growth temperatures (570 -- 630 ℃), and stabilized for 10 minutes.

3.4 FINFETS

The finFET is a transistor design, first developed by Chenming Hu and colleagues at the University of California at Berkeley, which attempts to overcome the worst types of short-channel effect encountered by deep submicron transistors, such as drain-induced barrer lowering (DIBL). These effects make it harder for the voltage on a gate electrode to deplete the channel underneath and stop the flow of carriers through the channel – in other words, to turn the transistor Off. By raising the channel above the surface of the wafer instead of creating the channel just below the surface, it is possible to wrap the gate around up to three of its sides, providing much greater electrostatic control over the carriers within it.

There are a number of subtly different forms of trigate transistor structure that are being described as finFETs. The architecture typically takes advantage of self-aligned process steps to produce extremely narrow features that are much smaller than the wavelength of light generally used to pattern devices on a silicon wafer. It is possible to create very thin fins - of 20 nm in width or less - on the surface of a silicon wafer using selective-etching processes, although they typically cannot currently be made less than 20 nm to 30nm because of the limits of lithographic resolution. The fin is used to form the raised channel. The gate is then deposited so that it wraps around the fin to form the trigate structure. As the channel is extremely thin the gate has much greater control over the carriers within it but, when the device is switched on, the shape limits the current through it to a low level. So, multiple fins are used in parallel to provide higher drive strengths.

Originally, the finFET was developed for use on silicon-on-insulator (SOI) wafers. Recent developments have made it possible to produce working finFETs on bulk silicon wafers and improve the performance of certain parameters. The steep doping profile used to control leakage into the bulk substrate has a beneficial impact on DIBL, although increased doping has a negative impact on variability.

Fully depleted SOI (*Guide*) transistors have been shown to offer comparable or better performance than finFETs. However, the relative compatibility of the bulk-silicon finFET with existing wafer fabrication processes and today's wafer-supply chain favors the finFET for high-volume IC production at 22 nm and below.

FinFETs have key advantages over planar bulk devices. They exhibit more drive current per unit area than planar devices, largely because the height of the fin can be used to create a channel with a larger effective volume but still take advantage of a wraparound gate.

The added performance capability of FinFETs can be used to achieve higher frequency numbers compared to bulk for a given power budget or lower power. The power reduces can come from two sources: reduces need for wide, high-drive standard cells; and the ability to operate with a lower supply voltage for a given amount of leakage.

What effect does the finFET have on design?

At such an early stage in its commercial development, the implications of the finFET are not entirely clear although results from Intel's work suggest that the impact on digital design need not be that great if conservative approaches are taken. At the International Solid State Circuits Conference (ISSCC) in 2012, Intel described its approach as being one largely of design migration from circuits created for planar processes, using modelling and simulation to assess how the transition from planar to trigate would affect circuit performance.

A key difference between finFET-based design and that using conventional planar devices is that the freedom to choose the device's drive strength is reduced, especially for devices that are close to the minimum size. Drive strength can only be improved during layout by adding more fins. The effective width of the device becomes quantized, and the quantization effect is worse for smaller transistors for which the next step up from the minimum-size device is one that is twice as wide. In addition, the minimum number of fins may be two in practical manufacturing processes. This is due to the self-aligned spacer processes that are used to create fins at tight pitches – each sacrificial spacer element that is deposited creates a pair of fins.

The Intel designers worked on the basis that whenever the optimum number of fins to achieve a particular drive strength was not an integer, they would round up to the next whole number – so that fractional fins were replaced with a full fin – rather than inserting transistors with less than optimal drive strength and risking the circuit not meeting timing.

A team from Infineon Technologies and Texas Instruments reported at the International Solid State Circuits Conference (ISSCC) in 2006 that the problem of fin quantization was potentially a bigger issue for SRAMs – as they would only use one fin to save space – than in analog circuits, where the use of minimum-sized transistors is far less crucial. The problem of using minimum-sized devices throughout an SRAM can create problems for static noise margin – reducing the ability of the system to reliable read a memory cell. Ideally, the pass gates would be weaker than the pullup and pulldown devices, particularly the latter.

One solution is to increase the fin count for pulldown devices but this increases area. Another is to weaken the pass gates by etching away the top surface of the gate – splitting the gate into a threshold-control and switching-control gate. This, however, increases process complexity. A third approach, as with sub-30nm planar CMOS processes is to use write-assist techniques – pushing the threshold voltage down temporarily by reducing the supply voltage.

Designers working on experimental finFET processes have reported other problems, such as self-heating – a problem noted again by Infineon researchers, this time at the International Electron Device Meeting (IEDM) in 2009. Recent work by IBM, albeit on SOI wafers, has indicated that self-heating is not likely to be a major issue.

FinFETs provide a number of advantages and several key disadvantages compared with bulk planar processes. Advantages include increased voltage headroom for circuits such as cascodes, lower gate resistance, which helps keep flicker noise under control, as well as improved matching, higher current drive and higher gain. However, the designer does not have the ability to control the channel as easily and the higher source/drain resistance cuts transconductance. On top of that, designers have little choice over voltages for I/O and have to develop more complex methods to achieve ESD immunity.

A further impact on design is the need to consider layout density in circuits that are usually quite sparse compared with digital layouts. Device density variation can lead to dishing – similar to the problems of copper metallization encountered in the move to 130nm processes. Similarly, the fins at the edges of a cluster suffer higher variability than those in the middle. These effects lead to greater need for the use of dummy-fill shapes to reduce the variation in density. Foundry processes tend to put dummy fins at the end of each transistor stack.

In terms of optimization for power, the finFET provides circuit designers with the opportunity to trade leakage for switching speed. Intel, for example, has deployed what it calls fast devices, with nominal leakage, medium-speed 'quarter-leakage' devices and slow 'tenth-leakage' devices. A problem facing process engineers is providing designers with a choice of threshold voltages to implement different circuits with different power-grade transistors at low cost.

At the International Electron Devices Meeting in December 2012, Intel presented details of a family of finFET designsthat were optimized for high speed, low leakage and high (1.8V and 3.3V) operation in SoC designs.

As the finFET was conceived to be a device with almost no channel doping and back biasing the gate is very area inefficient even where possible, the main technique for adjusting threshold is to manipulate the work function of the gate. An alternative that will push up variability and may have a knock-on effect on fin pitch – and therefore cell density – is to dope the channel.

The lack of back or forward body bias control is one of the handicaps of today's finFET structures versus FD-SOI. However, the larger ecosystem for finFET-based designs has made it more difficult for FD-SOI to compete.

Work is also underway at TSMC on introducing germanium into the fin of p-channel finFETs to improve the carrier mobility.

The finFET may have other, more subtle effects on design, at least at the cell-library level and for analog designers. Design rules will be further restricted to allow gates and fins to be placed on a regular grid. A key issue is compatibility between fin pitch and the pitch of the intra and intercell routing layers, leading to non-integer heights for standard cells if counted in terms of M2 tracks.

In their analysis of the finFET's influence on layout, Rob Aitken and colleagues and ARM found: "Fin and metal pitches have different scaling pressures, so they have not tended to line up. For example, at 14nm GlobalFoundries has stated that it uses a fin pitch of 48nm and a metal pitch of 64nm. The same values are used in TSMC's 16nm process."

They added: "[Using GlobalFoundries' numbers, only certain integral combinations of fin and M2 pitch are possible: six, nine, twelve, etc. A 6 track cell height is unlikely to be viable for two reasons. First, it will contain at most four active fins (2N and 2P), and second there is unlikely to be enough room to route internal signals for complex cells such as flip-flops. A library containing 6 active fins (3N and 3P) would be ten fins tall. This equates to 10x48=480nm, which is equivalent to 7.5 M2 tracks. This is likely to be the smallest feasible library in this type of technology, and comes with the obvious issues relating to non-integral track heights for physical design."

In their analysis of routing techniques for sub-28nm processes, CMU and IBM researchers performed simulations to look at analog designs on finFETs that revealed issues with restricted design rules. "Our design simulations based on preliminary models reveal that

FinFETs have a mixed impact on analog circuits. The restricted design rules expected to be seen in sub 20nm nodes greatly limit the allowable channel lengths for analog designers, which in turn can be worked around by stacking devices in series to emulate a long channel transistor, however, at the expense of increased parasitic capacitance.

"Conversely, FinFETs offer improved electrostatic control which translates to a higher intrinsic gain. Given these and several factors, some analog circuit topologies that have been considered obsolete may need to be revisited. For instance, topologies such as high gain linear amplifiers can be used in conjunction with switched capacitor circuits to balance performance for variation tolerance. Furthermore, emerging post-silicon tuning techniques such as self-healing and statistical element selection appear to be extremely valuable."

Synopsys has a useful discussion on the practicalities of designing with finFETs, which is summarised here.

When can we use finFETs?

- Unless you work for Intel or a research group with access to customized processes, there is no way to implement finFET-based designs commercially. This is expected to change with the move to 14 nm processes, with the Common Platform foundry alliance (Global Foundries, IBM, Samsung) effectively committing to this shift in early 2012. Global Foundries has said it will introduce finFETs in its 14 nm process the devices will be optimized for mobile systems. The world's largest foundry, TSMC, has yet to say when it will introduce finFETs although the technology is likely to be in place for the 14 nm and may be brought forward to 20 nm.

What are the risks of using finFETs?

- The difficulties of dealing with a new technology 3D transistor design in terms of parasitic extraction and physical behavior, the major issue is cost : cost of software is very expensive building a finFET uses a number of additional steps in a manufacturing flow that is already struggling to contain the cost of advanced lithography : double patterning in the next few years, and possibly a move to EUV lithography in the second half of the decade. Figures presented by Qualcomm at IEDM 2013 indicated that the jump in cost to finFET was lower than that caused by the shift to double patterning from 28 nm to 20 nm. The Back-End of Line (BEOL) processes are more or less the same for 20, 16 nm and 14 nm technologies provided by the foundries.

3.4.1 FinFET : The Promises and the Challenges

- While the new multi-gate or tri-gate architectures, also known as FinFET technology, deliver superior levels of scalability, design engineers face significant challenges in creating designs that optimize the promise of this exciting new technology. Jamil Kawa, group director of the Solutions Group, Synopsys, and Andy Biddle, product marketing manager, Galaxy Implementation Platform, Synopsys, explain how Synopsys is working with foundry partners and design teams to help them accelerate innovation and get the best out of their investments in FinFETs.

• Design metrics including performance, power, area, cost and time to market have not changed since the inception of the Integrated Circuit (IC) industry. In fact, Moore's law is all about optimizing those parameters by driving to the smallest possible transistor size with each new technology generation. However, as process technologies continued to shrink towards 20-nanometers (nm), it became impossible to achieve a similar scaling of certain device parameters, the power supply voltage, which is the dominant factor in determining dynamic power. When in additional optimizing for one variable such as performance automatically translated to unwanted compromises in other areas like power.

Given the new emerging metric of performance per unit power (Koomey's law), one major design optimization alternative designers have in FinFETs, as compared to planar technology, is much better performance at the same power budget, or equal performance at a much lower power budget.

From Moore's Law, we can infer that FinFETs represent the most radical shift in semiconductor technology in over 40 years. When Gordon Moore came up with his "law" back in 1965, he had in mind a design of about 50 components. Today's chips consist of billions of transistors and design teams strive for "better, sooner, cheaper" products with every new process node. However, as feature sizes have become finer, the perils of high leakage current due to short-channel effects and varying dopant levels have threatened to derail the industry's progress to smaller geometries.

The FinFET transistor structure promises to rejuvenate the chip industry by rescuing it from the short-channel effects that limit device scalability faced by current planar transistor structures.

3.4.2 FinFET : A Technology Primer

FinFETs have their technology roots in the 1990s, when DARPA looked to fund research into possible successors to the planar transistor. A UC Berkeley team led by Dr. Chenming Hu proposed a new structure for the transistor that would reduce leakage current.

The Berkeley team suggested that a thin-body MOSFET structure would control short-channel effects and suppress leakage by keeping the gate capacitance in closer proximity to the whole of the channel. They proposed two possible structures as shown in following Fig. 3.13.

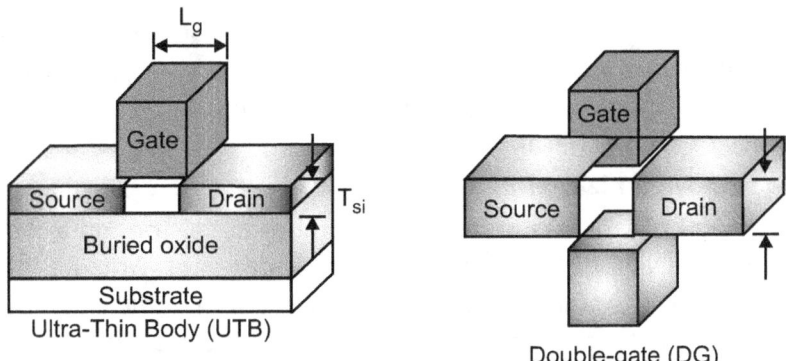

Fig. 3.13 : Thin-body MOSFETs are the origin of today's FinFET transistors

- Rotating the DG structure, which has the potential to provide the lowest gate leakage current, enables easier manufacturing using standard lithography techniques as the gate electrodes become self-aligned and the layout is similar to that of a planar FET as shown in Fig. 3.14.

- Modern FinFETs are 3D structures that rise above the planar substrate, giving them more volume than a planar gate for the same planar area. Planar area given to the excellent control of the conducting channel by the gate, which "wraps" around the channel, very little current is allowed to leak through the body when the device is in the off state. This allows the use of lower threshold voltages, which results in optimal switching speeds and power.

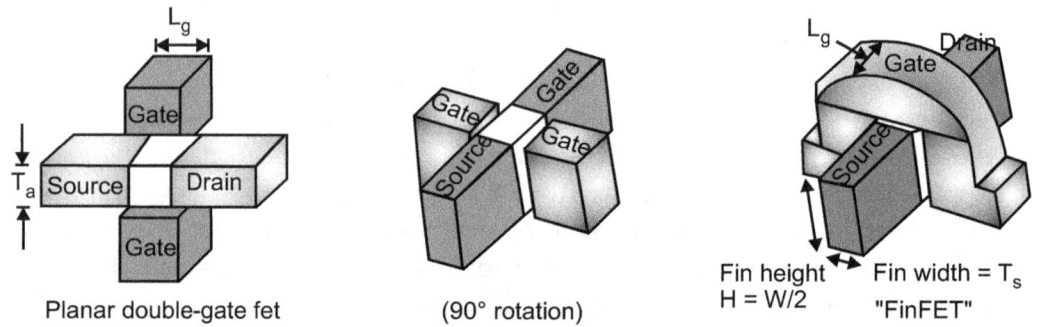

Planar double-gate fet   (90° rotation)   "FinFET"

Fig. 3.14 : From planar DG FET to FinFET

- Other research teams have shown that FinFETs are scalable as long as it is possible to scale the thickness of the channel. For example, KAIST has demonstrated a 3 nm FinFET in its lab.

The FinFET Promise :

- Leading foundries estimate the additional processing cost of 3D devices to be 2% to 5% higher than that of the corresponding Planar wafer fabrication. FinFETs are estimated to be up to 37% faster while using less than half the dynamic power or cut static leakage current by as much as 90%.

- FinFET also promise to problematic performance of the parameters such as power tradeoff etc. Designers can run the transistors faster and use the same amount of power, compared to the planar equivalent, or run them at the same performance using less power. This enables design teams to balance throughput, performance and power to match the needs of each application.

Design Challenges or Minimizing Impact :

- Increasingly, designers care less about packing more transistors on a die (Moore's Law) and more about delivering the best performance per Watt for the application. Interestingly, Jonathan Koomey has shown that the energy efficiency of computers has doubled nearly every 18 months since the first computers were built in the 1950s. Koomey's Law expands on Moore's law, especially given that quoting channel lengths is becoming less relevant. Given the abundance of transistors per unit area in advanced nodes, designers would use multi-processors at lower voltage to get the same throughput of a fewer number of processors at a higher voltage, sacrificing some additional area for the sake of saving power at the same throughput level.

- The foundries want to make the transition to FinFET processes as transparent and smooth as possible for the design community. In this case EDA and IP industries need to work behind the scenes to ensure that the tools understand and model the complexities involved. Design teams want to take advantage of the power, performance and area benefits that FinFETs offer while still getting to market quickly and painlessly through a familiar process of creating the RTL and taking it through a backend implementation process.

IP Design Challenges : Not Just Another Transistor :

- While developers can take a familiar design flow and work with FinFET technology in much the same way as their previous bulk CMOS designs, the quality of results they achieve will depend to a large extent on the quality of the IP they choose.

- Developing optimized memory and standard cells (physical IP) for FinFET requires expertise and experience. An experienced design team will be able to exploit the features that FinFET structures offer in order to create the best physical IP and not leave any power savings or performance on the table.

  In order to continue on the path of Moore's Law – and Koomey's Law – designers must be able to leverage the target technology for maximum benefit, and invariably, that means focusing on the details

- Synopsys has been working with industry and academic partners for several years to gain a detailed understanding of FinFET technology, and apply that knowledge to develop IP, tools and services for successful FinFET design.

As a leading tool and IP developer, Synopsys is uniquely qualified to provide specific FinFET tool methodologies and FinFET-based memory and standard cell IP to customers developing differentiated leading-edge products in a broad range of applications from mobile computing to enterprise.

As we move to FinFET, one of the challenges is the discrete size of the fin. Transistor width (W), which is one of the main variables for tweaking transistor sizes, is no longer a continuum. Discrete fin sizing brings a new variable in design, without any easy workarounds, that designers have never had to deal with before.

Furthermore, additional design levers usually utilized by the IP designer, such as varying the channel length or body biasing, are either much more restrictive or are of limited benefit due to the intrinsic characteristics of FinFET technology.

Another challenge has to do with the complexity of the model. The FinFET is a 3D structure that has a lot of subdivided resistance and capacitance compared with a planar structure. This 3D structure requires a more complex model and more data manipulation than planar transistors. The complexity of the model has implications for the whole backend flow including extraction, layout, DRC and LVS, for the engineers responsible for managing the design. Experience counts when it comes to optimizing FinFET designs efficiently in order to achieve the best quality of results.

Experience Counts :

- When it comes to IP design, getting the new FinFET technology requires experience. Synopsys has spent several years understanding the characteristics of FinFET technology and applying those to create new standard cell architectures and memory compilers. Synopsys has successfully navigated through complex FinFET issues. For example, there are specific challenges related to read-write access for memories. Synopsys has exploited the inherently low operating voltages of FinFETs to enable the design of memories with low retention voltages.

- Another fundamental issue that determines a transistor's performance is its stress profile – the mechanical stress that we deliberately introduce into the device to enhance its performance. Because of its vertical fin, the FinFET has a significantly different stress profile from a planar transistor. Synopsys has been collaborating with industry partners from an early stage to apply its Technology Computer-Aided Design (TCAD) tools to the task of accurately modeling FinFET stress profiles (for more information, see TCAD Tools).

- Synopsys continues to work closely with the major foundries to accurately capture all of the efficiency of FinFET technology, and to create models that we can use within the entire design flow from concept to implementation, including SPICE modeling, extraction and physical IP design.

3.4.3 The FinFET Tool Story

- The finFET tool is a transparent transition, it allows user to scale design to increasingly smaller geometry processes. This technology will require implementation of the tools to minimizing power consumption and maximize the clock speed and utilization.

- FinFETs require some specific enhancements made in the following areas :
    (1) TCAD Tools.
    (2) Mask Synthesis.
    (3) Transistor Models.
    (4) SPICE Simulation Tools.
    (5) RC Extraction Tools.
    (6) Physical Verification Tools.

1. TCAD Tools :

- To harness the full potential of 3D FETs, wafer processing technologies are being developed to controllably dope the fin sidewalls and stress the fins to boost device performance. To support these efforts, TCAD tools are used by the foundries during development to guide and optimize the semiconductor fabrication process. An important example of the need for 3D TCAD simulation is in the process optimization of

SRAM cells, where stress and doping proximity effects require that all transistors comprising the SRAM be simulated in a single structure. This is made possible by recent advances in 3D structure generation, mesh generation and parallel algorithms.

- The small geometries targeted for FinFETs have introduced a concern with the impact of process variability on device and circuit performance. While these effects were negligible on higher geometry processes, they are now becoming first order effects. These variations caused by random dopant fluctuations, line edge roughness, layout induced stress, and other process variations ultimately manifest themselves as variations in device performance, in particular with threshold voltage shifts and local currents that impact timing and power. TCAD tools are used to simulate these effects used by EDA tools.

- Synopsys has deployed Sentaurus TCAD in FinFET research and development since 2005 at leading foundries, Integrated Device Manufacturers (IDMs) and research universities, and has made highly complex and sophisticated refinements to these tools as a result of this collaboration. These refinements include changes to our plasma-doping model, fin dimensional optimization to achieve device performance targets and modeling of the random process variations to improve device performance. Fig. 3.15 shows an example of the 3D simulation performed by Sentaurus for p-channel FinFETs.

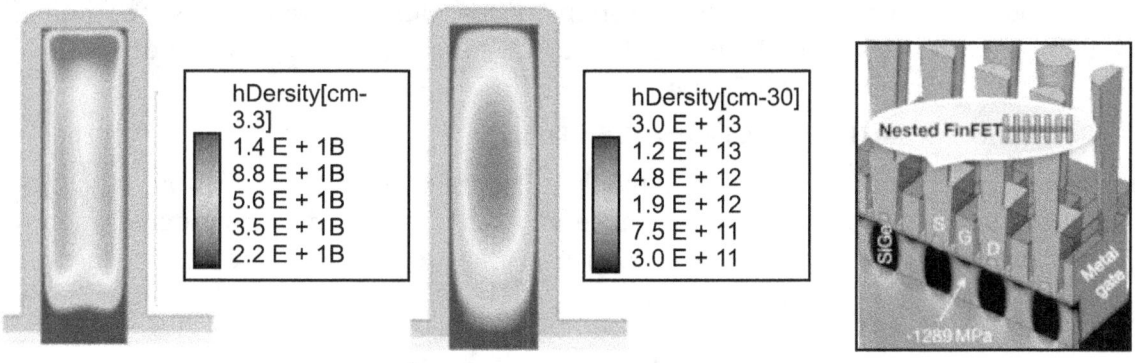

I_{on} (left) and I_{off} (right) in Fin cross section

Fig. 3.15 : Stress fields in pFinFETs simulated with TCAD Sentaurus

2. Mask Synthesis :

- Mask synthesis is a key component in advanced manufacturing. This mask synthesis process is used to post- process the resultant layouts produced by EDA tools and effects in the lithography process used in manufacturing. The advanced geometries targeted for FinFET are expected to require Self-Aligned Double Patterning (SADP) in deposition manufacturing steps to create the fins rather than defining the fins lithographically. As the fins are tall and thin, traditional lithography/OPC methods would result in line-edge roughness problems.

- The Synopsys product provides a comprehensive and powerful environment for performing full-chip proximity correction, building models for correction and analyzing proximity effects on corrected and uncorrected IC layout patterns. These products are the mask synthesis tool of choice for IDMs and foundries building FinFET-based designs. Synopsys is closely engaged with the foundries on refining and deploying the Proteus SADP solution.

3. Transistor Models :

- FinFETs introduce much higher complexities for resistance and parasitic capacitance. Additional information is needed in the model for source/drain resistance extensions, contact resistances fringing effects and the wider number of coupling capacitances introduced by the three dimensional structures. The new behaviors are captured in new standardized models used by spice simulators. The Berkeley Short-channel IGFET Model for Common Multi-Gate (BSIM-CMG) compact model is used by SPICE simulators to ensure accurate simulation of designs using these new devices.

4. SPICE Simulation Tools :

- The Synopsys of SPICE and Fast SPICE simulators have been used extensively by the leading FinFET foundries to validate correct and accurate functionality with the new BSIM-CMG models. These tools form the corner stone for transistor level library and circuit design. The Synopsys HSPICE simulator has been selected as the gold standard for foundries introducing FinFETs. Synopsys has multiple simulators supporting the BSIM-CMG models, HSPICE and FineSim SPICE for full SPICE accuracy and CustomSim and FineSim Pro for Fast SPICE use.

5. Resistance/Capacitance (RC) Extraction Tools :

- The 3D nature of FinFETs and the multiple fins making up the transistors introduce a large number of new parasitic resistance and capacitances to be considered, modeled and extracted from the FinFET-based designs. Fig. 3.16 shows some of the parasitics introduced by this technology.

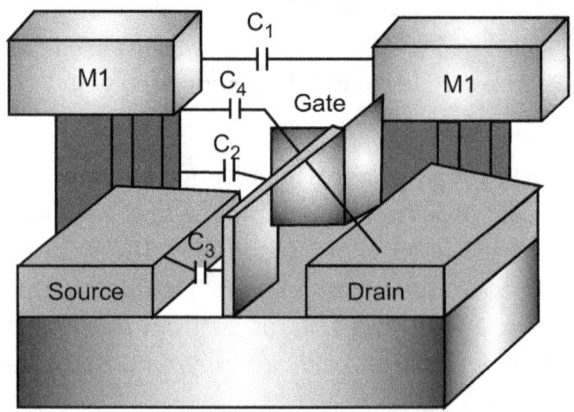

C_1 : S contact to D contact C_3 : Gate to S/D diffusion
C_2 : Gate to S/D contact C_4 : S contact to D diffusion

Fig. 3.16 : FinFET Parasitics

- The interconnect modeling of semiconductors has been standardized in the open source Interconnect Technology Format (ITF). This format has recently been extended to add the FinFET requirements.

- Synopsys' StarRC extraction tool has been enhanced to support the new ITF models and is extensively used in the extraction of FinFET-based designs. StarRC is certified by leading FinFET foundries and is the industry standard for signoff extraction.

6. Physical Verification Tools :

- Physical verification is another tools affected by FinFET technology. The new runsets used by the physical verification tools are used to verify Logic versus Schematic (LVS) correctness, and Design Rule Checks (DRCs). FinFETs require LVS enhancements to support recognition of these new devices in the layout and enable parameter extraction and identification of proximity effects. Other LVS enhancements include new source-drain resistance calculations. A number of new design rules have been introduced including fin-to-fin spacing and fin widths.

- Synopsy's IC Validator physical verification product has been enhanced to support LVS and DRC for FinFETs. It is currently being used for the development of FinFET- based designs and IP.

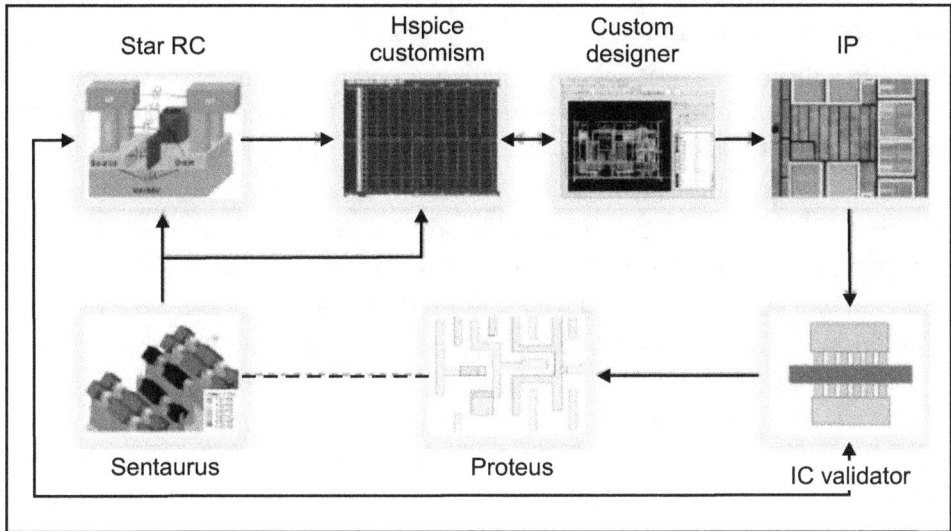

Fig. 3.17 : Synopsys FinFET Technology

- The Synopsys TCAD and complete Galaxy Implementation Platform of tools, including IC Compiler, Galaxy Custom Designer and PrimeTime, have already been used to tapeout 3D FET production designs and numerous test chips. Synopsys tools are ready for the next wave of FinFET technology adopters. Fig. 3.17 shows the entire design flow from concept to implementation, including SPICE modeling, extraction and physical IP design.

- Transition and significant benefits for circuit designer can be used finFET technology or synospys tools and IP. Synopsys is leading the industry in its efforts to create IP, tools, flows and expertise that will guide the design community towards the successful adoption of this radical shift in semiconductor technology.

- Historically, design teams have transitioned their IP from older planar technologies to the latest process nodes by using their in-house design capabilities and IP re-use. FinFET technology has created new challenges for many of these design teams because their current tools and techniques may not enable them to design their IP optimally for FinFET processes, delaying time to market. FinFETs require a new generation of design experience, expertise and tools in order to get the most from the technology.

- Synopsys has extensive experience and expertise with FinFETs and can help design teams to mitigate their risk in developing FinFET-based IP processes. As well as being an early developer of a vast portfolio of physical IP for FinFET, Synopsys is currently working alongside foundry partners and customer design teams to help them design highly differentiated products in order to win in highly competitive markets.

3.4.4 Construction of FinFET

- FinFET technology has been born as a result of the relentless increase in the levels of integration. According to Moore's law has held true for many years from the earliest years of integrated circuit technology. Essentially it states that the number of transistors on a given area of silicon doubles every two years.

- Some of the landmark chips of the relatively early integrated circuit era had a low transistor count even though they were advanced for the time. The 6800 microprocessor for example had just 5000 transistors. Todays have many orders of magnitude more.

- To achieve the large increases in levels of integration, many parameters have changed. Fundamentally the feature sizes have reduced to enable more devices to be fabricated within a given area. However other figures such as power dissipation, and line voltage have reduced along with increased frequency performance.

- There are limits to the scalability of the individual devices and as process technologies continued to shrink towards 20 nm, it became impossible to achieve the proper scaling of various device parameters. Those like the power supply voltage, which is the dominant factor in determining dynamic power were particularly affected. It was found that optimising for one variable such as performance resulted in unwanted compromises in other areas like power. It was therefore necessary to look at other more revolutionary options like a change in transistor structure from the traditional planar transistor.

3.4.5 Properties of FinFET

- FinFET technology takes its name from the fact that the FET structure used looks like a set of fins when viewed.

- The main characteristic of the FinFET is that it has a conducting channel wrapped by a thin silicon "fin" from which it gains its name. The thickness of the fin determines the effective channel length of the device.

- In terms of its structure, it typically has a vertical fin on a substrate which runs between a larger drain and source area. This protrudes vertically above the substrate as a fin.

- The gate orientation is at right angles to the vertical fin. And to traverse from one side of the fin to the other it wraps over the fin, enabling it to interface with three side of the fin or channel.

- This form of gate structure provides improved electrical control over the channel conduction and it helps reduce leakage current levels and overcomes some other short-channel effects.

- The term FinFET is used somewhat generically. Sometimes it is used to describe any fin-based, multigate transistor architecture regardless of number of gates.

3.4.6 Advantages of FinFET Technology

There are several advantages to IC manufacturers of using FinFETs.

- **Power :** Much lower power consumption allows high integration levels. Early adopters reported 150% improvements.

- **Operating Voltage :** FinFETs operate at a lower voltage as a result of their lower threshold voltage.

- **Feature Sizes :** Possible to pass through the 20nm barrier previously thought as an end point.

- **Static Leakage Current :** Typically reduced by up to 90%

- **Operating Speed :** Often in excess of 30% faster than the non-FinFET versions.

- The FinFET is a technology that is used within ICs. FinFETs are not available as discrete devices. However FinFET technology is becoming more widespread as feature sizes within integrated circuits fall and there is a growing need to provide very much higher levels of integration with less power consumption within integrated circuits.

SUMMARY

- Single-electron devices are devices that can control the motion of even a single electron and consist of quantum dots having tunnel junctions.

- Quantum theory is the theoretical basis of modern physics that explains the nature and behavior of matter and energy on the atomic and subatomic level

- A quantum dot is a semiconductor nanostructure that confines the motion of conduction band electrons, valence band holes, or excitons (bound pairs of conduction band electrons and valence band holes) in all three spatial directions

- Quantum dots are tiny particles or nanocrystals of a semiconducting material with diameters in the range of 2-10 nanometers (10-50 atoms).

- The luminescent properties of quantum dots arise from recombination of electron-hole pairs (exciton decay) through radiative pathways.

- Multi component quantum dots offer an alternative method to tune properties without changing crystallite size.

- Quantum dots are particularly significant for optical applications owing to their bright, pure colors along with their ability to emit rainbow of colors coupled with their high efficiencies, longer lifetimes and high extinction coefficient.

- A nanowire is a wire of dimensions of the order of a nanometer (10^{-9} meters). Alternatively, nanowires can be defined as structures that have a lateral size constrained to tens of nanometers or less and an unconstrained longitudinal size.

EXERCISE

1. What do you understand by the single-electron box? Explain.
2. Explain the history of quantum dots.
3. Discuss the applications of quantum dots in numerous fields.
4. What are the nano-wires? Write its construction methodology and applications?
5. Give an overview on finFET tool story.
6. Explain the quantum particle.
7. Write a short note on finFET properties.
8. State and explain the applications of the nanowires.
9. Explain the advantages of finFET.

INTRODUCTION TO MEMS

4.1 INTRODUCTION

- Micro-Electromechanical System (MEMS) is a process technology used to create tiny integrated devices or systems that combine mechanical and electrical components. They are fabricated using Integrated Circuit (IC) batch processing techniques and can range in size from a few micrometers to millimeters.

- These systems or devices have ability of the following parameters actuate, sense and control on the micro scale and effects generated on the micro scale.

- For their significant costs; their size also makes it possible to integrate them into a wide range of systems. Feature sizes may be made with size in the order of the wavelength of light, thus making them attractive for many optical applications.

- Microsensors (e.g., accelerometers for automobile crash detection and pressure sensors for biomedical applications) and microactuators (e.g., for moving arrays of micromirrors in projection systems) are examples of commercial applications of MEMS.

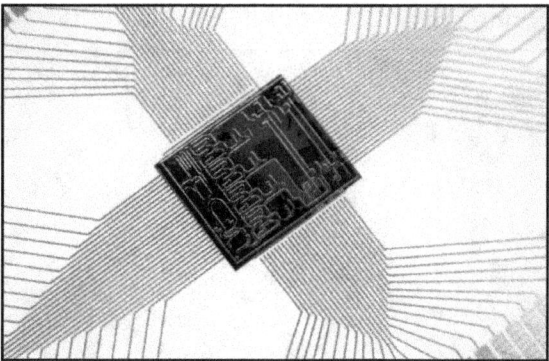

Fig. 4.1: Tiny integrated chip using MEMS

- Micro-optoelectromechanical Systems (MOEMS) is also a subset of microsystems (MST) and together with MEMS forms the specialized technology fields using miniaturized combinations of optics, electronics and mechanics. Both their microsystems incorporate the use of microelectronics batch processing techniques for their design and fabrication. Integrating technologies are considerable overlaps between the fields and their applications and tends which is very difficult to categorize. MEMS devices are in terms of their subset of MST or sensing domain.

- The difference between MEMS and MST is that MEMS tends to use semiconductor processes to create a mechanical part. In contrast, the deposition of a material on silicon, for example, does not constitute MEMS but is an application of MST.

- MEMS has several distinct advantages as a manufacturing technology. The interdisciplinary nature of MEMS technology and its micromachining techniques.

- MEMS with its batch fabrication techniques enables components and devices to be manufactured with increased performance and reliability, combined with the obvious advantages of reduced physical size, volume, weight and cost.

- MEMS provides the basis for the manufacture of products that cannot be made by other methods.

- These factors make MEMS potentially a far more pervasive technology than integrated circuit microchips.

4.2 OVERVIEW OF MEMS

- Micro-machined pressure sensors are variety of structure of building block and fabrication method. All these sensors can be based on capacitive, piezoresistive, electronics resonance, piezoelectric and optical detection methods.

- Advanced features for integrated pressure sensors include built-in vacuum for absolute pressure measurement, integrated telemetry link, close-loop control, insensitivity to contaminants, biocompatibility for integration into micro medical instruments and use of non-silicon membrane materials (e.g., ceramics, diamonds) for functioning in harsh and high temperature environments.

Fig. 4.2: PCB with mounting chips

- Microsensors detect changes in the system environment by measuring mechanical, thermal, magnetic, chemical or electromagnetic information or phenomena. Microelectronics processes this information and signals the microactuators to react and create some form of changes to the environment.

4.2.1 The Intrinsic Characteristics of MEMS

- This technology has two reasons one is development and other is commercialization.
- There are also included three generic distinct merits for MEMS systems. Microfabrication technologies: (1) Miniaturization, (2) Microelectronics Integration and (3) Parallel fabrication with high precision. MEMS products will compete in the market place on the grounds of functional richness, small sizes, unique performance characteristics (e.g., fast speed) and low cost.
- For advanced students of MEMS, it is important to realize that the three merits will not automatically lead to product and market advantages. One should understand the complex interplay between these elements to fully unleash the power of MEMS technology.

(1) Miniaturization:

- Generally, typical length scale of MEMS devices ranges from 1 μm to 1 cm. MEMS system may occupy entire system much bigger foot print or volume of large array. Small dimensions raise to many operational advantages. It gives soft springs, high resonance frequency, greater sensitivity, and low thermal mass.
- For example, the heat transfer of a micromachined device is generally fast. In this case please keep in case mind is the ink jet printer nozzle, with the time constant of droplet ejection being on the order of 20 ps.
- Small size allows MEMS devices to be less intrusive in biomedical applications (e.g., neuron probes). Small means that MEMS devices can be integrated non-intrusively in crucial systems, such as portable electronics, medical instruments, and implants (e.g., capsule endoscopes).
- This is ideal form but in practical form smaller device footprint leads to more devices per wafer and greater economy of scale. Hence, the cost of MEMS devices generally scales favorably with miniaturization.
- All these things are over-up in miniaturized. In physical phenomena do not scale favorably when the dimensions are reduced, while certain physical phenomena that work poorly at the macroscale suddenly become very practical and attractive at the microscale.
- Scaling laws are observed about how physics works at different sizes. A well-known example is that fleas can jump dozens of times its own height whereas elephants cannot jump at all, even though an elephant has far more muscle mass than a flea.
- A rigorous scaling-law analysis starts with the identification of a characteristics length scale (denoted as L) for a device of interest.
- For example, the length of a cantilever or the diameter of a circular membrane may be denoted as L of the respective element. Physical dimensions are assumed to the scale as a linearly and with characteristics of length scale locked ration. This is the remaining pertinent.

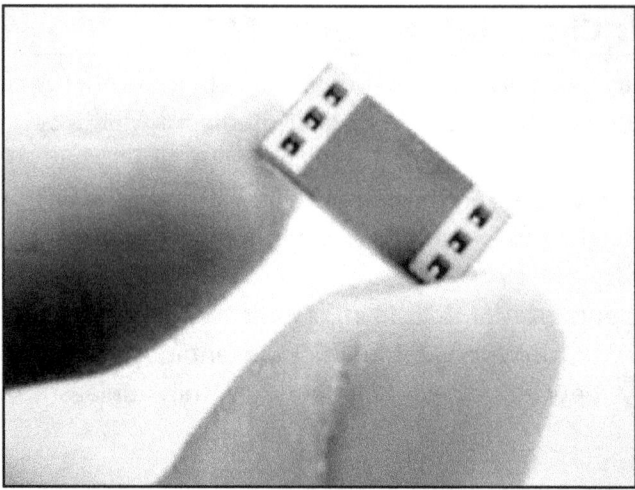

Fig. 4.3: MEMS sensor

- A performance merit of interest (e.g., stiffness of a cantilever or resonant frequency of a membrane) is expressed as a function of L, with dimension terms other than the characteristic length scale term expressed as a fraction or multiples of L. The expression is then simplified to extract the overall effect of L.

- In this process like so many scaling laws on several performance aspects must be evaluated simultaneously to determine the overall merit of scaling based on a combined figure-of-merit.

- Taking Analog Device accelerometer as an example; the following key performance metrics are variable by scale: spring constant of the support beam (related to sensitivity), resonant frequency of the support beam (related to bandwidth), and overall capacitance value (again related to sensitivity).

- Miniaturization generally leads to softer support beams (desired), higher resonant frequency, and bandwidth (desired), but at the expense of reduced capacitance value (undesired) and generally increased circuitry complexity (to accommodate smaller signals). Recently, electromechanical devices with a scale characteristics in the range of 1 to 10 nm are investigated to explore the scaling effect compared to traditional MEMS.

- Such devices and systems are referred to as nano-electromechanical systems or NEMS. Many NEMS devices are made using assembly of nanostructures, such as nanotubes or nanofabricated elements. High-frequency electromechanical resonators and filters have been made using lithography-patterned nanomechanical cantilevers.

- For example, a NEMS mechanical resonator with resonant frequency of 1.35 GHz and quality factor on the order of 20,000 to 50,000 has been demonstrated and used as a tool to validate fundamental quantum mechanical limits imposed by the Heisenberg uncertainty principle.

(2) Microelectronics Integration:

- Microelectronics integration circuit is used to sense process signal it provide the power and control to improve the signal qualities or interfacing with computer electronics also in control. MEMS products today are increasingly being embedded with computing, networking, and decision-making capabilities.

- By integrating micromechanical devices with electronics circuitry and offering the combined system as a product, significant advantages can be produced in a competitive market place.

- The ability to seamlessly integrate mechanical sensors and actuators with electronics processors and controllers at the single wafer level is one of the most unique characteristics of MEMS.

- This process paradigm is referred to as monolithic integration fabrication of various components on a single substrate in an unbroken, wafer-level process flow. (The word "monolithic" means "one stone". Hence, "monolithic fabrication" means fabrication on one piece of wafer). All MEMS devices should adhere or have adhered to the monolithic integration format, it is observed that silicon circuits that are monolithically integrated with mechanical elements have been involved in several successful commercial MEMS applications, such as Analog Devices, accelerometers, digital light processors, and ink jet printer heads.

- In monolithic process method do not involve assembly methods because of such method, robotics pick and place or any manual attachment of individual parts of the system. Dimensions and precision of placement are guaranteed by lithography.

- Monolithic integration improves the quality of signals by reducing the length of signal paths and noise.

- Monolithic integration with circuits is arguably the only way by which a large and dense array of sensors or actuators can be addressed. In the case of DLP, for example, each mirror is controlled by a CMOS logic circuit that is buried directly underneath. Without individual mirrors address it is impossible to get without the integration of the circuits such as a large and dense array.

(3) Parallel Fabrication with Precision:

- This technique can be realized two or three dimensional features and with small dimensions it cannot be provisionally reproducibly, efficiency and profitably making with traditional tool matching. Combined with photolithography, MEMS technology can be used to realize unique three-dimensional features such as inverted pyramid cavities, high aspect ratio trenches, through-wafer holes, cantilevers and membranes.

- These features are used in traditional machining or manufacturing methods. It is prohibitively difficult and inefficient. MEMS and Microelectronics are also different from traditional machining, in that multiple copies of identical dies are made on a same wafer.

- This happens practically to lower the cost of individual units. Modern lithography systems and techniques provide not only finely defined features, but also uniformity across wafers and batches.

4.3 SENSORS AND ACTUATORS

- Sensors and actuators are commonly used to interface between an engineering system and the physical world. The kingdom of MEMS actuators mainly consists of four families:

  (1) Electrostatic.

  (2) Piezoelectric.

  (3) Thermal.

  (4) Magnetic.

- The kingdom of MEMS displacement sensors can be structured into the families of capacitive, optical and electron tunneling. In analogous fashion, the kingdom of MEMS force sensors comprises the set of families of piezoresistive, piezoelectric and compliant sensors.

- For the family of compliant force sensors, a displacement sensor is used to measure the deflection of a compliant structure of known stiffness, and this family subdivides into classes of visual and capacitive sensing.

- In this case of the visual sensing, off-chip image capture is by optical microscopy, co-focal optical microscopy, electron microscopy and probe microscopy.

4.3.1 Energy Domains and Transducers

- MEMS technology enables revolutionary sensors and actuators. In general terms, sensors are devices that detect and monitor physical or chemical phenomenon, whereas actuators are ones that produce mechanical motion, force, or torque.

- Sensing can be broadly defined as energy transduction processes that result in perception, whereas actuation is energy transduction processes that produce actions. Sensors and actuators are collectively referred to as transducers, which serve the function of transforming signals or power from one energy domain to another.

- There are six major energy domains of interests:

  (1) Electrical domain (denoted E);

  (2) Mechanical domain (Mec);

  (3) Chemical domain (C);

  (4) Radioactive domain (R);

  (5) Magnetic domain (Mag) and

  (6) Thermal domain (T).

- These energy domains and commonly encountered parameters within them are shown in the following Fig. 4.4. The total energy within a system can coexist in several domains and can shift among various domains under right circumstances.

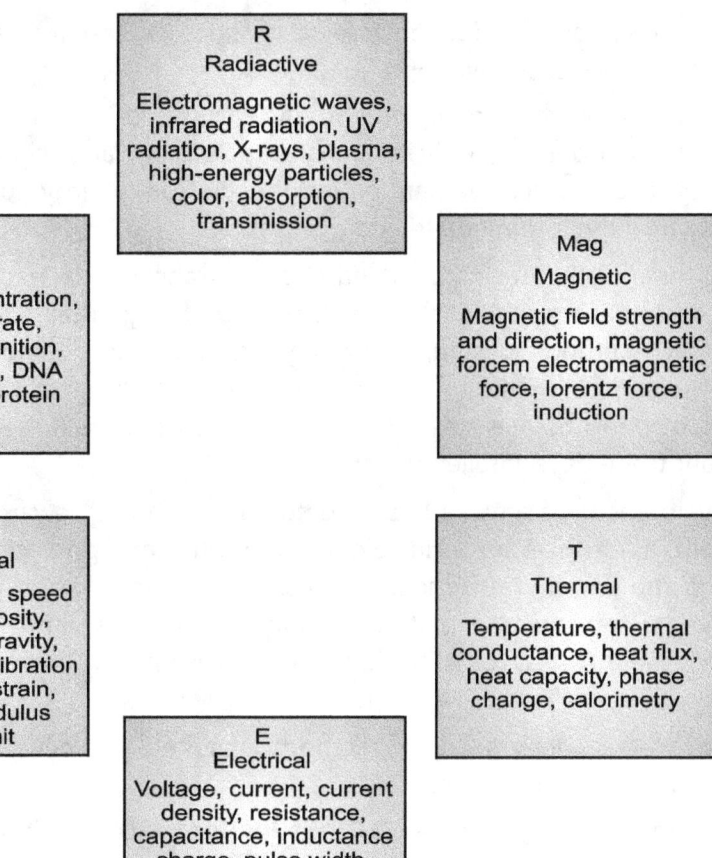

Fig. 4.4 : Major energy domains

- Generally, sensors transform stimulus signals in different energy domains to one is detectable by humans or the electrical domain for the interfacing with recorders or computers, electronics controllers etc.

- For example, a thermal-couple temperature sensor transforms a thermal signal, temperature, into an electrical signal (e.g., voltage) that can be read electronically.

- Often more than one sensing principles can be used for a transduction tasks. Temperature variation can be perceived via such phenomenon as resistance changes, volume expansion of fluids, increased radiation power of an object, color change of engineered dyes, shifted resonance frequency of resonant beams, or greater chemical reactivity.

- Energy transduction pathways for particular sensor and actuation tasks do not have to involve only two domains. Rather, the transduction process may incorporate multiple domains. Direct transduction pathways that involve the minimal number of domains do not necessarily translate into simpler device, lower cost, or better performances.

- Energy and signal transduction is a vast space of research and development and a continuing source of innovation.

- The desire to discover and implement efficient, sensitive, and low-cost sensing principles transcends the boundary of scientific and technological disciplines. Sensing task can be more than one way achievement either directly from energy domain to other domain or indirectly through intermediate energy domain.

- There is essentially an unlimited number of transduction pathways for achieving one sensor or actuator need. Each transduction pathway entails different sensing material, fabrication method, design, sensitivity, responsively, temperature stability, cross-sensitivity, and cost, among others. A trade-off study must be conducted, taking into account of performance, cost, manufacturing ease, robustness, and, increasingly more important these days, intellectual property rights.

- The development of sensors and actuators is a rich and rewarding research experience. To invent a new sensor principle for a particular application involves selecting or inventing the energy transduction paths, device designs, and fabrication methods that yield simple transduction materials, high performance, and low-cost fabrication. For example, the richness of this field and to exemplify the excitement involved with re-search and development activities.

- In many races new sensing methods resulted in new device capabilities and industrialization opportunities.

- **Acceleration Sensing (Mec → E Transduction):** Acceleration can be sensed in many different ways. A micro-machined proof mass suspended by cantilevers will experience an inertial force under an applied acceleration. The force will cause movement of the suspended proof mass. The movement can be picked up using piezoresistors, resistor elements whose resistance change under applied stress (Mec → E). The displacement can also be sensed with a capacitor (Mec → E). This is the principle of Analog Device accelerometers. These two methods involve moving mechanical mass. Can one build accelerometers without moving parts? The answer is yes. For example, inertial force can also move a heated mass, whose ensuing displacement can be picked up by temperature sensors (Mec → a → E). Thermal sensing does not provide as good as performance as capacitive sensing of moving air mass, but the fabrication is readily compatible with integrated circuits. This is the basic principle of a low-cost acceleration sensor (manufactured by MEMSIC Corporation) designed for low-sensitivity applications. No mass moving is required, eliminating concerns of mechanical reliability. Since no moving mass is needed, the device is compatible with mass batch microelectronics foundries, reducing the time to market significantly. Olfactory sensing (C → E transduction). Information about the presence and concentration of certain molecules responsible for smell or pertaining to environmental monitoring can be obtained using a number of strategies. A carbon-based material can be designed to specifically absorb certain molecules and alter the electrical resistivity (C → E direct transduction). The absorbance of certain molecules in the path of surface acoustic wave devices can alter mechanical properties such as frequency of surface acoustic wave transmission (C → M → E). These methods generally involve sophisticated electronics or algorithms. Can one build olfactory sensors that are simpler and more intuitive? The binding of chemical molecules can also alter the color of a specially designed chemical compound, which can be detected using low-cost optoelectronics diodes (C → R → E transduction) or directly by human beings without electronics (C → E).

- **DNA Sequence Identification (C → E Transduction):** This DNA molecules consists of a chain of base pairs, each with four possible varieties: A, C, G, or T. The sequence of base pairs in a DNA chain determines the code of synthesizing proteins. The ability to decipher base pair sequences of DNA molecules rapidly, accurately, and inexpensively is of critical importance for pharmaceutical and medical applications. There is a wide variety of innovative methods for detection of DNA sequence through their telltale binding (hybridization) events. DNA molecules may be modified chemically to incorporate (tagged) fluorescence reporters that lights or dims upon binding with another DNA strand. The chemical binding events are turned into optical signals first before transdused to the electrical domain (C → R → E). The fluorescent image is captured using high power fluorescent microscopes. However, fluorescent imaging requires sophisticated microscope and is not suitable for portable, field applications. DNA molecules attached to gold nanoparticles can report the event of hybridization through aggregation of gold particles, which can result in changes of optical reflectance (C → R → E) or electrical resistivity (C → E). The detection method with gold nanoparticles provides better sensitivity and selectivity compared with fluorescence methods while eliminating the need of cumbersome fluorescent imaging instruments.

4.3.2 Sensor Noise and Design Complexity

- Many sensors performance criteria need to be met for a product. However, it is often difficult to improve all performance characteristics simultaneously. Noise is very deep pertaining to so many areas including the practical measurement science, thermal dynamics and statistics. MEMS can be attributed as a noise in the following three major sources:

  (1) Electronic noise (2) Mechanical Noise and (3) Noise in the circuitry.

- In MEMS sensors, the major contribution of electronic noises comes from the following sources: the Johnson noise, the shot noise, and the 1/f noise. The Johnson noise is a white noise manifested as an open circuit voltage created by a resistor due to random thermal fluctuation of electrons and particles within. It is also called thermal noise and Nyquist noise.

- The RMS value of the Johnson noise is $V_{noise} = \sqrt{4kTRB}$,
  where k, T, R, B are the Boltzmann's constant, the absolute temperature, the resistance value and the bandwidth in hertz respectively. The equivalent noise current is V_{noise}/R. The amplitude of Johnson noise follows a Gaussian distribution. Thermal noise is present

in all resistors. One can normalize the Johnson noise figure by the bandwidth it is called as spectral noise figure, $C\sqrt{4kTR}$ with a unit of $V/\sqrt{Hz}$.

- The shot noise (rain-drop-on-a-tin roof noise), Gaussian and white noise are used in quantum fluctuation of the electric consent due to discrete passage charges aeros the energy barriers.

- The shot noise can be estimated as $I_{noise} = \sqrt{2qI_{dc}B}$, where q, I_{dc} and B are the single electron charge, the dc current, and the measurement bandwidth measured in hertz.

- The 1/f noise, also known as flicker noise, or pink noise, is the result of conductance fluctuation when a current passes through an interface (often with a semiconductor material). Current fluctuation stems from the trapping and releasing of charges through interface states.

- It derives its name from its characteristics 1/f spectrum dependence. It is called the pink noise following a color analogy. If an object has 1/f optical emission spectrum, it would appear to be pink to our eyes. One prominent source of 1/f noise is the Hooge noise, with the power 1/28 spectrum at a given frequency f given by $\dfrac{\alpha V_B^2}{Nf}$, where, V_g is the bias voltage across a resistor with a total number of carrier N, and f is an unitless constant.

- The total number of carriers of the 1/f noise to the volume of the resistor. Piezoresistor field effect transistors and carbon resistors this parameters exhibit 1/f but in metal film resistor does not get the 1/f noise. It is possible to optimize sensor design to reduce 1/f noise contributions.

- For many motion-based MEMS sensors (e.g., accelerometers and pressure sensors), the mechanical-thermal noise floor, which is vibration of micro structures under the impact of Brownian motion mechanical agitation, is another fundamental source of noise in addition to electrical ones.

- MEMS design, even considered in the absence of materials and processing issues, is complex. Many sensor performance characteristics, such as sensitivity, bandwidth, and noise, are interrelated. This makes design efforts very complex.

- An accelerometer; where the acceleration on a mass causes the mass to move. For such a device, a wider frequency response range (B) is a desirable product characteristic. It typically means a greater resonant frequency, which can be obtained by decreasing the mass and/or increasing the force constant k. However, such actions reduce the sensitivity to acceleration (due to smaller mass and stiffer spring) and increase the noise (due to larger B).

- One of the representative designs of accelerometer, the spring is made of silicon beams with doped piezoresistors.

- The dimensions of the piezoresistor, doping level, sensitivity, and noise are all closely related. To increase the piczoresistive effect, it is desirable to dope the silicon with lower concentration.

- However, this tends to increase the sensitivity to ambient temperature variation. It would also increase the resistance value for a given dimension, which would also elevate the noise level.

4.4 PACKAGING AND INTEGRATION

- MMMs is a new field which is tied so closed with silicon processing that most of the early packaging technologies will most likely use "off the shell" packaging borrowed from the semiconductor microelectronics field.

- Packaging of microelectronics circuits is the science and art of establishing interconnections and an appropriate operating environment for predominantly electrical (in this case, MEMS) circuits to process and/or store information.

- Packaging manifests itself in novel and unique creations that ingeniously reconcile and satisfy what seem to be mutually exclusive application requirements and constraints posed by the laws of nature and the properties of materials and processes. All applications can be summed up in three terms:

  (1) Cost (2) Performance (3) Reliability.

- Packaging can span from the consumer to midrange systems to the high performance and reliability applications.

- It must be noted that no sharp boundaries exist between the classes, only a gradual shift from optimization for parameters which control performance and cause the cost to increase.

- MEMS packages can contain many electrical and mechanical components. To be useful for the outside world these components need interconnections.

- A MEM die sawed from a wafer is extremely fragile and must be protected from mechanical damage and hostile environments.

- To function, electrical circuits need to be supplied with electrical energy, which is consumed and transformed into mechanical and thermal (heat) energy. Because the system operates best within a limited temperature range, packaging must offer an adequate means for removal of heat.

4.4.1 Functions of MEMS Packages

- The package serves to integrate all of the components required for a system application of in a manner that size, cost, mass and complexity.

- The package provides the interface between the components and the overall system.

- The following subsections present the three main functions of the MEMS package: mechanical support, protection from the environment, and electrical connection to other system components.

4.4.2 Types of MEMS Packages

- The MEMS application requires new package design to optimize its performance of the system. It is possible to loosely group packages into several categories.

Four of these categories are as follows:

1. **Metal Packages:**

- Metal packages are often used for microwave multichip modules and hybrid circuits because they provide excellent thermal dissipation and excellent electromagnetic shielding. While large internal volume still maintaining mechanical reliability.

- The package can use both an integrated base and sidewalls with a lid or it can have a separate base, sidewalls, and lid. Inside the package, ceramic substrates or chip carriers are required for use with the feed throughs.

- The selection of the proper metal can be critical. CuW (10/90), Silvar (a Ni-Fe alloy), CuMo (15/85), and CuW (15/85) all have good thermal conductivity and a higher CTE than silicon, which makes them good choices, Kovar a Fe-Ni-Co alloy commonly. All these materials required in additional Alloy-46, may be used for the sidewalls and lid. Cu, Ag, or Au plating of the packages is commonly done. Before final assembly, a bake is usually performed to drive out any trapped gas or moisture.

- This reduces the onset of corrosion-related failures. The highest temperature curing epoxies or solders should be used first and subsequent processing temperatures should decrease until the final lid seal is done at the lowest temperature to avoid later steps damaging earlier steps.

- Au-Sn is a commonly used solder that works well when the two materials to be bonded have similar CTEs. Au-Sn solder joints of materials with a large CTE mismatch are susceptible to fatigue failures after temperature cycling. The AuSn inter-metallic forms tend to be brittle and can accommodate only low amounts of stress. Welding (using lasers to locally heat the joint between the two parts without raising the temperature of the entire part) is a commonly used alternative to solders.

- The seal of this technology or misalignments can be tolerated by the compromise the package hermeticity. Hermeticity can also be affected by the feed throughs that are required in metal packages. These feed throughs are generally made of glass or ceramic and each method (glass seal or aluminium feed through) has its weakness. Glass can crack during handling and thermal cycling. The conductor exiting through the ceramic feed through may not seal properly due to metallurgical reasons.

2. **Ceramic Packages:**

- Ceramic packages have several features that make them especially useful for microelectronics as well as MEMS.

- They provide low mass and are easily mass produced, because of the low cost. They can be made hermetic and can more easily integrate signal distribution lines and feed through.

- They can be machined to perform many different functions. By incorporating multiple layers of ceramics and interconnect lines, electrical performance of the package can be tailored to meet design requirements.

- These types of packages are generally referred to as confirmed multilayer ceramic packages. Multilayer ceramic packages also allow reduced size and cost of the total system by integrating multiple MEMS or other components into a single hermetic package.

- These multilayer packages offer significant size and mass reduction over metal-walled packages. One of the advantages of ceramic packages is use of three dimensions instead of two for interconnects lines. Co-fired ceramic packages are constructed from individual pieces of ceramic in the green or unfired state.

- These materials are thin, pliable films. During a typical process, the films are stretched across a frame in a way similar to that used by an artist to stretch a canvas across a frame.

- On each layer, metal lines are deposited using thick-film processing (usually screen printing), and interlayer interconnects are drilled or punched.

- All of these layers have been fabricated and the unfired pieces are stacked and aligned using registration holes and laminated together. Finally, the part is fired at a high temperature.

- The MEMS and possibly other components are then attached into place (usually organically (epoxy) or metallurgically (solders), and wire bonds are made the same as those used for metal packages.

- The reliability of this package type can be affecting several problems. First, the green-state ceramic shrinks during the firing step.

- The amount of shrinkage is dependent on the number and position of via holes and wells cut into each layer.

- At the different layers, green state ceramic may shrink more than others creating stress in the final package.

- Second, because ceramic-to-metal adhesion is not as strong as ceramic-to-ceramic adhesion, sufficient ceramic surface area must be available to assure a good bond between layers.

- The possibility of continuous ground planes for power distribution and shielding. Instead, metal grids are used for these purposes.

- Third, the processing temperature and ceramic properties limit the choice of metal lines. To eliminate warping and the shrinkage rate of the metal and ceramic must be matched.

3. **Thin-Film Multilayer Packages:**

- There are two general technologies used in thin film multilayer packages. One is polyimide laminated and other is LTCC packages.

- One uses sheets of polyimide laminated together, in a way similar to that used for the LTCC packages described above, except a final firing is not required.

- Each individual sheet is typically 25 mm and is processed separately using thin-film metal processing. The second technique also uses polyimide, but each layer is spun onto and baked on the carrier or substrate to form 1 to 20 mm thick layers. In this method, holes are either wet etched or Reactive Ion Etched (RIE).

- The polyimide for both methods has a relative permittivity of 2.8 to 3.2. Since the permittivity is low and the layers are thin, the same characteristic impedance lines can be fabricated with less line-to-line coupling; therefore, closer spacing of lines is possible. The low permittivity results in low line capacitance and therefore faster circuits.

4. Plastic Packages:

- Plastic packages are used by the electronics industry for many years and for almost every application because of their low manufacturing cost.

- High reliability applications are an exception because serious reliability questions have been raised. Plastic packages are not hermetic, and hermetic seals are generally required for high reliability applications.

- The packages are also susceptible to cracking in humid environments during temperature cycling of the surface mount assembly of the package to the mother-board.

- Plastic packaging for space applications may gain acceptability as time goes on.

4.4.3 Integrating MEMS

- Micro-electromechanical Systems (MEMS) and emerging Nano-electromechanical Systems (NEMS). Both MEMS and NEMS refer as typical transducer systems that sense or control of the physical optical or chemical qualities such as fluids or radiation acceleration etc.

- A MEMS device typically interacts with a physical, chemical or optical quantity and has an electrical interface to the outside world. For MEMS sensors, the electrical output signal correlates with the physical, optical or chemical input quantity that is sensed.

- In the case of MEMS actuators, an electrical input signal is used to control one or more physical, optical or chemical quantities.

- To enable the MEMS transducer to perform useful functions, the electrical interface with the outside world is, in most cases, realized through integrated circuits (ICs) that provide the system with the necessary intelligence. ICs may provide signal conditioning functions such as analog-to-digital conversion, amplification, temperature compensation, storage or filtering as well as system testing and logic and communication functions.

MEMS and ICs can be integrated using two basic methods:

- In the general approach referred to: A multi-chip solution, MEMS and IC components are manufactured on separate substrates using dedicated MEMS and IC processes and are subsequently hybridized in the final system.

- Two-dimensional or side-by-side integrated systems are often referred to as multi-chip modules.

- When chips are vertically stacked in a package in this case a system is also referred to as a system-in-package or a vertical multi-chip module. Devices created through vertical stacking of several IC chips are also referred to as three-dimensional integrated circuits (3D ICs).

- Other general approach referred to a System-on-Chip (SoC) solution, MEMS and IC components are manufactured on the same substrate, using consecutive or interlaced processing schemes.

- For both multi-chip solutions and SoC solutions, numerous technological schemes have been proposed, and the research community and industry continue to develop new manufacturing and integration schemes at a rapid pace. Each of the two basic methods of combining MEMS and ICs offers distinct advantages and disadvantages, and the preferred solution depends on the device or the field of application and the product requirements.

- Based on recent MEMS market studies, we estimate that approximately half of all existing MEMS products (in terms of market value) are currently implemented as multi-chip solutions (including many accelerometers, gyroscopes, microphones, pressure sensors, RF MEMS and micro fluidic devices) and that the other half are implemented as SoC solutions (including digital mirror devices, infrared bolometer arrays, inkjet print heads, and certain gyroscopes, accelerometers and pressure sensors).

- Many of the MEMS products that are implemented as SoC solutions have the common feature that they consist of large transducer arrays in which each transducer is operated individually, and thus, the integration of each MEMS transducer and its associated IC on a single chip is the only practical way to implement these types of systems.

- However, there are also other products, including certain gyroscopes, accelerometers, microphones and pressure sensors that are implemented as SoC solutions. The commonality among these products is that they are relatively mature products that are manufactured and sold in very high volumes.

4.5 STRESS AND STRAIN

- The basic concepts of stress and strain is one of the most frequently encountered consequences of the Newton's Laws is that, for any stationary object, the vector sum of forces and moment (torque) on the object and on any part of it must be zero.

- These laws are used to analyze force distribution inside a material, which gives rise to stress and strain. Consider a bar firmly embedded in a brick wall with an axial force F applied at the end as shown in Fig. 4.5. The force is transmitted through the bar to the wall; the wall must produce a reaction according to the Newton's third Law.

- The wall would act on the left end of the bar with an unknown force. To expose and quantify this force, we imaginarily remove the wall, and replace it with the actions it imparts on the bar.

- This free-body diagram of the bar clearly reveals that the wall must provide an axial force with equal magnitude but opposite direction to the applied force, so that the total force on the bar is zero to maintain its stationary status (Newton's First Law).

- We can use this technique to expose and quantify hidden forces and stresses at any section. Since the bar is in equilibrium, any part of it must be in equilibrium as well.

- We can pick an arbitrary section of interest, and imaginarily cut the bar into two halves. (If this section is cut perpendicular to the longitudinal direction of the bar, it is called a cross section.) The convenient way to analyze the force on each of the two pieces is to start from the right-hand piece, since the loading condition on one of its ends is explicitly known.

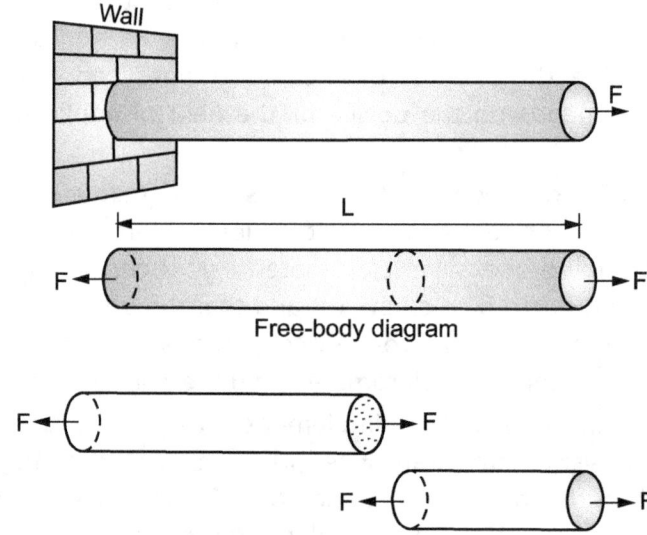

Fig. 4.5: Force balance Analysis

- Force applied at the free end of the bar, an equal but opposite force must develop at the cross section. The two opposite faces at the cut sections must have matched force and moment with opposite signs as dictated by the Newton's Third Law.

- Hence a force of magnitude F is believed to act on the right end of the left-hand piece, even if we have no way of measuring it experimentally since the surface is actually hidden. Now let us consider the same bar under a force acting in the transverse direction (Figure 4.3).

Again, we isolate the bar by imaginarily removing the wall.

- The sum of forces and moments acting on the isolated bar must be zero. For the net force to be zero, a force of same magnitude but opposite sign must act on the end of

---

the bar attached to the wall. The pair of force, however, creates a torque can refer to a couple or moment in mechanics.) with the magnitude being F times L, the length of the bar. A reactive torque, with the magnitude of F times L but opposite sign, must act on the end of the bar attached to the wall. To calculate the reactive force and torque at an imaginarily cut section, we can start from the piece to the right, since the loading on one of its ends.

- The cross section would experience an opposite force and a torque to balance the one created by the pair of force, separated by an arm of L'.

- This is the fact of the cross-sectional. The imaginarily cut section on the piece to the left would have exactly opposite force and torque as the opposing surface (according Newton's Third Law).

- The magnitude of the sum of torques on the left-hand piece is equal to $\sum M = FL - FL' = FL''$, which equals the force (F) multiplied by the length of the left-hand piece (L''). The net force and torque acting on the left-hand piece arc both zero.

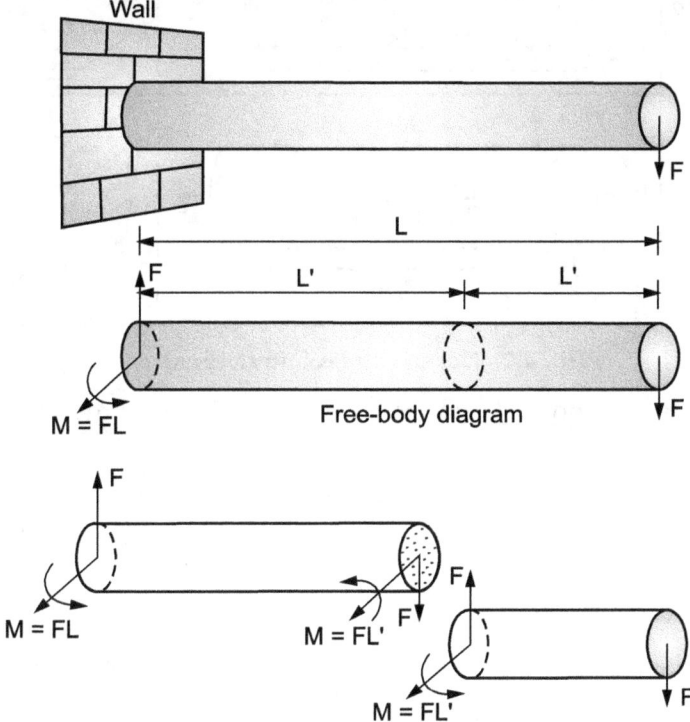

Fig. 4.6: Force and Momentum balance analysis

Mechanical stresses can be classified as two types:
   (1) Normal stress.
   (2) Shear stress.

- The definition of these two stresses using simple cases as shown in Fig. 4.7. For the simplest case of normal stress analysis, let us consider a rod with uniform cross-sectional area subjected to axial loading.

- If we pull on the rod in its longitudinal direction, it will experience tension and the length of the rod will increase. Internal stress in the rod is exposed in imaginary cut through the rod at an each section.

- At any chosen cross section, a continuously distributed force is found acting over the entire area of the section. The intensity of this force is called the stress. If the stress acts in a direction perpendicular to the cross section, it is called normal stress. The normal stress, commonly denoted as a, is defined as the force (F) applied on a given area (A),

The SI Unit of stress is N/m*m or pa.

$$\sigma = \frac{F}{A}$$

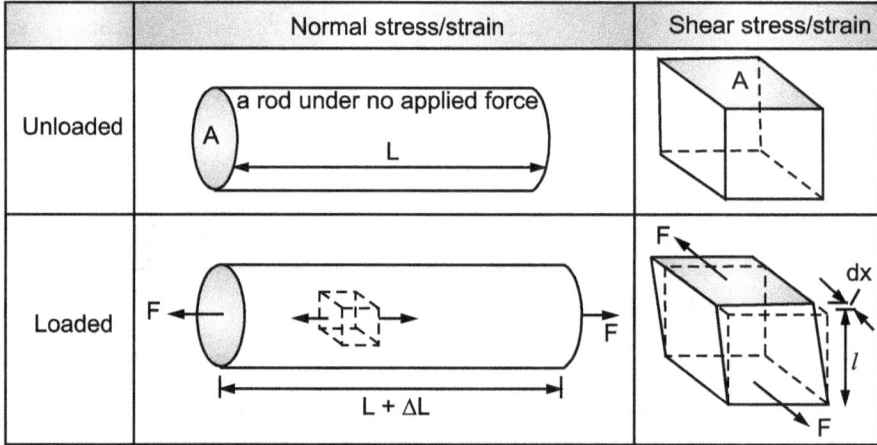

	Normal stress/strain	Shear stress/strain
Unloaded	a rod under no applied force, A, L	A
Loaded	F ← ... → F, L + ΔL	F, dx, l, F

Fig. 4.7: Normal stress and shear stress

- A normal stress can be tensile (as in the case of pulling along the rod) or compressive for the case of pushing the rod.

- The polarity of normal stress can also be determined by isolating an infinitesimally small volume inside the bar. If the volume is pulled in one particular axis, the stress is tensile; if the volume is pushed; the stress is compressive. The unit elongation of the rod represents the strain.

- In this case, it is called normal strain since the direction of the strain is perpendicular to the cross section of the beam. Suppose the steel bar has an original length denoted L0. Under a given normal stress, the rod is extended to a length of L. The resultant strain in the bar is defined as,

$$s = \frac{L - L_0}{L_0} = \frac{\Delta L}{L_0}$$

- The strain is commonly denoted as c in mechanics. However, it could easily be mistaken with the notation reserved for electrical permittivity (dielectric constant) of a material. In most cases the context of the piezoelectricity.

- In others, such as the discussion of piezoelectricity where the constitutive equations involve both strain and permitivity, the strain and permitivity terms must be assigned different notations to avoid confusion. Here, the strain is denoted as s to prevent any possible confusion.
- The applied longitudinal stress along the x-axis not only produces a longitudinal elongation in the direction of the stress, but a reduction of cross-sectional area as well. This can be explained by the argument that the material must strive to maintain constant atomic spacing and bulk volume.

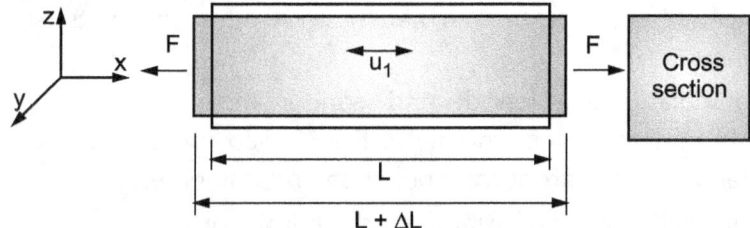

Fig. 4.8: Longitudinal elongation of a bar under an applied normal stress

- The relative dimensional change in the y and z directions can be expressed as E_x and s_y. This general material characteristic is captured by a term called the Poisson's ratio p, which is defined as the ratio between transverse and longitudinal elongations:

$$v = \left| \frac{s_y}{s_x} \right| = \left| \frac{s_z}{s_x} \right|$$

- Stress and strain are closely related. Under small deformation, the stress and the strain terms are proportional to each other according to the Hooke's law, i.e.

$$\sigma = Es$$

- The proportion constant, E is called the modulus of elasticity. The general relation between stress and strain over a wider range of deformation, however, is much more complicated.
- The modulus of electricity often uses young modulus according to intrinsic property of a material. It is a constant for a given material, irrespective of the shape and dimensions of the mechanical element. Atoms are held together with atomic forces. If one atom imagines inter-atomic force acting as springs to provide restoring force when atoms are pulled apart or pushed together, the modulus of elasticity is the measure of the stiffness of the inter-atomic spring near the equilibrium point.

4.5.1 Intrinsic Stress

- Thin film stress refers to an assortment of structural imperfections that result in the degradation or failure of microscopic layers of optical or conductive material. Any number of problems may occur when film is improperly produced or applied to a product. With layers sometimes only a few atoms thick, unplanned interactions between materials can have a pronounced effect on the performance of the film. In view of these many influences, several key types of thin film stress can occur. These include epitaxial stress, thermal stress, and growth stress, as well as other deformation processes.

- The thin film technology development challenges of manufacturing and deposition processes to a wide assortment of products. Scientific and household technologies rely on the thin film for a multitude of light wavelengths, such as in the optical components in copiers, scanners, and thin film solar panels.

- Products can also benefit from thin film material enhancements, such as scratch or impact resistance.

- Thin film manipulates wavelength and conductance properties and expands the capabilities of numerous technologies. It is varied manufacturing and deposition challenges offer a moving target for innovation and refinement.

- Thin film stress results from deposition issues, thermal processes, and laser technologies, and thin film is manufactured using methods that present unique characteristics, strengths and shortcomings.

- Film can crack or void, and sometimes lifts from its substrate medium, while other processes might interfere with characteristics like resistance to moisture or oxidation.

Intrinsic Stress Effects in Deposited Thin Films:

- Thin film deposition is a widely used for the fabrication of MEMS (Micro-Electro-Mechanical Systems). This method is required to manufacture free-standing structures which can induce or sense a mechanical movement.

- During the deposition process of thin layers and after an intrinsic stress is generated. The underlying sacrificial layer removal the subsequent process step the (stressed) deposited layer which is an important component of the desired MEMS device is left free-standing. As a consequence the process induced stress can relax and deform the deposited layer in an undesirable way.

- Polycrystalline silicon-germanium (poly-SiGe) has been promoted as an attractive material suitable as structural layer for several MEMS applications. Poly-SiGe is a good alternative to polycrystalline silicon (poly-Si), because it has similar properties.

- The same good mechanical and electrical properties can be obtained with poly-SiGe at much lower temperatures (down to 400°C) compared to poly-Si (above 800°C).

- These low processing temperatures enable MEMS post-processing on top of MOS without introducing significant changes in the existing MOS fabrication processes.

- This layer is normally made of silicon dioxide (SiO_2), because this material can then be etched with a high selectivity towards the structural layer by the use of hydrogen fluoride (HF).

- Different aspects of the connection between microstructure and stress have been investigated in the past 30 years. Mostly grain-grain boundary configuration early stage or mature of microstructure evolution.

- As a result of this models derived on the basis of continuum mechanics are applicable for highly simplified situations. On the other side a group of researchers, mostly mathematicians, has developed complex models for describing morphology of the micro-structural evolution, a development which culminates in multi-level set models of grain evolution.

- These models can reproduce the realistic grain boundary network in a high degree, but they do not include stress.

- The goal of this work is the integration of microstructure models which describe strain development due to grain dynamics in a macroscopic mechanical formulation.

- This strain loads the mechanical problem which provides a distribution of the mechanical stress and enables the calculation of displacements in the MEMS structure.

4.5.2 Types of Beams

- A beam is a structure member subjected to lateral loads, that is, forces or moments having their vectors perpendicular to the longitudinal axis. Here, we focus on planar structures beams that lie in single planes.

- In addition, all loads act in that same plane and all deflections occur in that plane. Beams are usually described by the manner in which they are supported. Boundary conditions pertain to the deflections and slopes at the supports of a beam.

- Consider a two-dimensional beam with movement confined in one plane. Each point along the length of the beam can have a maximum of two Linear Degrees Of Freedom (DOF) and one rotational degree of freedom.

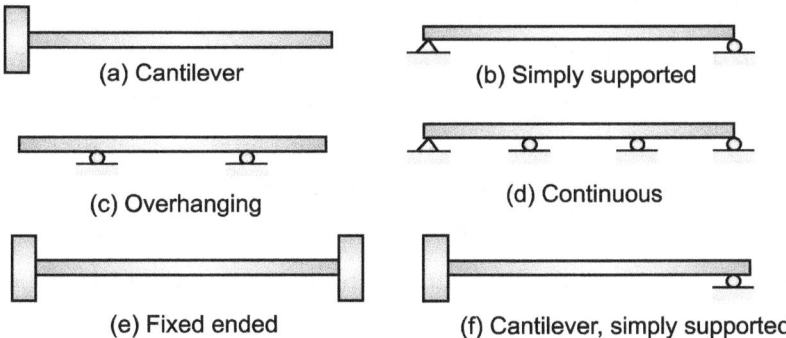

(a) Cantilever

(b) Simply supported

(c) Overhanging

(d) Continuous

(e) Fixed ended

(f) Cantilever, simply supported

Fig. 4.9: Types of beams

According to DOFs their are three possible boundary conditions as follows:

(1) The fixed boundary condition restricts both linear DOFs and the rotational DOF. No movement is allowed at the support. At the fixed support, a beam can neither translate

nor rotate. Representative examples include the anchored end of a diving board or the ground end of a flagpole.

(2) The guided boundary conditions allow two linear DOFs but restrict the rotational DOF.

(3) The free boundary conditions provide for both linear DOFS and rotation. At a free end, a point on beam may translate and rotate. For example free end of a diving board.

- Flexural beams can be classified according to the combination of two mechanical boundary conditions associated with it. For example, a beam fixed at one end and free at another is conveniently referred to as a fixed-free beam commonly called a cantilever.

The boundary beams of condition produced as follows:

- A fixed-free cantilever is parallel to the plane of the substrate, with the free tip capable of moving in a direction normal to the substrate. Lateral, in plane movement of the free end would encounter much significant resistance.

- A fixed-free beam (bridge) is parallel to the substrate plane.

- There are actually two ways to dimity this beam. It can be considered a fixed-fixed cantilever parallel to the substrate plane with a thick and stiff part in the middle. Alternatively, this beam can also be considered as two fixed-guided beams jointed in parallel to support a rigid part.

- A fixed-free cantilever is with the free end capable of movement perpendicular to the substrate.

- A fixed-free cantilever is with the free end capable of movement within the substrate plane. With its thickness greater than its width, the movement of the free end in a direction perpendicular to the substrate plane would encounter much greater resistance.

4.5.3 Deflection of Beams

- Stresses cause beam deflection, which is the bending, or twisting of the structural members due to building loads, movement of people, or changing weather.

- It can be exposed by structural beams to different varieties of stress. Tension is a force that pulls the beam apart, which steel can resist well, but concrete cannot. Rebar is placed inside reinforced concrete structures to resist tension forces.

- Compression is a force that pushes from both ends of a beam toward the middle. Any vertical wall or beam is under compression stress from the weight of the building above it. Concrete is very good at resisting compression forces, and steel somewhat less because it can bend. The structural steel is produced in a shape of like capital letter I, this is called as I-beam. These are designed with two steel plates placed 90 degrees to a main beam, and running the full length of it, to prevent twisting or bending.

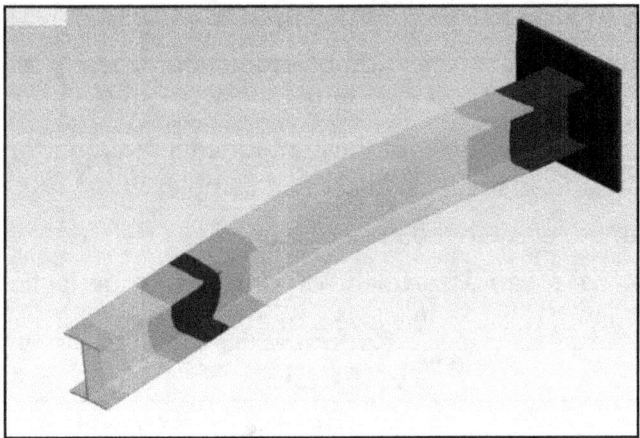

Fig. 4.10: Deflection of beams

- The beam deflection depends on the amount of size of the beam. This material used the weight and position of the object placed on it. A concrete floor poured on a steel beam structure may have little deflection, because the weight of the floor is distributed, or spread out evenly over the entire beam surface.

- Vertical wall beams must be designed to support the weight, called the load, of the steel and the concrete floor to prevent any deflection in the walls.

- A beam can deflect more if a large weight is placed at a point furthest away from where the beam is supported or attached to the building. This type of load is very important for beam deflection calculations. Beams or supporting walls at the maximum deflection point. Beams only supported on one end are also carefully analyzed for beam deflection.

SUMMARY

- A micro-electromechanical system (MEMS) is a process technology used to create tiny integrated devices or systems that combine mechanical and electrical components.

- Micro-optoelectromechanical systems (MOEMS) is also a subset of MST and together with MEMS forms the specialized technology fields using miniaturized combinations of optics, electronics and mechanics.

- MEMS have several distinct advantages as a manufacturing technology.

- Circuits are used to process sensor signals, provide power and control, improve the signal qualities, or interface with control/computer electronics.

- MEMS technology can realize two or three-dimensional features with small dimensions and precision that cannot be reproducibly, efficiently or profitably made with traditional machining tools.

- Sensors and actuators are commonly the interface between an engineering system and the physical world.

- MEMS technology enables revolutionary sensors and actuators. Sensors are devices that detect and monitor physical or chemical phenomenon, whereas actuators are ones that produce mechanical motion, force or torque.

- The package serves to integrate all of the components required for a system application in a manner that minimizes size, cost, mass and complexity.

- A normal stress can be tensile or compressive.

- Thin film stress refers to an assortment of structural imperfections that result in the degradation or failure of microscopic layers of optical or conductive material.

EXERCISE

1. Define micro-electromechanical system (MEMS).

2. What are the intrinsic characteristics of MEMS? Explain.

3. What are sensors and actuators? Also discuss the families of MEMS actuators mainly consist of.

4. Describe the applications of MEMS in industry. Also elaborate the types of MEMS packages.

5. Illustrate the types of stress and strain.

MEMS BASED SENSORS AND ACTUATORS

5.1 INTRODUCTION

- Microelectromechanical Systems (MEMS) Sensors and actuators are two dynamic components of every closed loop control system. This type of system is also known as a mechatronics system.

- A typical mechatronics system contains a sensing unit, a controller and an actuating unit. A sensing unit can be as modest as a single sensor or can comprise additional components like as filters, amplifiers, modulators, and other signal conditioners.

- The controller makes decisions based on the control algorithm taking the information from the sensing unit and outputs commands to the actuating unit.

- The actuating unit contains an actuator and additionally a power supply and a coupling mechanism.

- A Micro Electromechanical System (MEMS) refers to a collection of micro sensors and actuators that can sense its environment and is has the ability to react to the changes occurred in that environment with the use of a micro circuit control.

- The conventional microelectronics packaging has an integrating antenna structures for command signals in to micro electromechanical structures for desired sensing and actuating functions.

- The system may also require micro power supply, micro relay and micro signal processing units. Micro components make the system quicker, more consistent, economical, and capable of incorporating more complex functions.

- The utility of the development of integrated circuit (IC) fabrication processes, in which sensors, actuators, and control functions are fabricated in silicon. Since then, remarkable research progresses have been achieved in MEMS under the strong capital promotions from both government and industries. As well as the commercialization of some less integrated MEMS devices, such as micro accelerometers, inkjet printer head, micro mirrors for projection. It has more feasibility and more complex.

- MEMS devices have been offered and validated for the applications in various fields such as micro fluid, aerospace, biomedical, chemical analysis, wireless communications, data storage, display and optics as shown in Fig. 5.1.

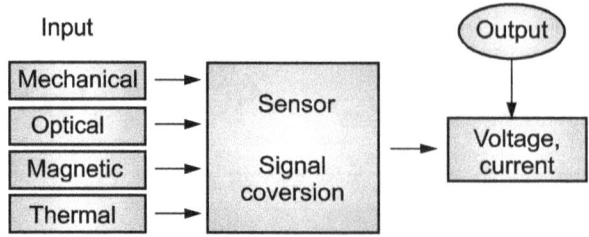

Fig. 5.1: MEMS block diagram

- Micro assembly and micro manipulation are commonly applied in numerous fields. Such as Micro gripper in the applications it acts as a chief element for handling objects for instance living cells and micro mechanical parts.

- In contrast Micro Electromechanical Systems (MEMS) technology permits the development of miniature devices just about millimeter, which allows the achievement of compact size, low cost and high resonant frequency.

- During the past two decades as the growth of interests in micro robotic systems increased, MEMS-based micro grippers with several types of actuators and sensors have been anticipated for more applications.

- Owing to different properties of actuators, the MEMS micro grippers exhibit diverse performances dedicated to various applications.

- For example, electrostatic actuation micro gripper can provide a large displacement with no hysteresis in a low operating temperature along with a simple structure. Specifically, two dissimilar kinds of movement configuration inter ms of lateral comb drive and transverse comb drive can fulfill the objective of high precision and large movement, respectively.

- Electro thermal actuator can generate a large output force and displacements by making use of its thermal expansion with a small voltage applied. The large force output, precision displacement and rapid response are the attractive points of the piezoelectric actuator. Also, electromagnetic actuator and pneumatic actuator driven micro gripper scan deliver are actively large output force and displacement.

- Mean while MEMS technology provides the solution to these challenges, it expected to play an increasingly important role in this sector. The industrial automation are wafer the opportunities to MEMS developers and providers to create and provide higher value MEMS-based sensors and actuating devices that could command a higher price compared to MEMS devices used in more price- sensitive, higher- volume applications.

5.2 ELECTROSTATIC SENSORS AND ACTUATORS

- Electrostatics refers to the study of electromagnetic phenomena that take place when there are no moving charges for instance, after a static equilibrium has been established. Charges reach their equilibrium positions rapidly because the electric force is extremely strong.

- The mathematical methods of electrostatics make it possible to calculate the distribution soft electric field and of the electric potential from a known configuration of charges, conductors, and insulators. Conversely, given a set of conductors with known potentials, it is possible to calculate electric fields in regions between the conductors and to determine the charge distribution on the surface of the conductors.

- The electric energy of a set of charges at rest can be viewed from the stand point of the work required to assemble the charges; alternatively, the energy also can be considered to reside in the electric field produced by this assembly of charges.

- Finally, energy can best or Edina capacitor; the energy required to charge such as device is stored in it as electrostatic energy of the electric field. Sensing characteristics are very important for electrostatic sensors. Optimal sensor designs are the key to obtaining better sensing characteristics.

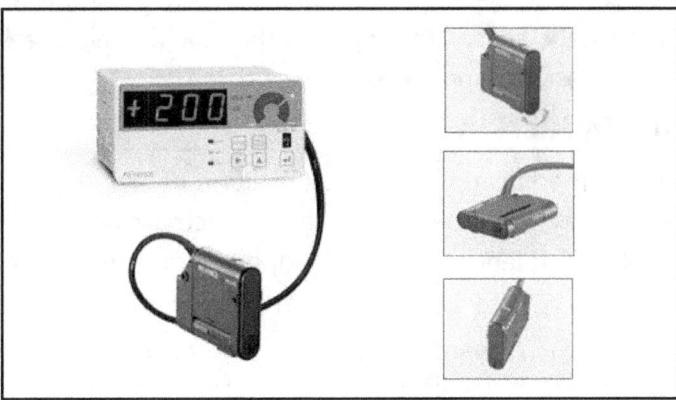

Fig. 5.2: Optimal sensors

For the sensor design, two important key points are given as follows:

- First, intrusive sensors have high spatial sensitivity, but they affect the gas flow. This contradiction raises difficult ties in the sensor design process. Generally trade off needs to be make between the spatial sensitivity and the gas flow disturbance. In order to achieve that, accurate sensor models have to be built.

- Second, while using these models to make optimal designs, analytical solutions are always difficult to obtain because of their irregular Dirichlet boundaries. Therefore, current designs of rod shaped sensors and intrusive round head screw shaped sensors always use Finite Element Modeling (FEM) methods.

- Electrostatic sensors have been widely used in many applications due to their some advantages like low cost and robustness. Their spatial sensitivity and time frequency characteristics are two performance parameters. (1) Around electric filed object, an electric field that is proportional in strength to the amount of charge is produced. (2) Electrostatic sensors detect the intensity of electric field and calculate the select potential. When a detection electrode is brought close to an electrified body, an electric charge that is proportional to the intensity of the electric field is induced in the detection electrode due to "electrostatic induction". The electrostatic sensor opens and closes a tuning for vibrating plate called a chopper in front of the detection electrode in order to cancel out DC noise and perform higher precision measurement. The sensor detects the intensity of the electric field by receiving the induced electric charge as a communication signal.

- Electric potential is proportional to the intensity of the electric field, but the intensity of the electric field gets smaller as it gets further away from an electrified object. Therefore, the electrostatic sensor sets a distance between the electrified object and the sensor using a controller and a corrected calculation of the electric potential is performed. Since an electric field relies on the measurement distance, you need to fix the sensor at a set distance in order toper form a high precision measurement. The electric field that is produced by an electrified object spreads concentrically out from the electrified object. Therefore, the electrostatic sensor that detects the electric field measures a wider range as them measurement distance increases.

5.2.1 Electrostatic Induction

- Electrostatic induction modification in the distribution of electric charge on one material under the influence of nearby objects that have electric charge. Electrostatic induction machines, also called influence machines, operate on the principle of charge by induction.

- The electric force between charged particles that constitute materials, a negatively charged object brought near an electrically neutral object induces a positive charge on the near side and a negative charge on the far side of the neutral object.

- The neutral object may become charged positively by induction, if its negative part is grounded momentarily to permit the negative charge to escape. Electrostatic induction occurs whenever any object is placed in an electric field.

- This process, a charged object can impart an opposite charge to another object simply by being placed near the second object.

- This process is coupled with some type of mechanical operation, like a rotating disk of glass, to continually adding of charge to the storage object.

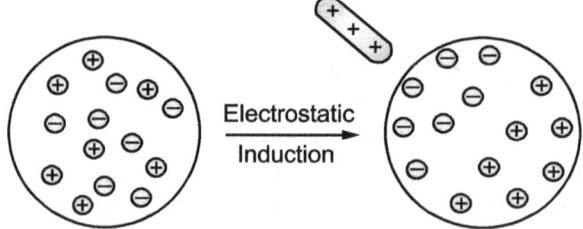

Fig. 5.3: Disk electrostatic induction

5.2.2 Electrostatic Actuators

Any electric charge creates around it an electric field. Any electric field applies a force to any charged particle. This principle, widely known since Maxwell's era, has not been so much used during the past decades, but MEMS have a high interest in using electrostatic actuators: The main problem of electrostatic effect is that it decreases with the square of the distance between the two charged bodies. In microscopic scale, this is a huge advantage, because most of the structures have a very low aspect ratio (*i.e.* width and length are large before thickness and gap in z direction), so the distance between bodies is really very small. Electrostatics is the most widely used force in the design of MEMS. In industry, it is used in microresonators, switches, micromirrors, accelerometers, etc. Almost every kind of microactuator has one or more electrostatic actuation based version.

Pros and cons

Electrostatic force depends largely on the size of the structures and the distance between electrodes. So, for large electrode surface compared to distance to travel, electrostatic actuation has a large advantage. But the equation of the force gives a dependency to the square of the distance. This means that the longer the distance is, the higher the actuation voltage is. This is one of the main problem with this physics principle: actuation voltage are often quite high, easily reaching tens, and even hundreds of volts to be used. High voltages are easy to get on a large device, but not on a very compact integrated system. An interesting point is the fact that the electric circuit is capacitive, meaning the power consumption is very low, despite of any high voltage. Very few current is needed to load the capacity formed by electrodes.

Another consideration to take care of is the electric field itself: the nature of the material between electrodes: water, for example, is conductive at low frequencies, so electrostatic actuation cannot be used in these conditions. Void and neutral gases are the best environments.

Finally, the hysteresis behaviour of straight actuators can be as well an advantage and a problem, depending on the application. It reduces sensitivity of devices to electrical noise, but it also means larger voltage variation for a complete actuation cycle when pull-in/pull-out is desired.

This example shows an electrostatic actuator in which one plate is electrostatically attracted toward another. You can consider this an electrostatic tunable capacitor if you wish, since some of them use the same principle. But remember real systems are often more complicated!

Electrostatic Actuation Systems

- Straight actuation
- Comb-drives actuators
- Microresonators

Straight actuation

By straight actuation, i.e. actuation between two electrodes in which the mobile parts moves along the electric field paths. This is the most simple actuation technique you can imagine, though the architectures used are often not so simple to optimize it.

The tunable capacitor is an example of straight actuation. But there are others. Microswitches devices make a large use of electrostatic actuation, depending on the characteristics required for the device. Micromirrors devices are almost all based on electrostatic force.

In a straight actuation, the exact movement of the mobile parts is ruled by the electric field path and the mechanical constrains of the structure. So, tunable capacitor will translate along a straight line, micromirrors will rotate around their anchor axis, etc. The actuation is not always really straight, but it is as well as possible. This technique is probably the most efficient in terms of forces, and so required voltage.

The straight actuation is the one in which pull-in/pull-out hysteresis cycle can be met.

Comb-Drive Actuators

Another widely used architecture for electrostatic actuation is a lateral translation of the mobile parts. This is mostly achieved with *comb-drive actuators*

In this configuration, the force is equally and symmetrically applied on both side of beams, and the mobile part moves along the beams direction.

The total displacement is rather shorter than what is possible in straight actuation, but the force is constant, meaning an easier control of the displacement. This kind of system offers a very high precision level, and a simpler electronic control. Systems like microaccelerometers make high use of comb-drive.

In theory, comb-drive would require higher voltage than straight actuation because of the electric-field direction being different than displacement one. But most of the time, theses structures are geometrically optimized, so the gap between electrodes and the distance to travel are also shorter.

In a comb-drive, there is no pull-in effect, unless a design error make electrodes reach each others. The displacement is linear, contrary to straight actuation. But the design is limited by the needs to place electrodes beams opposite to each other. Designer must also take care of the end stop to avoid contact between mobile part and fixed part, and to keep forces quite symmetric so that the direction of the displacement is kept as planned.

Microresonators

Microresonators are structures not planned to be displaced, but, as their name tells, to vibrate. They're planned to replace electronic resonators, being used in electronic filter systems, so select a particular frequency chosen amongst several ones. This is highly used in telecommunications. For example, in mobile phone communication: each telephone uses a precise frequency included in a range depending on the protocol. The filter must keep only the chosen frequency, so that you're not disturbed by other people conversations during your own calls!

All mechanical systems have specific resonance frequencies. Most of time, only the first one are useful. Think of it as guitar cords: if you stimulate it, it is, from a frequency point of view, as if you were applying a signal containing all frequencies at once on the cord, but only one note comes out: it is the *eigen frequency* of the cord.

So, microresonators use mechanical vibrating parts to filter signals so that only one frequency, the eigen frequency of the structure, is kept. The application is for electronic signal treatment, so, there must be a way to convert electrical signal into mechanical stimulation, and then back again mechanical vibration into electrical signal. This way is the electrostatic principle.

The top schematics is always the same: the vibrating part includes as well the electrode for stimulation, and the electrode for measurement. Then, a lot of architectures are under studies in research laboratories, including different shapes and electrodes configuration for mechanical and electrical parts.

The vibration is made by the incoming electrical signal. Then, the amplitude of the vibration depends on how close the input frequency is to the eigen value. On the output, a *polarization* (constant voltage) between the resonator and the output electrode allows the measurement of the amplitude of vibration. Since the amplitude difference obtained between the eigen frequency and other ones is very high, the electrical output signal for any non-selected frequency is considered as neglectible, while the eigen frequency signal is kept. Note that this is a quite simple explanation of the behaviour of the system. In real development a lots of parameters are taken in account.

The photos show microresonators architecture vibrating in the range of tens of MHz, that corresponds to *Intermediate Frequencies* (IF). Intermediate frequencies are a convenient way of treating a signal between low frequency (ex: human voice frequency) and really high frequencies (at which mobile phones communicate). The distance between mobile parts and fixed parts here is about 60 nm.

Micro resonators should enter the market quite soon from now. They will replace electronic devices, especially in mobile devices, and allow greater autonomy and more integrated functions thanks to the save of space and power consumption.

Actuation in MEMS is commonly achieved through electrostatic devices known as comb drive actuators. Two sets of inter digitized electrodes are manufactured through bulk or surface micro machining techniques, one of which is released from the substrate, and in-plane actuation is achieved through the application of alternately similar and opposing polarity voltages to the two combs. Out of plane motion, termed as electrostatic levitation, is also possible by wiring up the device in a different fashion with appositive voltage applied to the stationary comb drive, and all other parts of the device grounded. The generated vertical force is amount come of presence of the substrate beneath the electrodes, which creates an asymmetry in the electric field between the top and bottom of the comb drive.

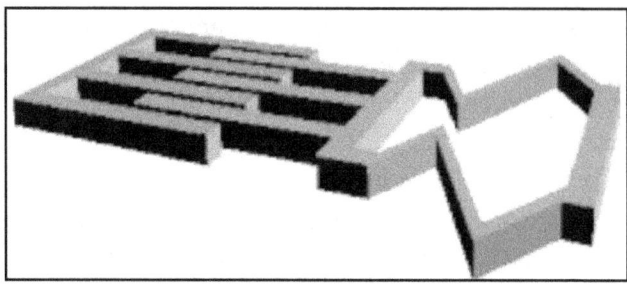
Fig. 5.4: Comb drive

- To move or control mechanical components, actuators frequently use an energy source. They are commonly used in motors and various machines.

- Mechanical devices have been miniaturized over the years, but this process normally entails the individual components to be much smaller as well.

- The calibration of micro phones using an electrostatic actuator is applied to laboratory method for determination of frequency response characteristics of measurement microphones. The actuator produces an electrostatic force which simulates sound pressure acting on the microphone diaphragm.

- In other way compare to sound based methods, the actuator method has a great advantage it provides a simpler means of producing a well defined calibration pressure over a wide frequency range without the special facilities of an acoustics laboratory.

- The actuator method cannot be used for micro phone sensitivity, as it absolute accuracy is not sufficiently high. Therefore, an actuator frequency response calibration is combined with an absolute sensitivity calibration reference frequency. This can be performed using a piston phone and a sound level calibrator.

- Electrostatic actuation practice electrostatic force using by the potential difference between a micro actuator and its electrode. When Electrode is applied voltage and then increases electrostatic force results in more displacement. Generally, both DC bias and AC signal are used to displace a micro actuator at the same time. While the dynamics of a micro actuator can be linearized within small displacement, an electrostatic micro actuator is inherently non-linear and making it is more difficult for feedback control to be implemented while achieving a large displacement.

- Although electrostatic actuation requires higher actuation voltage than that of other actuation methods, electrostatic actuation does not require complicated fabrication methods, piezoelectric materials or ferromagnetic materials deposited on a micro actuator.

- In most cases electrostatic actuators need very small current, depending on the size and geometry of micro actuators.

- The limited operation range due to the effect of in pull and non-linear behavior in response to applied voltage and high actuation voltage and electrostatic actuation is one of the most popular actuation methods because of its low power consumption and fast response time (less than 0.1 ms) and the easiness of integration and testing with electrical control circuitry

- Electrostatic actuators depend on the force between two conducting electrodes when a voltage is parametric between them. The arrangement of the electrodes is dependent on several types of actuators.

- The electrode arrangement and if there exists mutual capacitance and there will also be an attractive force when a voltage is applied between the electrodes.

- Electrostatic forces are a favorite for surface micro machined structures. This stems in part from ease of implementation and in part from favorable scaling laws for electrostatic forces.

- Electrostatic forces are surface forces, hence their favorable scaling. Further, extremely large electric field scan be created with modest voltage because of the small distances involved.

- The gaps between components and large electric fields are easily realizable. One of the main disadvantages of electrostatic actuators is the large voltages necessary. Voltages of several hundred volts are not uncommon.

- This high-voltage electronics requires for control and is a barrier to integration with standard electronics.

- Miniaturization in the 21st has advanced to the point that micro actuators and other parts are so small that powerful microscopes often have to be used to see them.

- Industrial processes such as lithography and micro machining are used to make a micro actuator and there are numerous types that can be made also. An electrostatic micro actuator is one common variety, but scientist can also build electromagnetic varieties that can produce more power to energize a device like a motor.

- This method typically used for making integrated circuits. Motors as small as about 0.04 inches (1 millimeter) across have been made and have often been used by researchers to insert tiny catheters into biological cells.

- There is also a piezoelectric micro actuator with composite materials that react similar to crystals, which when pushed on and create an electrical voltage. Thin film scan be deposited onto silicon that can produce motion over very short distances.

- Ultrasonic micro actuators are frequently used in small motors built into piezoelectric devices. These can be integrated into auto focus mechanisms of small cameras.

- Moving mechanical constituent can be built on a small scale, but an electrostatic micro actuator is normally made of a material that bends on the basis of electrical charges.

- Motion is generally microscopic in scale and a small amount of force is produced. Some rotational motors and linear motion comb drives have been developed based on this principle. Micro actuator scan be used to build tiny mirrors for displays and projectors.

- Microscopic current transmits and small mechanisms to control hard drive soften make use of such miniature devices. They are often called Micro Electromechanical Systems (MEMS) and a category which include many kinds of miniature moving parts. Production of micro actuator scan is accomplished by etching parts into silicone. Lithography is often used for making circuits.

- Lights and chemicals and a layer composed of the parts to be added are typically combined in this process. The finished product is usually produced in layers and while micro machining often involves lasers and scanning electron microscopes for example, top lace individual atoms and cells.

Applications of Actuators

- A vertical levitation electrostatic comb drive actuator was manufactured for the purpose of measuring the properties of small scale piezoelectric.

- The force measured by the sensors is affected by the relative height of the central plate in the device and the substrate an increase in force is observed by pushing the probe tip of the sensor into the MEMS device.

- There are a number of studies already using FEA to model the levitation effect in comb drive actuators and however these have focused on the electric field generated in poly silicon films ~2 μm thick, with the aim of reducing the levitation in order to minimize the effects on in plane motion.

- In these devices, the comb structure were manufactured from 20 μm electroplated Ni, with a large (25 μm) trench created beneath the released structure through chemical wet etching.

- Not only is the geometry therefore different to that studied before, it is possible for to study the effect of 'negative' levitation for the first time.

5.2.3 Electrostatic Type Instruments Construction Principle Torque Equation

The electrostatic type instruments practice the static electrical field to produce the deflecting torque. These types of instrument are generally used for the measurement of high voltages but in some cases they can be used in measuring the lower voltages and powers of a given circuit. Now there are two possible ways in which the electrostatic force can act.

The two possible conditions are as follows:

- When one of the plates is fixed and other plate is free to move and plates are oppositely charged in order to have attractive force between them. Now due this attractive force movable plate will move towards the stationary or fixed plate till the moving plate stored maximum electrostatic energy.

- In other way there may be force of attraction or repulsion or both and due to some rotary of plate.

Force and Torque Equation of Electrostatic Type Instrument

To derive force equation for the linear electrostatic type instruments and let us consider two plates as illustrated in the given Fig. 5.5.

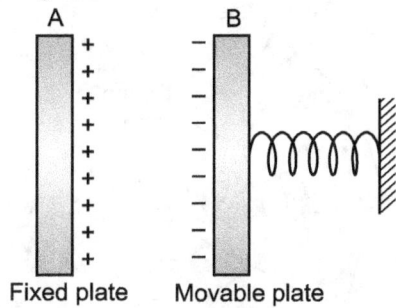

Fig. 5.5: Two plates electrostatic

When plate A is positively charged and then plate B is negatively charged. As mentioned above as per the possible condition, we have linear motion between the plates. The plate A is fixed and plate B is free to move. Consider exist some force F between the two plates at equilibrium when electrostatic force becomes equal to spring force. At this case the electrostatic energy stored in the plates is,

$$\frac{1}{2} CV^2$$

Now suppose we increase the applied voltage by an amount dV, due to this the plate B moves towards the plate A by a distanced x. The work done against the spring force due to displacement of the plate B is F dx. The applied voltage is related to current as

$$i = C\frac{dV}{dt} + V\frac{dV}{dt}$$

From this value of electric current them in put energy can be calculate d as

$$V_{idt} = V^2dC + CV\, dV$$

From this we can calculate the change in the stored energy and that comes out to be

$$\frac{1}{2}V^2dC + CDdV$$

By neglecting the higher order terms that appears in the expression. Now applying the principle of energy conservation we have input energy to the system = increase in the stored energy of the system + mechanical work done by the system. From this we can write,

$$V^2dC + CVdV = \frac{1}{2}V^2dC + CVdV + Fdx$$

From the above equation the force can be calculated as

$$V = \frac{1}{2} V^2 \frac{dC}{dx}$$ ...(5.1)

Now let us derive force and torque equation for the rotary electrostatic type instruments.

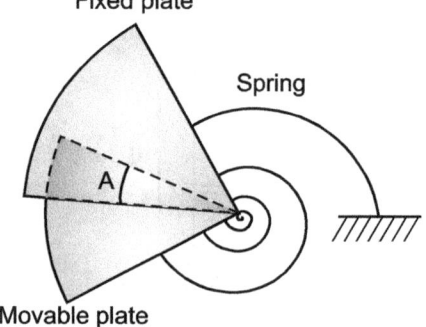

Fig. 5.6: Rotary electrostatic instrument

The expression for deflecting torque incase of rotary type electrostatic instruments, just replace the in the equation (5.1) F by Td and dx by dA. Now rewriting the modified equation we have deflecting torque is equals to

$$T_d = \frac{1}{2} V^2 \frac{dV}{dA}$$

Now at steady state we have controlling torque is given by the expression $T_c = K*A$. The deflection A can be written as,

$$A = \frac{1}{2} V^2 \frac{dV}{K \cdot dA}$$

From deflection of the pointer is directly proportional to the square of the voltage to be measured hence the scale will be non-uniform. Let us now discuss about Quadrant electrometer. This instrument is generally used in measuring the voltage ranging from 100 V to 20 kilovolts. A gain the deflecting torque obtained in the Quadrant electrometer is directly proportional to the square of the applied voltage; one advantage of this is instrument can used to measure both the ac and dc voltages. One advantage of using the electrostatic type instruments as volt meters is that we can extend the range of voltage to be measured. Now there are two ways of extending the range of this instrument.

By using resistance potential is as shown in the following Fig. 5.7.

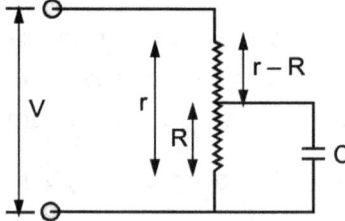

Fig. 5.7: Resistance potential

To measure voltage is applied across the total resistance and the electrostatic capacitor is connected across the portion of the total resistance which is marked as the applied voltage is DC, then we should make one assumption that the capacitor which is connected to having infinite leakage resistance. In this case the multiplying factor is given by the ratio of resistance/R. The AC operation on this circuit can also be analyzed easily a gain in case of AC operation we multiplying factor equal to r/R.

By using capacitor multiplier technique: We can increase the range of voltage to be measured by placing a series of capacitors as shown in the given Fig. 5.8.

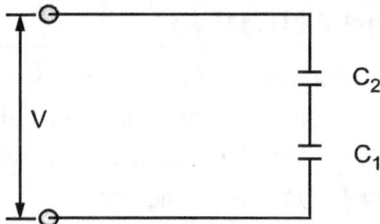

Fig. 5.8: Series capacitors using capacitor multiplier

The expression for multiplying factor for the circuit Fig : 5.8 Let us mark the capacitance of the voltmeter be C_1 and series capacitor be C_2 as shown in the Fig. 5.8. Now the series combination of these capacitor be equal to

$$C = \frac{C_1 C_2}{C_1 + C_2}$$

The total capacitance of the circuit is the impedance of the voltmeter is equal to $Z_1 = 1/j\omega C_1$ and thus total impedance will be equal to

$$Z = \frac{C_1 + C_2}{j\omega C_1 C_2}$$

Now the multiplying factor can be defined as the ratio of Z/Z1 which is equal to $1 + C_2/C_1$. Likewise the multiplying factor can also be calculated. Hence by this way we can increase the range of voltage to be measure.

Advantages of Electrostatic Type Instruments

Now we look at some advantages of electrostatic type instruments. These are given as follows:

- The first and the most important advantage is that we can measure both ac and dc voltage and the reason are very obvious the deflecting torque is directly proportional to the square of the voltage.

- Power consumption is quite low in these types of instruments as the current drawn by these instruments is quite low.

- We can measure high value of voltage.

Disadvantages of Electrostatic Type Instruments

As opposed to various advantages, electrostatic instrument have few disadvantages and these are written as follows:

- These are quite costly as compared to other instruments and also these have large size.
- The scale is not uniform.
- The various operating forces involved are small in magnitude.

5.2.4 Thermal Sensing and Actuation

A **MEMS thermal actuator** is a micromechanical device that typically generates motion by thermal expansion amplification. A small amount of thermal expansion of one part of the device translates to a large amount of deflection of the overall device. Usually fabricated out of doped Single Crystal Silicon or Polysilicon as acomplex compliant member, the increase in temperature can be achieved internally by electrical resistive heating or externally by a heat source capable of locally introducing heat. Microfabricated thermal actuators can be integrated into micromotors

- The conversion of a signal or other physical variable and from one form to another usually into a form that can be utilized more efficiently by the system that organizes the sensor.
- A sensor is termed as a transducer; i.e. it translates a physical signal from that cannot be read by the process and to one which allows to be interrogated successfully.

Fig. 5.9: Thermal sensing

- Now a day, many are equipped with more electronic systems than in the past. Today, vehicles are equipped with hundreds of miniature sensing systems, such as temperature, tire pressure, accelerometer and speed sensors.
- Actuators are also installed as components of advanced systems for optimized braking and assisted steering and although the market for really intervening systems is not mature yet.

The sensors are grouped into three different categories:

- General in-vehicle sensors
- Perception sensors
- Virtual sensors

Most of the general in-vehicle sensors are already available in the automotive market in the majority of commercial cars. On the other hand, the market penetration rate of perception sensors and except for ultrasonic sensors is very low mainly because of their cost.

5.2.4.1 Thermocouple

A Thermocouple is a sensor used to measure temperature and comprised of at least two metals joined together to form two junctions.

- One is connected to the body and temperature is to be measured; this is the hot or measuring junction.
- The other junction is connected to a body is known as temperature; this is the cold or reference junction.

The thermocouple measures unknown temperature of the body with reference to the known as temperature of the other body. There are many types of thermocouples, each with its own unique characteristics interims of temperature range, durability, vibration resistance, chemical resistance, and application compatibility. Type J, K, T, and E are "Base Metal" thermocouples and Type R, S, and B thermocouples are "Noble Metal" thermocouple are used in high temperature applications, industrial, scientific, and OEM applications.

They can be found in nearly all industrial markets like as:

- Power Generation
- Oil/Gas
- Pharmaceutical
- Biotech
- Cement
- Paper and Pulp

Thermocouples are also used in every day appliances like stoves, furnaces, and toasters.

Working Principle of Thermocouple

The working principle of thermocouple is divided into a three effects such as follows:

- Seebeck
- Peltier
- Thomson
- **Seebeck Effect:** The Seebeck effect states that when two different metals are joined together at two junctions, an electromotive force (emf) is generated at the two junctions. The amount of emf generated is different for different combinations of the metals.

- **Peltier Effect:** As per the Peltier effect, when two dissimilar metals are joined to get here to form two junctions and the emf is generated within the circuit due to the different temperatures of the two junctions of the circuit.
- **Thomson Effect:** As per the Thomson effect, when two unlike metals are joined together forming two junctions and the potential exists within the circuit due to temperature gradient along the entire length of the conductors within the circuit.

In most of the cases the emf suggested by the Thomson effect is very small and it can be neglected by making proper selection of the metals. The Peltier effect plays a prominent role in the working principle of the thermocouple.

The Operating Principle

- A thermocouple is a device made by two different wires joined at one end, called junction end or measuring end.
- The two wires are called as thermo elements or legs of the thermocouple: the two thermo elements are distinguished as positive and negative ones.
- The junction end is immersed in the environment whose temperature T_2 has to be measured, which can be for instance the temperature of a furnace at about 500°C, while the tail end is held at a different temperature T_1, e.g. at ambient temperature.
- The thermocouple cannot be formed if there are not two junctions. Since the two junctions are maintained at different temperatures the Peltier emf is generated within the circuit and it is the function of the temperatures of two junctions.
- If the temperature of both the junctions is same then the equal and opposite emf will be generated at both junctions and the net current flowing through the junction is zero.
- If the junctions are maintained at different temperatures, the emf's will not becomes zero and there will be a net current flowing through the circuit.
- The total emf flowing through this circuit depends on the metals used within the circuit as well as the temperature of the two junctions.
- The total emf or the current flowing through the circuit can be measured easily by the suitable device is as shown in Fig.5.10.

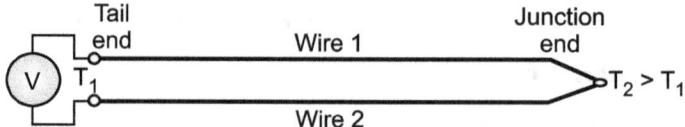

Fig. 5.10 : Schematic drawing of a thermocouple

The temperature difference between junction end and tail end a voltage difference can be measured between two thermo elements at the tail end: so the thermocouple is a temperature voltage transducer.

$$Emf = \int_{T_1}^{T_2} S_{12} \cdot dT = \int_{T_1}^{T_2} (S_1 - S_2) \cdot dT \qquad \ldots(5.2)$$

The Electro Motive Force or Voltage produced by the thermocouple at the tail end, T_1 and T_2 are the temperatures of reference and measuring end respectively, S_{12} is called Seebeck coefficient of the thermocouple and S_1 and S_2 are the Seebeck coefficient of the two thermo elements; the Seebeck coefficient depends on the material. As given equation (5.1)

A null voltage is measured if the two thermo elements are made of the same materials: different materials are needed to make a temperature sensing device.

A null voltage is measured if no temperature difference exists between the tail end and the junction end: a temperature difference is needed to operate the thermocouple,

When a temperature difference is applied between the two ends of a single Ni wire a voltage drop is developed across the wire itself. The end of the wire at the highest temperature, T_2, is called hot end, while the end at the lowest temperature, T_1, is called cold end.

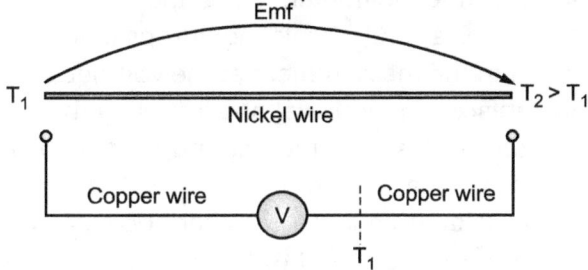

Fig. 5.11 : Emf produced by a single wire

- When a voltmeter, with Cu connection wires, is used to measure the voltage drop across the Ni wire and two junctions need to be made at the hot and cold ends between the Cu wire and the Ni wire; assuming that the voltmeter is at room temperature T_1, one of the Cu wires of the voltmeter will experience along it the same temperature drop from T_2 to T_1 the Ni wire is experiencing. In the attempt to measure the voltage drop on the Ni wire a Ni Cu thermocouple has been made and so the measured voltage is in reality the voltage drop along the Ni wire plus the voltage drop along the Cu wire.

- The Emf along a single thermo element cannot be measured: the Emf measured at the tail end in Fig. 5.11 is the sum of the voltage drop along each of the thermo elements. As two thermo elements are needed, the temperature measurement with thermocouple' is a differential measurement.

- The temperature measurement with thermocouples is also a differential measurement because two different temperatures, T_1 and T_2, are involved. The desired temperature is the one at the junction end, T_2. In order to have a useful transducer for measurement, a monotonic Emf versus junction end temperature T_2 relationship is needed, so that for each temperature at the junction end a unique voltage is produced at the tail end.

- However, from the integral in Equation (5.12) it can be understood that the Emf depends on both T_1 and T_2: as T_1 and T_2 can change independently, a monotonic Emf vs T_2 relationship can not be defined if the tail end temperature is not constant.

- The tail end is maintained in an ice bath made by crushed ice and water in a Dewar flask: this produces a reference temperature of 0°C. All the voltage versus temperature relationships for thermocouples is referenced to 0°C.

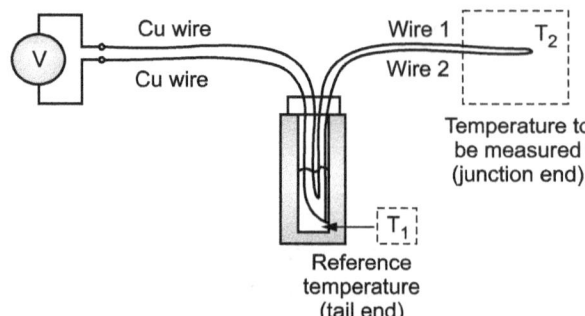

Fig. 5.12 : A measuring system for thermocouples

- So as to measure the voltage at the tail end, two copper wires are connected between the thermo elements and the voltmeter: both the Cu wires experience the same temperature difference and as a result the voltage drops along each of them are equal to each other and cancel out in the measurement at the voltmeter.

- The ice bath is usually replaced in industrial application with an integrated circuit called cold junction compensator: in this case the tail end is at ambient temperature and the temperature fluctuations at the tail end are tolerated; in fact the cold junction compensator produces a voltage equal to the thermocouple voltage between 0°C and ambient temperature, which can be added to the voltage of the thermocouple at the tail end to reproduce the voltage versus temperature relationship of the thermocouple.

- The cold junction compensation cannot reproduce exactly the voltage versus temperature relationship of the thermocouple, but can only approximate it: for this reason the cold junction compensation introduces an error in the temperature measurement.

- Fig. 5.13 show the filtering and amplification of the thermocouple. Being the thermocouple voltage a DC signal and removal of AC noise through filtering is beneficial; furthermore the thermocouples produce voltage of few tens of V and forth are reason amplification is required.

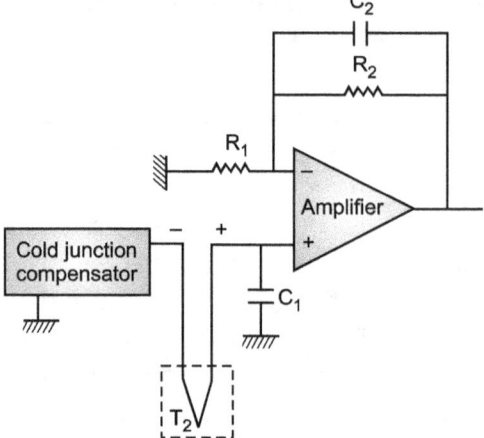

Fig. 5.13 : An example of cold junction compensation

- Type R, Sand B thermocouples use Pt base thermo elements and they can operate at temperature up to 1700 °C; however they are more expensive and their voltage output is lower than type K and type N thermocouples, which use Ni base thermo elements. However, Ni base thermocouples can operate at lower temperatures than the Pt base ones.

SOLVED EXAMPLE

Example 5.1 : The output voltage of a particular thermocouple sensor is registered to be 42.3 mV at temperature 105 °C. It had previously been set to emit a zero voltage at 0 °C. Since an output/input relationship exists between the two temperatures, determine:

(a) The transfer function of the thermocouple

(b) The temperature corresponding to a voltage output of 15.8 mV.

Solution

(a) We know that $S = C + ms$

Where S is the output signal; s is the stimulus; C is the output value at a stimulus value of zero; and the constant of proportionality between s and S.

Therefore: 42.3 mV $= 0 + m (105 °C) = m (105 °C)$

Or $m = 0.4028571429$

$\rightarrow$ $S = 0.4028571429(s)$

(b) Using the relationship from $(S = 0.4028571429(s))$ above, were place S with the voltage output given, i.e. 15.8 mV.

$\rightarrow$ 15.8 mV $= 0.4028571429(s)$

$\rightarrow$ $\dfrac{15.8}{0.4028571429} = S$

$\rightarrow$ $S = 39.22°C$

5.2.4.2 Bimorph

- When two piezoelectric crystals cemented together so that an applied voltage cause so net expands and the other to contract, converting electrical signals into mechanical energy.

- An Instrument used in the calibration procedure and the corresponding output data were further analyzed to determine the static and dynamic characteristics of the piezoelectric bimorph.

- The piezoelectric bimorph showed appropriate static operating range, repeatability, hysteresis, and frequency response for application in lower prosthesis, with a force range of 0 to 100 N.

- To further valid at this finding, an experiment was conducted with a single transfer moral amputee subject to measure the stump/socket pressure using the piezoelectric bimorph embedded inside the socket.

- The results showed that a maximum interface pressure of about 27 kP occurred at the anterior proximal site compared to the anterior distal and posterior sites, consistent with values.

The applications of the bimorph are given as follows:

- Oil exploration
- Machine and equipment monitoring
- Automotive engines
- Feedback sensors
- High temperature accelerometers
- Rate and gyroscope sensors
- Intrusion alarms

These bimorphs are also frequently used as actuators in fine micro manipulation mechanisms such as computer hard drive indexing and aerospace valves.

Bimorph Characteristics

In order to assess the overall characteristics of the piezoelectric bimorph and a calibration procedure was conducted to estimate the static and dynamic behavior of the piezoelectric bimorph. The piezoelectric bimorph consists of two layers:

- Sandwiched by brass layer and
- Sandwiched with supporting layer

A series of input signals were applied to the input of piezoelectric bimorph and its corresponding outputs were recorded. In the current approach, static and dynamic calibrations were performed on the piezoelectric bimorph. The machine consists of two lower and upper heads, while the bimorph was fixed on the lower head with the force exerted from the upper head. The purpose of the bimorph calibration is to set the static and dynamic behavior of the bimorph that is used in development and fabrication of the active amputee's socket. The calibration procedure was conducted by applying specific loads to the piezoelectric bimorph in both static and cyclic form to mimic the real situation of pressure dynamics inside the socket.

5.2.4.3 Resistive

- The electrical resistivity of a material is also known as its specific electrical resistance. It is a measure of how strongly a material opposes the flow of electric current. It is used for the specified temperature.

- It is define the resistivity of a substance as the resistance of a cube of that substance having edges of unit length, with the understanding that the current flows normal to opposite faces and is distributed uniformly over them. The SI unit for electrical resistivity is the ohm meter.

- Electrical resistance of a conductor of unit cross sectional area and unit length. A characteristic property of each material and resistivity is useful in comparing various materials on the basis of their ability to conduct electric currents.

- High resistivity design at poor conductors. Resistivity, commonly symbolized by the Greek letter rho, ρ, is quantitatively equal to the resistance R of a specimen such as a wire, multiplied by it is cross sectional area A, and divided by its length; $\rho = RA/l$.

- The unit of resistance is the ohm. In the meter kilogram second (mks) system, the ratio of are an in square meter stolen thin meters simplifies to just meters. Thus, in the meter-kilogram-second system, the unit of resistivity is ohm-meter. If lengths are measured in centimeters then the resistivity may be expressed in units of ohm centimeter.

- The resistivity of an exceedingly good electrical conductor, such as hard drawn copper, at 20 °C (68 °F) is 1.77×10^{-8} ohm meter, or 1.77×10^{-6} ohm-centimeter. At the other extreme, electrical insulators have resistivity in the range 10^{12} to 10^{20} ohm-meters. The value of resistivity depends also on the temperature of the material; tabulations of resistivity usually list values at 20°C.

- Resistivity of metal lid conductors generally increases with a rise in temperature; but resistivity of semiconductor such as carbon and silicon and generally decreases with temperature rise.

- Conductivity is the reciprocal of resistivity and it, too, characterizes materials on the basis of how well electric current flows in them.

- The meter-kilogram second unit of conductivity is ampere meter, or amperes per volt-meter.

- Good electrical conductors have high conductivities and low resistivity. Good insulators, or dielectrics, have high resistivity and low conductivities. Semiconductors have intermediate values of both.

5.2.4.4 Thermal Actuation

- Thermal actuators are non-electric motors that produce linear motion upon temperature change. Thermal sensitive material inside the thermal actuator expands pushing the piston to the designed length and hence the temperature increases.

- When the temperature drops thermal sensitive material inside the thermal actuator contracts or shrinks, it is provide that the piston tore turn. Thermal actuators can actuate at any temperature within the range of 30° F to 300° F (86° C to 572° C). Simply choose an actuation temperature.

- Actuators is used to convert energy into motion or thermal actuator is a type of non-electric motor containing components such as a piston and a thermal sensitive material capable of producing linear motion in response to temperature changes.

- These devices can be used for many applications such as the aerospace, automotive, agricultural industries all widely employ thermal actuator devices.

- A thermal actuator is one of the few devices that require no outside power source to produce motion. In a thermal actuator system, temperature changes can be used to perform certain tasks such as release latches, operate switches and open or close valves.

- These devices are very sensitive and can be used for applications that require actuation even at very slight temperature changes. The thermal sensitive materials used in a thermal actuator react to fluctuations in temperature, causing the actuator's piston component to move.

- These materials are engineered to expand as temperatures rise and driving a piston out of the actuator.

- When a thermal actuator is exposed to decreases in temperature and the thermal sensitive materials inside contract and allowing the device's piston to retract.

- Stroke refers to the distance a piston travels outward from an actuator. Many of the more common thermal actuators feature pistons that can extend between 0.015 inches (0.381 millimeters) and 0.500 inches (12.7 millimeters). Most thermal actuators are made to react to temperatures anywhere between 86 °F (30 °C) and 572 degrees Fahrenheit (300 °C).

- Manufacturers produce thermal actuators in a wide range of sizes and configurations, making them ideal for many different applications.

- Many thermal actuators are designed for use in pressurized or vacuum, gas, or liquid environments. They can be constructed out of durable and rugged materials such as brass, aluminum or stainless steel and feature custom mounting configurations.

- Thermal actuators are easily machined and can be designed to feature any thread type or valve end. A well-constructed thermal actuator is resistant to shock and vibration.

5.2.4.5 Precision Temperature Controller

A temperature control system is to maintain a device at a constant temperature. There are types of actuators are commonly used to precisely control the temperature of optics, lasers, biological samples.

- One is a thermo electric or Peltier device.

- The other is a resistive heater.

This is used to a current or voltage source to drive power through these actuators based on feedback from a temperature sensor. The temperature sensors are typically thermistors, RTDs, or linear devices such as the LM335 or AD590. With these types of sensors, stabilities of 0.01 °C to 0.001 °C are commonly achievable. Less precise sensors thermocouple can also be used for stabilities of about 1°C. If the stability of sensor, actuator, and device being stabilized are poorly connected to the best controller. The following Fig. 5.14 Shows the basic temperature control system.

This Fig. 5.14 shows the preventative sample, meant to familiarize the users with terminology and basic elements and not an exhaustive evaluation of what is available on the market.

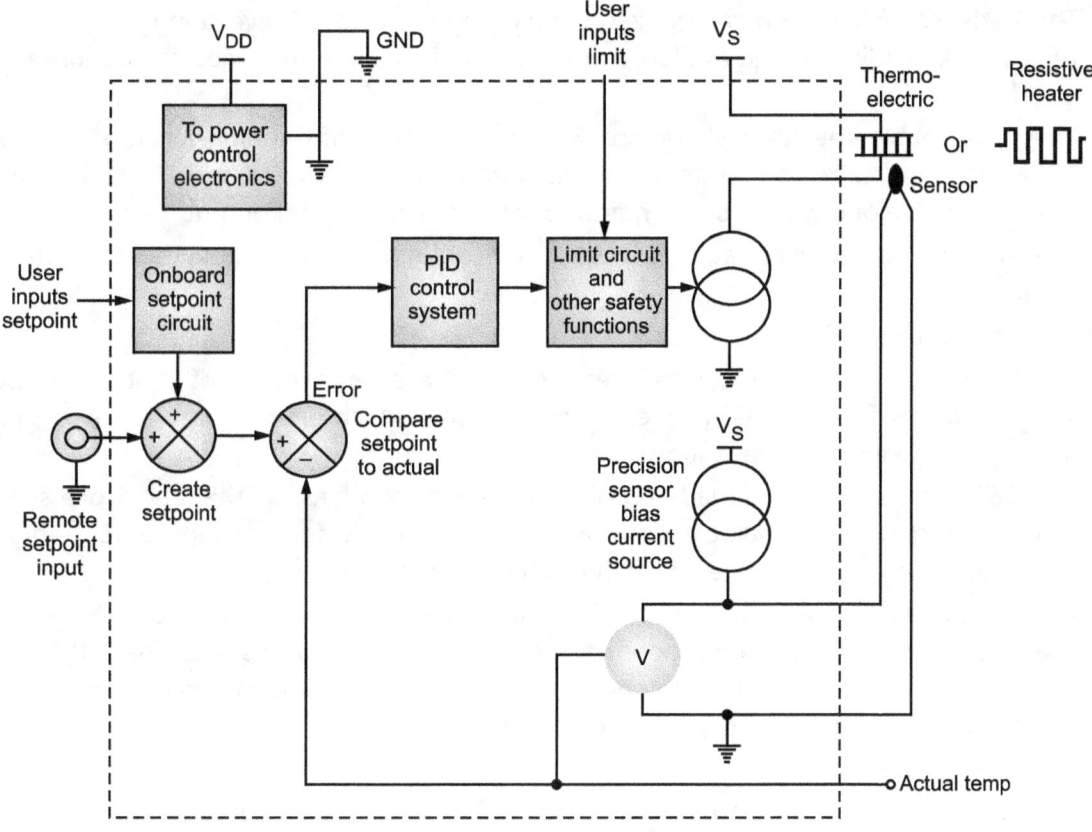

Fig. 5.14 : Temperature controller within the dashed lines

Presence Detection using MEMS Thermal Sensor

- MEMS Thermal Sensors are using as upper-sensitive infrared temperature sensor that makes full use of MEM sensing technology.

- Typical piezoelectric human presence sensors that rely on motion detection and the thermal sensor is able to detect the presence of stationary humans by detecting body heat and can be used to automatically switch off unnecessary lighting, air conditioning, etc.

- Detection using MEMS thermal sensors is an intelligent way of controlling and managing the loads in a building.

- Intelligent load management under constrained energy availability is away of extending the backup and there by reducing the installation size of renewable energy sources like solar energy and wind energy systems in buildings.

- When reducing the cost of initial installation of such systems. Many times majority of the loads in the buildings can be categorized as critical loads and noncritical loads.

- The loads may fall in both categorized pending on the comfort level and convenience of the user. Depending on the availability of a person in a room the loads can be turned on or off.

- These are enable detection of stationary human presence of the high sensitivity sensors. These are high precision at temperature detection with low cross talk field of view characteristics along with superior noise performance and digital output.

- The sensor was installed at a location and continuously provided the temperature readings.

5.2.4.6 Omron D6T-44L

- This is a high sensitivity sensor that detects the surface temperature of a radiating body. This is different from traditional piezoelectric sensors which detect only change of signal (i.e. moving bodies, not the stationary one).

- The D6T series sensors are made up of a cap with silicon lens, MEMS thermopile sensor chips, and dedicated analog circuit and a logic circuit for converting to a digital temperature value on a single board through one connector.

- As the D6T sensor is also able to monitor the temperature of a room and it can also be used to continually maintain optimal room temperature levels and instantly sense unusual changes in temperature there by detecting factory line stoppages, or discover areas of overheating for early prevention of fire out breaks.

Operating Principle

- The Seebeck Effect. The silicon lens collects radiated heat (far-infrared ray) emitted from an object on to the thermopile sensor in the module. The radiated heat (far-infrared ray) produces an electromotive force on the thermopile sensor.

- The analog circuit calculates the temperature of an object by using the electromotive force value and a measured temperature value inside the module. The measured value is outputted through an I^2C bus which can be used for further processing using STM32L Discovery Board. D6T - 44L - 06 has sensor chip arrays of 16 channels (4×4).

- Each channel corresponds to a pixel and measures temperature independently. In the Field of view of the sensor that includes all the pixels, whenever an object appears the temperature of corresponding pixel changes.

- The signal processing circuit closely to the sensor chip and allow noise temperature measurement is realized.

Application in Human Detection

- The sensitivity area is wider than the FOV specified area. When an object to be measured is smaller than the sensitivity area, the background temperature effects the measurements.

- Though Omron's D6T sensor corrects a temperature measurement value by using a reference heat source (black body furnace) and the measurement's value is influenced by the emissivity of the specific material of the object to be measured, and the surface shape of the occupant relative to the sensitivity area as shown in following Fig. 5.15.

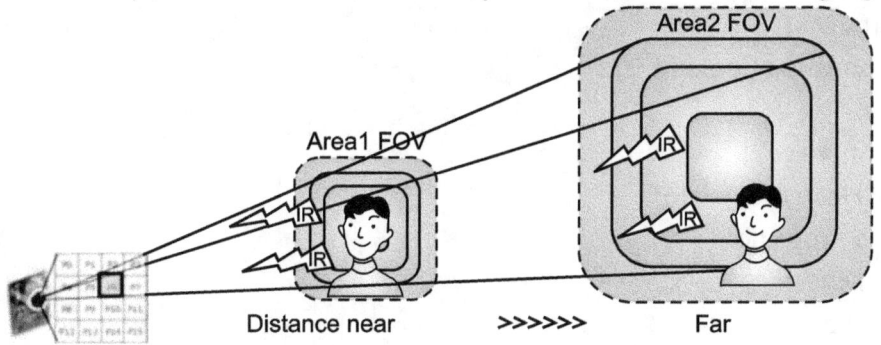

Fig. 5.15 : Omron's D6T

- OV becomes smaller with increasing distance and the back ground temperature prevails.
- Detecting human beings, the application will be limited to closer a when the detection programming scheme only judges by temperature value.
- The detection distance, improvements to the judgment accuracy can be made via software programming, considering time change, heat source location and human being movement.

5.2.5 Thermal Actuator Applications

Electro thermal (E-T) actuators have been developed to complement the capabilities of electrostatic actuators. The thermal actuators can be used as an arrayed to generate high forces. Equally significant is that the single actuators and arrays of actuators operate at voltages and currents that are directly compatible with standard micro electronics.

The thermal actuator is used in many fields. There are limitless applications for thermal actuators given as follows:

Aerospace

- Auxiliary Power Units (APUs)
- Engine Lubrication Systems
- Fuel Temperature Control
- Hydraulic Fluid Temperature Control
- Safety Shut Off Devices

Agriculture

- Automatic Green house Ventilation
- Live stock Watering System Freeze Protection

Automotive

- Formula 1 Oil Temperature Regulation
- Heavy Equipment Oil Temperature Control

- Oil Cooler Bypass
- Oil Cooler Automatic Regulation
- Thermostat
- Transmission Cooler

HVAC

- Mixing Valve
- Pool Heater Regulator
- Pump Protection
- VAV Diffuser
- Zone Valve

Medical

- Thermal Relief
- Scaled Protection
- UV Purification

Solar

- Solar Thermal/Hot Water Freeze Protection Systems
- Hot Water Heating Bypass
- Solar Tracking

Misc

- Cellular Equipment Cooling
- Fuel Cell Temperature Control
- Education (University)
- Various Military Applications

5.2.6 Piezo Resistive Sensing

Piezoresistive sensors are among the earliest micromachined silicon devices. The need for smaller, less expensive, higher performance sensors helped drive early micromachining technology, a precursor to microsystems or microelectromechanical systems (MEMS). The effect of stress on doped silicon and germanium has been known since the work of Smith at Bell Laboratories in 1954. Since then, researchers have extensively reported on microscale, piezoresistive strain gauges, pressure sensors, accelerometers, and cantilever force/displacement sensors, including many commercially successful devices. In this paper, we review the history of piezoresistance, its physics and related fabrication techniques. We also discuss electrical noise in piezoresistors, device examples and design considerations, and alternative materials. This paper provides a comprehensive overview of integrated piezoresistor technology with an introduction to the physics of piezoresistivity, process and material selection and design guidance useful to researchers and device engineers.

- The change in electrical resistance that occurs when an external force is applied to a semiconductor i.e. the piezo resistive effect.

- This affects material's electrical resistivity unlike the piezoelectric effect and it cannot be used to generate a voltage across the device.

- The applied force impacts the material's band structure, which makes it easier or more difficult for electrons to be excited into the conduction band.

- Consequently, the density of current carriers is altered and the material's resistance changes.

- The piezo resistive effect also involves pressure or stress. However, changes in resistance across the piezo material are the product of a charge or voltage.

- It is a change in electrical resistance of a semiconductor material due to mechanical stress.

- Probably the most basic piezo resistive devices are, obviously, piezo resistors form factors include integrated resist or networks, potentiometers, and accelerometers.

- Made from semiconductor materials, piezo resistive devices most commonly are used in pressure measurement.

- A piezo resistive sensor is a device which makes use of changes in the resistivity of certain semiconductor materials when subjected to mechanical stress to effect an electronic action.

- This piezo resistive phenomenon is based on these materials tendency to undergo changes in the latent resistive characteristics when flexed by exposure to pressure or stress.

- This electrical current passing through the device which translates into a measurement or readout. Semiconductor materials commonly used in piezo resistive devices are generally the same basic metallic and silicon families used in most electronic components.

- These components are available with a wide range of sensitivity characteristics to suit the requirements of diverse industries.

- When certain semiconductor materials are exposed to mechanical stress, their resistivity, or basic ability to oppose electrical current flow changes. This change in the materials resistive character obviously changes its specific resistance value.

- This result in a rise or fall in any current passed through the device which is then used to indicate or measure the stress involved.

- The piezo resistive effect is harnessed to create a range of deflection sensitive semiconductor devices used to record and measure stress inducing forces such as acceleration and pressure as shown in Fig. 5.16.

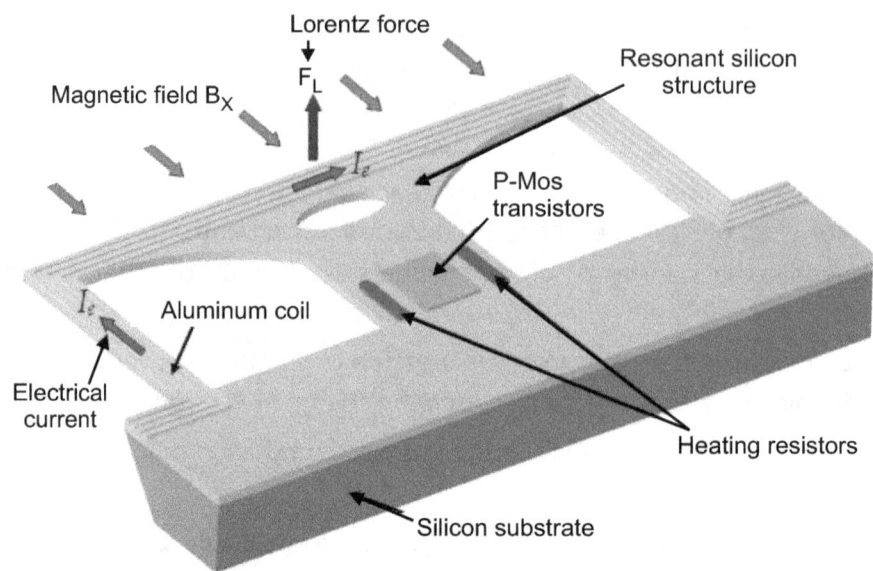

Fig. 5.16 : Piezo resistive sensor

- This is typically constructed of semiconductor substrates such as germanium, polycrystalline silicone, amorphous silicon, and single crystal silicone. A typical sensor consists of a pressure sensitive semiconductor diaphragm with several n+ and p+ contacts attached to it.

- Electrical current is passed through the wafer at a rate depending on its resistance. This current transfer result and tread out differs according to the resistance changes in the component when the diaphragm is exposed to pressure.

- These sensors range in complexity from simple piezo resistors with limited range and temperature stability to highly stable and accurate Piezo-FETs.

- The piezo resistive sensor is used in numerous applications involving mechanical stress measurement. The automotive industry employs them as vacuum and pressure sensors or to give in dictation of oil and gas levels.

- They are also useful in medical field devices such as blood pressure measurement equipment. Depth gauges used by deep sea divers also employ piezo resistive sensor technology to produce accurate depth readings.

- These devices are also used in aircraft time and barometric pressure instruments. Pressure dependent sensors of this type are also often used in electronic measurement instruments which use circuits and components such as the Wheatstone bridge and bipolar transistors.

- Accelerometers used to measure positional orientation, acceleration, and vibration forces also utilize piezo resistive sensor technology to produce their readouts.

- This technology has also found its way into the domestic environment with many dishwashers, vacuum cleaners, and washing machine manufacturers using the mint heir products.

5.2.7 Areas of Applications

Piezo resistive Pressure Sensors

- Valued for their high sensitivity and linearity, piezo resistive pressure sensors were some of the first MEMS devices to come to market.

- These are devices in their products as a means to measure pressure. For example, the biomedical field uses piezo resistive sensors as tools to measure blood pressure, while the automotive industry uses them to gauge oil and gas levels in car engine.

- In a piezo resistive pressure sensor, a piezo resistor is usually implanted in the surface of a thin silicon diaphragm.

- As pressure is applied, the diaphragm deforms and the resulting strain impacts the carrier mobility and number density.

- Pressure sensors have been in demand since the advent of the steam age. Billions of such sensors are used daily to monitor the pressure of fluids in pipes, engines, hydraulics, or in nature.

- It is used to determine the pressure of solids or gases. A typical pressure sensor is about a cubic inch in size, though some may be a hundred or more times smaller, for example those used in micro electromechanical systems. Pressure causes a material to conduct electricity at a certain rate, leading to a specific level of charge flow associated with a specific level of pressure.

- This charge is fed to a wire which leads to a control panel and display for human analysis.

- Conventional pressure sensors use film resistors, strain gauges, metal alloys, or polycrystalline conductors as the resistive media.

- These materials conduct more or less electricity based on geometric deformations in their structure. Because a linear increase in pressured ones not lead to a linear magnitude in deformation, calibration techniques must be used to determine the true pressure.

- In more sensitive pressure sensors based on mono crystalline semiconductors, which are fabricated using conventional semiconductor technology, tiny deformations can give rise to large changes in resistance.

- The change in resistance is not based on geometric deformations in the conducting material, but on smaller and more delicate structural war page.

Accelerometers

- Many types of accelerometers also make use of the piezo resistive effect. Designed for high frequency shock measurements, these devices have an advantage over their piezo electric counter parts as they are able to measure accelerations down to reaching 0 Hz.

- This capability to measure very low frequencies means that the device can provide an accurate static measurement of acceleration.
- Piezo resistive accelerometers are often used to analyze shock and vibrations in automotive safety testing, including safety air bag and anti-lock brake systems.
- Accelerometers are devices that are utilized in measuring acceleration and the impact of gravity on the acceleration.
- The process of measuring acceleration, the accelerometer will also yield information on such important factors as vibrations, inclination, and shock.
- The devices were once only large and relatively bulky in construction, modern technology has made it possible to produce accelerometers that are relatively portable and easy to setup for operation.
- One of the more common examples of the modern accelerometer is known as a MEMS device.
- Essentially, the MEMS or micro electro mechanical system is a simple device that functions mainly with the use of a cantilever beam and circuits that are designed for the purpose of detecting the presence of deflection sensing.
- An accelerometer of this type may be produced in single, dual, and triple axis designs, each one helpful in measuring vibrations, locomotion and shock in different situations.
- The accelerometer is also an important component in personal gaming and media devices as well. Helpful in maintaining a reasonable degree of interactive control between the user and the program, the accelerometer moves along the process of switching modes and display angles quickly.

5.3 MAGNETIC SENSING AND ACTUATION

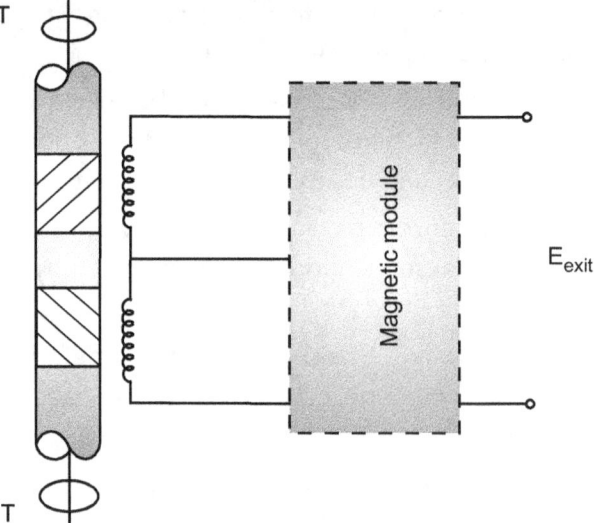

Fig. 5.17 : Magnetic sensor

A **MEMS**-based **magnetic field sensor** is a small-scale microelectromechanical (MEMS) device for detecting and measuring magnetic fields. Many of these operate by detecting effects of the Lorentz force: a change in voltage or resonant frequency may be measured electronically, or a mechanical displacement may be measured optically. Compensation for temperature effects is necessary. Such instruments have medical and biomedical applications.

Magnetic sensors

Magnetic sensors are used for the detection of positions without contact or wear and tear in control technology. They come into their own where inductive sensors reach their limits.

Advantage: Magnetic sensors offer small designs with very long sensing ranges. Depending on the orientation of the magnetic field the sensor can be damped from the front or from the side.

Since magnetic fields penetrate all non-magnetisable materials, the sensors can detect magnets through walls made of non-ferrous metal, stainless steel, aluminium, plastic or wood.

In gate systems, for example, the magnet sensor only detects the magnet which is to be detected. Any possible influences by aluminium in the environment do not impact or reduce the sensing range.

In the food industry the magnetic sensor is often used in connection with pigs (cleaning devices which pass through the inside of pipes). By means of magnetic sensors their exact position can be detected from the outside through the wall of the stainless steel pipe.

Operating principle

Magnetic sensors from ifm electronic use GMR (Giant Magneto Resistive Effect) technology. The measuring cell consists of resistors with several extremely fine, ferromagnetic and non-magnetic layers. Whereas in a conventional Wheatstone bridge circuit two GMR resistors are used, a large signal proportional to the magnetic field is produced if a magnetic field is present. As from a defined threshold value an output signal is switched via a comparator.

- Detection even through non-magnetisable metals
- Small housings with very long sensing ranges up to 100 mm
- Cylinder and rectangular designs for demanding applications
- High mechanical stability in case of shock or vibration
- Flush or non-flush installation in non-magnetisable metals

Magnetic Field Sensing

Magnetic field sensors, or "magnetometers", can be categorized into four general types[1] depending on the magnitude of the measured field. If the targeted B-fieldis larger than the earth magnetic field (maximum value around 60 μT), the sensor does not need to be very sensitive. To measure the earth field larger than the geomagnetic noise(around 0.1 nT), better sensors are required. For the application of magnetic anomaly detection, sensors at different locations have to be used to cancel the spatial-correlated noise in order to achieve a better spatial resolution. To measure the field below the geomagnetic noise, much more sensitive magnetic field sensors have to be employed. These sensors are mainly used in medical and biomedical applications, such as MRI and molecule tagging.

There are many approaches for magnetic sensing, including Hall effect sensor, magneto-diode, magneto-transistor, AMR magnetometer, GMR magnetometer,magnetic tunnel junction magnetometer, magneto-optical sensor, Lorentz force based MEMS sensor, Electron Tunneling based MEMS sensor, MEMS compass, Nuclear precession magnetic field sensor, optically pumped magnetic field sensor, fluxgate magnetometer, search coil magnetic field sensor and SQUID magnetometer.

Advantages of MEMS-based sensors

A MEMS-based magnetic field sensor is small in size, and so it can be placed close to the measurement location and thereby achieves higher spatial resolution. Additionally, constructing a MEMS magnetic field sensor does not involve the microfabrication of magnetic material. Therefore, the cost of the sensor can be greatly reduced. Integration of MEMS sensor and microelectronics can further reduce the size of the entire magnetic field sensing system.

Lorentz-Force-Based MEMS Sensor

This type of sensor relies on the mechanical motion of the MEMS structure due to the Lorentz force acting on the current-carrying conductor in the magnetic field. The mechanical motion of the micro-structure is sensed either electronically or optically. The mechanical structure is often driven to its resonance in order to obtain the maximum output signal. Piezoresistive and electrostatic transduction methods can be used in the electronic detection. Displacement measurement with laser source or LED source can also be used in the optical detection. Several sensors will be discussed in the following subsections in terms of different output for the sensor.

Voltage Sensing

Beroulle fabricated a U-shape cantilever beam on silicon substrate. Two piezo-resistors are laid on the support ends. There are 80-turns Al coil passing current along the U-shape beam. Wheatstone bridge is formed by connecting two "active" resistor with another two "passive" resistor free of strain. When there is an external magnetic field applying to the current carry conductor, motion of the U-shape beam will induce strain in two "active" piezo-resistors and thereby generating an output voltage across the Wheatstone bridge which is proportional to the magnetic field flux density. The reported sensitivity for this sensor is 530 m Vrms/T with a resolution 2 µT. Note that the frequency of the exciting current is set to be equal to the resonant frequency of the U-shape beam in order to maximize the sensitivity.

Herrera-May fabricate a sensor with similar piezoresistive read-out approach but with different mechanical motion. Their sensor relies on the torsional motion of a micro-plate fabricated from silicon substrate. The exciting current loop contains 8 turns of aluminum coil. The location of the current loop enables a more uniform Lorentz force distribution compared with the aforementioned U-shape cantilever beam. The reported sensitivity is 403 mVrms/T with a resolution 143 nT.

Kádár also chose the micro-torsional beam as the mechanical structure. Their read-out approach is different. Instead of using piezoresistive transduction, their sensor relies on electrostatic transduction. They patterned several electrodes on the surface of the micro-plate and another external glass wafer. The glass wafer is then boned with the silicon substrate to form a variable capacitor array. Lorentz force generated by the external magnetic field results in the change of capacitor array. The reported sensitivity is 500 Vrms/T with a resolution of a few mT. The resolution can reach 1 nT with vacuum operation.

Emmerich fabricated the variable capacitor array on a single silicon substrate with comb-figure structure. The reported sensitivity is 820 Vrms/T with a resolution 200 nT at the pressure level of 1mbar.

Frequency Shift Sensing

Another type of Lorentz force based MEMS magnetic field sensor utilizes the shift of mechanical resonance due to the Lorentz force applying to certain mechanical structures.

Sunier et al.[6] change the structure of aforementioned U-shape cantilever beam by adding a curved-in support. The piezoresistive sensing bridge is laid between two heating actuation resistors. Frequency response of the output voltage of the sensing bridge is measured to determine the resonant frequency of the structure. Note that in this sensor, the current flowing through the aluminum coil is DC. The mechanical structure is actually driven by the heating resistor at its resonance. Lorentz force applying at the U-shape beam will change the resonant frequency of the beam and thereby change the frequency response of the output voltage. The reported sensitivity is 60 kHz/T with a resolution of 1 μT.

Bahreyni et al.[7] fabricated a comb figure structure on top of the silicon substrate. The center shuttle are connected to two clamped-clamped conductors used to change the internal stress of the moving structure when external magnetic field is applied. This will induce the change of the resonant frequency of the comb finger structure. This sensor use electrostatic transduction to measure the output signal. The reported sensitivity is improved to 69.6 Hz/T thanks to the high mechanical quality factor (Q = 15000 @ 2 Pa) structure in the vacuum environment. The reported resolution is 217 nT.

Optical Sensing

The optical sensing is to directly measure the mechanical displacement of the MEMS structure to find the external magnetic field.

Zanetti fabricated a Xylophone beam. Current is flowing through the center conductor and the Xylophone beam will be deflected as the Lorentz force is induced. Direct mechanical displacement is measured by an external laser source and a detector. The resolution of 1 nT can be reached. Wickenden[9] had tried to shrink the footprint of this type of device by 100 times. But a much lower resolution of 150 µT was reported.

Keplinger et al.[10][11] were trying to use an LED source for optical sensing instead of using an external laser source. Optical fibers were aligned on the silicon substrate with different arrangements for the displacement sensing. A resolution 10 mT is reported.

Temperature Effects

When the temperature increases, the Young's modulus of the material used to fabricate the moving structure decreases. This will leads to the softening of the moving structure. Meanwhile, thermal expansion and thermal conductivity will increase with the temperature inducing an internal stress in the moving structure. These effects can result in the shift of the resonant frequency of the moving structure which is equivalent noise for resonant frequency shift sensing and the voltage sensing as well. In addition, temperature rise will generate larger Johnson noise (affect the piezoresiative transduction) and also large mechanical fluctuation noise(affects the optical sensing). Therefore, advanced electronics for temperature effect compensation have to be used to improve the sensitivity.

- The magnetic field is typically generated by electromagnets or permanent magnets. The magnetic field in the air gap of an electromagnet depends on the electrical current in the coil and the turns of the coil and the ferromagnetic material used in the core so called metallically hard materials have a high conductivity. After the magnetizing process, they deliver a permanent magnetic field.

- The concerning mechanic and mechatronical systems, demands for designing area of keeping constant advances in development and improvement of structures, and consequently, accurate analysis and tests more representative and rigorous and pointing out the evident importance of determining dynamics properties of such as structures, mainly: natural frequencies, damping factors and vibration mode shapes, among others.

- The analysis, of an external excitation force necessarily must be applied to the structure, being usually obtained from electro mechanic exciters, named shakers.

- The application of the electro mechanic exciter demands a mechanical connection between this device and the structure (flexible stick, technically named stinger).

- The connection is done; the exciter can be controlled by a signal generator, capable of introducing signals of different kinds and characteristics to the structure.

- The connection between exciter and structure, as well as the kind of signal generated, consist in parameters with expressive importance concerning the quality of results to be obtained during the tests.

- There is a lack in experimental part, involving modal analysis in rotating machinery, which is precisely the application of an external excitation force without contact, one of the several factors which can be able to minimize the noise signal.

- The noise influence occurs in part due to the journal / bearing friction, as noticed in experiments with shaker application.

- The electromagnetic actuator, constituting, in this way, the main focus of this work, once these devices enable the external excitation by electromagnetic force, destitute of any kind of mechanical contact.

- The ferromagnetic forces are generated by permanent magnets or controlled electromagnets. An electromagnetic actuator is any device that provides working motion courtesy of an internal electromagnetic field. These devices fall into two broad categories solenoid sand linear electromagnetic motors both of which function according to the same principle, but differ significantly in design.

- The movement used for actuation by exposing a free moving plunger or armature to the magnetic field created by energizing a static wire coil.

- The field attracts the plunger or armature that, in turn, moves, thus providing the required actuation.

- Actuation functionality can be achieved with an electromagnetic actuator, ranging from single cycle, and single speed actions to fairly sophisticated control of both actuation time and positioning.

- Electromagnetic switching is one of the most widely utilized remote actuation methods available and may be found in heavy industrial manufacturing and domestic applications of all descriptions. The basic principle of electromagnetic switching or actuation may be clearly seen when a simple bar magnetic used to pick up spilled sewing pins off of the floor.

- The basic requirement in remote switching and actuation is movement and, in the case of the electromagnetic actuator, a static coil is used to attract a ferrous metal plunger or armature that, in turn, provides the movement required.

- This movement can, depending on the actuator design, be a fairly simple single directional, single speed movement, or fully controllable in terms of speed and extent.

- The term electromagnetic actuator can be applied to two basic categories of devices. The first are solenoids, which are the more simple and common of the two types.

- These devices consist of a static, hollow centered wire coil and a movable ferrous metal plunger.

- In the neutral state, the solenoid plunger is positioned in such a way in relation to the opening of the core that, when the coil is energized by an electric current, the magnetic field created in the coil attracts the plunger.

- This pulls it smartly into the center of the coil and provides the movement necessary to actuate a secondary mechanism.

- The linear electromagnetic motor is the second and more sophisticated of the electromagnetic actuator types.

- They consist of a hollow tube with a wire coil wound around the inside surface. A permanent magnet armature is positioned inside the core with the actuator arm attached to it.

- When the core is energized, the armature reacts to the magnetic field moving up or down the tube, the movement being transferred by the actuator arm to a secondary device.

- By manipulating the way that the electric current is applied to the static coil and a far more complex range of movement in terms of extent and duration can be achieved with this type of actuator.

5.3.1 Magnetic Materials for MEMS

- A variety of magnetic materials have potential applications in magnetic MEMS including familiar hard and soft materials as well as more exotic magneto astrictive, thermo-reversible and shape memory materials.

- While soft materials such as perm alloy (FeNi) are relatively easy to prepare in film form by electrode position and sputtering, the processing of the other materials is more challenging.

- The core of this lecture will deal with the preparation of high performance hard magnetic materials based on rare earth transition metal (RE-TM) alloys (Nd FeB, Sm Co) or L10 alloys (Fe Pt, CoPt).

5.3.2 MEMS Switch uses Magnetic Actuation

- MEMS RF switches provides much lower insertion loss, higher isolation, better linearity, use lower power and are potentially cheaper.

- The conventional electromechanical switches and relays in terms of switching speed, integration capabilities, power and cost.

- MEMS RF work has focused on electrostatic actuation, presumably because other actuation mechanisms, such as magnetic and thermal actuation, consume much power and thus are not suitable for many applications.

- The switch is non-volatile and bi-stable. Because of the long range magnetic forces, the switch it has been named Mag Latch require slow operation voltage (less than 5 V).

- The design consists of a cantilever, an embedded planar coil, a permanent magnet and the necessary electrical contacts.

- As an electrical switch, the cantilever is a two layer composite consisting of a soft magnetic material NiFe perm alloy on it stop side and a highly conductive material, such as gold, at the bottom surface. The cantilever is supported by torsion flexures from the two sides.

- The contact end to the right of the cantilever can be deflected up or down by applying a current through the coil.

- When down, the cantilever makes select recall contact with the bottom conductors and the switch is on, or closed; when the contact end is up, or opened, the switch is off.

- The permanent magnet holds the cantilever up or down after switching, making the device a latching relay. Single pole double throw and RF switches can be designed. Latching optical switches can be made based on similar principles.
- The principle behind the latching characteristics is the preferential magnetization of a cantilever made of soft magnetic material (for example, perm alloy).
- In a constant, nearly perpendicular magnetic field, a cantilever can have a clockwise or a counter clockwise torque depending on the angle between the cantilever and the field, which leads to the bi-stability.
- To switch the relay, a second magnetic field, in this case generated by a short current pulse through a coil, realigns the magnetization of the cantilever causing it to flip.
- A static external magnetic field instantly latches the switch in the closed or open position, respectively. The switch maintains this state until the next switching signal realigns the cantilever. The relay consumes no power to maintain the latched state.

5.4 COMPARISON OF MAJOR SENSING AND ACTUATION METHODS

The relative advantages and disadvantages of electrostatic sensing and thermal sensing. Piezo resistive sensing and piezo electric sensing are interpreted as follows:

	Advantage	Disadvantage
Electrostatic Sensing	Electrostatic sensing technology in combination with correlation signal processing offers a promising solution to the online continuous measurement of velocity of particulate solids in pneumatic pipelines. Electrostatic sensors respond only to moving particles. Circular thin plate electrostatic sensors are prom singing as path monitoring due to their advantages of non-intrusiveness and easy installation. In rotational speed measurement using electrostatic sensors with single or double electrodes. Electrostatic sensors have been widely used in many applications due to their advantages of low cost and robustness.	Large footprint of device necessary to provide sufficient capacitance. Sensitive to particles and humidity. Sensors require carefully designed circuits to measure capacitance change in presence of noise and interference.

	Advantage	Disadvantage
Thermal Sensing	Manufacturing high precision mass flow sensors requires the use of two high resolution temperature sensors High temperature operation Point temperature sensing Fastest response to temperature changes	Temperature sensors are very expensive and must be handled with care. Low sensitivity to small temperature changes. Wire may pick up radiated electrical noise if not shielded. Lowest accuracy.
Piezoresistive Sensing	Low cost sensor fabrication opportunity. Mature processing technology. Different pressure levels can be achieved according to the application. Also, various sensitivities can be obtained. Read-out circuitry can be either on-chip or discrete. Piezo resistive sensors are abet more sophisticated in their design and the piezo they employ. Good linearity at constant temperature. Ability to track pressure changes without signal hysteresis, up to the destructive limit	The piezo resistive sensor is a main stay in pressure measurement applications. Strong non-linear dependence of the full scale signal on temperature (up to 1 %/Kelvin). Large initial offset (up to 100 %of full scale or more) Strong drift of offset with temperature.
Piezoelectric Sensing	The device generates its own voltage. These materials generate electric potential or voltage across their dimensions if any mechanical strain is applied to the dimensions. High stability, High output insensitivity to the extreme temperature and humidity Ability to be formed into most desirable shape. Quartz is most stable piezoelectric	Piezoelectric materials is very small The piezoelectric crystals have high impedance.

	Advantage	Disadvantage
	crystal but with small output. Rochelle salt gives high Output but can work over limited humidity.	

- Electrostatic sensing and piezo resistive sensing are the most common methods used in commercial MEMS products. When designing a MEMS product, it is perhaps one of the biggest decisions to make.

- Many issues including noise, sensitivity, temperature crosstalk, and processing should be consider Edina comprehensive manner when making a decision.

- The noise issue alone is rather complex, giving capacitive sensing's light but not decisive advantage.

- Capacitive sensing is used formulation is inertia sensing devices, for example. Simply because capacitors can be formed on surfaces parallel to the substrate or side walls, where as piezo resistive are traditionally only formed on front surfaces.

- Relative advantages and disadvantages of electrostatic actuation, thermal actuation, piezoelectric actuation, and magnetic actuation are summarized in the following table:

	Advantage	Disadvantage
Electrostatic Actuation	Low power consumption Fast response time Easy to integrate and implement with CMOS technology Compatible with most fabrication methods	High actuation voltage. Limited operation range due to the pull-in.
Thermal Actuation	Capable of achieving large displacement. (angular or linear); Moderately fast actuation response.	Relatively large power consumption; Sensitivity to environmental temperature changes.
Piezoelectric Actuation	Higher switching speed Low power consumption	Small displacement range High actuation voltage
Magnetic Actuation	Relatively large power consumption; Sensitivity to environmental temperature changes.	Moderately complex processes: Difficulty to for mono-chip .high-efficiency solenoids.

5.5　CASE STUDIES OF SELECTED MEMS: ACCELERATION SENSORS

Inertial sensors are micro electro mechanical systems (MEMS) this technology was first applied for commercial drives in the 1990's, and allowed new applications through high miniaturization and cost reduction.

5.5.1 Simple Steps to Selecting the Right Accelerometer

Technology have shape, size, and sensing range, novices as well as more experienced users can be intimidated when examining an accelerometer manufacturer's catalog or Website.

Technology Selection

The selection process is to determine the type of measurement to be made. There are three popular technologies used for acceleration measurements these are given as follows:

Piezoelectric (PE): accelerometers are the most widely used accelerometers for test and measurement applications. These devices offer a very wide measurement frequency range (a few Hz to 30 kHz) and are available in arrange of sensitivities, weights, sizes, and shapes. They are appropriate for both shock and vibration measurements.

Piezo Resistive (PR): Accelerometers generally have low sensitivity making them desirable for shock measurements and less useful for vibration measurements. They are also used extensively in transportation crash tests. PR accelerometers generally have a wide bandwidth (from a few hundred Hz to > 130 kHz) and the frequency response goes down to 0 Hz (often called "DC was responding") or steady state, so they can measure long-duration transients.

Variable capacitance (VC): It is among the newer accelerometer technologies. Like piezo resistive accelerometers, VC accelerometers are DC responding. They have high sensitivities, an arrow bandwidth (from 15 Hz to 3000 Hz), and outstanding temperature stability. Thermal zero and sensitivity shifts can be as low as 1.5% over a temperature range of 180°C. These devices are suited for measuring low-frequency vibration, motion, and steady-state acceleration.

5.5.2 Type of Measurement

Acceleration measurements can be divided into the following categories:

1. **Vibration:** An object is said to vibrate when it executes an oscillatory motion about a position of equilibrium. Vibration is found in the transportation, aerospace, and industrial environments as well as when simulated by a shaker system.

2. **Shock:** A sudden transient excitation of a structure that generally excites the structure's resonances. A shock pulse can be produced from an explosion, a hammer striking an object, or a vehicle crash.

3. **Motion:** Motion is a slow-moving event lasting from < 1 s to several minutes, such as the movement of a robotic arm or an automotive suspension.

4. **Seismic:** As low-motion or a low-frequency vibration. This measurement usually requires a specialized, low-noise and high-resolution accelerometer. Seismic accelerometers are used to measure the motion of bridges, floors, and earthquakes.

- Frequency response is the accelerometer's electrical output versus a mechanical excitation over a frequency range with fixed amplitude and it is an important parameter when considering any accelerometer.

- The frequency range will usually be determined by the test specifications or by the user. It is usually specified within ± 5% of the reference frequency (usually 100 Hz).

- Many devices will have the specifications extended to ± 1 dB and in some cases ± 3 dB. The preceding limits express the accuracy that can be expected over a given frequency range. Most data sheets will have a typical frequency response curve to assist the user.

- The accelerometer's accuracy varies over a specified frequency range. Another consideration is the number of axes to be measured. Accelerometers are available in single-axis and tri axial (3-axis) versions.

- A three-axis measurement is to mount three accelerometers on a tri axial mounting block. Both methods allow for the measurement of three orthogonal axes simultaneously.

1. Vibration

Piezoelectric accelerometers are the first choice for most vibration measurements since they have a wide frequency response, good sensitivity and resolution, and are easy to install.

There are two types of piezoelectric accelerometers:

(a) The basic charge-mode accelerometer

(b) The voltage-mode Internal Electronic Piezoelectric (IEPE) accelerometer.

- The IEPE type has become the most commonly used accelerometer type because of its ease of use. IEPE sensors are often sold under different trademarked names, but most comply with a pseudo industry standard and are interchangeable between brand names.

- Basically, an IEPE accelerometer has a charge amplifier built into the accelerometer. As a result, the sensor requires no external charge amplifier and uses ordinary, low-cost cable.

- The accelerometer does require a constant current power source and many DA systems have built-in power sources.

- For a known vibration range and an operating temperature that lies within the range of – 55C°C to 125°C consider using an IEPE device.

- Note that high-temperature versions of some models have a maximum operating temperature of 175°C.

- The advantages of charge-mode piezoelectric accelerometers include high-temperature operation and an extremely wide amplitude range, which is largely determined by the charge amplifier setting.

- An IEPE accelerometer has a fixed amplitude range. A typical charge-mode accelerometer will have an operating temperature range of −55°C to 288°C. Special-purpose accelerometers are available for extreme environments also were −269°C to as high as 760°C. Special radiation-hardened charge-mode accelerometers are available for use in a nuclear environment.

- Unlike the IEPE accelerometer, the charge-mode accelerometer requires the use of a special low-noise cable, which is expensive when compared to the standard commercial coaxial cable.

- A charge amplifier or an in-line charge converter is also required for operation. Charge-mode accelerometers are preferred for high-temperature operation (above 175°C) or in cases where the maximum acceleration is unknown.

- In instances where vibration measurements at very low frequencies are required, consider choosing a VC accelerometer.

- VC accelerometers have a frequency response from 0 Hz to 1 kHz, depending on the sensitivity required.

- When making very low frequency measurements, a VC accelerometer with a frequency range from 0–15 Hz will provide sensitivity of 1 V/g. VC accelerometers are useful on electro hydraulics hakes, to make flutter measurements, and for many transportation applications, such as testing automotive and suspension systems and making rail road ride and sway measurements.

2. **Shock**

- Shock Is depending on the shock level sand the final data required, you can choose from a variety of accelerometers. It is important to know the expected shock even, since this will determine the type of accelerometer to be used. Here is a rough guide to assist the reader in choosing the proper accelerometer.

- For low-level shock measurements, a general-purpose accelerometer will usually do the job.

- The accelerometer will need a linear range of at least 500 g and a shock survivability rating of 500 g.

- An IEPE type is usually preferred because they are less susceptible to producing erroneous results from cable motion. Use an amplifier with a low-pass filter to attenuate the accelerometer resonance.

- For automotive crash testing, a rather specialized area of shock testing, piezo resistive accelerometers is usually used. For far-field shock measurements, a special shear-mode accelerometer with a built-in electronic filter is often adequate. These are usually light weight IEPE types with solder connections.

- The electronic filter attenuates the resonance frequency of the accelerometer to prevent over loading of the DA equipment. Near-field measurements are often in excess of 20,000 g. Here the choice of accelerometers is dependent on the type of test being conducted.

- Specialized accelerometers of either piezoelectric (charge-mode and IEPE) or piezo resistive may be appropriate. Typically, an IEPE with characteristics similar to the far-field accelerometer is appropriate, but with the addition of an internal mechanical filter. The mechanical filter will ensure the survivability of the accelerometer and will generally eliminate zero shifts.

3. Motion, Constant Acceleration, and Low-Frequency Vibration

- VC accelerometers should be considered for applications with in this category. This technology allows for the measurement of low-level, low frequency vibration with a high output level.

- They also provide a high degree of stability over a broad temperature range. When a VC accelerometer is placed in a position where the sensitive axis is parallel to the earth's gravity, an output equal to 1 g will be produced. This phenomenon is often referred to as "DC responding." Because of this characteristic, VC accelerometers are very useful for measuring centrifugal force or for measuring acceleration and deceleration of devices such as elevators.

- In the real m of vibration testing, VC accelerometers are used in applications where low-frequency events are to be studied and where preservation of phase data is important.

- VC accelerometers have found their niche in the area of aircraft flutter testing.

- Their low-frequency characteristics make VC accelerometers ideal for ride quality measurements in automobiles, trucks, and rail road equipment. A wide band frequency response is not a characteristic of VC devices.

4. Mounting

- There are a number of ways to mount an accelerometer to the Unit Under Test (UUT), and methods include everything from permanent mounting to temporary methods. Here are a few of the most common mounting methods.

- The best mounting method uses a threaded stud or screw. Stud/screw mounting provides the best transmissibility at high frequencies since the accelerometer is virtually fused to the mounting surface.

- High-frequency response can be enhanced by the application of light oil between the accelerometer and the UUT. If this method of mounting is desired, accelerometers should be purchased that are designed for stud and/or screw mounting.

- Adhesive mounting is often required, especially on small surfaces and PC boards. The preferred mounting adhesive, because it can be easily removed (with the proper removal techniques).

- Many accelerometers are specifically designed for adhesive mounting and this fact will be noted on the data sheet.

- As mount accelerometer may be mounted using an adhesive, but a cementing stud should be used to prevent the adhesive from damaging the accelerometer's threads.

5.5.3 Ground Isolation

- A difference in ground voltage levels between the electronic instrumentation and the accelerometer may cause a ground loop resulting in erroneous data.
- Accelerometers are available with ground isolation or with the ground connected to the accelerometer's case.
- Accelerometers with ground isolation usually have an isolated mounting base and, where applicable, an isolated mounting screw. In some cases the entire accelerometer case is ground isolated.

Sensitivity and Resolution

- When either a low-level signal and/or a wide dynamic range are required, the accelerometer's resolution and sensitivity become important. An accelerometer converts mechanical energy into an electrical signal (the output).
- The output is expressed in terms of mill volts per g (mV/g), or, in the case of a charge-mode accelerometer, the output is expressed in terms of Pico Coulombs per g (pC/g).
- Accelerometers are offered in a range of sensitivities and the optimum sensitivity is dependent on the level of the signal to be measured e.g., in the case of a high shock test, low sensitivity is desirable.
- In the case of low-level signals, the best approach is to use an accelerometer of high sensitivity to provide an output signal well above the amplifier's noise level.
- For example, if the expected vibration level is 0.1 g and the accelerometer has a sensitivity of 10mV/g, then the voltage level of the signal would be 1 mV, and a higher sensitivity accelerometer may be desirable.
- Resolution is related to the accelerometer's minimum discern able signal. This parameter is based on the noise floor of the accelerometer (and in the case of an IEPE type, the internal electronics) and is expressed in terms of grams.

Acceleration (Vibration) Sensors

An **accelerometer** is a device that measures proper acceleration ("g-force"). Proper acceleration is not the same as coordinate acceleration (rate of change of velocity). For example, an accelerometer at rest on the surface of the Earth will measure an acceleration g= 9.81 m/s^2 straight upwards. By contrast, accelerometers in free fall (falling toward the center of the Earth at a rate of about 9.81 m/s^2) will measure zero.

Accelerometers have multiple applications in industry and science. Highly sensitive accelerometers are components ofinertial navigation systems for aircraft and missiles. Accelerometers are used to detect and monitor vibration in rotating machinery. Accelerometers are used in tablet computers and digital cameras so that images on screens are always displayed upright. Accelerometers are used in drones for flight stabilisation. Pairs of accelerometers extended over a region of space can be used to detect differences (gradients) in the proper accelerations of frames of references associated with those pointsThese devices are called gravity gradiometers, as they measure gradients in the gravitational field. Such pairs of accelerometers in theory may also be able to detect gravitational waves.

Single- and multi-axis models of accelerometer are available to detect magnitude and direction of the proper acceleration (or g-force), as a vector quantity, and can be used to sense orientation (because direction of weight changes), coordinate acceleration (so long as it produces g-force or a change in g-force), vibration, shock, and falling in a resistive medium (a case where the proper acceleration changes, since it starts at zero, then increases). Micromachined accelerometers are increasingly present in portable electronic devices and video game controllers, to detect the position of the device or provide for game input.

One of the most common inertial sensors is the **accelerometer**, a dynamic sensor capable of a vast range of sensing. Accelerometers are available that can measure acceleration in one, two, or three orthogonal axes. They are typically used in one of three modes:

- As an intertial measurement of velocity and position;
- As a sensor of inclination, tilt, or orientation in 2 or 3 dimensions, as referenced from the acceleration of gravity (1 g = 9.8m/s^2);
- As a vibration or impact (shock) sensor.

There are considerable advantages to using an analog accelerometer as opposed to aninclinometer such as a liquid tilt sensor – inclinometers tend to output binary information (indicating a state of on or off), thus it is only possible to detect when the tilt has exceeded some thresholding angle.

Working Principle of an Accelerometer

The design of an accelerometer is based on the application of physics phenomenon. In aviation, accelerometers are based on the properties of rotating masses. In the world of industry, however, the design is based on a combination of Newton's law of mass acceleration and Hooke's law of spring action. This is the most common design applied to the making of accelerometers, and therefore, in this wiki page I will focus on explaining the accelerometer's working principle based on this combination of Newton's law and Hooke's law. Figure 5.18 shows a simplified spring-mass system. In figure 1a, the mass of mass m is attached to a spring at equilibrium position x0 which in turn is attached to the base. The mass can slide freely on the base. Suppose that the base friction is negligible. Figure 1b shows the mass is moving to the right by a displacement of $\Delta x = x - x0$. Since the mass is slowing down, the direction of acceleration vector is to the left. In this case, the mass is subject to the force according Newton's second law and Hooke's law.

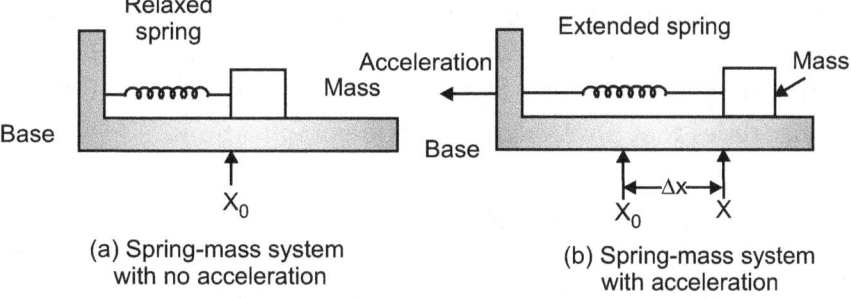

(a) Spring-mass system with no acceleration

(b) Spring-mass system with acceleration

Fig. 5.18 : A simplified spring-mass system accelerometer

According to Newton's second law, if a mass, m, is undergoing an acceleration, a, then there must be a force, F, acting on the mass with a magnitude of

Most accelerometers are Micro-Electro-Mechanical Sensors (MEMS). The basic principle of operation behind the MEMS accelerometer is the displacement of a small proof mass etched into the silicon surface of the integrated circuit and suspended by small beams. Consistent with Newton's second law of motion (**F = ma**), as an acceleration is applied to the device, a force develops which displaces the mass. The support beams act as a spring, and the fluid (usually air) trapped inside the IC acts as a damper, resulting in a second order lumped physical system. This is the source of the limited operational bandwidth and non-uniform frequency response of accelerometers.

Types of Accelerometer

There are several different principles upon which an analog accelerometer can be built. Two very common types utilize capacitive sensing and the piezoelectric effect to sense the displacement of the proof mass proportional to the applied acceleration.

Capacitive

Accelerometers that implement capacitive sensing output a voltage dependent on the distance between two planar surfaces. One or both of these "plates" are charged with an electrical current. Changing the gap between the plates changes the electrical capacity of the system, which can be measured as a voltage output. This method of sensing is known for its high accuracy and stability. Capacitive accelerometers are also less prone to noise and variation with temperature, typically dissipate less power, and can have larger bandwidths due to internal feedback circuitry.

Piezoelectric

Piezoelectric sensing of acceleration is natural, as acceleration is directly proportional to force. When certain types of crystal are compressed, charges of opposite polarity accumulate on opposite sides of the crystal. This is known as the piezoelectric effect. In a piezoelectric accelerometer, charge accumulates on the crystal and is translated and amplified into either an output current or voltage.

Piezoelectric accelerometers only respond to AC phenomenon such as vibration or shock. They have a wide dynamic range, but can be expensive depending on their quality

Piezo-film based accelerometers are best used to measure AC phenomenon such as vibration or shock, rather than DC phenomenon such as the acceleration of gravity. They are inexpensive, and respond to other phenomenon such as temperature, sound, and pressure

Overview of other types that are less used in audio applications

Piezoresistive

Piezoresistive accelerometers (also known as Strain gauge accelerometers) work by measuring the electrical resistance of a material when mechanical stress is applied. They are preferred in high shock applications and they can measure acceleration down to 0Hz. However, they have a limited high frequency response.

Hall effect

Hall effect accelerometers work by measuring the voltage variations caused by the change in magnetic field around them.

Heat transfer

Heat transfer accelerometers consist in a single heat source centered in a substrate and suspended accross cavity. They include equally spaced thermoresistors on the four side of the heat source. They measure the internal changes in heat due to an acceleration. When there is zero acceleration, the heat gradient will be symmetrical. Otherwise, under acceleration, the heat gradient will become asymmetrical due to convection heat transfer

Other

There are many other types of accelerometer, including:

- Null-balance
- Servo force balance
- Strain gauge
- Resonance
- Optical
- Surface acoustic wave (SAW)

Specifications

A typical accelerometer has the following basic specifications:

- Analog/digital
- Number of axes
- Output range (maximum swing)
- Sensitivity (voltage output per g)
- Dynamic range
- Bandwidth
- Amplitude stability
- Mass

Analog vs. digital: The most important specification of an accelerometer for a given application is its type of output. Analog accelerometers output a constant variable voltage depending on the amount of acceleration applied. Digital accelerometers output a variable frequency square wave, a method known as pulse-width modulation. A pulse width modulated accelerometer takes readings at a fixed rate, typically 1000 Hz (though this may be user-configurable based on the IC selected). The value of the acceleration is proportional to the pulse width (or duty cycle) of the PWM signal.

For use with ADCs commonly used for music interaction systems, analog accelerometers are usually preferred.

Number of axes: Accelerometers are available that measure in one, two, or three dimensions. The most familiar type of accelerometer measures across two axes. However, three-axis accelerometers are increasingly common and inexpensive.

Output range: To measure the acceleration of gravity for use as a tilt sensor, an output range of ±1.5 g is sufficient. For use as an impact sensor, one of the most common musical applications, ±5 g or more is desired.

Sensitivity: An indicator of the amount of change in output signal for a given change in acceleration. A sensitive accelerometer will be more precise and probably more accurate.

Dynamic range: The range between the smallest acceleration detectable by the accelerometer to the largest before distorting or clipping the output signal.

Bandwidth: The bandwidth of a sensor is usually measured in Hertz and indicates the limit of the near-unity frequency response of the sensor, or how often a reliable reading can be taken. Humans cannot create body motion much beyond the range of 10-12 Hz. For this reason, a bandwidth of 40-60 Hz is adequate for tilt or human motion sensing. For vibration measurement or accurate reading of impact forces, bandwidth should be in the range of hundreds of Hertz. It should also be noted that for some older microcontrollers, the bandwidth of an accelerometer may extend beyond the Nyquist frequency of the A/D converters on the MCU, so for higher bandwidth sensing, the digital signal may be aliased. This can be remedied with simple passive low-pass filtering prior to sampling, or by simply choosing a better microcontroller. It is worth noting that the bandwidth may change by the way the accelerometer is mounted. A stiffer mounting (ex: using studs) will help to keep a higher usable frequency range and the opposite (ex: using a magnet) will reduce it.

Amplitude stability: This is not a specification in itself, but a description of several. Amplitude stability describes a sensor's change in sensitivity depending on its application, for instance over varying temperature or time (see below).

Mass: The mass of the accelerometer should be significantly smaller than the mass of the system to be monitored so that it does not change the characteristic of the object being tested.

Other specifications include:

- Zero g offset (voltage output at 0 g)
- Noise (sensor minimum resolution)
- Temperature range
- Bias drift with temperature (effect of temperature on voltage output at 0 g)
- Sensitivity drift with temperature (effect of temperature on voltage output per g)
- Power consumption

Output

An accelerometer output value is a scalar corresponding to the magnitude of the acceleration vector. The most common acceleration, and one that we are constantly exposed to, is the acceleration that is a result of the earth's gravitational pull. This is a common reference value from which all other accelerations are measured (known as g, which is ~9.8m/s^2).

Digital output

Accelerometers with PWM output can be used in two different ways. For most accurate results, the PWM signal can be input directly to a microcontroller where the duty cycle is read in firmware and translated into a scaled acceleration value. (Check with the datasheet to obtain the scaling factor and required output impedance.) When a microcontroller with PWM input is not available, or when other means of digitizing the signal are being used, a simple RC reconstruction filter can be used to obtain an analog voltage proportional to the acceleration. At rest (50% duty-cycle) the output voltage will represent no acceleration, higher voltage values (resulting from a higher duty cycle) will represent positive acceleration, and lower values (<50% duty cycle) indicate negative acceleration. These voltages can then be scaled and used as one might the output voltage of an analog output accelerometer. One disadvantage of a digital output is that it takes a little more timing resources of the microcontroller to measure the duty cycle of the PWM signal. Communication protocols could use I2C or SPI.

Analog Output

When compared to most other industrial sensors, analog accelerometers require little conditioning and the communication is simple by only using an Analog to Digital Converter (ADC) on the microcontroller. Typically, an accelerometer output signal will need an offset, amplification, and filtration. For analog voltage output accelerometers, the signal can be a positive or negative voltage, depending on the direction of the acceleration. Also, the signal is continuous and proportional to the acceleration force. As with any sensor destined for an analog to digital converter, the value must be scaled and/or amplified to maximally span the range of acquisition. Most analog to digital converters used in musical applications acquire signals in the 0-5 V range.

The image at right depicts an amplification and offset circuit, including the on-board operational amplifier in the adxl 105, minimizing the need for additional IC components. The gain applied to the output is set by the ratio R2/R1. The offset is controlled by biasing the voltage with variable resistor R4. Accelerometers output bias will drift according to ambient temperature. The sensors are calibrated for operation at a specific temperature, typically room temperature. However, in most short duration indoor applications the offset is relatively constant and stable, and thus does not need adjustment. If the sensor is intended to be used in multiple environments with differing ambient temperatures, the bias function should be sufficient for analog calibration of the device. If the ambient temperature is subject to drastic changes over the course of a single usage, the temperature output should be summed into the bias circuit. Smart sensors may even take this into consideration.

The resolution of the data acquired is ultimately determined by the analog to digital converter. It is possible, however, that the noise floor is above the minimum resolution of the converter, reducing the resolution of your system. Assuming that the noise is equally distributed across all frequencies, it is possible to filter the signal to only include frequencies within the range of operation. The filter required depends upon both the type of acquisition as well as the location of the sensor. The bandwidth is primarily influenced by the three different modes of operation of the sensor.

Uses

The acceleration measurement has a variety of uses. The sensor can be implemented in a system that detects velocity, position, shock, vibration, or the acceleration of gravity to determine orientation (Doscher 2005)

A system consisting of two orthogonal sensors is capable of sensing pitch and roll. This is useful in capturing head movements. A third orthogonal sensor can be added to the network to obtain orientation in three dimensional space. This is appropriate for the detection of pen angles, etc. The sensing capabilities of this network can be furthered to six degrees of spatial measurement freedom by the addition of three orthogonal gyroscopes.

5.3.4 Gyroscope

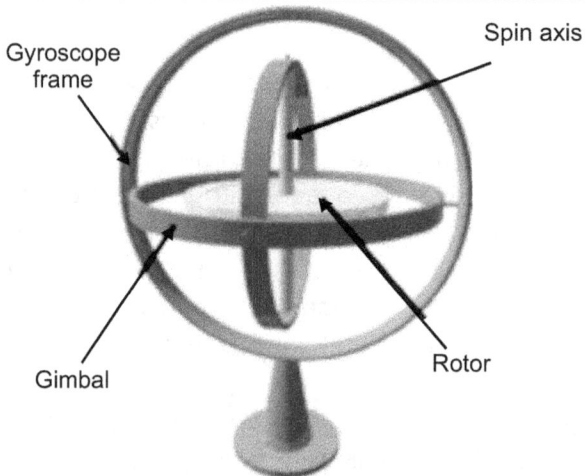

Fig 5.19 : Gyroscope

A gyro sensor, angular rate sensor or angular velocity sensor is a device that can sense angular velocity. Gyro sensors can sense rotational motion and changes in orientation and therefore augment motion. Vibration gyro sensors can sense angular velocity due to the Coriolis force which is applied to a vibrating element. This motion produces a potential difference from which angular velocity is sensed. The angular velocity is converted into an electrical signal output.

Types of Gyro Sensors

There are several different kinds of gyro sensors. At Future Electronics we stock many of the most common types categorized by output type, supply voltage, supply current, sensing range, operating temperature range and packaging type. The parametric filters on our website can help refine your search results depending on the required specifications.

The most common sizes for supply voltage are 2.7 to 3.6 V. We also carry gyro sensors with supply voltage up to 5 V. The output type can be analog, digital, linear or ratiometric, with the most common chips having an analog output.

Applications for Gyro Sensors:

The main applications for gyro sensors are:

- Angular velocity sensing: to sense the amount of angular velocity produced, which is the motion itself. An example would be the sensing of athletic movement.
- Angle sensing: to sense the angular velocity produced by the movement of the sensor itself. Angles are detected by a CPU. Thus, the moved angle is fed to and reflected in an application. Examples are car navigation systems, video game controllers and mobile phones.
- Control mechanisms: to senses the vibration produced by external factors. This vibration data is then transmitted as electrical signals to a CPU. This is used in correcting the balance or orientation of an object. Some examples include camera-shake correction and vehicle control.

Choosing the Right Gyro Sensor:

When you are looking for the right gyro sensors, you can filter the results by various attributes with the FutureElectronics.com parametric search: by Sensing Range (± 2000 °/s, ± 300 °/s, ± 100 °/s, 500 °/s,...), Output Type (Analog Output, Digital Output, Linear, Ratiometric) and Supply Current (from 4.2 mA to 10 mA) to name a few. You will be able to find the right high speed op amps to design a 3 axis gyro sensor or mems gyro sensor.

- A gyroscope is used to sense and measure angular motion using vibrating mechanical elements. It works on coriolis component of applied force to sense angular rates. A vibratory gyroscope has one or more proof masses that are excited by means of a feed-back control device.
- The amplitude of excitation is carefully controlled and frequency of vibration is set to natural resonant frequency.
- When the proof mass is made to rotate about an axis perpendicular to the plane of vibration, the coriolis component of the force sets the proof mass into vibration along the axis perpendicular to the excitation direction but in the plane of vibration.
- This secondary vibration is dependent on the angular rate of rotation and thus, is employed to find out the angular rate.

The two indices selected for performance measure are as follows:

- (M_1 = rf/E) (Maximization of this index means that the component will possess a higher cut-off frequency thereby increasing it supper limit of functionality)
- (M_2 = k/Ea2) (Maximization of this index means that the component will have a higher deflection for a given frequency) thereby improving its sensitivity.

Hence required materials need larger values of M_1 and M_2. So as to give quantitative ranking to the materials, we combine the two indices to from a third index (M_3 = M_1 M_2). Thus, an overall higher value of M_3 indicates better performance of a given alternative. M_3 can be interpreted as area under the plot of M_1 versus M_2. This method is similar to weighted product method (MADM approach) when we assume unit weights for both the indices.

The desirable properties for the selection of material for a vibratory gyroscope are: a lower value of Young's modulus and coefficient of thermal expansion while a higher value of failure strength and thermal conductivity are required. These are the properties which form the positive ideal solution and vice versa are done for negative ideal solution.

SUMMARY

- Sensors and actuators are two critical components of every closed loop control system.
- Micro Electro Mechanical Systems (MEMS) refer to a collection of microseconds and actuators that can sense its environment and have the ability to react to changes in that environment with the use of a microcircuit control.
- Electrostatics is the study of electromagnetic phenomena that occur when there are no moving charges i.e., after a static equilibrium has been established.
- Electrostatic induction machines, also called influence machines, operate on the principle of charge by induction.
- Actuation in MEMS is commonly achieved through electrostatic devices known as comb drive actuators.
- A sensor allows for the transformation of a signal, or other physical variable, from one form to another generally into a form that can be utilized more efficiently by the system that deploys the sensor.
- A thermocouple is a device made by two different wires joined a tone end, called junction end or measuring end.
- The electrical resistivity of a material is also known as its specific electrical resistance. It is a measure of how strongly a material opposes the flow of electric current.
- Thermal actuators are non electric motors that produce linear motion upon temperature change.
- The piezo resistive effect describes the change in electrical resistance that occurs when an external force is applied to a semiconductor.
- The magnetic field is typically generated by electromagnets or permanent magnets. The magnetic field in the air gap of an electromagnet depends on the electrical current in the coil, the turns of the coil and the ferromagnetic material used in the core.

EXERCISE

1. Define the electrostatic induction and electrostatic actuators.
2. What are the advantages of electrostatic type instruments?
3. Write your views on the thermal sensing and actuation.
4. What do you understand by the thermal actuation?
5. Write a short note on piezo resistive sensing and magnetic actuation

MEASUREMENTS, METHODS AND TOOLS

6.1 INTRODUCTION

- Measurement systems are the systems used in the process of associating numbers with physical quantities and phenomena.

- While the concept of weights and measures today comprises such factors as pressure, temperature, luminosity, and electric current, it once comprised of only four basic measurements: mass, distance or length, area and volume; last three are closely related. Basic to the whole idea of weights and measures are the concepts of uniformity, units and standards.

- A unit is the name of a quantity, for example, kilogram or pound. A standard is the physical example of a unit.

- Electrical measurements are those that quantity the voltage, current, and power and resistance in an electric circuit. Additionally, electrical measurements are those measurements made of the electromagnetic field surrounding a conductor carrying an electric current.

- All types of electrical measurements involve methods, devices, and calculations specific to the measurements being made.

- All these measured quantities most commonly used in electrical circuit are determined with a meter. An ammeter measures current in amperes, a voltmeter measures voltage in volts, and an ohmmeter measures resistance in ohms.

- The electrical power circuit measured in watt. It is product of voltage and current. It can be calculated as two quantities, if the resistance of the quantities is known to according to ohms law.

- The functions of ammeter, voltmeter, and ohmmeter are combined in a device known as a multimeter. It has a switch on the front that allows the user to select the function of the meter and the sensitivity of measurement.

- The electrical field around a conductor can affect other conductors in its vicinity, and electrical measurements of its characteristics can often be deduced from the effect it has on these conductors.

- If the electric current in a conductor is changing, or is in flux, it generates a magnetic field capable of inducing a current in any other conductor within the field.

- The magnetic field around a conductor with a changing electric current, such as one carrying an alternating current in a constant state of flux, can be measured with a Hall sensor. A stationary current, on the other hand, generates an electrostatic field that can be determined with an electrometer, which measures the force of repulsion induced by the field in two similar conductors.

- Electrical circuits and their components have characteristics that affect the ability of the circuit to conduct a current and generate a magnetic field.
- Electrical measurements of these characteristics are often determined by calculations based on measurable quantities of the circuit, like voltage, current, and resistance.
- For example, the capacitance of an electrical device designed to hold a charge, like a battery, is determined from measurements of the electrical power and time taken to charge it.
- Inductance circuit ability to generate a voltage when in a magnetic field can be inferred by strength of the field measuring with hall sensor and generated amount of current in ammeter circuit.

6.2 ELECTRICAL METHODS

- Electrical methods include electrical resistivity, Induced Polarization (IP), and spontaneous or Self Potential (SP).
- Electrical surveys are used for mapping the geological framework of aquifers, locating concentrated plumes of ground–water contamination, mapping the subsurface thickness of unconsolidated sediments and the depth to consolidated bedrock, and mineral exploration.
- The Electrical Resistivity method measures the apparent bulk electrical resistivity by injecting current into the ground through current electrodes that are grounded at the earth's surface and measuring the difference of the electrical potential between the potential electrodes.
- The amount of current (Ampere) and the potential difference (V) is used to calculate the apparent resistivity (Ω m) at the midpoint of the array of the electrodes.
- When the electrical resistivity specified electrical resistance or volume resistivity is a quantifies intrinsic property that material given oppose the flow of electric current.
- A low resistivity indicates a material that readily allows the movement of electric charge.
- MEMS elements having some sort of mechanical functionality whether or not these elements can move. The term used to define MEMS varies in different parts of the world.

In the United States they are predominantly called MEMS, while in some other parts of the world they are called "Microsystems Technology" or "micromachined devices". While the functional elements of MEMS are miniaturized structures, sensors, actuators, and microelectronics, the most notable (and perhaps most interesting) elements are the microsensors and microactuators. Microsensors and microactuators are appropriately categorized as "transducers", which are defined as devices that convert energy from one form to another. In the case of microsensors, the device typically converts a measured mechanical signal into an electrical signal.

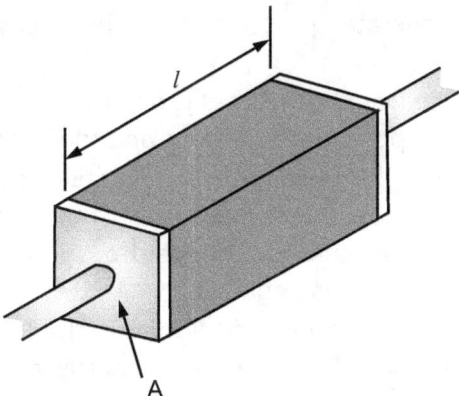

Fig. 6.2: Mechanical functionality of MEMS element

6.2.1 Hot Probe Method

- Electrical, optical, and mechanical properties of thin films significantly differ from bulk materials. Therefore, characterization methods for evaluation of thin film properties became highly important.

- The conventional Hot Probe characterization method enables only the definition of a semiconductor type, P or N, by identifying the majority charged carriers.

- According to the new Hot Probe technique, one can measure and calculate the majority charged carriers concentration and its dynamic parameters. The traditional hot-probe method, which is developed from the transient hot-wire method, can only be applied to determine thermal conductivity. This kind of method is based on the idealized 'one-dimensional radial heat flow' model. As a matter of fact, the finite length influence of a hot probe on measurement is remarkable when the hot probe is not sufficiently long.

- The corrected term of finite length for a hot probe is nonlinearly dependent on the thermal diffusivity of the measured sample and the length of the hot probe. In this work the long/short hot–probe method (LSHPM) is developed which can simultaneously determine the thermal conductivity, thermal diffusivity and specific heat of the measured sample.

- The simple "hot–probe" experiment consists of a soldering iron and a standard voltmeter to distinguish between n–type and p–type semiconductors.

- A semiconductor wafer is contacted with a "hot" probe such as a heated soldering iron and room temperature "cold" probe. Hot probe is connected to the positive terminal of the meter and the cold probe is connected to the negative terminal and then it is measured the direction of current flow between the two probes. Positive current reading or positive voltage reading on the meter determines the material is n- type and the reverse is p-type. Current flows from the hot probe to the cold probe for the n-type wafer, while current flows in the opposite direction for the p-type wafer. The explanation is that the thermally excited majority free charged carriers are diffused within the semiconductor from the hot probe to the cold probe.

- A temperature gradient generates potential difference between probes called Seebeck voltage.
- For n–type, electrons diffuse from hot to cold probe throughout the sample setting up an electric field that produces a potential difference and then detected by voltmeter.
- Actually, electrons flow through the cold probe (negative) and current (hole) flows in the opposite direction with the hot probe positive, so that the meter reading is positive. Similarly, for p–type, holes flow through the cold probe (negative) with the hot probe positive, so that the meter reading is negative.
- If the current meter has zero resistance with ignoring the (small) thermoelectric effect in the metal wires, one can justify that the Fermi energy does not vary throughout the material.
- The corresponding energy band diagram illustrates the specific case in which the temperature variation causes a linear change of the conduction band energy as measured relative to the Fermi energy.
- As the effective density of states decreases with decreasing temperature, the conduction band energy decreases with decreasing temperature yielding an electric field which causes the electrons to flow from higher to lower temperature.

The Hot–Probe Experiment

- The conventional Hot–Probe experiment provides a simple yet efficient way to distinguish between n–type and p–type semiconductors using a heated probe and a standard multimeter.
- The experiment is done by attaching a couple of cold probe and hot probe to a semiconductor surface. Both probes are wired to a sensitive electrometer.
- The hot probe is connected to the positive terminal of the meter while the cold probe is connected to the negative terminal.
- When the cold and hot probes to an n–types semiconductor positive voltage is obtained in meter and p–type semiconductor like negative voltage obtain this experiment is that the thermally excited majority free charged carriers are translated within the semiconductor from the hot probe to the cold probe.
- The mechanism for this motion within the semiconductor is of a diffusion type since the materialist uniformly doped due to the constant heating in the hot probe contact.
- These translated majority carriers define the electrical potential sign of the measured current in the multimeter. Thus, the hot probe surrounding zone becomes charged with minority carriers and the cold probe remains neutral.
- Hot Probe experiment may be realized following three various methods:
  1. To heat a probe and connect it to the sample under evaluation for a short period while keeping the second electrode (the cold one) constantly connected; variation of

the multimeter to the positive or negative direction indicates type of the semiconductor (the old "Hot–Probe" method).

2. To connect two electrodes to the sample under evaluation and heat one of them; this way we obtain information on the type of semiconductor as in the thermo–electrical voltage dependence on temperature.

3. To heat a mediator probe for a pre-defined temperatureand attach it to one of the two probes for a certain time.Two electrodes are constantly held attached to thesurface. Attachment is maintained until a steady state isobtained. Then the mediator probe heater is removedfrom the heated electrode. In this way one gets additional information concerning the majority charged carriers concentration and the dynamic parameters of the semiconductor material. In our actual work we concentrate efforts on the majority charged carriers concentration only.

4. The "hot-probe" experiment provides a very simple way to distinguish between n-type and p-type semiconductors using a soldering iron and a standard multimeter. The experiment is performed by contacting a semiconductor wafer with a "hot" probe such as a heated soldering iron and a "cold" probe. Both probes are wired to a sensitive current meter. The hot probe is connected to the positive terminal of the meter while the cold probe is connected to the negative terminal

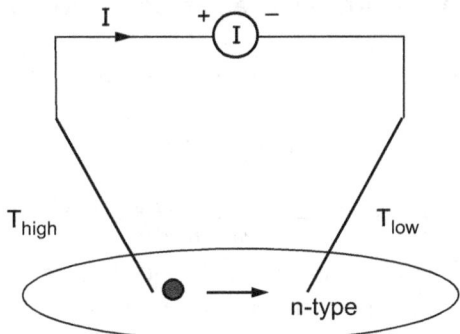

Fig. 6.3: Semiconductor wafer

- When applying the probes to n–type material one obtains a positive current reading on the meter, while p–type material yields a negative current. This experiment is that the carriers move within the semiconductor from the hot probe to the cold probe. While diffusion seems to be a plausible mechanism to cause the carrier flow it is actually not the most important mechanism since the material is uniformly doped.

- Starting from the assumption that the current meter has zero resistance, and ignoring the (small) thermoelectric effect in the metal wires one can justify that the Fermi energy does not vary throughout the material.

- This energy band diagram illustrates above Fig. 6.4 in which the temperature variation causes a linear change of the conduction band energy as measured relative to the Fermi energy, and also illustates the trend in the general case.

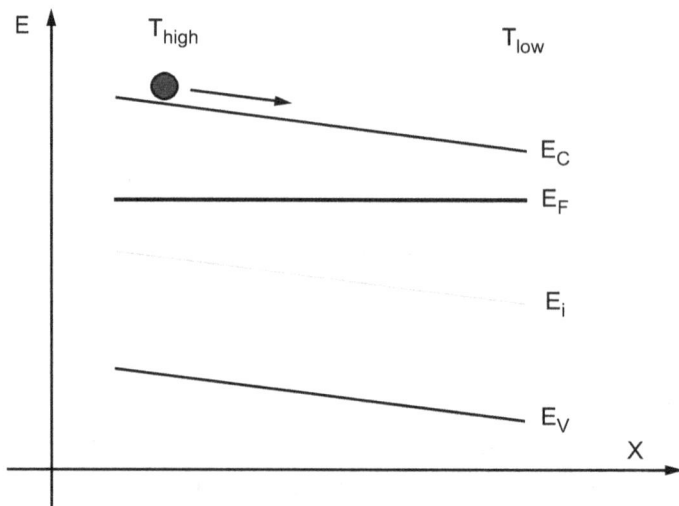

Fig. 6.4: Thermo electric effect

- As the effective density of states decreases with decreasing temperature, one finds that the conduction band energy decreases with decreasing temperature yielding an electric field which causes the electrons to flow from the high to the low temperature.
- The same reasoning reveals that holes in a p–type semiconductor will also flow from the higher to the lower temperature.

The current can be calculated from the general expression

$$J = \mu_n n \left(\frac{\partial E_F}{\partial x} - qp \frac{\partial T}{\partial x} \right)$$

where

$$qP = -k \left(\frac{5}{2} - \frac{T}{\mu_n} \frac{\partial \mu_n}{\partial T} + \ln \frac{N_c}{n} \right)$$

The current will increase with doping and with the applied temperature gradient as long as the semiconductor does not become degenerate or intrinsic within the applied temperature range.

6.2.2 Sheet Resistance

- Sheet resistance should be in terms of electronic thin film. It is the bulk resistivity of a metallic film and thickness.
- The sheet resistance has a meaning for the polymer thin films, not the solution.
- The thin films by some deposition technique (dip–coating, spin–coating, printing, doctor blade, etc.) on some insulating substrate (glass, polymer foil, etc.) you can measure the total resistance. In this case of the square shape, the sheet resistance (resistance for one square).
- The sheet resistance depends on various material parameters (i.e. polymer conductivity, solvent evaporation process annealing time, atmosphere, etc. as well as film properties such as film thickness higher thickness means lower sheet resistance.

For the emitter layer, the resistivity as well as the thickness of the layer will often be unknown, making the resistance of the top layer difficult to calculate from the resistivity and thickness. However, a value known as the "sheet resistivity", which depends on both the resistivity and the thickness, can be readily measured for the top surface n–type layer. For a uniformly doped layer, the sheet resistivity is defined as:

$$\rho_m = \frac{\rho}{t}$$

Where,

ρ is the resistivity of the layer; and t is the thickness of the layer.

The sheet resistivity is normally expressed as ohms/square or Ω/m.

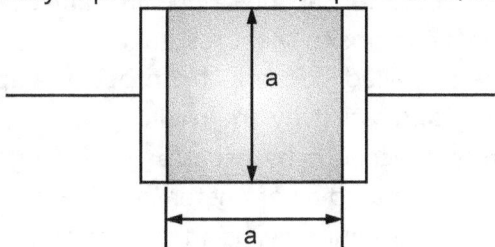

Fig. 6.5: Resistivity

The resistance of a square conductive sheet is the same no matter what size it is so long as it remains a square.

For non–uniformly doped n–type layers, i.e. if ρ is non–uniform:

$$\rho_m = \frac{1}{\int_0^t \frac{1}{\rho(x)} dx}$$

The sheet resistivity of an emitter layer is typically measured with a four–point–probe.

Four point probe based instruments use a long established technique to measure the average resistance of a thin layer or sheet by passing current through the outside two points of the probe and measuring the voltage across the inside two points.

If the spacing between the probe points is constant, and the conducting film thickness is less than 40% of the spacing, and the edges of the film are more than 4 times the spacing distance from the measurement point, the average resistance of the film or the sheet resistance is given by:

$$₹ = 4.53 \times V/I$$

The thickness of the film (in cm) and its resistivity (in ohm cm) are related to Rs by:

$$₹ = resistivity/thickness$$

Therefore one can calculate the resistivity if the thickness of a film is known, or one may calculate the thickness if the resistivity is known.

Sheet Resistance and Sheet Conductance as Functions of Frequency

• It is not often considered is that sheet resistance is a function of frequency. Applied in the RF world, errors can result from using the DC definition.

- The assumption of constant sheet resistance is only valid for conductors that are thin compared to skin depth (which is often the case for thin–film resistors, but never the case for transmission lines.)
- Knowing RF sheet resistances versus frequency of interconnect metals for example copper or gold it can be a very useful short–cut for evaluating attenuation of strip conductors such as microstrip.

Calculating Maximum Sheet Conductance (Minimum Sheet Resistance)

- Sheet conductivity is the inverse of sheet resistance; its units are Siemen–squares, or mho–squares. This quantity is useful when you are dealing with multiple–layer conductors, as their conductivities can be added in parallel, then the sum can be re–inverted and expressed in a composite sheet resistance.
- When RF is involved, the so called skin–effect can become apparent, and therefore DC calculations of conductivity and resistivity are invalid.
- The skin effect is taken into account by using a decreasing exponential factor whose exponent is inversely proportional to a parameter called skin depth.
- The skin effect is taken into account by using a decreasing exponential factor whose exponent is inversely proportional to a parameter called skin depth. Maximum sheet conductance is the best you can do, and is a function of frequency.
- At the surface, complete conduction takes place, and the resistivity of the metal is 100% of its value at DC, equal to ρ.
- At one skin depth, the metal's conductivity has been reduced to 36.8% of ρ, at 2 skin depths, 13.5%, etc.
- By the time you reach five skin depths the metal's conductivity is reduced to just 0.7% of its full value. After reaction fire skin depth adding to in of metal beyond five skin depth it reduce RF resistance.
- The incremental RF conductivity, it is the conductivity at a given depth, reduced by the skin depth equation:

$$\text{Incremental RF conductivity } = \text{ Bulk conductivity } \times \exp\left(-\frac{t}{\delta_s}\right) \text{ (Siemens/meter)}$$

$$\text{Incremental RF conductivity } = \frac{1}{\rho} \times \exp\left(-\frac{t}{\delta_s}\right) \text{ (Siemens/meter)}$$

$$\rho = \text{ Bulk resistivity (Ohm – meters)}$$
$$t = \text{ Depth into metal}$$
$$\delta_s = \text{ Skin depth}$$

This is different from DC sheet conductivity, which can be quite a bit higher since every free electron in the metal contributes to conduction during direct current. Although we have pledged never to use integrating an exponential function is so easy that even we can do it. The maximum sheet conductance is:

$$\text{Maximum RF sheet conductance} = \sqrt{\frac{1}{\rho \, \pi f \, \mu_0 \, \mu_r}} = \frac{1}{\rho} \sqrt{\frac{2\rho}{2\pi \, f \mu_0 \, \mu_r}}$$

$$= \frac{\delta_s}{\rho} \text{ (Siemen –squares)}$$

where δ_s = Skin depth

                                         ρ = Bulk resistivity (Ohm–meters)

The maximum RF sheet conductance is in units of Seimen–squares (or mho–squares) which is the inverse of sheet resistance (units of ohms/square). Similarly, the minimum RF sheet resistance is just the reciprocal of the above equation:

$$\text{Minimum RF sheet resistance} = \frac{\rho}{\delta_s} \text{ (Ohms / square)}$$

The DC sheet resistance equation except the skin depth is now in the dominator instead of the conductor's thickness.

Remember, this is the best you can achieve, no matter how much more metal you add to the transmission line. The plot below compares aluminum, gold, copper and silver. Silver is best, followed by copper, then gold, then aluminum. At DC you can achieve nearly zero sheet resistance, because the skin depth is infinite. But to get truly zero sheet resistance, you'd need infinite metal thickness.

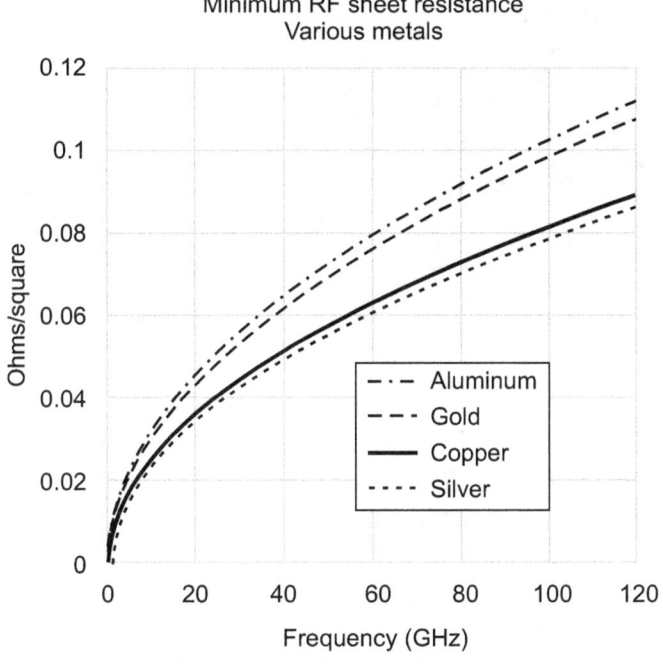

Fig. 6.6: DC sheet resistance

6.2.3 Hall Effect

- Hall Effect, development of a transverse electric field in a solid material when it carries an electric current and is placed in a magnetic field that is perpendicular to the current.

- This phenomenon was discovered in 1879 by the U.S. physicist Edwin Herbert Hall. The electric field, or Hall field, is a result of the force that the magnetic field exerts on the moving positive or negative particles that constitute the electric current.
- When current is a movement of positive particles then negative particles in the opposite direction or mixing together a perpendicular magnetic filed displace the moving electric charge at the same direction.
- At right angles to both the magnetic field and the direction of current flow. The accumulation of charge on one side of the conductor leaves the other side oppositely charged and produces a difference of potential.
- An appropriate meter may detect this difference as a positive or negative voltage. The sign of this Hall voltage determines whether positive or negative charges are carrying the current.
- In metals, the Hall voltages are generally negative, indicating that the electric current is composed of moving negative charges, or electrons. The Hall voltage is positive, however, for a few metals such as beryllium, zinc, and cadmium, indicating that these metals conduct electric currents by the movement of positively charged carriers is called as holes. as shown in Fig. 6.7.

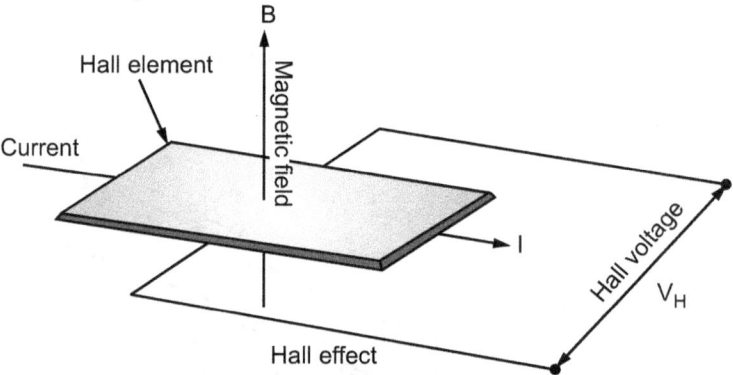

Fig. 6.7: Hall effect

- In semiconductors, in which the current consists of a movement of positive holes in one direction and electrons in the opposite direction, the sign of the Hall voltage shows which type of charge carrier predominates.
- The Hall effect can be used to measure the density of current carriers, their freedom of movement, or mobility, as well as to detect the presence of a current on a magnetic field.
- The hall effect develops across a conductor is directly proportional to the current to a magnetic field at a particular conducting material.
- Then hall voltage is inversely proportional to the thickness of the material in the direction of magnetic field.
- Because various materials have different Hall coefficients, they develop different Hall voltages under the same conditions of size, electric current, and magnetic field. Hall coefficients may be determined experimentally and may vary with temperature.

- The Hall Effect occurs when an electrical charge passing through an electrical conductor produces an asymmetric distribution of charge resulting in a voltage difference and a magnetic field perpendicular to the current.
- If a current carrying conductor placed in a perpendicular magnetic field, a potential difference will generate in the conductor which is perpendicular to both magnetic field and current.
- This phenomenon is called Hall Effect. Hall effect is an important tool to characterize the materials especially semiconductors. It directly determines both the sign and density of charge carriers in a given sample.
- Consider a rectangular conductor of thickness *t* kept in XY plane. An electric field is applied in X–direction using Constant Current Generator (CCG), so that current *I* flow through the sample. If *w* is the width of the sample and *t* is the thickness. There for current density is given by

$$J_x = I/wt$$

Hall Effect Sensor

A Hall effect sensor is a small device, mounted to a circuit board, which can measure a magnetic field. It is designed around the principles of the Hall effect, in which a magnetic field perpendicular to an electrical current on a circuit produces voltage on the other side. The sensor can be in the form of a single chip, along with components to compensate for temperature changes. An amplifier for the signal is needed to output accurate measurements as well. Analog and digital output Hall effect sensors are available, and both are used in computer, automobile, and industrial control systems

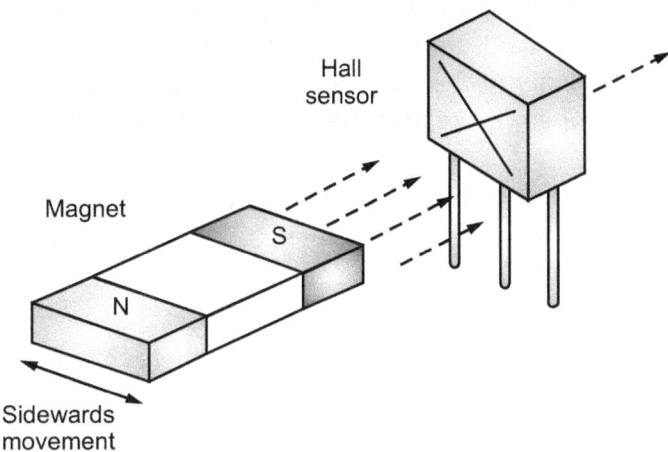

Fig. 6.8: Hall effect sensors

- In an analog Hall effect sensor, the voltage from the output is always directly related to the magnetic field, which can be either positive or negative.
- Voltage rises with magnetic field intensity, and if no field is turned on then a null voltage represents the value of the power going through.

- In digital output Hall effect sensor, the output is only defined by on and off states. An analog sensor can be converted to a digital one using a specific circuit, the Schmitt trigger circuit.

- The states change only when a predetermined level is reached; otherwise the output doesn't increase or decrease unless the magnetic field changes significantly enough.

- Also, digital sensors can be powered by supplies that are either regulated or unregulated, depending on a tiny integrated circuit package is all that is needed to house a Hall effect sensor along with its associated electronics.

- The actual sensors are almost too small to see and can be placed anywhere on a circuit board. At the same time, they can tolerate shock, vibration, and extreme temperature ranges, so Hall effect sensors can be used for speed sensing in industrial control systems.

- They can also detect the strength and direction of a magnetic field, allowing for direction detection. Use as a position sensor is possible as well.

Hall Effect Sensors as Two Basic Types:

- **Threshold (Alternatively called Digital, or On–off),** which produce a constant hall voltage when the field strength reaches a certain amplitude and/or polarity. There are many different threshold device configurations such as latching devices which turn on when a positive field strength reaches the threshold but only turn off under the negative field of the same strength, or devices which turn on when only a positive field reaches a certain threshold and are off otherwise, or devices which turn on when either a positive or negative field reaches the threshold and are off.

- **Linear (Analog Output Sensor),** which produced a hall voltage proportional to the strength of the magnetic field around it. The orientation of the surrounding magnetic field determines the polarity of the voltage swing. Linear devices are more often used in musical applications, when expressive gestures must be sensed as tiny changes in position.

Hall sensors are commonly used to time the speed of wheels and shafts, such as for internal combustion engine ignition timing or tachometers. In the pictured wheel carrying two equally spaced magnets, the voltage from the sensor will peak twice for each revolution.

Hall Effect Measurements

- Electrical characterization of materials evolved in three levels of understanding. In the early 1800s, the resistance R and conductance G were treated as measurable physical quantities obtainable from two-terminal I-V measurements (i.e., current I, voltage V).

- The resistance alone was not comprehensive enough since different sample shapes gave different resistance values. This led to the understanding (second level) that an intrinsic material property like resistivity (or conductivity) is required that is not influenced by the particular geometry of the sample. This allowed scientists to quantify the current–carrying capability of the material and carry out meaningful comparisons between different samples.

- The electrical conduction theory were constructed with varying degrees of success, but until the advent of quantum mechanics, no generally acceptable solution to the problem of electrical transport was developed. Carrier density n and mobility μ which are capable of dealing with even the most complex electrical measurements today.

The Hall Effect and the Lorentz Force

- The Hall effect is the Lorentz force, when an electron moves along a direction perpendicular to an applied magnetic field, it experiences a force acting normal to both directions and moves in response to this force and the force effected by the internal electric field. The Lorentz force is given by

$$F_{lorentz} = q \ (E + (v + B)]$$

- The Hall effect is shown in Fig. 6.9 bar–shaped sample in which charge is carried by electrons. A constant current I flow through the bar and the entire bar is subject to a uniform magnetic field **B**, which is directed into the screen, perpendicular to the current flow.

- Since the electrons are travelling through a magnetic field, they are subject to an upwards Lorentz force and so drift to the top of the bar whilst maintaining their horizontal motion.

- This leads to a build up of negative charge on one side of the bar and positive charge on the other due to the lack of electrons. This is build up negative charge on one side of a bar and potential difference between the other two sides it can be measured as hall voltage.

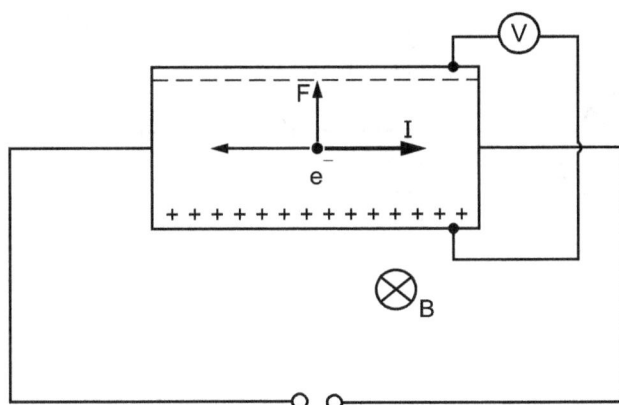

Fig. 6.9 : Illustration of the Hall effect in a bar of conducting material

This transverse voltage is the Hall voltage V_H and its magnitude is equal to IB/q_{nd}, where I is the current, B is the magnetic field, d is the sample thickness, and q (1.602×10^{-19} C) is the elementary charge. In conventional layer is used to layer or sheet density ($n_s = n_d$) instead of bulk density.

$$n_s \ = \ \frac{qB}{q|V_H|} \hspace{3cm} ...(6.1)$$

The Hall voltage V_H and from the known values of I, B, and q, one can determine the sheet density n_s of charge carriers in semiconductors. If the measurement apparatus is set up as shown, the Hall voltage is negative for n–type semiconductors and positive for p–type semiconductors. The sheet resistance R_S of the semiconductor can be conveniently determined by use of the Van der Pauw resistivity measurement technique. Since sheet resistance involves both sheet density and mobility, one can determine the Hall mobility from equation (6.1).

$$\mu = \frac{|V_H|}{R_S IB} = \frac{1}{qn_s R_s} \qquad \qquad ...(6.2)$$

If the conducting layer thickness d is known, one can determine the bulk resistivity ($r = R_S d$) and the bulk density ($n = n_S/d$).

The Van der Pauw Technique

In order to determine both the mobility μ and the sheet density n_s, a combination of a resistivity measurement and a Hall measurement is needed. We discuss here the Van der Pauw technique which, due to its convenience, is widely used in the semiconductor industry to determine the resistivity of uniform samples (References 3 and 4). As originally devised by Van der Pauw, one uses an arbitrarily shaped (but simply connected, i.e. no holes or nonconducting islands or inclusions), thin-plate sample containing four very small ohmic contacts placed on the periphery (preferably in the corners) of the plate.

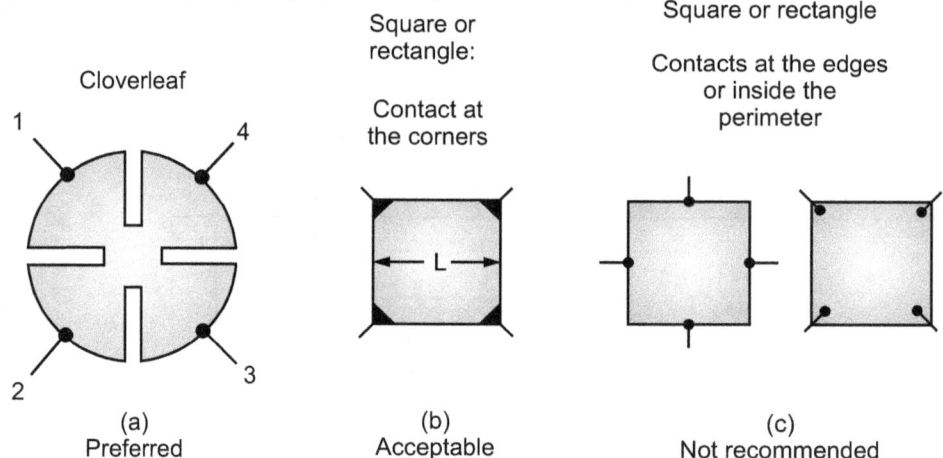

Fig. 6.10 : **Examples of possible Van der Pauw configurations and their preference**

The resistivity measurement objective is to determine the sheet resistance R_S. Van der Pauw demonstrated that there are actually two characteristic resistances R_A and R_B, associated with the corresponding terminals shown in Fig. 6.10. R_A and R_B are related to the sheet resistance R_S through the van der Pauw equation

$$e^{\frac{-pR_A}{R_s}} + e^{\frac{-pR_B}{R_s}} = 1 \qquad \qquad ...(6.3)$$

Which can be solved numerically for R_S.

The bulk electrical resistivity r can be calculated using

$$r = R_s \, d \qquad \qquad ...(6.4)$$

To obtain the two characteristic resistances, one applies a dc current I into contact 1 and out of contact 2 and measures the voltage V_{43} from contact 4 to contact 3. Next, one applies the current I into contact 2 and out of contact 3 while measuring the voltage V_{14} from contact 1 to contact 4 using a geometry shown in Fig. 6.11. R_A and R_B are calculated by means of the following expressions:

$$R_A = \frac{V_{43}}{I_{12}} \text{ and } R_B = \frac{V_{14}}{I_{23}} \qquad \qquad ...(6.5)$$

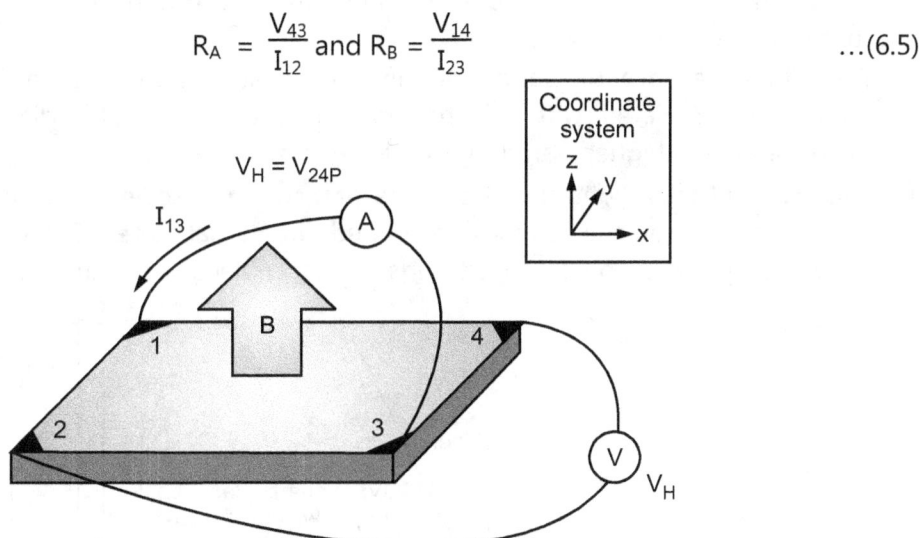

Fig. 6.11: Geometry contact

- The objective of the Hall measurement in the Van der Pauw technique is to determine the sheet carrier density n_s by measuring the Hall voltage V_H.
- The Hall voltage measurement consists of a series of voltage measurements with a constant current I and a constant magnetic field B applied perpendicular to the plane of the sample.
- To measure the Hall voltage V_H, a current I is forced through the opposing pair of contacts 1 and 3 and the Hall voltage V_H (= V_{24}) is measured across the remaining pair of contacts 2 and 4.
- Once the Hall voltage V_H is acquired, the sheet carrier density n_s can be calculated via $n_s = IB/q|V_H|$ from the known values of I, B, and q.

6.3 PHYSICAL MEASUREMENTS

- The limits of the measuring device necessarily involve some estimation of the final digit in the value for the measured quantity.
- When some instruments with digital outputs, it is because the meter is rounding for you and the true limit of "precision" for the instrument is being obscured by this rounding.

- In this case, reproducibility in measurements is a critical aspect of the measurements and often is reported. In engineering or production this is commonly referred to as "the tolerance."
- For example, furniture construction might be done to a tolerance of 1/64th of an inch while machining of an engine component might be done to a tolerance of 1/10,000th of an inch.

6.3.1 Fourier Transform Infrared Spectroscopy

- Fourier Transform–Infrared Spectroscopy (FTIR) is an analytical technique used to identify organic materials. This technique measures the absorption of infrared radiation by the sample material versus wavelength.
- The infrared absorption bands identify molecular components and structures when a material is irradiated with infrared radiation, absorbed IR radiation usually excites molecules into a higher vibrational state.
- The wavelength of light absorbed by a particular molecule is a function of the energy difference between the at-rest and excited vibrational states. The wavelengths that are absorbed by the sample are characteristic of its molecular structure as shown in Fig. 6.12.

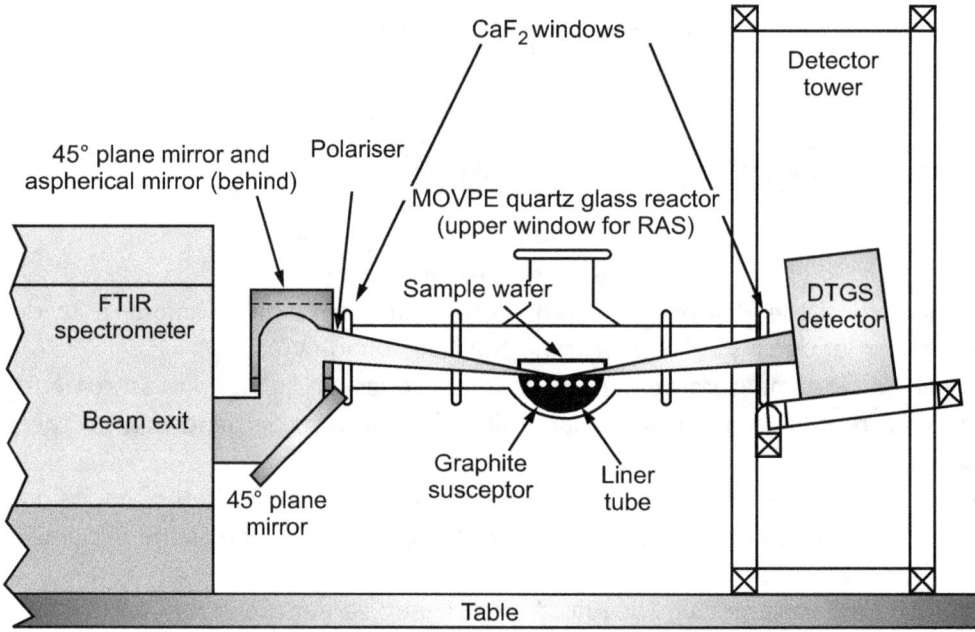

Fig. 6.12: FTIRS method

- The FTIR spectrometer uses an interferometer to modulate the wavelength from a broadband infrared source. A detector measures the intensity of transmitted or reflected light as a function of its wavelength.
- The detector is an interferogram, obtained the sign with computer using Fourier transforms to obtain a single–beam infrared spectrum. The FTIR spectra are usually

presented as plots of intensity versus wavenumber (in cm^{-1}). Wave is the reciprocal of the wavelength.

- The intensity can be plotted as the percentage of light transmittance or absorbance at each wavenumber. Since FTIR spectrometers can be hyphenated to chromatography, the mechanism of chemical reactions and the detection of unstable substances can be investigated with such instruments.

- The range of Infrared region is 12800 ~ 10 $cm^{-1}$and can be divided into near–infrared region (12800 ~ 4000 cm^{-1}), mid–infrared region (4000 ~ 200 cm^{-1}) and far–infrared region (50 ~ 1000 cm^{-1}). The discovery of infrared light can be dated back to the 19th century.

- Since then, scientists have established various ways to utilize infrared light. Infrared absorption spectroscopy is the method which scientists use to determine the structures of molecules with the molecules' characteristic absorption of infrared radiation. Infrared spectrum is molecular vibrational spectrum.

- When exposed to infrared radiation, sample molecules selectively absorb radiation of specific wavelengths which causes the change of dipole moment of sample molecules. Consequently, the vibrational energy levels of sample molecules transfer from ground state to excited state. The frequency of the absorption peak is determined by the vibrational energy gap. The number of absorption peaks is related to the number of vibrational freedom of the molecule. The intensity of absorption peaks is related to the change of dipole moment and the possibility of the transition of energy levels. Therefore, by analyzing the infrared spectrum, one can readily obtain abundant structure information of a molecule. Most molecules are infrared active except for several homonuclear diatomic molecules such as O2, N2 and Cl2 due to the zero dipole change in the vibration and rotation of these molecules. What makes infrared absorption spectroscopy even more useful is the fact that it is capable to analyze all gas, liquid and solid samples. The common used region for infrared absorption spectroscopy is 4000 ~ 400 cm-1because the absorption radiation of most organic compounds and inorganic ions is within this region. .

FTIR spectrometers are the third generation infrared spectrometer. FTIR spectrometers have several prominent advantages given as follows:

- The signal–to–noise ratio of spectrum is significantly higher than the previous generation infrared spectrometers.
- The accuracy of wavenumber is high. The error is within the range of ± 0.01 cm^{-1}.
- The scan time of all frequencies is short (approximately 1 second).
- The resolution is extremely high (0.1 ~ 0.005 cm^{-1}).
- The scan range is wide (1000 ~ 10 cm^{-1}).
- The interference from stray light is reduced. Due to these advantages, FTIR Spectrometers have replaced dispersive IR spectrometers.

Development of IR Spectrometers

Up till FTIR spectrometers, there have been three generations of IR spectrometers. These are given as follows:

1. The first generation IR spectrometer was invented in late 1950s. It utilizes prism optical splitting system. The prisms are made of NaCl. The requirement of the sample's water content and particle size is extremely strict. Further more, the scan range is narrow. In that repeatability is fairly poor. As a result, the first generation IR spectrometer is no longer in use.

2. The second generation IR spectrometer was introduced to the world in 1960s. It utilizes gratings as the monochrometer. The performance of the second generation IR spectrometer is much better compared with IR spectrometers with prism monochrometer, but there are still several prominent weaknesses such as low sensitivity, low scan speed and poor wavelength accuracy which rendered it out of date after the invention of the third generation IR spectrometer.

3. The invention of the third generation IR spectrometer, Fourier transform infrared spectrometer, marked the abdication of monochrometer and the prosperity of interferometer. With this replacement, IR spectrometers became exceptionally powerful. Consequently, various applications of IR spectrometer have been realized.

Dispersive IR Spectrometers

*   FTIR spectrometer is used to information of dispersive IR spectrometer. The basic components of a dispersive IR spectrometer include a radiation source, monochromator, and detector.

*   The common IR radiation sources are inert solids that are heated electrically to promote thermal emission of radiation in the infrared region of the electromagnetic spectrum.

*   The monochromator is a device used to disperse or separate a broad spectrum of IR radiation into individual narrow IR frequencies.

*   This spectrometer double–beam design with two equivalent beams from the same source passing through the sample and reference chambers as independent beams.

*   These reference and sample beams are alternately focused on the detector by making use of an optical chopper, such as, a sector mirror.

*   One beam will proceed, traveling through the sample, while the other beam will pass through a reference species for analytical comparison of transmitted photon wavefront information.

*   After that incident radiation travels through and sample species, the emitted wavefront of radiation is dispersed by a monochromator into its component frequencies. A combination of prisms or gratings with variable–slit mechanisms, mirrors, and filters comprise the dispersive system.

- Narrower slits gives better resolution by distinguishing more closely spaced frequencies of radiation and wider slits allow more light to reach the detector and provide better system sensitivity.

- The emitted wavefront beam hits the detector and generates an electrical signal as a response.

- The analog spectral output into an electrical signal this conversion use for electrical signals are further processed by the computer using mathematical algorithm to arrive at the final spectrum.

- The detectors used in IR spectrometers can be classified as either photon or quantum detectors or thermal detectors.

- It is the absorption of IR radiation by the sample, producing a change of IR radiation intensity, which gets detected as an off–null signal. This change is translated into the recorder response through the actions of synchronous motors.

- Each frequency that passes through the sample is measured individually by the detector which consequently slows the process of scanning the entire IR region. A block diagram of a classic dispersive IR spectrometer as shown in following Fig. 6.13.

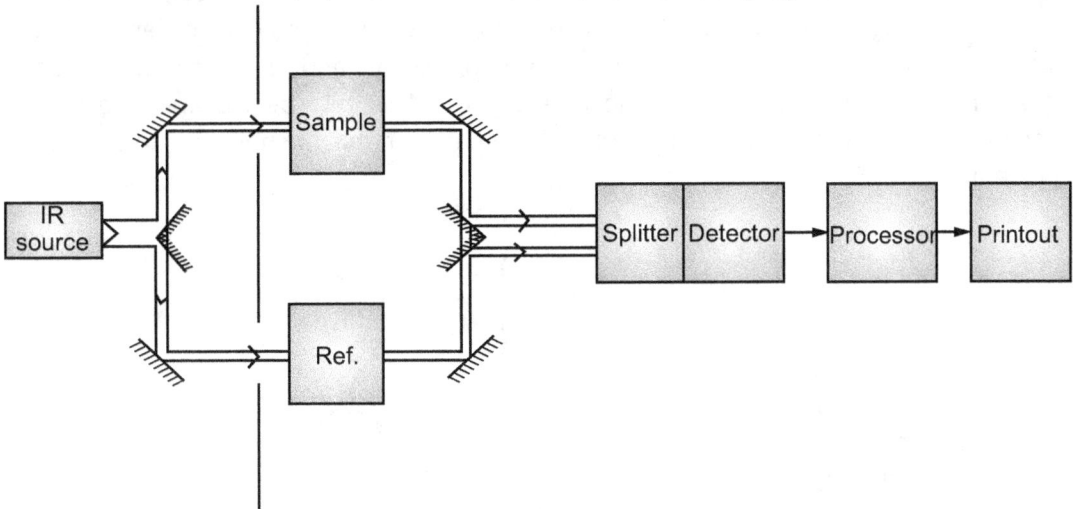

Fig. 6.13: IR spectrometer

The Components of FTIR Spectrometers

- In Fig. 6.14 consists of a source, interferometer, sample compartment, detector, amplifier, A/D convertor, and a computer.

- The source generates radiation which passes the sample through the interferometer and reaches the detector. Then the signal is amplified and converted to digital signal by the amplifier and analog–to–digital converter, respectively. Hence, the signal is transferred to a computer in which Fourier transform is carried out.

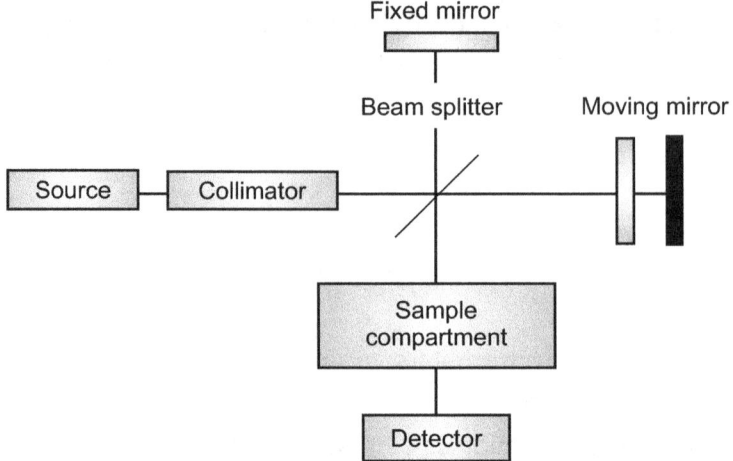

Fig. 6.14: Difference between FTIR and IR spectrometer

The major difference between an FTIR spectrometer and a dispersive IR spectrometer is the Michelson interferometer.

Michelson Interferometer

- The Michelson interferometer, which is the core of FTIR spectrometers, is used to split one beam of light into two so that the paths of the two beams are different. Then the Michelson interferometer recombines the two beams and conducts them into the detector where the difference of the intensity of these two beams are measured as a function of the difference of the paths Schematic of the Michelson Interferometer as shown in Fig. 6.15.

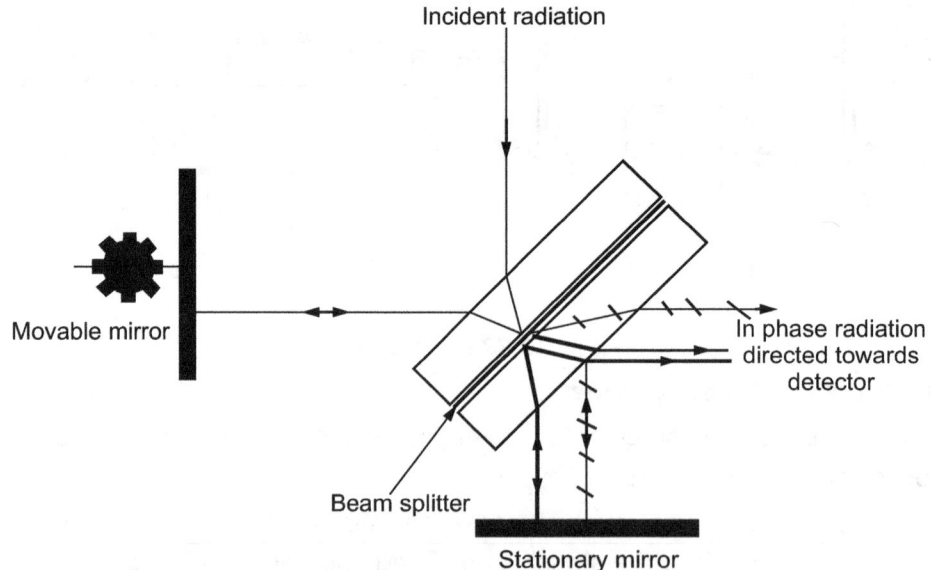

Fig. 6.15: Michelson interferometer

- Michelson interferometer consists of two perpendicular mirrors and a beamsplitter. One of the mirrors is a stationary mirror and another one is a movable mirror.

- The beamsplitter is designed to transmit half of the light and reflect half of the light. The transmitted light and the reflected light strike the stationary mirror and the movable mirror, respectively.

- When reflected back by the mirrors, two beams of light recombine with each other at the beam splitter. If the distances travelled by two beams are the same which means the distances between two mirrors and the beamsplitter are the same, the situation is defined as zero path difference (ZPD).

- If the movable mirror moves away from the beamsplitter, the light beam which strikes the movable mirror will travel a longer distance than the light beam which strikes the stationary mirror.

- The distance which is the movable mirror is away from the ZPD is defined as the mirror displacement and it is represented by Δ. It is obvious that the extra distance travelled by the light which strikes the movable mirror is 2Δ. OPD is defined as the extra distance represented by delta. Therefore,

$$\delta = 2\Delta \text{ (1) (1) } \delta = 2\Delta$$

When OPD is the multiples of the wavelength, constructive interference occurs because crests overlap with crests, troughs with troughs. As this condition result maximum intensity signal is observed by the detector. This situation can be described by the following equation:

$$\delta = n\lambda(2) \text{ (2) } \delta = n\lambda$$

With $n = 0, 1, 2, 3...$

In contrast, when OPD is the half wavelength or half wavelength add multiples of wavelength, destructive interference occurs because crests overlap with troughs. A minimum intensity signal is observed by the detector.

$$\delta = (n + 12)\lambda \text{ (3) (3) } \delta = (n + 12) \lambda$$

With $n = 0, 1, 2, 3...$

If the OPD is neither n–fold wavelengths nor (n + 1/2)–fold wavelengths, the interference should be between constructive and destructive. The signal should be between maximum and minimum. Since the mirror moves back and forth, the intensity of the signal increases and decreases which gives rise to a cosine wave. This plot defined as interferogram when detecting the radiation of a broad band source rather than a single–wavelength source, a peak at ZPD is found in the interferogram.

Fourier Transform of Interferogram to Spectrum

The interferogram is a function of time and the values outputted by this function of time are said to make up the time domain. The time domain is Fourier transformed to get a frequency domain, which is deconvolved to product a spectrum.

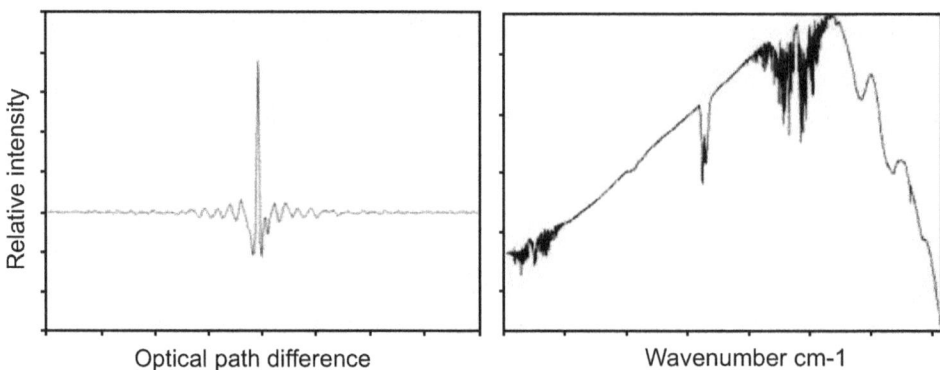

Fig. 6.16: FTIR spectrum

Operation of an FTIR Spectrometer

Step 1

The first step is sample preparation. The standard method to prepare solid sample for FTIR spectrometer is to use KBr. About 2 mg of sample and 200 mg KBr are dried and ground. The particle size should be unified and less than two micrometers. Then, the mixture is squeezed to form transparent pellets which can be measured directly. For liquids with high boiling point or viscous solution, it can be added in between two NaCl pellets. Then the sample is fixed in the cell by skews and measured. For volatile liquid sample, it is dissolved in CS_2 or CCl_4 to form 10% solution. Then the solution is injected into a liquid cell for measurement. Gas sample needs to be measured in a gas cell with two KBr windows on each side. The gas cell should first be vacuumed. Then the sample can be introduced to the gas cell for measurement.

Step 2

The second step is getting a background spectrum by collecting an interferogram and its subsequent conversion to frequency data by inverse Fourier transform. We obtain the background spectrum because the solvent in which we place our sample will have traces of dissolved gases as well as solvent molecules that contribute information that are not our sample. The background spectrum will contain information about the species of gases and solvent molecules, which may then be subtracted away from our sample spectrum in order to gain information about just the sample. The background spectrum also takes into account several other factors related to the instrument performance, which includes information about the source, interferometer, detector, and the contribution of ambient water (note the two irregular groups of lines at about 3600 cm^{-1} and about 1600

cm^{-1} in Fig. 6.17and carbon dioxide (doublet at 2360 cm^{-1} and sharp spike at 667

cm^{-1} in Fig. 6.17) present in the optical bench.

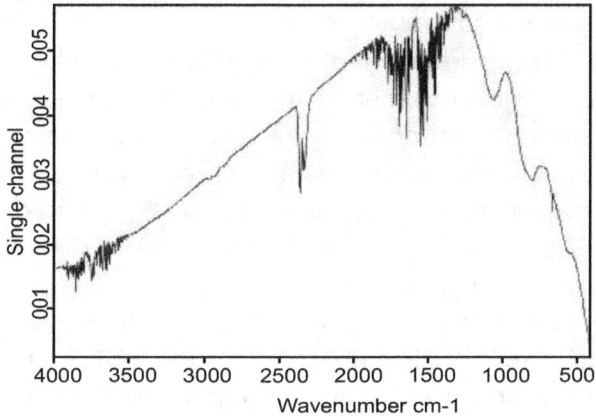

Fig. 6.17: Water contribution

Step 3

A single–beam spectrum of the sample, which contain absorption bands from the sample as well as the background (gaseous or solvent).

Step 4

The ratio between the single–beam sample spectrum and the single beam background spectrum gives the spectrum of the sample.

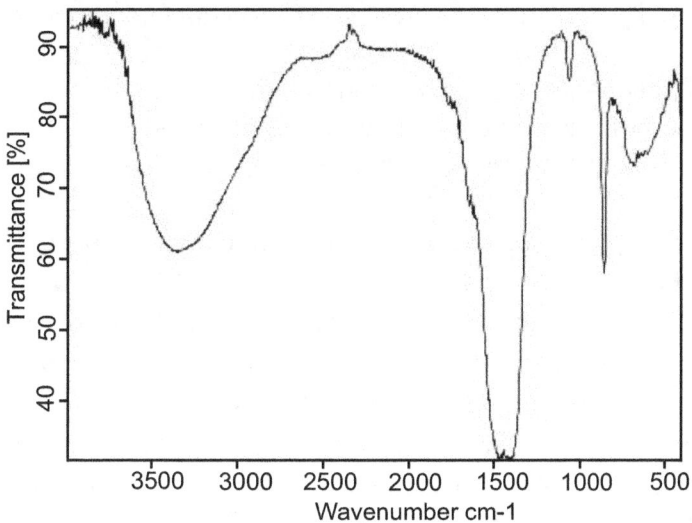

Fig. 6.18: Single beam spectrum

Step 5

Data analysis is done by assigning the observed absorption frequency bands in the sample spectrum to appropriate normal modes of vibrations in the molecules.

Portable FTIR Spectrometers

Despite of the powerfulness of traditional FTIR spectrometers, they are not suitable for real-time monitoring or field use. So various portable FTIR spectrometers have been developed.

Here two examples are given as follows:

- Ahonen *et al* developed a portable, real–time FTIR spectrometer as a gas analyzer for industrial hygiene use. The instrument consists of an operational keyboard, a control panel, signal and control processing electronics, an interferometer, a heatable sample cell and a detector. All the components were packed into a cart. To minimize the size of the instrument, the resolution of FTIR spectrometer was sacraficed. The use of industrial hygiene and correlation coefficient of hygienic effect between the analyzer and adsorption tubes is about 1 mg/m^3.
- Korb *et al* developed a portable FTIR spectrometer which only weighs about 12.5 kg. The energy source of the instrument is battery so that the mobility is significantly enhanced. The instrument can function well within the temperature range of 0 to 45 °C and the humidity range of 0 to 100%. Consequently, this instrument is excellent for the analysis of radiation from the surface and atmosphere of the Earth. The instrument is stable. After a three–year operation, it did not lose optical alignment. The reduction of size was implemented by a creative design of optical system and accessory components. Two KBr prisms were used to constitute the interferometer cavity. Optical coatings replaced the mirrors and beam splitter in the interferometer. The optical path is shortened with a much more compact packaging of components.

Applications of FTIR

- Identification of simple mixtures of organic and inorganic compounds both as solids or liquids.
- Identification of polymers and polymer blends.
- Indirect verification of trace organic contaminants on surfaces.
- Routine qualitative & quantitative FTIR Analysis.
- Thin film analysis.
- Analysis of adhesives, coatings and adhesion promoters or coupling agents.
- Small visible particle chemical analysis.
- Analysis of stains and surface blemishes remnant fromcleaning and degreasing processes combined withoptical microscopy, SEM/EDX, XPS and SIMS techniques.
- Analysis of resins, composite materials and release films.
- Solvent extractions of leachables or contaminants, plasticisers, mould release agents and weak boundary layers coupled with XPS surface chemical analysis techniques.
- Identification of rubbers and filled rubbers.
- Determination of degrees of crystallinity in polymers (eg LDPE and HDPE).
- Compararive chain lengths in organics.
- Extent of thermal, UV or other degredation or depolymerisation of polymers and paint coatings.
- Analysis of gaseous samples using a gas cell for headspace analysis or environmental monitoring.
- Analysis of unknown solvents, cleaning agents and detergents.

6.3.2 Electron Microscopy

- The electron microscope is a type of microscope that uses a beam of electrons to create an image of the specimen. Microscope is higher magnifications and has a greater resolving power than a light microscope.

- They are large, expensive pieces of equipment, generally standing alone in a small, specially designed room and requiring trained personnel to operate them.

- An electron microscope is a type of microscope that uses electrons rather than photons as a conventional light microscope does for imaging.

- Because electrons have a much smaller wavelength than photons, they provide much greater magnification. Electrons are the tiny "satellites" that orbit the atomic nucleus and carry electric charge these particles are so small that in physics they are often modeled as points.

- Yet light waves are much larger, with a wavelength of around 500 nanometers for the color green, for instance.

- The best optical microscopes only offer about 2000X magnification of a sample, whereas some electron microscopes can magnify a sample by 50 million times; in contrast, 2 million times is more typical.

- This works out to a resolution limit of about 0.1 nanometers, allowing the observation of individual atoms on a surface.

The History of EM

- By the middle of the 19th century, microscopists had accepted that it was simply not possible to resolve structures of less than half a micrometer with a light microscope because of the Abbe's formula of the cathode ray tube was literally about to change the way they looked at things; for the development progress by using electrons instead of light! Hertz (1857–94) suggested that cathode rays were a form of wave motion and Weichert, in 1899, found that these rays could be concentrated into a small spot by the use of an axial magnetic field produced by a long solenoid. But it was not until 1926 short solenoid converges beam of electro in the same glass then light of the sun directly made between light and electrons beam.

- Busch should probably therefore be known as the father of electron optics. In 1931 the German engineers Ernst Ruska and Maximillion Knoll succeeded in magnifying and electron image.

- This was, in retrospect, the moment of the invention of the electron microscope but the first prototype was actually built by Ruska in 1933 and was capable of resolving to 50 nm. Although it was primitive and not really fit for practical use, Ruska was recognized some 50 years later by the award of a Nobel Prize.

- The first commercially available electron microscope was built in England by Metropolitan Vickers for Imperial College, London, and was called the EM1, though it never surpassed the resolution of a good optical microscope.

- The early electron microscopes did not excite the optical microscopists because the electron beam, which had a very high current density, was concentrated into a very small area and was very hot and therefore charred any non–metallic specimens that were examined.

- Electron microscope treating for biological specimens with osmium and cutting very slices. Viable proposition at the University of Toronto, in 1938, Eli Franklin Burton and students Cecil Hall, James Hillier and Albert Prebus constructed the first electron microscope in the New World.

- This was an effective, high–resolution instrument, the design of which eventually led to what was to become known as the RCA (Radio Corporation of America) range of very successful microscopes.

Types of Electron Microscopes

- All electron microscopes use electromagnetic and/or electrostatic lenses to control the path of electrons. Glass lenses, used in light microscopes, have no effect on the electron beam. The basic design of an electromagnetic lens is a solenoid (a coil of wire around the outside of a tube) through which one can pass a current, thereby inducing an electromagnetic field.

- The electron beam passes through the centre of such solenoids on its way down the column of the electron microscope towards the sample. Electrons are very sensitive to magnetic fields and can therefore be controlled by changing the current through the lenses. The faster the electrons travel, the shorter their wavelength.

- The resolving power of a microscope is directly related to the wavelength of the irradiation used to form an image. Reducing wavelength increases resolution.

- The resolution of the microscope is increased if the accelerating voltage of the electron beam is increased. In modern electron microscopes can magnify objects up to about two million times, they are still based upon Ruska's prototype and the correlation between wavelength and resolution. The electron microscope is an integral part of many laboratories such as the John Innes Centre. Researchers can use it to examine biological materials, a variety of large molecules, medical biopsy samples, metals and crystalline structures, and the characteristics of various surfaces. They can be used as part of a production line, such as in the fabrication of silicon chips, or within forensics laboratories for looking at samples such as gunshot residues.

There are four types of this microscope the first two being the most common:

1. The Transmission Electron Microscope (TEM),

2. Scanning Electron Microscope (SEM),

3. Reflection Electron Microscope (REM),

4. Scanning Transmission Electron Microscope (STEM)

1. Transmission Electron Microscope (TEM)

In a transmission electron microscope or TEM, a beam of electrons hits a very thin sample like 100 nm thick. The electrons are transmitted through the sample. The electrons hit a fluorescence screen that forms an image with the electrons that were transmitted. By imagining how a movie projector works. In a projector, you have a film that has the negative image that will be projected. The projector shines white light on the negative and the light transmitted forms the image contained in the negative. The TEM is the electron microscope as it was originally invented. Using a sample that is semi–transparent to electrons, an electron beam is fired directly through the sample. A receiver on the other side measures the density of electrons at each individual point and compiles them into a grayscale image.

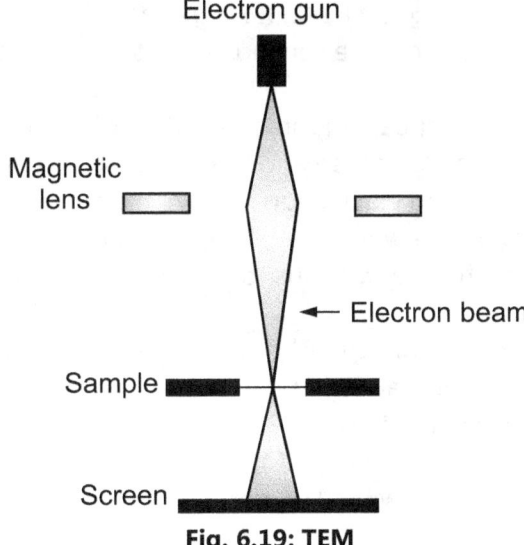

Fig. 6.19: TEM

The Transmission Electron Microscope (TEM) works as follows:

*   A high–voltage electricity supply powers the cathode.

*   The cathode is a heated filament, a bit like the electron gun in an old–fashioned cathode–ray tube (CRT) TV. It generates a beam of electrons that works in an analogous way to the beam of light in an optical microscope.

*   An electromagnetic coil (the first lens) concentrates the electrons into a more powerful beam.

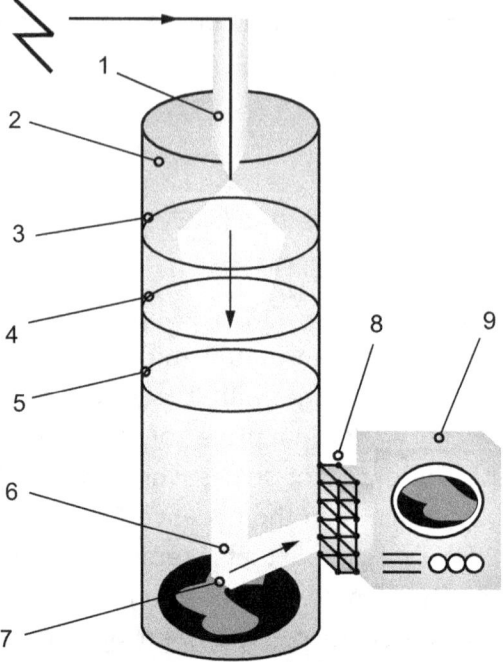

Fig. 6.20: Monitoring of TEM

- Another electromagnetic coil (the second lens) focuses the beam onto a certain part of the specimen.
- The specimen sits on a copper grid in the middle of the main microscope tube. The beam passes through the specimen and "picks up" an image of it.
- The projector lens (the third lens) magnifies the image.
- The image becomes visible when the electron beam hits a fluorescent screen at the base of the machine. This is analogous to the phosphor screen at the front of an old–fashioned TV .
- The image can be viewed directly (through a viewing portal), through binoculars at the side, or on a TV monitor attached to an image intensifier.

2. **Scanning Electron Microscope (SEM)**
- In a scanning electron microscope or SEM, a beam of electrons scans the surface of a sample. The electrons interact with the material in this was triggers the emission of secondary electrons.
- These secondary electrons are captured by a detector the direction of the emission of the secondary electrons depends on the orientation of the features of the surface.
- The image formed will reflect the characteristic feature of the region of the surface that was exposed to the electron beam. SEM required less resolution than a TEM.
- This microscope scans an electron beam across the sample. Instead of analyzing the original beam for information about the makeup of the sample, sensors pick up secondary electrons released from the surface of the sample via excitation from the primary beam.

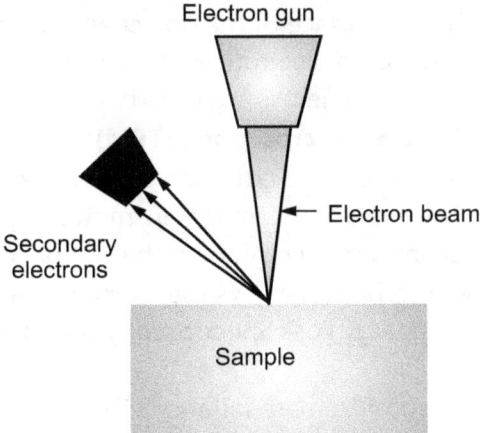

Fig. 6.21: SEM

The Scanning Electron Microscope (SEM) works are given as follows:

- Electrons are fired into the machine.
- The main part of the machine (where the object is scanned) is contained within a sealed vacuum chamber because precise electron beams can't travel effectively through air.

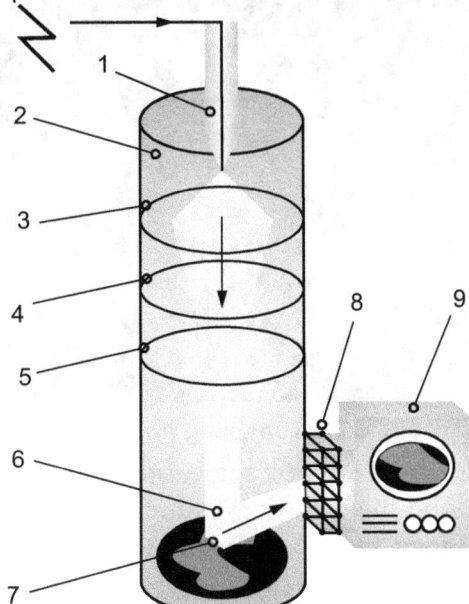

Fig. 6.22: Monitoring of SEM

- A positively charged electrode (anode) attracts the electrons and accelerates them into an energetic beam.
- An electromagnetic coil brings the electron beam to a very precise focus, much like a lens.
- Another coil, lower down, steers the electron beam from side to side.
- The beam systematically scans across the object being viewed.

- Electrons from the beam hit the surface of the object and bounce off it.
- A detector registers these scattered electrons and turns them into a picture.
- A hugely magnified image of the object is displayed on a TV screen.

3. Scanning Transmission Electron Microscope (STEM)

- In a scanning transmission electron microscope or STEM combines the capabilities of both an SEM and a TEM. The electron beam is transmitted across the sample to create an image (TEM) while it also scans a small region on the sample (SEM).
- The ability to scan the electron beams allows the user to analyze the sample with various techniques such as Electron Energy Loss Spectroscopy (EELS) and Energy Dispersive X–ray (EDX) Spectroscopy.
- TEM produce images of the inside material and SEM show 3D surfaces, it designed to make images of the atoms or molecules.
- They work differently to TEMs and SEMs too: they have an extremely sharp metallic probe that scans back and forth across the surface of the specimen. Electrons try to wriggle out of the specimen and jump across the gap, into the probe, by an unusual phenomenon called "tunneling".

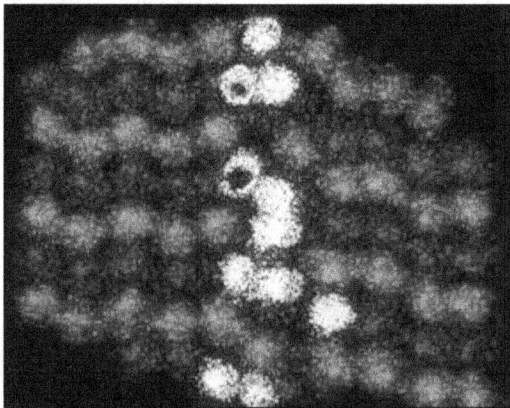

Fig. 6.23: Tunneling Phenomenon

- The closer the probe is to the surface, the easier it is for electrons to tunnel into it, the more electrons escape, and the greater the tunneling current. The microscope constantly moves the probe up or down by tiny amounts to keep the tunneling current constant.
- The probe has to move, it effectively measures the peaks and troughs of the specimen's surface.
- A computer turns this information into a map of the specimen that shows up its detailed atomic structure.

Disadvantages of Electron Microscopy

- Electron microscopes are very expensive to buy and maintain. They are dynamic rather than static in their operation: requiring extremely stable high voltage supplies, extremely stable currents to each electromagnetic coil/lens, continuously–pumped high/ultra–high vacuum systems and a cooling water supply circulation through the lenses and pumps. As they are very sensitive to vibration and external magnetic fields, microscopes aimed at achieving high resolutions must be housed in buildings with special services.

- A significant amount of training is required in order to operate an electron microscope successfully and electron microscopy is considered a specialized skill.

- The samples have to be viewed in a vacuum, as the molecules that make up air would scatter the electrons. This means that the samples need to be specially prepared by sometimes lengthy and difficult techniques to withstand the environment inside an electron microscope. Recent advances have allowed some hydrated samples to be imaged using an environmental scanning electron microscope, but the applications for this type of imaging are still limited.

6.3.3 Atomic Force Microscope

- Atomic Force Microscopy (AFM) is a form of scanning probe microscopy (SPM) where a small probe is scanned across the sample to obtain information about the sample's surface.

- The information gathered from the probe's interaction with the surface can be physical topography or as diverse as measurements of the material's physical, magnetic, or chemical properties.

- These data are collected as the probe is scanned in a raster pattern across the sample to form a map of the measured property relative to the X–Y position.

- The AFM microscopic image shows the variation measurement for example height of magnetic domains over the area of image. The AFM probe diameter 100A° at the end of cantilever beam.

- The probe is attached to a piezoelectric scanner tube, which scans the probe across a selected area of the sample surface.

- Interatomic forces between the probe tip and the sample surface cause the cantilever to deflect as the sample's surface topography (or other properties) changes. A laser light reflected from the back of the cantilever measures the deflection of the cantilever.

- An Atomic Force Microscope (AFM) is an extremely precise microscope that images a sample by rapidly moving a probe with a nanometer–sized tip across the surface.

- This is quite different than an optical microscope used to reflected light to image a sample.

- An AFM probe offers a much higher degree of resolution than an optical microscope because of the size of probe is much smaller than the finest wavelength of visible light. In an ultra–high vacuum, an atomic force microscope can image individual atoms.

- Its extremely high resolution capabilities have made the AFM popular with researchers working in the field of nanotechnology. The scanning tunneling microscope (STM), which images a surface indirectly via measuring the degree of quantum tunneling between the probe and sample, in an atomic force microscope the probe either makes direct contact with the surface or measures incipient chemical bonding between probe and sample.

- The AFM uses a micro scale cantilever with a probe tip whose size is measured in nanometers.

AFM operates two modes:

1. Contact (static) mode and
2. Dynamic (oscillating) mode.

In static mode, while in dynamic mode it oscillates. When the AFM is brought close to or contacts the surface, the cantilever deflects. The cantilever is a mirror which reflects a laser. The laser reflects onto a photodiode, which precisely measures its deflection. When the oscillation or position of the AFM tip changes, it is registered in the photodiode and an image is built up, such as optical interferometer, capacitive sensing or piezoresistive (electromechanical) probe tips.

Working AFM

- AFMs operate by measuring force between a probe and the sample. Normally, the probe is a sharp tip, which is a 3 to 6 μm tall pyramid with 15 to 40 μm end radius.
- Though the lateral resolution of AFM is low (~30 vm) due to the convolution, the vertical resolution can be up to 0.1 nm. AFMs use a laser beam deflection system where a laser is reflected from the back of the reflective AFM lever and onto a position–sensitive detector. AFM tips and cantilevers are micro fabricated from Si or Si_3N_4. Typical tip radius is from a few to 10s of nm.

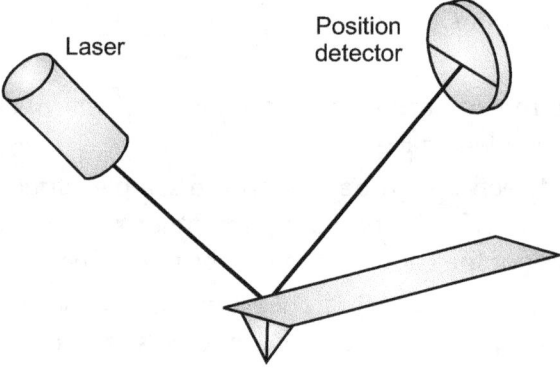

Fig. 6.24: AFM

Measuring Forces

AFM relies on the forces between the tip and sample, these forces impact AFM imaging. The force is not measured directly, but calculated by measuring the deflection of the lever, knowing the stiffness of the cantilever.

Hooke's law gives

$$F = -k\,z$$

where F is the force, k is the stiffness of the lever, and z is the distance the lever is bent.

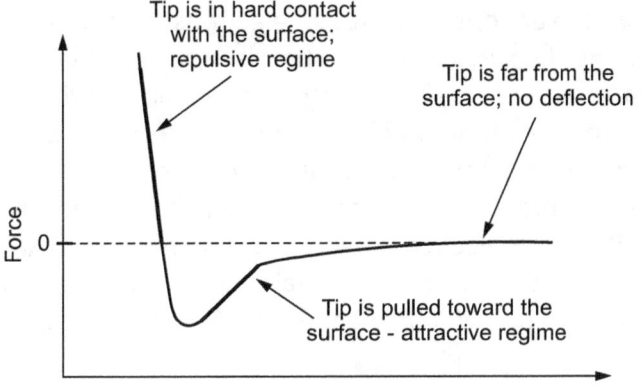

Fig. 6.25: Hooke law

6.3.4 X–Ray Photoelectron Spectroscopy

- X–ray Photoelectron Spectroscopy (XPS), also known as ESCA (electron spectroscopy for chemical analysis) provides both elemental and chemical state information virtually without restriction on the type of material which can be analyzed.
- Monochromatic or unfiltered Al Ka or Mg Ka and photoelectrons are emitted from the surface.
- The kinetic energy of these emitted electrons is characteristic of the element from which the photoelectron originated.
- The position and intensity of the peaks in an energy spectrum provide the desired chemical state and quantitative information. This technique analysis of with sampling volume extends from a surface to depth 50 to 70 A.
- XPS analysis can be utilized for sputter depth profiling to characterize thin films by quantifying matrix–level elements as a function of depth. XPS is an elemental analysis technique that is unique in providing chemical state information of the detected elements, such as distinguishing between sulfate and sulfide forms of the element sulfur.
- The process works by irradiating a sample with monochromatic X–rays, resulting in the emission of photoelectrons whose energies are characteristic of the elements within the sampling volume.
- The sample is placed in an ultrahigh vacuum environment and exposed to a low–energy, monochromatic X–ray source. The incident X–rays cause the ejection of core–level electrons from sample atoms.
- The energy of a photo emitted core electron is a function of its binding energy and is characteristic of the element from which it was emitted. Energy emitted photoelectrons is the primary data used for XPS this is the analysis of energy. When the core electron is ejected by the incident x–ray, an outer electron fills the core hole.
- This transition is balanced by the emission of an Auger electron or characteristic x–ray Auger electrons can be used in XPS, emitted photoelectrons.
- The photoelectrons and Auger electrons emitted from the sample are detected by an electron energy analyzer, and their energy is determined as a function of their velocity entering the detector.

- The number of photoelectrons and Auger electrons as a function of their energy, a spectrum representing the surface composition is obtained. The energy corresponding to each peak is characteristic of an element present. The area under a peak in the spectrum is a measure of the relative amount of the element represented by that peak.
- The peak shape and precise position indicates the chemical state for the element. XPS is a surface sensitive technique hence those electrons generated near the surface escape and are detected. The photoelectrons of interest have relatively low kinetic energy.
- Due to inelastic collisions within the sample's atomic structure, photoelectrons originating more than 20 to 50 °A below the surface cannot escape with sufficient energy to be detected.

For Example

1. The XPS spectrum of Pd metal

The Fig. 6.26 below shows a real XPS spectrum obtained from a Pd metal sample using Mg K_α radiation.

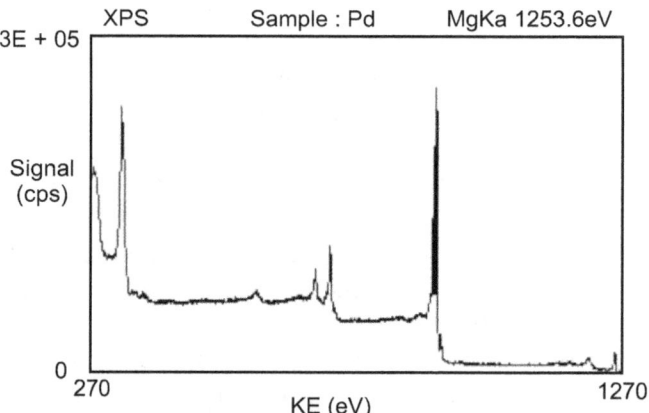

Fig. 6.26: XPS spectrum

The main peaks occur at kinetic energies of ca. 330, 690, 720, 910 and 920 eV.

Since the photon energy of the radiation is always known it is a trivial matter to transform the spectrum so that it is plotted against BE as opposed to KE.

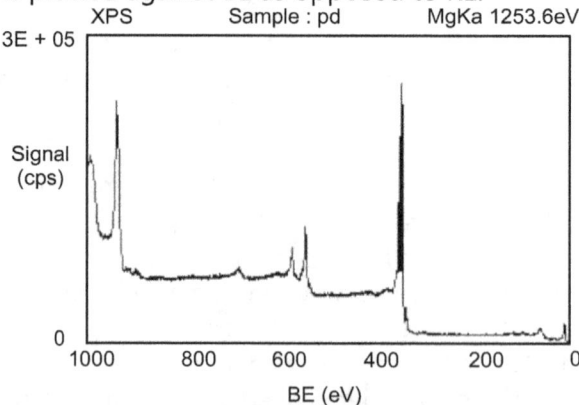

Fig. 6.27: Trivial spectrum

The most intense peak is now seen to occur at a binding energy of ca. 335 eV

Working downwards from the highest energy levels:

1. The valence band (4d, 5s) emission occurs at a binding energy of ca. 0 – 8 ev (measured with respect to the Fermi level, or alternatively at ca. 4 – 12 ev if measured with respect to the vacuum level).

2. The emission from the 4p and 4s levels gives rise to very weak peaks at 54 ev and 88 ev respectively

3. The most intense peak at ca. 335 ev is due to emission from the 3d levels of the pd atoms, whilst the 3p and 3s levels give rise to the peaks at ca. 534/561 ev and 673 ev respectively.

4. The remaining peak is not an xps peak at all! – It is an auger peak arising from x–ray induced auger emission. It occurs at a kinetic energy of ca. 330 ev (in this case it is really meaningless to refer to an associated binding energy).

These assignments are summarized as follows:

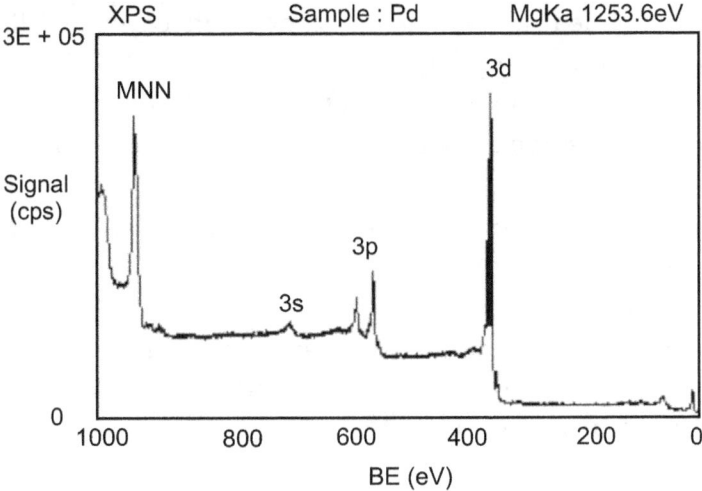

Fig. 6.28: Sample assignment

6.3.5 Profilometers

- A profilometer is a device used to measure the roughness of a surface. There are two classes of profilometers: (1) contact and (2) non–contact.

- This device also used for vertical difference between the high and low point of a surface in nanometers. This tight measurement readily illustrates the difference in objects that look or feel the same without direct measurement. While a profilometer is common in many fields, one of their main uses is measuring the roughness of road surfaces.

- A Profilometer is a measuring device used to measure relative surface roughness, peak to valley, in order to quantify its roughness.

- They may operate in either contact or non–contact modes and may use optical or stylus techniques to make the actual measurements.

- A contact profilometer uses technology much like that of a record player. A stylus with a diamond tip is run over a sample of a material. The records styles groves as a wave pattern and send the information to a computer.

- This computer can be used at the wave to directly model of the stylus moves.

- The process is done; the system will have an accurate model of every location measured. The first types of profilometers and are still very common. The non–contact tools, but it is limited to use on samples.

- They are generally difficult to use in the field since the surface being examined needs to fit under the reading needle.

- A non–contact profilometer uses beams of light to read a surface. Much like the common range finder, they shoot a beam out and measure the time it takes to return.

- This gives two major advantages to this style of profilometer over the contact version.

- First, it easily works in the field, as it can just sit on a surface and it suffers almost no wear since none of its parts touch anything.

- This profilometer style has one major disadvantage. Since it sends data to the central system using digital code, the surface modeling for the area needs to be translated into human–usable data.

- This requires an additional step that the contact version doesn't need, and it can greatly increase the modeling time. One area where profilometers are very common is in measuring a road's roughness.

- When used for this purpose, the profilometer, along with several other measurement tools, connects to a moving test system. This system can be specialized by the tools these are used in profilometers filed over a distance they are in non-contact device.

Laser Profilometer

A profilometer is an instrument that measures a surface profile to determine its roughness. A surface's vertical resolution is normally measured at the nanometer level, with lateral resolutions being measured to a less accurate degree. Over the past decade, profilometers have started using laser technology in order to improve the degree to which a surface can be measured without having to physically touch the profile being measured. The most recent laser profilometers have been able to map surfaces in 3D, thereby displaying form and texture over a large area.

6.3.6 Reflectrometers

A reflectometer, also referred to as a spectrophotometer, is an optical instrument used to measure the intensity of light through a solution or object as a function of the light's wavelength. They are typically used to measure how reflective a particular solution, glass object, or gas is. Reflectometers also measure the diffusivity of light for each of the known wavelength ranges.

There are two different parts to a fully functional reflectometer

1. The spectrometer
2. The photometer

1. The Spectrometer

- The spectrometer produces light of any wavelength, and the photometer records the intensity of the light. The instrument used to the test subject is placed between the spectrometer beam and the photometer.
- The intensity of the light is absorbed by the photometer, which then sends a voltage signal to a galvanometer, a device used to display scientific results.
- Time Domain Reflectometers (TDRs) on telephone cables since the late 1960s, but only the best technicians' impedance of the discontinuities incident the signal to be sent back towards the source.
- The advanced capabilities offered by the TDR. This one piece of equipment can triple efficiency and reduce call backs.
- A TDR is a test set used to characterize and locate faults in metallic cables. It transmits a short rise time pulse along the cable pair.
- If the cable pair is of a uniform admittance and properly terminated, the entire transmitted pulse will be absorbed in the far–end termination and no signal will be reflected toward the TDR.
- It is possible to find the proportional relationship between the concentration of the solute and the intensity of the light from the spectrometer.
- The intensity of transmitted light through a mixed solution, i.e. one with a colored solute, equals the intensity of transmitted light through the pure solvent, multiplied by ten to the negative power of the concentration of the mixed solution, times a constant and the distance that the light passes through the solution.
- In industry and teaching lab different types of reflectometers are used. One type of reflectometer that is frequently employed in academic settings is called the Spectronic 20 reflectometer or the Spectronic 20 spectrophotometer.
- To use, the instrument is warmed about 15 minutes before use. For wavelengths in the more outlying ranges, special instruments, such as corvettes, must be used to accurately analyze the light sample.
- Once the wavelength has been set, the reflectometer is tarred to zero in order to ensure the most accurate spectrophotometric results. The holding tube is wiped clean and the sample is placed in the tube. The light control knob is tarred to zero on the absorbance scale.
- Before performing tests on desired solutions, scientists usually perform tests on a reference solution to provide a benchmark for future results.

SUMMARY

- Electrical measurements are those that measure the voltage, current, and power and resistance in an electric circuit.

- Electrical methods include electrical resistivity, induced polarization (IP), and spontaneous or self potential (SP).

- According to the new Hot Probe technique, one can measure and calculate the majority charged carriers concentration and its dynamic parameters.

- The term sheet resistance should be familiar if you work with electronic thin films. It is a function of the bulk resistivity of a metallic film, and its thickness.

- Hall effect, development of a transverse electric field in a solid material when it carries an electric current and is placed in a magnetic field that is perpendicular to the current.

- All measurements that are made to the limits of the measuring device necessarily involve some estimation of the final digit in the value for the measured quantity.

- Fourier Transform–Infrared Spectroscopy (FTIR) is an analytical technique used to identify organic (and in some cases inorganic) materials.

- The electron microscope is a type of microscope that uses a beam of electrons to create an image of the specimen.

- Atomic Force Microscopy (AFM) is a form of scanning probe microscopy (SPM) where a small probe is scanned across the sample to obtain information about the sample's surface.

- X–ray photoelectron spectroscopy (XPS), also known as ESCA (electron spectroscopy for chemical analysis) provides both elemental and chemical state information virtually without restriction on the type of material which can be analyzed.

- A profilometer is a device used to measure the roughness of a surface. There are two classes of profilometers: contact and non–contact.

EXERCISE

1. Discuss about the hot probe method and sheet resistance?
2. Define the Hall Effect sensor
3. Explain about the Hall Effect measurements
4. Discuss about the Fourier Transform infrared spectroscopy.
5. What are the types of electron microscopes?
6. Explain automic force microscope
7. Describe X ray photoelectron spectroscopy
8. Explain Profilometers
9. Explain reflectrometers.

REFERENCE

1. Fundamentals of Nanoelectronics, by Hanson

2. Nanoelectronics and Information Technology, by Rainer Waser

3. Introduction to Nanoelectronics: Science, Nanotechnology, Engineering, and by Vladimir V. Mitin, Viatcheslav A. Kochelap, Michael A. Stroscio

4. MEMS and MOEMS Technology and Applications, by P. Rai-Choudhury

5. Adleman, L. 1994. Molecular computation of solutions to combinatorial problems. Science 266:1021.

6. Alivisatos, A.P., et al. 1996. Organization of 'nanocrystal molecules' using DNA. Nature 382:609.

7. Aviram, A., and M. Ratner, eds. 1998. Molecular electronics: Science and technology. Annals of the New

8. York Academy of Sciences, Vol. 852. New York: New York Academy of Sciences.

9. Balzani, V., M. Gomez-Lopez, and J.F. Stoddart. 1998. Molecular machines. Acc. Chem. Res. 31:405.

10. Bockrath, M., et al. 1997. Single electron transport in ropes of carbon nanotubes. Science 275:1922.

11. Bumm, L.A., J.J. Arnold, M.T. Cygan, T.D. Dunbar, T.P. Burgin, L. Jones II, D.L. Allara, J.M. Tour, and P.S. Weiss. 1996. Are single molecular wires conducting? Science 271:1705-1707.

12. Chen, J., M.A. Reed, A.M. Rawlett, and J.M. Tour. 1999. Large on-off ratios and negative differential resistance in a molecular electronic device. Science 286:1550-1552.

13. Chou, S., and P.R. Krauss. 1996. Quantum magnetic disk. J. Magn. Magn. Mater. 155:151.

14. Collier, C.P., E.W. Wong, M. Belohradský, F.M. Raymo, J.F. Stoddart, P.J. Kuekes, R.S. Williams, and J.R. Heath. 1999. Electronically configurable molecular-based logic gates. Science 285:391-394.

15. Collins, P.G., A. Zettl, H. Bando, A. Thess, and R.E. Smalley. Nanotube nanodevice. Science 278:100.6. Applications: Nanodevices, Nanoelectronics, and Nanosensors 95

16. Cuberes, M.T., et al. 1996. Room temperature repositioning of individual C60 molecules at Cu steps. Operation of a molecular counting device. Appl. Phys. Lett. 69:3016.

17. Credi, A., V. Balzani, S.J. Langford, and J.F. Stoddart. 1997. Logic operations at the molecular level. An XOR gate based on a molecular machine. J. Am. Chem. Soc. 119:2679

18. Stroscio, J.A., and Eigler, D. 1991. Atomic and molecular manipulation with the STM. Science 254: 1319.

19. Tans, S.J., et al. 1997. Individual single-wall carbon nanotubes as quantum wires. Nature 386:474.

Sample Question Paper for
In-Semester Examination (30 Marks)

Time: 1 Hour   **Marks: 30**

Q. 1.   **(a)** Draw and explain the CMOS technology   **[6]**

        (b) Explain the band structures in silicon   **[4]**

OR

Q. 2   **(a)** Write a short note on MOSFET   **[6]**

        (b) Write a I-V/C-V characterization   **[4]**

Q. 3   **(a)** Describe in short: (i) Optic (ii) Photoresist (iii) Wafer exposure system   **[6]**

        (b) Explain the thermal oxidation techniques   **[4]**

OR

Q. 4   **(a)** Differentiate between Dopant diffusion and Ion implantation   **[6]**

        (b) Dram and explain the sputtering methods.   **[4]**

Q. 5   **(a)** Write short notes on (i) Quantum particle (ii) Quantum dot.   **[8]**

        (b) State the nanowires construction .   **[2]**

OR

Q. 6.   **(a)** Explain the FinFET construction   **[6]**

        (b) What are the properties of FinFET?   **[4]**

Sample Question Paper for
End-Semester Examination (70 Marks)

Time: 2:30 Hours   **Marks: 70**

Q. 1. **(a)** Explain the crystal growth and wafer fabrication.   **[6]**

   (b) State the working principal of N and P MOSFET transistor.   **[8]**

   (c) What are ongoing challenges of removal of contamination faced by semiconductor industry?   **[6]**

OR

Q. 2. **(a)** What are the nano-wires? Write its construction methodology and applications?   **[6]**

   (b) What do you understand by the single-electron box? Explain..   **[8]**

   (c) Define lithography. Why is it used in forming devices?   **[6]**

Q. 3   **(a)** Discuss various sensors and actuators.   **[9]**

   (b) Describe packaging and integration methods   **[9]**

OR

Q. 4. **(a)** Explain deflection beams   **[9]**

   (b) Explain the instrinsic characteristic of MEMS.   **[9]**

Q. 5. **(a)** Write a short note on piezo resistive sensing and magnetic actuation   **[8]**

   (b) Define the electrostatic induction and electrostatic actuators.   **[8]**

OR

Q. 6. **(a)** Write your views on the thermal sensing and actuation..   **[8]**

   (b) Explain acceleration sensors and gyros.   **[8]**

Q. 7   **(a)** Discuss about the Fourier Transform infrared spectroscopy.   **[8]**

   (b) Explain the microscope and X-ray photoelectron   **[8]**

OR

Q. 8   **(a)** Discuss about the hot probe method and sheet resistance?   **[8]**

   (b) Explain about the Hall Effect measurements   **[8]**

Time : $2\frac{1}{2}$ Hours   Max. Marks : 70

Instructions to the candidates :

(1) Answer any one questions out of Q. 1 or Q. 2, Q. 3 or Q. 4, Q. 5 or Q. 6, Q. 7 or Q. 8.

(2) Neat diagrams must be drawn wherever necessary.

(3) Use of electronic pocket calculator is allowed.

(4) Assume suitable data, if necessary.

1. **(a)** Explain temperature effects in semiconductor.   **[7]**

    (b) What is Lithography? Write different methods which are used for IC fabrication.   **[7]**

    (c) What is Fin FET? How it is different than normal FET?   **[6] OR**

2. **(a)** What are the different technologies which are used for silicon crystal growth?   **[7]**

    (b) What is etching? What do you mean by wet etching and dry etching?   **[7]**

    (c) Write short notes on   **[6]**

    　　(i)   Dopant diffusion

    　　(ii) Sputtering

3. **(a)** Discuss three different approaches for circuits that can be integrated with MEMS. **[9]**

    (b) What is Encapsulation? Explain Importance of it.   **[9] OR**

4. **(a)** Explain experimental methods for measuring intrinsic stress.   **[9]**

    (b) Write a short note on   **[9]**

    　　(i)   Sensor   (ii) Actuator   (iii) Transducer

5. **(a)** What is direct and inverse effect of piezo electric sensors?   **[8]**

    (b) Compare electrostatic and thermal actuation methods.   **[8] OR**

6. **(a)** What are the aspects, which should be considered for successful design of accelerometer.   **[8]**

    (b) Write short note on comb drive devices.   **[8]**

7. **(a)** Write short note on   **[8]**

    　　(i)   Profilo meter

    　　(ii) Reflectometer

    (b) What are the advantages and disadvantages of Transmission Electron Microscopy (TEM) in comparison to Scanning Electron Microscopy (SEM).   **[8] OR**

8. **(a)** What is FTIR? Explain advantages, limitations and applications FTIR.   **[8]**

    (b) Write short note on Atomic Force Microscope. (AFM)   **[8]**

✳ ✳ ✳

END SEM. EXAM. NOVEMBER 2016

Time : $2\frac{1}{2}$ Hours   **Max. Marks : 70**

Instructions to the candidates :

(1) Answer any one question out of Q. 1 or Q. 2, Q. 3 or Q. 4, Q. 5 or Q. 6, Q. 7 or Q. 8.

(2) Neat diagrams must be drawn wherever necessary.

(3) Use of electronic pocket calculator is allowed.

(4) Assume suitable data if necessary.

1. **(a)** What are the advantages and disadvantages of Silicon as a material for semiconductor?   **[7]**

    (b) Explain why contamination should be taken very seriously while fabrication of IC? **[7]**

    (c) What is Single Electron Transistor (SET)? Draw the circuit model of a SET.   **[6]**

OR

2. **(a)** What is the importance of silicon from semiconductor point of view?   **[7]**

    (b) Write various levels of contaminations.   **[7]**

    (c) Write applications of semiconducting quantum dots.   **[6]**

3. **(a)** What are the important intrinsic characteristics of MEMS? Enlist them.   **[9]**

    (b) What do you mean by sensor, actuator and tranducer?   **[9]**

OR

4. **(a)** Enlist six major energy domain of interest for MEMS description.   **[9]**

    (b) What are three major sources of noise in MEMS that needs to be considered by designers?   **[9]**

5. **(a)** Explain Basic Principle of Electrostatic sensors and actuators.   **[8]**

    (b) Explain working principle of Electrostatic motor with necessary diagrams.   **[8]**

OR

6. **(a)** What are the major advantages of electrostatic sensors and actuators?   **[8]**

    (b) Explain operation principle of scratch drive actuator with suitable sketches.   **[8]**

7. **(a)** Write down different methods of measurement of parameters of silicon wafer.   **[8]**

    (b) Explain hot probe method of measurement with neat diagram.   **[8]**

OR

8. **(a)** Explain sheet Resistance method of measurement with neat diagram.   **[8]**

    (b) Explain principle of working of contact type profilometer.   **[8]**